EDENGLASSIE

MELISSA LUCASHENKO

Melissa Lucashenko is a Goorie (Aboriginal) author of Bundjalung and European heritage. Her first novel was published in 1997 and since then her work has received acclaim in many literary awards. Her sixth novel, *Too Much Lip*, won the 2019 Miles Franklin Literary Award and the Queensland Premier's Award for a work of State Significance. It was also shortlisted for the Prime Minister's Literary Award for Fiction, the Stella Prize, two Victorian Premier's Literary Awards, two Queensland Literary Awards and two NSW Premier's Literary Awards. Melissa is a Walkley Award winner for her non-fiction, and a founding member of human rights organisation Sisters Inside. She writes about ordinary Australians and the extraordinary lives they lead.

Sydney 2024

Also by Melissa Lucashenko

Steam Pigs
Killing Darcy
Hard Yards
Too Flash
Mullumbimby
Too Much Lip

MELISSA LUCASHENKO

EDENGLASSIE

UQP

First published 2023 by University of Queensland Press
PO Box 6042, St Lucia, Queensland 4067 Australia

University of Queensland Press (UQP) acknowledges the Traditional Owners and
their custodianship of the lands on which UQP operates. We pay our respects to their
Ancestors and their descendants, who continue cultural and spiritual connections to
Country. We recognize their valuable contributions to Australian and global society.

uqp.com.au
reception@uqp.com.au

Cover design by Jenna Lee
Author photograph by Glenn Hunt
Typeset in 12/16 pt Bembo Std by Post Pre-press Group, Brisbane
Printed in Australia by McPherson's Printing Group

 University of Queensland Press is supported by the
Queensland Government through Arts Queensland.

  University of Queensland Press is assisted by
the Australian Government through the
Australia Council, its arts funding and
advisory body.

A catalogue record for this book is available from the National Library of Australia.

ISBN 978 0 7022 6612 6 (pbk)
ISBN 978 0 7022 6773 4 (epdf)
ISBN 978 0 7022 6774 1 (epub)

University of Queensland Press uses papers that are natural, renewable and recyclable
products made from wood grown in well-managed forests and other controlled
sources. The logging and manufacturing processes conform to the environmental
regulations of the country of origin.

Aboriginal and Torres Strait Islander readers are respectfully cautioned that this
publication contains mentions of people who have passed away.

For Cec

'You fool', she said, 'this is England.'
'I don't believe it,' I said, 'and I will never believe it.'

Jean Rhys, *Wide Sargasso Sea*

NOTE

This book draws on extensive research into colonial Queensland history, both written and oral. The timing of some real events, such as Tom Petrie's expedition to establish Murrumba Downs, has been changed to suit the narrative. Other historical details have been omitted, or in rare cases, embellished. In other words, this is a work of fiction, and should be read as such.

Edenglassie was a colonial name briefly applied to the area of inner Brisbane now called Newstead. It is used as the title for this novel in a nod to paths not taken.

More information on sources, informants and languages can be found in the Author's Note.

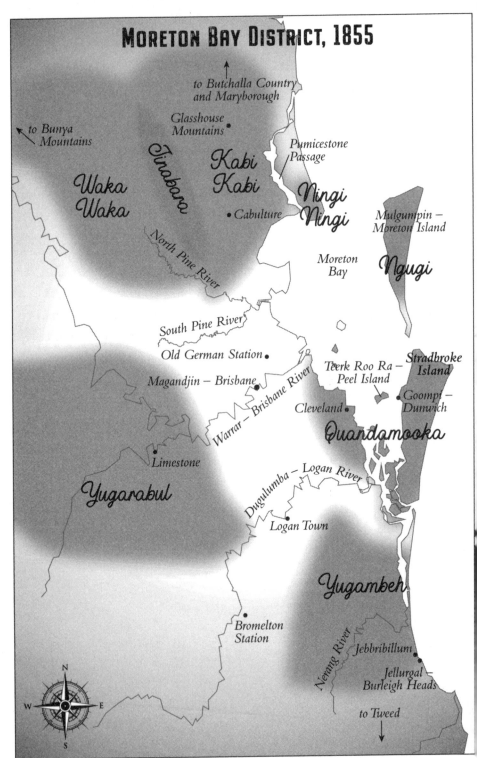

MORETON BAY DISTRICT, 1855

to Butchalla Country
and Maryborough

to Bunya
Mountains

Glasshouse
Mountains

Jinabara

Kabi
Kabi

Waka
Waka

• Caboolture

Pumicestone
Passage

Ningi
Ningi

Mulgumpin –
Moreton Island

Ngugi

Moreton
Bay

North Pine River

South Pine River

Old German Station •

Magandjin – Brisbane

Teerk Roo Ra –
Peel Island

Stradbroke
Island

Goompi –
Dunwich

Cleveland •

Warrar – Brisbane River

Quandamooka

Limestone •

Yugarabul

Dugulumba – Logan River

Logan Town •

Yugambeh

Bromelton
Station •

Nerang River

Jebbribillum

Jellurgal
Burleigh Heads

to Tweed

N
W   E
S

All language group boundaries are approximations.

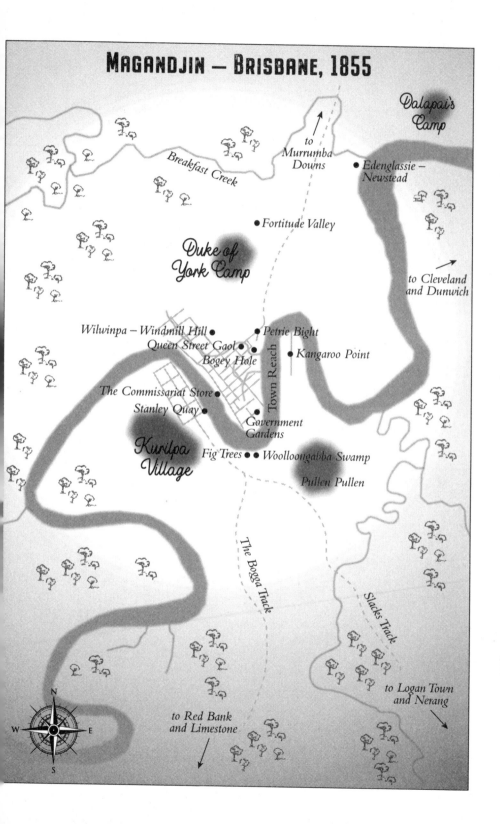

MAGANDJIN — BRISBANE, 1855

Dalapai's Camp

to Murrumba Downs

Breakfast Creek

• Edenglassie – Newstead

• Fortitude Valley

Duke of York Camp

to Cleveland and Dunwich

Wilwinpa – Windmill Hill •
Queen Street Gaol •
Bogey Hole •
• Petrie Bight
• Kangaroo Point

Town Reach

The Commissariat Store •
Stanley Quay •

Kurilpa Village

Government Gardens

Fig Trees • • Woolloongabba Swamp

Pullen Pullen

The Bogga Track

Slacks Track

to Logan Town and Nerang

to Red Bank and Limestone

N W E S

1. The Fall

2024

Eddie Blanket was falling, falling, falling towards the good Yagara earth.

A calamity. At her great age, a fall meant the end, simple as that. Broken hip, pneumonia, kaput.

Even as she lost the vertical, though, Granny Eddie was rejecting the whole stupid idea. You didn't live to her age by damn well accepting things. So: she was definitely *not falling*. Toppling, well yes, possibly. Or teetering – oh! – like the teeter-totter in the schoolyard, remember? Hot yellow sunshine in the playground, thumping up and down with Lizzie Norman on the other end, terrible buckteeth bared in joy. Lizzie was dead and buried now, of course. Nearly everyone was. Eddie had buried her own kids, and her husband, too. Sisters and brothers, she'd outlived the lot. And now here she was at South Bank, poised on the edge of the precipice herself.

Eddie observed with a kind of detached dismay her right knee buckling to the footpath outside the maritime museum, her walking stick betraying her to skid across the grass and into the nearest garden bed. There was a solid three inches of cement between Granny Eddie's person and the good Yagara dirt of the Ancestors, but that was of no concern to gravity, or indeed to Granny Eddie, for she was knocked cold by her fall.

~

Everything had buggered-up, gorn skewiff. Blurred trees grew out of wavering buildings; human-shaped blobs stood at a right angle to normality. Something else was off, too. The traffic on Vulture Street had frozen in its lanes, the CityCat didn't move midstream, even the Qantas jet roaring over the river had decided to pull up and have a jolly old breather, its shadow flung down onto the maritime museum in the shape of a giant warped bird, an albatross or pelican. Granny Eddie blinked in confusion. Then her brain slowly began to crochet together a looped understanding of events: her stupid fall outside the museum, that was right, she'd tripped on the tiniest jutting tree root and in outrage the earth had flung itself up at her, insisting she join it. This act of remembering made time begin thumping sharply in her left temple: *ouch, ouch, ouch.*

Eddie Blanket lay there, registering her injuries, for two minutes and twenty-seven seconds. An Elder, mind you, laid low in the middle of the path – oh terrible, terrible! – and the whitefellas walking well out of their way to avoid her, to avoid even looking at her. There they go – bugger you Jack I'm alright, that's your motto, ay? Christ Almighty, *drunk?* Can't you see I'm hurt, and someone needs to stop and help an old black woman, and instead you go an turn yer nose up at me as a drunk on metho! Good go! Bugger off then! Useless! And you, I can just about see ya moot, missy, didn't the shop have a skirt your size, to make you go and buy a child's one? No shame at all. Yeah, I can hear ya, never mind yer *alco* and *homeless.* And in a sudden burst of rage: who dragged youse mob up? A person could be dead fer all you care. You, I'm talking to you – this is my country too, don't I count? So never mind walking past like I don't exist …

When all of a sudden some youngsters stopped, knelt down and murmured in concern. A flooding relief of tears, because everything hurt and somebody cared. Oh, thank God. Thank you, Jesus. A girl and a boy with broad brown faces the pair of them, bending and exclaiming over her. Students with foreign eyes in their heads to see she was hurt, and foreign brains in their heads to know she was an old, old Goorie woman who needed some blooming help, quick smart.

Granny Eddie surrendered to the kindness of the students. Her head was hurting, her eyesight was all wrong and she was suddenly very, very tired.

~

In her long life, Granny Eddie reflected from her hospital bed that afternoon, she had seen a great deal of time. A lot of time, and more than one variety of it, but this sort of time – or life (which amounted to the same thing) – was altogether new. The blurred colours of the hospital ward were far too bright, everything shining and glowing with colours a person had never imagined before. All colour and no detail, and a pain in her temple that had taken a fair whack of morphine to knock over. At first Eddie thought it was the hospital lighting making everything glow and shimmer, but when the nurse drew the curtains apart, revealing the brown Warrar snaking around the City Botanic Gardens with the Story Bridge in the distance – a silver brooch joining the two banks of the river – she realised it was the same outside. Brighter. Newer. Blurry. The world was like it always was, and yet different. Hard to put your finger on it. Most things a lot less clear, and yet some things as clear as day.

Take Old Grandad Charlie. She'd never in all her born days been able to recall his face. Grandad had ploughed Mr Bolitho's Phantom Continental smack bang into the shopfront at McDonnell & East just before the war. Finally pushed it too far that day, bless. Just turned eleven, young Edwina had kept the memory of Charlie's voice and smell, nothing more. But strange, lying here in crisp sheets in what was doubtless a whiteman hospital overlooking the river – and as to why she could hear so many little babies crying so loud on the floor below was yet another mystery – strange that she could all of a sudden picture Old Man Charlie, his thick dark eyebrows and Fred Astaire hat, the cheeky old darlin as clear as anything in her mind. The fall must have shaken some of the dust out of the crannies in her head and made room up top for the old bloke to come visiting her.

As the nurses rabbited on about blood pressure and bedpans and suchlike, Eddie focused her mind on the serious matter of dirt. She had been concerned with dirt all her life, and with being dispossessed of same, not to mention treated like dirt, which is to say, trampled over and disregarded as a general rule. And what with being *a dirty black*, so-called, it was only common sense that dirt – meaning earth, meaning also Country – was something of a constant and compelling interest to her, unlike the whitefellas who so very rarely looked at the ground beneath their feet, for fear of remembering where it had come from and what it had cost, and where they themselves would undoubtably end up.

She was dirty on them mob, truth be told.

Yes, yes, there were plenty of exceptions, like Rob's dear wife, Cathy, an actual human being for all them squatters she come down from, and wotsername Judy. But the Judys and the Cathys of the world were hard put to cancel out the likes of Bridget in Grade One, her with the short little stick at school just long enough to keep your black hand from touching hers in the line-up outside the classroom, and Margaret too, the sour-faced bitch, running your family down when she thought you couldn't hear her. So, all your Murri life, your Goorie life, it was a matter of learning the hard way to be just like the earth, unmoving and unchanging, in the face of white people and their never-ending provocations.

Despite the ache in her head and neck, Granny Eddie smiled. That was the funny thing, the really hilarious thing – white people thinking she was stupid, when they were the ones walking around with blinkers on, hah! Stupid as sheep for the most part, never noticing a damn thing. Looking at their phones for the last two hundred years. What was it Grandad Charlie had said? *Never say no to a white person. Say yes, yes, yes and always smile.* Watch them relax, watch them believe they have it over you, that you are malleable, stupid, not a troublemaker, nothing to lose sleep over. Nothing to see here.

The door began to open. With a burst of fright, Granny Eddie remembered the dirt beneath her fingernails. She curled her hands into quick fists to protect the precious dark grains from strangers. Never know who's in there, see. Never know whose ancestors you might be carrying around in the palm of yer hand. She fell at the maritime museum they said earlier, well, well. You might as well say Mary time museum. May as well say Murri time museum, meaning back in the day, back before Grandad Charlie even, so long ago the land didn't recognise the sound of an English word. How many Marys Murris Murrdis would you need to go back to … for it was well known, of course, that part of every blackfella who ever lived went back to the good jagun, the good earth. Who was she holding on to, below her nails? Who was holding on to her, as the door to her room in Ward B swung wide for all the world to see?

Eddie uncurled her fingers then and peered at her shimmering nails, wishing for Grandad Charlie to come, or her big sister, or her poor old dead ma. But it was a man with a stethoscope who entered the room. Not very tall, and not particularly dark, but handsome enough, yes, in a blurry sort of fashion.

'Who're you?' Granny Eddie demanded. 'State yer damn business! Where's Winona?'

Doctor Johnny Newman startled. He was used to being sworn at, spat on and even punched by the unfortunates in Emergency, but Eddie's centenarian aggression was a novelty. He pointed to his ID badge.

'As if I can read that!' Granny Eddie huffed. The silly brat! Even with her glasses on, she could barely make him out, let alone his badge. And who was to say it was the truth written there? They could make anything up. What if he was one of them serial killers? Look at Daniel Morcombe. What chance did a hundred-year-old black woman stand, alone in the world, her husband and their three daughters finished up, and her blind as a damn bat it seemed. Someone needed to fix that and fix it fast.

'I'm Doctor Johnny,' the handsome blur said gently. 'My damn business is to see what's up with your eyesight, Aunty. Did you know you had a fall? Hit your noggin on the footpath?'

'Noggin – is that a medical term then? I reckon you got your doctor's licence out of a cornflakes box, mate. It's my neck that hurts,' Eddie grumbled. 'Where's Winona got to?'

'Winona? Is that your daughter?' Johnny looked around in vain for a flower-shaped family chart pinned to the wall.

'Not my dort, my grannie – my daughters've all passed. Watcha doing now? Are you a student, ay? Don't I warrant a real doctor?'

Johnny assessed her: hip – bruised but by some miracle not broken; limbs – sound; head and neck – very sore for no obvious reason, likely soft tissue damage, but also needing an X-ray pronto, especially given the sudden change in vision; diabetes no doubt a complicating factor, and quite possibly the reason for the fall in the first place.

'Nice to meet you, Aunty,' he said several minutes later, handing her over to the X-ray orderly.

'I don't remember saying you can call me Aunty,' Eddie snapped. Somebody ran a cultural awareness seminar somewhere and she magically acquired a million white nephews. 'Call me Mrs Blanket. And find my Winona!'

2. Kurilpa Village, Moreton Bay

1840

The Ancestors sent no warning. The first inkling of the arrival was the thing itself – a great white curve headed upriver. Dawalbin had seen this sight in her youth, but never here on her husband's bend of the Warrar. She scrambled to her feet.

'Yerrin! Look!'

Her husband was mending a wallaby net with his brother. As they worked, the men were absorbed in a discussion about how high to shift their oompies before storm season arrived. The dingoes had pupped early. The magpies had hatched four chicks: a big flood was coming.

'Yerrin! The river! Look!'

It was mid-afternoon. As Dawalbin called out, a cry went up from the women in the bungwall patch. Most of the men were away, harvesting honey or cutting sheets of ironbark to sell to the white people. Some were checking their fish traps or finding game at the Woolloongabba Swamp, but those who remained in the village halted, mesmerised.

A handful of boats rested on the sandy beach below the village and so it took some manoeuvring for the newcomers to find space to land. The visitors – two bearded men – remained seated, waiting for an invitation. When Yerrin signalled welcome, they came up the riverbank, leaving their great white curve behind

7

them. As the men reached the first row of huts, their shadows stretched behind them, almost touching the children who had clustered near the canoes and were examining the strange white object.

'Hello, Uncle.' Yerrin embraced the older man. 'It's been a while.'

'Good to see you, Nephew! Dalapai wanted to catch up,' the Old Man said, gesturing to his companion. Like him, Dalapai bore the scarrings of seniority on his chest and arms. His hair was streaked white and his face was grooved with the lines of habitual worry.

'Of course, of course,' Yerrin said, easing himself down onto the sand and preparing to hear what had been happening north of the Warrar. He refrained from asking about, or even looking at, the gift these men had brought.

'Welcome, Dalapai. Will you eat?' Dawalbin asked, opening the neck of her dillybag. The visitors laughed with pleasure and Dawalbin passed her toddler, Murree, over to his big sister, Ada, so she could prepare the crayfish.

'Your hospitality feeds more than just our bellies, Nephew,' the Old Man announced some time later. He threw his last cray shell in the fire and wiped the juice from his beard and whiskers. 'To sit with our relatives, eating the gifts of Biame, it reminds us to enjoy life. Especially now our Countries are returning to us.'

Yerrin nodded. The end of the Catastrophe was in sight. Soon their Federation would be at peace again. The havoc the English brought would never be forgotten, of course. But the clanking of iron chains on Sufferer's legs was now rarely heard. The screams from the flogging triangle in Queen Street had ceased last Oyster Season, and less than three hundred foreigners remained in Magandjin. Soon this tiny band of invaders would return across the ocean, and the Kurilpa, along with their neighbours, would have a normal existence again. Yerrin wondered if the peace he had known as a child would feel the same as a middle-aged man. He had seen so much destruction.

'When these last dagai have returned to Muttakundrei,' the Old Man predicted, 'we will have sanity. A life where lunatics don't go around pretending to own other people's land and calling themselves *masters*.'

Yerrin and Dalapai grunted in disgust at the word.

'I doubt this one's children will even believe the nightmare was real,' Dawalbin commented, kissing her son's curls and throwing a fish wrapper onto the coals. The paperbark briefly flared before crumbling to powdery white ash.

'I hope they leave by the Time of the Whales,' she dreamed aloud. To travel to the ocean without fear; to journey home to her grandfather's people and see the whales spouting off the Island Countries knowing that her safe return home was assured; how wonderful that would be!

'They will be gone by the Mullet Run,' predicted the Old Man. 'And there we can discuss our Federation's recovery. What say you, cousin?' He was addressing Dalapai, who had remained silent and was gazing down at the children splashing in the river.

'It will be a blessing from the Ancestors to see them gone,' Dalapai agreed. 'But, cousin, don't speak too soon. Our neighbours beyond the mountains report that dagai continue to arrive uninvited. They still come from the south with their Sufferers and their hole makers, driving great flocks of munkies before them, and there they camp and wait for word from their Queen.'

'Word?' asked Yerrin, looking up sharply. 'What word?'

'Word that free white men are now welcome in our lands.'

The group fell silent, pondering this grim revelation. On the opposite side of the Warrar, a cutter left the Commissariat Store dock and slid into the outgoing tide, heading for Dunwich.

At that moment a mob of panting kids raced up the bank and tumbled into the conversation. The youngsters giggled and clutched at Dawalbin and Yerrin, all wet hair and smiles. They rubbed their bellies and made extravagant sniffs at the roasted bream Dawalbin had set aside for them. Yerrin smiled and handed the parcels over. While they ate cross-legged on the sand, the children talked sixteen to the dozen over the top of one another.

'A stick touched sister's foot and she thought it was a shark, and she jumped clear out of the water like a mullet!'

'Did you see how long I stayed underwater the last time, Grandmother?'

'Brother caught this one in his bare hands, look!'

A grinning lad at the centre of the group was holding a large bream. Yerrin praised him. It was quite common for adults to catch fish this way at low tide – even the off-duty diamonds sometimes managed it – but this child was young, his slender body unmarked by ceremony.

'Time you headed home, though, Tom,' Yerrin chided, pointing at the lowering sun. 'Nellie will cook that fellow up for your dinner. Don't pout – you can come back in the morning.' It was a constant battle to persuade the boy to don clothing and return to his parents' house. Once, when Tom was in trouble for some small misdemeanour, he had camped with them for three nights, prompting a gruff appearance from Mister Andrew Petrie himself.

It was arranged that Young Tom would return home with the visitors. Down at the shoreline, the boy folded himself into the Old Man's canoe, looking as natural there as any Goorie boy, even with his trousers restored.

'Come to our village on the full moon,' said the Old Man to Yerrin. 'There's more to discuss before we hear from Dundalli. And my sisters ask that Dawalbin comes to visit, your daughter also.'

The visitors' canoes, now minus their strange cargo, were edged out into the current. The Old Man climbed in beside Young Tom and dipped his paddle to steady the craft.

'You know you are always welcome in my Country,' Dalapai

turned to add, floating alongside, 'and please, Nephew, hark my words. The dagai's numbers may seem to grow less. But he is a mothar – and like a mothar his web spreads and spreads.'

'Yoway.' Yerrin nodded. 'We must use all our wits to avoid being tangled in it.'

With that, the visitors were away. They left behind them the gift – a set of whale ribs which would never again plumb the depths of the ocean. The giant bones, bleached white in the sun since being harvested by Dawalbin's people near Dunwich, would become the girders of Yerrin's new home. This gift symbolised a new phase in the alliance between saltwater and freshwater Goories.

Later that afternoon, Dawalbin took Murree onto her hip and sat beside the fire with him, deep in thought. She suckled the little boy, imagining as her milk passed into the child what his life would be like when the dagai had gone, and also what it would mean if Dalapai was right. If life never returned to normal. If the rule of Law was never restored. What would her son see as a man? Would he be free to travel their Federation, or would he, too, have to live in fear of displeasing the invaders? Would her daughters be subject to the terror the dagai brought? Grim imaginings filled Dawalbin's mind. She took Murree's hands in hers and held them closer to the glowing coals of her fire. The boy yawned in her lap as she resumed the day's lesson. It was the same lesson all infants learnt. *Be generous. But never steal. Taking what isn't yours will burn your hands.*

She next held ten chubby toes towards the fire.

Walk strong. Don't step where you aren't invited. Stepping where you aren't invited will burn your feet.

Dawalbin took Murree's curls in her hands and turned his head sideways to the glowing coals. Warming first one ear, then the other.

Listen well. Don't listen to bad talk or lies, son. Listening to bad words or lies will burn your ears.

As his wife instructed their son, Yerrin stepped away and stood facing west. The sun had just slipped below the mountains. Early stars were beginning to show in the Sky Camps. He looked up, wondering what advice the Ancestors, wheeling above the earth in their great ellipses, might give him in times like these. Times when things could go either way – a return to peace, or the ongoing turmoil of undeclared war. Civilisation or unending chaos. What should we do, my Old People? he asked. Which road will lead us back to freedom? Where is the honourable path in seasons as strange as these?

After long minutes, Yerrin finally lowered his gaze to the village. What he saw there made him laugh aloud in astonishment. There, in the fast-fading light, stood what looked like an entire forest. But the trees he saw in front of him were not bloodwoods, nor palms, nor the distant grove of sacred figs downstream. He was looking, rather, at a trick of the twilight. A vast field of smoke plumes rose from the fires of his people. Two hundred white pillars stretched from where he stood opposite the Queen's Wharf all the way down to the ridge above the Woolloongabba Swamp. It seemed to Yerrin, standing there, that for every star that had just emerged in the night sky, a twin fire blazed among his people. The rising pillars of smoke joined the Sky Camps to the earth, knitting the past and the present together in one tremendous tableau. It was answer enough. He was not alone; he was never alone. The Kurilpa were still so many, and their Ancestors were always watching.

3. Mulanyin's Fish

Season of the Cold Winds, Kombumerri Country, 1854

The lad sat shivering on a rock platform that jutted over the ocean. Salt spray flew up and his limbs goose-pimpled in the breeze, but he persisted. He was a hunter; his weapon was endurance. For hours his mind had been concentrated on the rising tide of the burragurra and the great prize he sensed it was going to bring him. A short distance away, his fathers stood on the grassy slope below Jellurgal; they too were scanning the ocean. The boy knew without being told that these older men, quietly murmuring, gesturing minutely to each other at each swelling of the waves or tilting of the osprey in flight, were expertly gathering information on him along with everything else.

Finally unable to resist, he glanced over at them. The men felt the boy's gaze without returning it, and he understood very well the message in their refusal. It was the same message given by the cold unyielding rock beneath him; by the constant swell of the burragurra where he daily sought his prey.

Patience. You are not the centre on which the world turns.

The boy swallowed his irritation and went back to work, determined to impress the men. He would catch a fine big fish, a tailor or mulloway so gigantic that they would stagger with shock at the very sight of it, telling his whole family that he, Mulanyin, had fed them once again. The men would slap him on the back, marvelling that here was a boy who hunted like a grown maibin, a boy fully deserving of elevation to the rank of kippa. He vowed that he would be given his ceremony by the time of the next Mullet Run and take his place at the fire beside his fathers and waijungs when decisions were made.

But first he had to catch his fish.

Mulanyin pulled his possum skin close around him. He did this with utmost care, making only tiny movements, because fish had eyes, and fish had Law, and the fish he intended to kill that day had a life that it no doubt valued in its own fishy fashion. Minutes passed, and the sea calmed. Warm in the embrace of the fur cloak, Mulanyin fell into a kind of trance. He daydreamed that rather than simply being an ordinary Yugambeh boy holding a fishing line, he was some type of powerful Ancestor, holding the giant expanse of the burragurra by a taut magic cord; imagining that he, and not the ocean, was in control of what happened next.

The boy was jerked out of this fantasy when the line pulsed in his hand. In an instant the universe shrank to the place between his index finger and thumb where the wagoi had quivered.

Another pulse.

On the grassy hill above him, the watching men's gaze sharpened. The boy's Waijung, keeping one eye on the bungwall damper slow roasting on her fire, commented that they would have some tricky parenting to do very soon.

'Let's see,' Big Father answered. For his son was about to be severely tested.

Mulanyin breathed out carefully for one breath, two breaths – then, when the third bite came, he ripped his right hand back, jagging the mulloway onto his hook. As he leapt up to haul the line in, his numb legs wobbled. For a second he was in real danger of joining the fish in the waves below. But he had been training all his young life for this moment and knew how to win his prize.

As he headed uphill soon afterwards, his stride was proud. The head of the mulloway was at his shoulder, while its tail flapped wetly against the back of his knees. It was by far the largest fish he had ever caught; it was almost the largest he had seen. Anticipation made his stomach talk as he struggled back to the fire with his catch. He imagined the aroma of the fillets sizzling as they cooked and the feel of hot white flakes of flesh melting on his tongue.

He lay the flapping giant down beside the fire where ugari steamed in their open shells. He grinned at Waijung and his fathers and waited for praise.

To Mulanyin's astonishment, Small Father bent to grab the mulloway up by the gills. Then the man sprinted with it back down to the rock ledge, his glistening trophy flapping from side to side as Small Father ran.

Mulanyin screeched in horror as his wonderful fish got further and further from the cooking fire.

'Hurry and get down here,' Small Father yelled.

'This fish is not for us, son,' Waijung called, as Big Father hustled him downhill.

Stumbling and tripping, the boy gnashed his teeth in rage. He knew no reason that the mulloway couldn't be eaten; it wasn't his totem and nor was it one of the fishes who had grown shy since the dagai boats arrived.

'But why not?' he erupted. Even as he spoke, he realised what Father would answer.

'Why do you think?' Big Father countered. There it was again. *You work it out.* Big Father gestured at the mulloway, lying where Small Father had put her on the very rim of the rock ledge. Mulanyin's hands had taken the fish from her home, and so it was right that his hands returned her to it. His mistakes were not for others to remedy.

'Hurry up', Small Father instructed, 'and with luck she might survive your ignorance.' The boy shot him a look of pure anguish.

15

Insulted as well as denied: was this why he had sat freezing his arse on the hard rock all afternoon?

'Be quick,' Big Father agreed. 'And mind you apologise to her, while you're at it.'

Mulanyin stared in disbelief at the fish, now gasping on the rock where he had sat unmoving for all those painful hours. Hot tears prickled behind his eyes. Don't be such a baby, he scolded himself. But he struggled to discard his trophy. All that effort, all those long cold hours of waiting and watching! All for naught. Why would they do this? Was it a test? Or did they hate him?

The men waited, frowning at the delay.

Something clicked and whirred inside Mulanyin's brain as he inched towards the fish.

She might survive.

Apologise to *her*.

'Because she's a Matriarch,' he sighed. 'Possibly even now bearing eggs.'

'Yoway. Good. Do you understand?' Big Father probed, scanning the boy's face for petulance, for signs that his son was not yet ready to meet the burdens of coming months and years. 'How can we ask for the lives of the fish clan if we destroy their Old Ones out of greed? There is no honour in that, and no future either.'

'Yoway,' the boy said heavily, lifting his face to meet the question. This time his voice was clear of childish anger. Yes. Yes, he had been too eager to impress, to bring something grand to the fire, illicitly borrowing majesty from the huge Matriarch, blind and deaf to the consequences for others.

Mulanyin bent down and half-heaved, half-rolled the enormous fish over the lip of the rock ledge, apologising to her for his mistake. There was a splash, and the mulloway vanished.

'Will she live?' he asked, as guilt came flooding in.

Probably, the men assured him. The Matriarch was strong and had not been very long in the Dry World. She might lose any eggs she carried. But if she survived, she would have many more in years to come, and those offspring – and their offspring in turn – would feed the whole clan in future seasons. His grandchildren would eat of her descendants.

'Baugal gungalehla,' Big Father told his crestfallen son. 'Your question shows good character. And your behaviour does you credit. Now go, Fishing Man. Help your Waijung with the ugari.'

'Fishing Man?' the boy echoed in astonishment. He had never been called a *man* before.

'Yoway, Maibin Jalumbira,' his father repeated with a smile. Yes, Fishing Man. 'Or soon to be one, at least.'

'Ngaya maibin jalumbira,' the boy whispered to himself in secret delight. I am a Fisherman; I will feed my people with my hand and my heart.

The boy had always known that he was Goorie, one of thousands of citizens who belonged to the five Yugambeh rivers, which fell like wide blue ribbons from the western range. He knew that he'd been born a son, a grandson, a brother, a father, an uncle, a grandfather; through a web of unbreakable connections, he belonged to everyone amongst his coastal nation. Now the future shimmered like early dawn breaking silver and gold upon the burragurra, for he knew his destiny as well. He gazed down at his hands. The palms were calloused, his young fingers already strong from thousands of hours wielding the tow-row net, the spear and the fishing line. His wit was sharp and his body strong. He knew the shadows of the different fishes on the ocean floor, the different waves which held them, the phases of the moon that summoned them or kept them away. He had been taught by his Waijung where to find the correct bait for every species in every season; had been instructed by his fathers of those fish and creatures expressly forbidden him. The clan's Big River, too, had few mysteries to reveal. He had lived beside it for nearly fifteen Mullet Runs, and it was as dear to him as a sweetheart.

That evening, as his young brother and sisters lay asleep inside the family's hut, the boy stood apart from them, felt set apart from them. 'Ngaya maibin jalumbira,' he whispered to the Southern Cross in wonder. I am almost a man, a burragurra man. I will know the shark and the dolphin and the stingray as kin, and more than kin – and they will all know me. It occurred to him to wonder where the Matriarch was at that moment. He imagined her swaying in the heavy swell beneath the cliff, asleep or perhaps simply resting. Whatever she was doing, whatever the mulloway ever did from this day onwards, would be partly due to his actions today.

With that thought, the boy had the electric realisation that all his life he had been eating the decisions of his Ancestors. Every fish, every mudcrab, every ugari or turtle or vegetable or egg or fruit, they all came to him – to all his people – from generations of nurture. None of it was accidental, or random. And if his Old People hadn't cherished the biggest fish and the female turtles, if they hadn't sung up the Country, and protected the fecund of every species since the dawn of time, then he would not have eaten the results from the fire that night. Just as his children and grandchildren still unborn had needed him to release today's Matriarch. The thought consumed him with wonder; it made him feel small, yet at the same time as though he belonged in a universe of meaning; part of a web of ceaseless and sacred connection across thousands of generations.

Next day, Waijung watched her children collecting shellfish from the rocky foreshore: their dillybags filling quickly with limpets, cockles and succulent oysters. Mulanyin gave a quick shout and turned, holding something high.

'A cowrie for you, Mother!'

'Good work, my clever boy.' Waijung smiled, pleased. She was very fond of the beautiful spotted shells. Her curly-haired son stood on the beach, facing her and grinning back. She was close enough to see his finely carved nose and jaw and his shapely lips. His black eyes were large, burning with dreams. A realisation dawned on her as she counted the boy's life on the segments of her left hand. Mulanyin would soon see his fifteenth Mullet Run. He had grown tall, with the muscled arms and shoulders of his fathers. The lad carried food to the fire each night, just as a grown man must, given a little luck. And his response to the previous day's disappointment – when the fish he expected to bring celebration and praise instead brought condemnation – had not been that of a child.

That night she told Big Father: 'Mulanyin is ready to go to Coriki for ceremony.'

'I expected you to resist,' Big Father said in mild surprise. They had lost two children to the skin-eating Death Spirit, and so held their remaining jarjums especially close. His wife gave a small smile. It was hard enough to let any child go, let alone a fine handsome lad like Mulanyin. But there was news she had not yet told her husband.

'I have these ones still.' Mulanyin's younger sister Ngaburay would see her tenth Mullet Run when the next Oyster Season had been and gone. There was another girl of seven. And the youngest jarjum, a merry little boy, was still occasionally tugging at her breast.

'Coriki Bora won't meet for many moons, but the Yagara are putting kippas through soon,' Big Father mused. 'Small Father heard it from some Black Earth People over near Nindooinbah. It's a good time to take him – the girls begin to look hard at our son now. Even the waymerigan notice him.'

Waijung sat bolt upright.

'Waymerigan? Not Miss Compigne?'

'No, no.' Big Father soothed. 'But that daughter of Ivory, Miss Katherine – *she* looks. And so does her sister, who rides the white pony.'

19

Waijung stared in wordless horror.

The local dagai – the Ivorys and the Mallards, and the rough croppies who touched their hats and called Mister Ivory *boss*, at least to his face – these people were nothing if not unpredictable, one day offering you smiling friendship and the next shooting your cousin in the throat for harvesting a sheep on his own Country. What price, then, would a white man's daughter exact?

'He must go to the Yagara Bora! Quickly, before disaster strikes.'

'When the oodgeroo blooms,' Big Father agreed, 'we'll travel north to Yerrin's pullen pullen and our boy will become a kippa. And in another Mullet Run or two, prepare for marriage.'

4. The Woolloongabba Pullen Pullen

Season of Oodgeroo Blossom, Yagara Country, 1854

'Stick close to me,' Big Father warned as they rounded a small hill and approached the end of the Slacks Track. Mulanyin stared. He was familiar with the oompies of white men, yes. But he couldn't have counted on all his finger joints the number of shops and shanties lining the road they now walked. And with barely room to turn a bullock dray between most of them! Workers both black and white hauled sacks of corn into the shops from wagons, while other men stood beneath bullnose verandas, watching them labour and puffing on clay pipes. Grubby boys played in the dirt and threw sticks at lizards. Nobody in Woolloongabba paid him any heed, but Mulanyin did as his father ordered and clung to his side.

A minute later the two travellers halted beside a grove of large fig trees, one spear's throw from a large river. Here Mulanyin's mouth fell open.

A stretch of flat open ground stood before them, flanked by high ridges. This was the Yagara pullen pullen ground his father had told him about, where the tournament and the public parts of his kippa ceremony would be held. To its west lay a giant wetland, lush with reeds and waterfowl, fed by a freshwater stream running down to meet the glistening blue of the large river. Paperbark trees, heavy with lemon-coloured blossom, stood like enormous pale sentries along the banks of the creek. Humming with bees, these paperbarks dotted the edges of the One Mile Swamp along with the needle-leafed billa billa and great perfumed clumps of golden wattle. Everywhere between the fig grove and the swamp was alive with movement. Hundreds of Goorie people were busy preparing for the pullen pullen. The noise of this crowd laughing and gossiping and flirting filled the air, along with the pounding of bungwall mortars, and songbirds carolling from the scrub. These happy sounds drowned out the clip-clop of horse-drawn wagons making their way along the Bogga Track to the wharf, and the moaning of thirsty bullocks yoked half a mile away outside the Commercial Hotel.

'Keep clear in your mind why we have walked four days to get here. All these people – many, many citizens of many clans – are watching us, wondering exactly who we belong to and whether we are worthy of our invitation.'

Big Father swung his arm, then, in a wide arc that took in a thousand dark faces. People from every direction had gathered at Woolloongabba, some marching through the night from Limestone and Esk, and even as far as Warwick, to attend Yerrin's ceremony. The clans were assembled beside the wetland to dance, to feast and flirt, to assess the current crop of kippas, to share news of the British and most important of all, to resolve any internal conflicts which threatened the order of their Goorie Federation.

On the eastern ridge, a cluster of young Coorparoo women preparing bread had noticed Mulanyin arrive. As they pounded their bungwall they teased each other about the handsome stranger partly hidden by the fig trees. Mulanyin noticed them as well, laughing with wattle sprigs in their hair and romance in their eyes. In the boy's racing mind, the sweetness of the girls' smiles merged with the scent of the yellow blossom which blazed all around him. These feelings mixed together – the scent of the nectar, the sight of the beautiful laughing girls, the swirl of hundreds of warriors around the pullen pullen – made him faint with excitement. For a moment he thought dizziness might fell him and make a fool of him in front of the jalgany.

'And don't think you can go wandering off to sweet-talk those cheeky jalgany, either,' Big Father added. 'It's bad enough that we got here late for the opening.'

Mulanyin ducked his head. He was desperate to edge closer to the girls with their inviting eyes and shapely limbs, but to approach strange women without the blessing of their families could only lead to trouble and shame. Even worse, he risked being sent home still a child, denied the chance to go through his ceremony. That would mean even longer before he could woo a jalgany of his own, marry her, and sit with the adults around the decision-making waibara at home.

Mulanyin tore his attention from the girls and looked to the arena. Smoke billowed from scores of campfires on the surrounding ridges, the white cloud drifting down across the flattened acres where the ceremonial court would be held. Dozens of workers were preparing the tournament ground. The top layer of earth had been dug out earlier in the week by Yagara women, Big Father explained. Now the men were busy smoothing and decorating it. Other men – and a few women too – were having their bodies ochred and greased with goanna oil in preparation for combat. Mulanyin watched in fascination as a young Kurilpa man allowed his brothers to daub his face and body, and place red and green parrot feathers in his coiled dreadlocks. The man held a fighting burrang in his right hand and a shield of intricately carved corkwood in his left. He was a full-grown maibin of about thirty Mullet Runs, with the scars of battle as well as those of initiation on his chest and arms. Glistening with oil, his sinewy frame was a testament to a life of action and discipline. As he was being prepared for his duel, the man laughed easily with his companions as though nothing on earth worried him.

Mulanyin was mesmerised by the man's courage. Would he feel

that bold, he wondered, if he was about to face the Court of the Federation in front of a thousand onlookers? Or would he quake in fear, shaming himself and his people? For the chance to claim one of the watching girls on the ridge, he might muster enough courage, he thought.

'Are they fighting for wives?' he asked.

Big Father smiled. At his son's age all he thought of was women and how to get one. Some things never changed.

'Not for women. For honour,' he replied, 'And to make peace.' The men would engage in regulated combat between the clans, he explained, to restore order in the Federation. If a long-promised wife had run off with another man, causing insult and offence between families, there might indeed be a duel. But generally, marriage was not taken so lightly by anyone. Pairings were carefully negotiated, so that the correct young people always married partners from distant regions. This year would see eligible Coorparoo women, for example, matched with men from the western range, far beyond Limestone. At the previous pullen pullen, eligible Coorparoo girls had been matched with Dalapai's kippas north of the Warrar. And Coorparoo kippas going through ceremony this year would one day marry Waka girls from the northern seacoast, whereas last year their wives had come from Dalapai's people. It was not yet decided which clan the saltwater Yugambeh kippas like Mulanyin would be paired with; decisions about those matches, which would be formalised two years hence, would be a central part of the business of this year's pullen pullen.

Mulanyin's head whirled with these different scenarios.

'So even if you were able to sweet-talk those Coorparoo girls watching us you could not possibly marry one,' Mulanyin's father said, glancing at his crestfallen son. 'Tell me why.'

'Because of the Law,' came the boy's glum reply. Everything desirable in his life that was forbidden, or delayed, or out of bounds, or impossible, was always because of the damn Law.

The ancient spider web of obligations and restrictions bound all Goories together, protecting their civilisation but suffocating him, and stopping him from running to the lovely girls on the ridge. The beautiful girls were still staring at him and giggling behind their hands. Mulanyin resented the chafing bonds of the Law. At the same time, he longed to be an initiate of its mysteries and judged worthy of an invitation into the realm of adulthood. To sit at the fire with the other men and women and be listened to with respect; to be privy to the decisions affecting his clan and his life – this was the status he ached for. It was still two ceremonies distant for him; as an adolescent he was only beginning on the path to citizenship.

'Why, though? Why is this our Law? To marry into distant clans?' his father probed. The boy shrugged. Surely it couldn't just be because the adults liked ordering young men and women around – though they certainly did enjoy that. His father waited.

'To make the babies strong,' Mulanyin suggested at last, remembering a brace of stunted dingo pups whose parents had been littermates.

'That is the skin of it,' Father said with a short nod, and paused. 'Now show me the bone.'

He offered no further comment, turning instead to greet a brother-in-law among the throng of passing Kurilpa. Mulanyin twisted his mouth in dismay. This was yet another of the endless puzzles set by his Elders, and such puzzles were never solved except by his own effort. He was deliberately focusing his breathing and calming himself before turning his mind to the deeper aspects of the question – the bone of the matter – when a great cooee sounded. It came a second time, this time from near the centre of the arena, ricocheting off the surrounding ridges and stilling the entire crowd.

One thousand sets of eyes turned to where the four headmen of the major clans stood in their magnificent kangaroo skin cloaks.

Musicians stood beside them, loudly rattling their ceremonial burrang, before gradually allowing the clatter to fade to silence.

A hush settled over the arena.

'Let the disputants of the Green Frog clan come forward,' announced Dalapai.

The pullen pullen was one thing while the sun shone, but when the moon rose that evening and fires blazed on the flat ground, the gathering was transformed. The night itself became alive, dancers shimmering out of the darkness like a shoal of whiting caught by sunlight in a cresting wave. Mulanyin saw men turn to flame, turn to sparks. He had never known his people could be – that they were – so very beautiful. The sights he saw that night filled him up. They made him feel holy.

5. Granny Eddie's Yarning Rectangle

2024

Winona lay in bed at six a.m. with a thin cotton sheet pulled up over her cornrows. She was Blak, beautiful and fighting to hold on to her sanity.

You're such a loser, the Voice sneered.

'Fuck *orf*. I made one mistake, so what?'

Nah. Yer a dumb dawg world champion, gold medal, numbawan DUUUUUMB DAAAAWWWWGGG.

'Ooh, Lordy, will ya just RACK OFF? I ain't got time for yer cousin-fucking shit today!'

And ya ain't as hot as you wanna go thinkin ya are, neither. How much fat ya gorn and put on lately? Five kay gee? Ten? (grunting pig sounds)

'I might not be no oil painting, but at least I'm drawn inside the mothafucken lines, BITCH!'

Aw bless. Nah, but serious — ya seen ya reflection there lah? Muffin top! Lookin like some lopsided doughy bread, leaking outta ya jeans. Shamejob, ay. Nobody wants a fat ugly chick who can't even set an alarm clock.

'No, no, no, NO. No shamejob ere. Truesgod, bra, ya wanna shut ya maggoty hole. Fuckwit.'

Winona threw back the sheet and swung her caramel-brown legs out of bed, fuming. Late for work again, and the Voice in fine fucking form to boot. She picked up her alarm clock and shook it. The el cheapo slut of a thing started screaming out the noise it shoulda made three hours ago. Useless mothafucker. Winona pegged it at the clothes basket in the bathroom and missed, hitting the tiled wall instead.

The clock busted dramatically open, screws flying south, plastic face skidding west and the guts of the mechanism coming to a spinning stop against the mouldy shower cubicle. But by some ancestral curse the loud beeping kept on going. And going. And going.

As she jammed her fingers in her ears Winona had an epiphany.

Right.

Got it.

Busted clock blaring at the world. Debt piling up. Head full of her own private demons, running her down real bad. And late for work, *again*.

Today was gonna be one of them *stupid days*.

~

At the exact moment Winona hurled her offending alarm clock, Granny Eddie was waking up in hospital. She blinked at the fluorescent ceiling lights of Ward B, wondering where her husband, Terry, was, and what in the name of sweet baby Jesus had happened to her eyesight. Then it dawned on her where she was, and that Terry was decades dead, and why her eyes weren't working properly. Brought down by the vagaries of history, yes, and the many demands and nuisances of the Murri Time Museum, that's right. Granny Eddie harumphed in displeasure. Despite her headache and the strange numbness of her neck, she hauled her small mountain of pillows into order and decided that a revolution on Ward B would definitely be the go, just as soon as somebody thought to bring an old black woman a nice strong cuppa tea.

~

Winona emerged from the hospital lift with Granny Eddie's walking stick, a packet of mint leaves lollies and no job, having just been sacked by the Logan Plaza Bakers Delight. Cos yeah, verily, it was one of them *stupid days*.

'I don't mind them corncobs, bub,' Eddie said. She squinted at Winona's cornrows, running in neatly regimented lines away from her granddaughter's obviously Aboriginal face. 'Flash as a rat with a gold tooth, you are. But how come they went and sacked ya?'

'Alarm clock let me down, Nan,' Winona told her grandmother. 'But I was wanting a new job anyways, stuff getting up at three in the morning. I just seen all these whitefellas on the train cruising in ta work at like eight-thirty, nine o'clock. Why's Murri gotta get up in the middle of the night for, ay?'

Winona rolled her eyes. They both knew the answer to that question, but she was gonna change them coloniser rules, onetime. Get herself a uni degree and a cushy office job, too, with no aching back from sliding heavy trays of dough into a hot oven that never stopped needing its gaping maw fed. A cushy desk job that paid off a piece of her own land, and once she had it, she'd tell the bank and the government to kiss her caramel arse, cos she was gonski, man, gonski.

Winona drifted into a reverie, seeing her plan replicated all over Australia. She imagined endless offices filled with endless Blak bodies, mob all around typing emails and having meetings and doing whatever the fuck else office workers did, (not much in her experience), until each Blak body in turn closed their laptop, stood up and walked out the door never to return. Because the whole mob of em had bought back the farm, over and over and over, in their tens of thousands, till they once more owned the continent they had never agreed was lost. Imagine it. Streets and suburbs and country towns, all owned by happy blackfellas. No more eviction notices, no more house inspections or head-shaking real estate agents. Just mobs with roofs over their heads and food in the fridge, and something to leave their kids. And the tut-tutting dagai could *love it or leave.*

'Your Nan won't be wanting that,' interrupted a man's voice.

Winona turned to see a stringy fifty-something dagai in the hall. He was peering in like they were a fucking circus.

Exhibit A: two native gins.

'What?'

'She won't be needing her walking stick. Heard the nurses yesterday. She's got to stay in bed for a fortnight, minimum.'

The man grinned and Winona instantly hated him. Hated his jolliness, hated his ugly Boomer haircut, hated his facial mole, hated his insufferable belief that he had the right to talk to her uninvited, and above all hated his conceit that he knew anything whatsoever about her Blak family. Who the fuck you even think you is, brah?

'In the land of nod again, is she?'

Winona glanced at Granny Eddie, suddenly feigning sleep.

'She's a hundred years old. Course she's asleep.' *Ya fuckstick.*

The man's eyes widened.

'A hundred? Literally?'

The faint whisper of a snore came from the figure in the bed.

'She turns a hundred and three next month, actually,' Winona lied, just because it pleased her to lie to pushy gammon dogs who poked their nose in uninvited. The man's mouth fell open and he stammered in his haste.

'Oh my God! I knew she was an Elder, but a hundred and three! She must have been born just after the First World War ... my name's Dartmouth Rice – I'm a journalist – I'd love to do a feature article on what she's seen over the course of her life – the Depression, the Second World War, the Stolen Generations – I could give her a real voice! Was she stolen herself, do you know?'

The man's eyes gleamed expectantly till the very moment Winona banged the door in his face.

'Good girl,' said Granny Eddie, magically resurrected. 'That whitefulla keeps sniffing round. Wants to talk about the "fullbloods he knew in the Territory".'

Winona groaned a loud groan.

'Yeah – oh, and it gets better – he reckon's he's Archibald Meston's great-nephew. I'd be keeping that pretty blooming quiet if it was me.'

'Will I go club him to death?' Winona asked, brandishing the walking stick.

'Oh! My jabree! Ain't you a darlin.' Granny was delighted, clutching her stick to her chest and crooning to it like it was a baby. 'I was telling Sammy I needed it back, I'm not much chop without my jabree. But she reckoned they couldn't find it, I dunno why …'

Winona silently tried and failed to place Sammy in her constellation of distant cousins. That's what she got for not visiting her nan more than once a year at Christmas. Shamejob.

'Yeah, I got the message you wanted it, Nan. It was under that hedge there, lah.' Winona pointed out the window at the top end of South Bank, where Griffith University ended and a small grassy park with a war memorial statue began.

Granny Eddie stroked the jabree, nodding. It was no good her looking out the damn window; everything looked as though it was under water.

'So's Sammy taking care of you, mmm?' Winona ventured, hoping for enlightenment on her identity.

'Yeah, she's real good … oh, I mean she goes walkabout a bit,' Eddie admitted. 'But we manage okay. She's a good girl. When she's around.'

'What about Denzel and Matt, though? And Aunty Elise and wotsername, all that crowd?'

'Denzel and Matt went ages ago bub, they got ranger work on the island. Aunty Elise's having dialysis and Jared's off with his dirt bikes every weekend, never see him from one month to the next. Linda and Dave are good neighbours though. And Zainab downstairs looks in on me when Sammy can't come.' Granny Eddie was not about to fess up to any lack of regular care, Winona could tell, for fear of being put away. And fair enough too. Bugger being put in a Home after doing time in one at ten years old.

'Now I'm not on early shifts, I'll come see ya more, Nan,' Winona promised. 'We'll cook up a storm, make everyone's birthday cakes ay? Take ya ta bingo too.' Although if Nosey Parker Dartmouth Rice – and what kind of a gammon name was that, anyway? – was on the money, it'd be the hospital she'd be visiting for the next few weeks, not Nan's tiny flat in Fairfield Road.

There was a brisk knock on the door and both women blanched.

'Darwin whitefellas are the pushiest mob out, true's god!' declared Granny Eddie.

'Fuck orf,' Winona barked. 'Doncha ever know when ya not fucken wanted?'

Dr Johnny Newman opened the door and fell in love.

~

'Grandad Charlie,' announced Granny Eddie several days later with a faraway look in her eye, 'was *by far* the handsomest man in German Bridge. To hear him tell it, anyway. And yarn! He could yarn for days. He'd pick us up Friday arvo and start telling us stories on the road to the coast, still be going when we got back home Sunday dinnertime ...'

'What sort of things would he yarn about?' Dartmouth licked his lips. 'The war? The Depression?'

'Oh, you know,' Eddie gestured vaguely. 'Just people he used to know and that. Dogs maybe. Funny little things that happened. He never went to the first war, and course he was dead by the second.'

Dartmouth adjusted the iPhone secreted in his pocket, making sure the microphone was pointing at Eddie.

'I wonder why that was?' he probed delicately. 'Why he never enlisted?'

'We never knew if it was because he was too black,' Eddie mused. 'They took Uncle Ted, he was lightskin though, see, Irish father. Grandad Charlie was dark cos of his Punjabi blood, but I don't think it was his colour, somehow. I think it musta been that he was such a deadly driver for Mr Bolitho. They were as thick as thieves, them two, and I think Mr Bolitho might have pulled a string or two to keep Grandad outta harm's way—'

'Mr Bolitho being?'

'Oh, he was the bigwig, the top man!' Granny Eddie looked askance, as though he'd asked who the Queen was. 'Everybody knew him! Thought you said you grew up in East Brisbane? Mr Bolitho owned half the houses in Annerley Junction and donated the land for the community hall, too. Old Charlie used to wear a fancy cap and an ironed white shirt every day to drive him around in his Rolls!'

'*Driving Miss Daisy*,' muttered Dartmouth to himself, making a note.

'No,' Granny corrected. 'They were *mates*. Not servant and master, real special mates.'

'My mistake,' Dartmouth soothed her. 'It must have been quite a sight, an Aboriginal man driving a Rolls in the 1920s …'

'Nearly killed him more than once, the old Phantom. Mr Bolitho had the poultry farm at Salisbury, that was his main hobby, see, fancy chickens. Well, this one day they turn up at the farm and the blooming house paddock had just caught fire! Mr Bolitho bolts out of the Rolls in his fancy suit and tie, races straight into the chicken shed and starts rescuing roosters! Cage after cage, he chucks them out onto the grass, yelling for Grandad to come help him. He was screaming out, the roosters was screaming out, the firefront was getting wider and wider, and oh my Lawd, what a circus!'

33

'And did he?' Dartmouth leant forward. 'Go in the shed and help Mr Bolitho?'

'No!' Eddie shook her head vehemently. 'No, Old Charlie knew better. It was September and the paddock was as dry as that there sheet, lah.' She pointed to the crisp white cotton covering her legs. 'Once the fire took off towards the farmhouse Grandad knew there'd be no stopping it.'

'So, he didn't go in?'

'No, cos if it reached the house, they'd lose a lot more than damn prize roosters. So, what do ya think he did?' She stopped abruptly, peering at Dartmouth.

'Called the fire brigade?' he suggested. 'Or ran for the neighbours?'

Granny Eddie let out a triumphant cackle. 'He *drove!*' she cried. 'It was in the paper the next day. He drove the bloomin Rolls round and round the chicken shed at top speed, spraying dust and dirt and putting out the flames with the car tyres! I don't know how many laps he done, but by the time he finished, he was dripping with sweat and his ironed white shirt was as black as his face, he reckoned. But it did the trick – it put the fire out. Risky as hell, cos all four of them tyres caught fire eventually. When he realised they were flaming up beneath him he went oh, bugger this, and he drove into the middle of the burnt ground with them blazing away like billy-o. Then as he jumped out and sprinted away from the car – kaboom! – the petrol tank exploded like a bomb behind him. Tore the trousers right off of him! He was lucky to get away alive, they was picking up bits of Rolls-Royce for weeks.'

'Incredible,' said Dartmouth, feverishly composing paragraphs.

'That was Charlie all over, see. He never did what anyone expected; it was like an unwritten rule he had. They give him some sorta medal for it, too. My sister Rose showed me it once before she went away to Wolston Park, poor darlin.' Granny Eddie turned to greet the nurse bringing her dinner. 'Ooooh, I'm glad to see you, luv. Me stomach thinks me throat's cut, I'm that hungry. Oh, and the roosters was all safe in the end, too. I forgot to say that bit.'

'You must be on the mend, Aunty.' Nurse Xi smiled.

'I'll leave you to eat in peace,' said Dartmouth, getting up on the crutches that had recently replaced his walker.

'Cheerio!' Granny Eddie said, full of goodwill from the memory of Old Man Charlie saving the day and the fifty milligrams of Pethidine coursing through her veins.

6. A Fine Shillelagh

Newstead, Moreton Bay District, Colony of New South Wales, 1854

'I cannot devote myself just now,' Captain John Wickham addressed his drawing room at his Newstead house, 'to the matter of the unfortunate Foreman boy. I have one thousand Bavarian emigrants on the horizon, blacks committing outrages on the Pine and the Logan, and our water supply *still* not secured. Let me turn to these more pressing issues, I beg you.'

'Mr Petrie?' invited the other official in the room. Andrew Petrie dug in his satchel for his plans. His son Tom took the blueprint from him and opened it across Wickham's cedar table for the second time that week. Wickham bent over Petrie's vision that would replace the current arrangement that saw North Brisbane compete with shitting livestock for its water. Only last month, Mrs Ross had let a steer escape and drown in the Horse Pond. The rotted carcass had caused a sensation, and incidentally created a bonanza for the owners of drays and wheelbarrows, as the price of clean drinking water rocketed to a shilling per bucket. Queen Street merchants claimed to still be retching three weeks later. Not to mention the congregation of town blacks routinely found bathing in the stream. No, the situation was dire. Water had to take priority, *clean* water with no yellow mud at the bottom of its barrels. All other matters beyond North Brisbane would need to wait.

'How is the schedule? Will our water-joeys be redundant by Christmas?' Wickham asked optimistically.

Andrew Petrie winced. Designing a water tank was one thing. Finding enough willing workmen to stick at the job of building it was quite another.

'Perhaps by Easter. It will depend on finding the labour of course, and the rains.'

Captain Wickham bent to the document once more. Like Andrew Petrie, he found solace in the neatness and order of the blueprint. Both were educated men, who enjoyed using their technical skills to carve their new town from the wilderness. Although Petrie was a builder here in the Moreton Bay district, an artisan rather than an important public official like Wickham, he also knew the feeling, welcome yet burdensome, of having responsibility for men under his command. To safeguard North Brisbane from drought, disease and the depredations of the myalls; these were the necessary steps towards building a Christian civilisation in Moreton Bay, and he would willingly play his part.

Petrie reached out a hand to touch the mullion windows he had personally installed at the Newstead house more than a decade earlier. Their solidity had meant something to him then, and it meant something still.

'I eagerly anticipate the day my bamboos are made safe,' Wickham announced, straightening and allowing the plans to curl back into loose tubes. 'Those pilfering wretches in Frog Hollow seem not to understand the concept of the Government Botanic Garden. Or not to want to understand, more likely. A botanic exhibition is a place of science and education – it is not there to provide free guttering for their damned shanties.'

'The Garden will be restored to its scientific purpose very soon,' Andrew Petrie assured the blustering captain, remembering well the look of Frog Hollow before sandy blight had robbed him of his vision. Frog Hollow was a veritable democracy of squalor and vice, a jumble of crowded wooden humpies, canvas tents and ramshackle shops, many with timbers dangerously rotten from the boggy conditions near the river. Decayed or not, the miserable dwellings had bodies spilling from every door and window. Irish and Chinese rubbed shoulders in the swamp with the very lowest class of British emancipists; there was a sprinkling of Hindoos and blackfellows, too, to season the mix. The theft of bamboo canes from the Botanic Garden would seem only obvious to these inhabitants. Why pay dearly for barrels of rainwater when you could catch it off a shanty roof and channel it into a bucket for free? Petrie could never condone thieving, of course, but the pragmatic Scot was inclined to overlook the slum-dweller's initiative in raiding the Gardens. God helped those who helped themselves, after all.

'And the Hollow, too, will be so much the safer from fire once our tank is built,' Petrie added tactfully. Engineering was civilisation and cleanliness, and order. It was reclaiming the shantytown from disease and imposing a proper semblance of British decency.

Wickham grunted. 'Let's fill North Brisbane's water barrels before we begin to worry about infernos,' he answered shortly, placing the rolled blueprint in the blind Petrie's hand and signalling to Tom that their conversation was over. He turned to his secretary. 'Now, about this business of the unionists ...'

Andrew Petrie took his son's elbow and allowed himself to be led to the small wharf below Newstead.

'Show me the river, Tom,' Andrew asked his son, turning his face to feel the breeze coming off the water. 'I hear hammering – Jeay's men, I suppose. Dr Ballow told me yesterday that his patients here in Edenglassie say they are disgusted now at the sight of two houses side by side. They all talk of lighting out for less crowded parts.'

As Tom dutifully rowed home, he described the houses being erected in the newly cleared paddocks, and the various vessels they passed on their way.

'What in the name of our Lord and Saviour is that unholy racket?' Tom's father asked as they pulled in at Petrie Bight. A great yowling had filled the vicinity of the Bogey Hole, and only grew louder as they climbed up from the stone landing.

'Catchpenny,' said Young Tom. 'With a load of screaming felines over her shoulder, it would seem.'

'Where on earth did she ... Catchpenny! Catchpenny!' Petrie called out to his old acquaintance. The woman hung her screeching dillybag on a paperbark tree beside Bribie's bridge and made her way to where the elder Petrie stood leaning on his walking stick, tilting his best ear to the source of the cacophony.

'Fancy a kittijen, Mister Petrie?' she propositioned. 'Guarantee he'll be a budgeree mouser in no time, this fellow, and he's the prettiest little kittijen in all Moreton Bay, too.'

'Thank you, no. I have my Gilbert for the last of the infestation, and busy with it he is. But Catchpenny, where on earth did you come upon a spare kitten?' A mouse plague had lately been upon North Brisbane and those lucky enough to own cats could name their price. Only last week Nellie had been in despair about the rodents in the ceiling.

'Not one, Mister Petrie,' Catchpenny gloated, 'seven! York's Hollow mob traded me the lot yesterday for some baccy and half a pail of flour. There's just the two gingers left. I turned down a sovereign apiece for em this morning, but I'd take that very same price from you right now, sir, no word of a lie. Given their colour, like, and you being the gentleman you are, and seeing as how you, Young Tom, has allus been like a—'

'A sovereign each?' Andrew Petrie interrupted, feigning outrage. 'Whist woman! Are these *talking* kittens? I tell you what, let me ask my good wife to cast an eye over them. If she gives her blessing to yet more mouths to feed, I'll give you a pound for the pair.'

'Baal him budgeree,' Young Tom added drily, disputing her claims, 'Gammon! Kuril bin finish dis pfella budgigan more likely!'

Catchpenny laughed, undeterred by Young Tom's cynicism. 'My price one sovereign till noon, Midja Petrie.'

Andrew Petrie paused. The Sydney steamer would arrive at noon, bearing British and Bavarian emigrants, doubtless wanting to establish themselves in decent homes free of vermin. Petrie put out his hand to feel the mewling scraps in the bag. Catchpenny expertly guided it so that the lively kittens latched onto Petrie's pinkie finger and began to suck at it in vain.

'Gunnan-gunnan, no milk for him, poorfella kittijen,' Catchpenny grieved loudly and insincerely on the kitten's behalf.

Petrie withdrew his hand, wiping it on his handkerchief. He knew when he was bested. 'A sovereign for the pair. That's my final offer.'

'Oh, you drive a hard bargain to an old friend, Midja Petrie.' Catchpenny put on a show of reluctance. 'But nevermine. I'll take your price as a favour to you and be done with it.'

Young Tom spluttered with laughter, having just estimated Catchpenny's exorbitant overnight profit.

'This gin believes she's the match of any white man in New South Wales,' Young Tom told his father, before adding, 'and she could be right at that.'

'Catchpenny, you're a natural wonder for humbug,' Andrew Petrie agreed with a shake of his head. 'Not to mention you get around this town like you own the place.'

'Indeed, that's God's truth you speak there, Midja Petrie!' Catchpenny said over her shoulder as she headed to where the emancipist Bribie was emptying his fish trap. 'No word of a lie!'

An hour later, as his family were sitting down to lunch on boiled cabbage and dugong, Andrew Petrie suddenly paused, fork in the air, and laughed. He had just caught the full meaning of Catchpenny's reply. What, he wondered, headshaking, was to be done with such a person?

~

Grenier's Hotel overflowed with workers intent on swallowing their wages and swallowing them fast. Sickly Jamaica rum perfumed the South Brisbane air. It filled the nostrils of the drinkers, overpowering the stench of the slaughter yard across the road and the dozens of mangy curs in the street, lured by the blood and offal running down into the river. Gallons of grog flowed all day at Grenier's, allowing the men there to briefly forget that they lived in a colonial shithole not of their choosing, their lives at the mercy of bosses, squatters and unelected officials who enjoyed nothing better than licking the monied arses of those who'd put them there.

Grog flowed, pushing away the prospect of starvation in this muddy backwater, three days sail from Sydney and ten thousand miles from home. Grog flowed, buying sweet amnesia, blotting out for a few hours the terrifying knowledge of myall blacks lurking beyond the town's boundary stones, and the hideous memories of what had come before '42. The rough men at Grenier's drank and laughed, and sang their native Gaelic tunes, and fought each other for no good reason at all. They boasted that they were about to chuck it all in, bugger the bosses, and strike out for the diggings! They'd bring back great lumps of gold the size of a man's fist. Hadn't a jolly cove struck it rich that very week at Cedar Creek, or was it Esk? Wasn't the scrub all about them riddled with quartz and likely to send them back to Glasgow or Dublin millionaires? They drank and sang and dreamed; the hotel heaved with their passions and, as Friday afternoon crawled towards dusk, Thomas Grenier's purse swelled with their scripts.

From the footpath, Nita observed this mayhem with a keen eye. She'd been sent across the river by Missus Petrie, to fetch Murree. He was wanted to haul lumber, but Nita didn't like her chances of returning to Petrie Bight with him in tow. She could glimpse her quarry inside, yarning merrily with several other working men and looking like any obligation to haul heavy timber was the furthest thing from his mind. Nita sighed and prudently shifted away from the propositions coming at her thick and fast through the hotel's open door.

'Murree!' she called through a window on the other side of the building, 'Murree, come now, Murree, Mister John bin want you!'

Murree waved her away, promising to come on a later ferry. Reluctantly, with an anxious glance at the dagai filling the room, Nita stepped inside the hotel. Murree was wanted at Petrie Bight now, not later.

'Tell yer master Dundalli did slip his'n bracelets and did grab Murree,' one of the drinkers said and laughed. 'And did skin im alive afore roasting im fer supper.' The drinker poked a blunt finger into Murree's stomach, testing his suitability for a feast.

The loud laughter that followed this suggestion was shrill with fear. Yes, laugh all you want from the safety of South Brisbane town, thought Nita in scorn. If the warrior Dundalli escaped his cell and caught you ten miles from here, you brute, you'd be gone like shit through a goose. You'd never laugh again.

'Mister John bin want you for yakka long Queen Street,' she repeated to Murree.

Various lewd interpretations of the work in question were offered by the crowd, and Nita's alarm grew. She was alone at the hotel. Though she lived with the protection of the Petrie name over her, South Brisbane was a very different kettle of fish from Petrie Bight. She was about to skedaddle when a gaunt croppie smoking in the corner spoke up.

'I'll put him on the next ferry for ye, lass.'

Nita looked at the man's grizzled features. The man was fifty if he was a day and looked like hunger and hardship had been his natural state of being for every one of those years. Even the other drinkers were giving him a wide berth, as if worried his air of permanent suffering and rotten luck might rub off.

'Are you up to it, mister? Not meaning to be rude ...' Nita trailed off.

Murree was a muscular young kippa just through his Second Law and this ragged fellow had obviously known better days. The old Irishman straightened up and a queer expression, a kind of faded pride overlain with newer despair, came over his face. For a moment Nita was almost ashamed of her question. Then she spied the tremor in his left arm and her doubts redoubled.

The man tapped his clay pipe against the sill of the open window and blew glowing ash onto the mucky ground outside. Then he fossicked for the few crumbs of tobacco that remained in his pouch. 'I'm to collect a flock of ewes at Cowper's tomorrer,' he told Nita, 'then drive the beggars to Red Bank and keep em safe till near Christmas, all without a spear decorating me gizzards. I reckon I can manage yer young friend.' He nodded at Murree with thinly veiled contempt.

'Mister John would thank you for yer trouble, I'm sure,' Nita said, with a rush of gratitude.

The Irishman gave a hoarse laugh. 'I tell ye lass, be it father or son, any Petrie's more likely to look down his long Scotch nose like he's smelt his own shit for the first time, than he is to thank the likes of me. But it's your thanks I'm after anyhow, colleen.'

The croppie got to his feet and reached for Nita. She realised in horror what the man expected and fled from his outstretched arm while the pub roared with laughter. Cursing herself for a fool and Murree for a knave, Nita bolted outside. She skirted the snapping mongrels in the street before catching the ferry back over to North Brisbane. Safe on the water, she pondered whether to tell her employer the truth of Murree's refusal, or instead wait and see if he got himself to Queen Street in time. She decided in the end that she would simply say she had delivered the message, which was no more and no less than the truth. A Ngugi adopted by the Petries at a young age, she owed no special favours to Murree of the Kurilpa, and even fewer since the scoundrel had exposed her to the dangers of the hotel.

Later that night, Nita pulled her wool blanket up against the cool air of the veranda. She snuggled into Goldie's soft ginger fur. The cat's dear little pink nose rested on her chin as they both drifted off to sleep. She was secure from molestation under the Petrie roof, but her dreams were unhappy, the frightening kind she thought she'd left behind in childhood. Nightmare mobs of dagai circled her, laughing in derision at her terror. They spoke the unlovely guttural tongue of the English and their dream wrists which grasped at her were, like those of the croppie, ringed with purple scarring from the irons.

~

Deep in the scrub beyond Canoe Creek, a man crouched by a fire, intently focused on the weapon he was carving. Earlier in the day he had selected exactly the right branch, careful to choose it for the correct length and shape, not just settling for any convenient lower limb as a lazy man might. Now he squatted on his haunches, stripping the fibrous stringybark from the branch and rotating it over the low flames to dry the timber. He worked patiently, shaping the branch with the rude stub of a broken knife blade he had happened upon, knowing that the effort he put in now was essential to his task. His very life might depend on it. Satisfied at last with his work, the man gathered leaves from a sandpaper fig tree nearby. The rough leaves did their job well. In a few short minutes the still-warm wood was silken to his touch. Then, holding a weapon that was fire-hardened and smooth, as well as convincing to his enemies, the man stood and balanced it lightly in his palms. He frowned a little as he held it, shifting its weight from one hand to the other to judge his work. He had gotten the form and the balance perfect, but the colour was wrong, and that could be his undoing.

44

He considered this problem a moment. Then his gaze fell on the tar pot which sat warming on the coals. Exclaiming at the obviousness of the solution, the man took up the tar brush and blackened the breech and barrel of his new wooden rifle. When the tar had dried and hardened, the result – a matte black closely resembling old steel – made him smile a grim smile. His gun was now indistinguishable at a spear's distance from the real McCoy. Delighted with his work, the man sighted along the barrel at the sheep grazing innocently in front of him. Then he brandished the weapon high, addressing his woolly companions.

'There's a fine shillelagh wouldn't yer say, friends! But yer in no danger from it nor from me, don't yer worry my lovelies.'

Several ewes responded with doubtful bleats.

'Oh, it's contradicting me you'd be, is it? I tell you plain, Miss Molly – yer safe as houses with old Tim Shea in charge.' The Irishman waved his rifle in demonstration.

Despite this assurance, one which he repeated to the herd every ten minutes throughout the day, Shea kept his weapon close to hand. He spent nearly every waking moment scanning the brush for danger. There were smokes two ridges to the south, towards the River Darling, and Shea had no earthly way of knowing if they belonged to the Native Police or to the heathen black buggers that Freddy Walker was meant to be dispersing. He prayed it was the former, but slept always with one eye open, knowing that the sapsucker Walker had lately grown a lot more fond of the bottle than he was of his job hunting the myalls away from Godfearing folk like him.

7. Bingkin Business

1854

'Come on, will you!' urged Murree, jostling his leather pails in the direction of the river. Mulanyin shook his head as he reached to fill his own bucket from Kingfisher Creek. His law-brother was always in a hurry, provided he was calling the shots, that is. Given orders, Murree turned into a creature as slow as Harry the Galapagos bingkin, lumbering around the garden at Newstead. But today his fellow kippa was itching to be done with water-joeying. The boat regatta offered two-pound purses for the winners of each race – and Murree knew that Mulanyin was as at home in a boat as he was on dry land. Riches beckoned.

'But the Warrar doesn't know me like it knows you,' Mulanyin objected, as they carried their final load of drinking water to Missus Ross.

Murree instantly poo-pooed this. Hadn't Mulanyin lived at Kurilpa ever since the Bora made them into brothers months ago? And hadn't Mulanyin, like all of Murree's people, used the Warrar for everything from bathing to ceremony? Couldn't his thick southern skull comprehend that an arm with an oar on the end of it shifted a boat the same, regardless of whether the water it dipped into was salt or sweet? Maybe, Murree proposed, his new law-brother was just secretly afraid that the Amity mob would beat them and humiliate the Kurilpa men in front of all Brisbane?

'You were braver during our Bora,' Murree noted. 'And anyway brother, it's about time you realised you belong here too, now, in my father's Country.'

'As a welcome guest, yes. But my blood is of the Nerang, and always will be.'

They were still debating when Missus Ross opened her gate to them. Mulanyin shuffled sideways through the narrow opening she created, turning away his muscled body, glistening with sweat and creek water, to spare the waymerigan a close-up view of his privates. Most dagai saw water-joeys as just another beast of burden, their nakedness as natural as that of a cow or a dog. Others, like Missus Ross, apparently enjoyed the sight in an earthier fashion. Nobody seemed to have ever taught the woman any decorum, and so Mulanyin turned his back.

'Two-shilling, missus,' Murree said cheerfully once they had poured their final buckets into the water barrel beside the kitchen.

Missus Ross dug in her apron for coins, emerging with a battered Spanish dollar.

'Baal chilling!' objected Mulanyin in alarm, spotting the unfamiliar currency. 'Baal budgeree bungoo!'

Murree assured him that the Spanish coin Missus Ross offered was equal to a British shilling. Mulanyin felt, though, that Missus Ross was not to be trusted; why else was she always staring so hard and smiling so directly at him, a virtual stranger? He escaped out onto the rutted dirt of Grey Street seeking refuge from her foreignness and her skewering eyes.

While he waited, Mulanyin turned to face Yerrin's village. The Kurilpa huts clustered on the hill separating South Brisbane from One Mile Swamp. According to Murree, the village in his youth held many more scores of families, mostly Magandjin people who had been hunted away from their home in central Brisbane. In his childhood their campfires had stretched all the way from the ridge down to the very riverbank itself, where the ferry was now moored. In Murree's short lifetime the Kurilpa and Magandjin had been rudely shoved back from their river, often at gunpoint. They'd been forced onto the high sloping ground, and now lived there, watching strangers enjoying their old home. His people's ancient footpaths had transformed into tracks for the bullock drays bringing wool and tallow and hides from the outstations beyond Red Bank. Wooden bungalows dotted the river flats where Murree had played and slept as a child. Now paling fences surrounding each cottage made sure the true landowners stayed well back from the river. That hallowed ground had become the province of the dagai.

Mulanyin sometimes saw the burning injustice of this in his brother's face. But Murree was in the habit of turning his thoughts to tomorrow, not yesterday. Mulanyin wondered about this, for it was only in Yerrin's whale rib hut, surrounded by the easy comfort of the Goories, that South Brisbane made any sense to him at all. There was no sanity down among the aliens where he was forced to work. Doubtless growing up alongside so many dagai had shaped Murree in ways different to himself, who had neither seen white skin nor heard English spoken until his sixth Mullet Run.

'I'd itch to finish them,' he blurted when Murree had first told him of the war which had raged when he had been a newborn. 'Spear the lot and send their women and jarjums back over the seas to their own damn Country.'

Murree had turned his face away at this and fallen silent. Mulanyin felt awkward, as though he'd accused the Kurilpa clan of cowardice. He knew the battles to keep their Country must have been brutal.

'I understand, brother,' Mulanyin added quickly. 'Their diamonds have the muskets and powder, and their Death Spirit has sent so many warriors to the Star Country.' This was true. And yet secretly, he wondered. There were many stories of the Goorie

Generals and the troops they led. The giant Dundalli – a prisoner, now, in the Queen Street gaol – and the others like him who were dead. Men who had warred to defend their lands; legends of warriors in the mould of Mulrobin, Eulopy and Multuggerah, unbowed by the weapons of the invaders, striking back against the dagai even in their towns. The Butchulla had recently come close to driving the whites from Maryborough, it was said. Was it really too late to take back what had been thieved in Magandjin? It was a mournful thought; it rankled. But Mulanyin knew that this war – if it *was* still a war – was the proper business of Yerrin and Dawalbin, and those Elders who had always called Magandjin home.

He was a newcomer north of Nerang Creek, and a young newcomer at that. His Big Father had impressed on him – do only what his hosts asked, because to do anything more, or less, would shame his family and risk a spear through his thigh from a vast range of landowners into the bargain. As soon as Mulanyin spoke of killing the British, he regretted his words. It wasn't his business.

The breeze shifted direction. From where he stood in Grey Street Mulanyin could hear the village women pounding bungwall. The syncopated drumming drifting down from the ridge flung him a hundred miles south, transporting him to his home beside Nerang Creek. All Mulanyin's youth, his waijungs and grandmothers had tended the bungwall root, roasted the tubers they grew, and pounded them into flour for daily sustenance. It was the happy sound of normal life, he mused, the driving heartbeat of Kombumerri people, along with the tumbling of waves in the endless dance between burragurra and shore. The comforting thumps of bungwall preparation were rhythmic and ever-present, but never mechanical; the women paused, often in laughter, to comfort a child or simply to rest. There was no need for any hurry. Bungwall was straightforward to grow and harvest – and life was for enjoyment, otherwise why bother?

'Your mate a bit myall, is he? Cat got his tongue?' Missus Ross quizzed Murree on the other side of her paling fence. 'Or he just no savvy English?'

'Me sabby English,' Mulanyin said stiffly from the rutted clay road. He had learnt enough of the dagai tongue to understand when he was being discussed. This woman was making him very uncomfortable, laughing merrily with Murree as though she had no husband of her own.

'Let's go to the regatta,' he suggested abruptly in Yagara. 'The races will be over if you insist on standing around gossiping with waymerigan while their husbands are away.'

Murree bounced into the street and clapped his mate on the back, grinning in triumph. His strategy had worked. Mulanyin loved being the centre of attention when it came to Goorie girls, but he was rather shy around dagai women. Murree had schemed that by leaving Missus Ross's delivery till last, he could shepherd Mulanyin towards the boat race, just as sure as any mob of wallabies being funnelled into the netted gully behind the Woolloongabba Swamp.

'Two pounds for the winner!' he shouted as he began to run towards the river, 'Think of what a feast two pounds will buy us, brother!'

Mulanyin soon reached the new wool dock on Stanley Quay. He turned around to find Murree some distance behind him, dragging his heels.

'What's up?' Mulanyin panted. 'I thought we were in a hurry?'

He could already hear the regatta crowd. Pistol shots marked the beginning and end of the heats and distant waves of applause and encouragement followed the progress of each boat along Town Reach. Apparently, somebody had thought it a splendid idea to bring a set of bagpipes out for the festivities. Anything happening in South Brisbane today was clearly happening at the regatta.

Murree halted, pointing his lips at three unremarkable eucalypts with wool drays parked beneath them. If the kippas continued on, they would walk directly into the shadow of the gum trees.

'No good,' said Murree, jogging westward. 'Come this track, brother.' He leapt aside as he went, avoiding a deep bog where the heavy drays had churned the road into a thick brown liquid.

'Why go away from the river?' Mulanyin asked – although from the weathered timber platform he could glimpse in the canopy of the eucalypts, he was pretty sure he already knew.

His companion's reply was lost in a loud burst of applause from the regatta crowd. Their jog west to avoid the burial trees cost the boys a couple of minutes, and when they arrived along the riverbank they saw the colourful flags of the competitors fluttering against a cloudless blue sky. People from South Brisbane and Kangaroo Point and further afield had turned out for the festivities. Ketches and wager boats milled merrily about in Town Reach, getting in each other's way. The familiar government steamer, *Kate*, was there, along with the *Dove*, the *Swiftsure* and the *Sylph*. The kippas could see Tom Petrie with his brothers, John and James, readying the *Lucy Long* to race Mr Byrne. Byrne had his sleeves rolled up to skipper the *Medora*, determination written all over his face, but in the end was outdone by the dogged Scots.

Dalapai and Yerrin had also mustered crews and the Amity Goories sailed back and forth, showing off their beloved *Pirate,* the whaleboat given to them for rescuing survivors off the shipwrecked *Sovereign* seven years earlier.

'I don't know that Goorie pilot,' Mulanyin said, as a clinker swept past with a black man in European clothing at the prow, while another worked the rigging.

'He's not Goorie,' Murree answered. 'He's from a far-off place called Fiji. And that boat he skippers belongs to the Curragee oyster camp.'

The two kippas climbed up onto a handy tree stump and sat

down on it together to enjoy the spectacle. Mulanyin drew his knees up beneath his chin, entranced. The regatta was almost as big as the Wolloongabba pullen pullen and he was secretly hoping to see the Coorparoo girls among the crowd. Nearly all of Yerrin's people, barring the women grinding bungwall back at the village, had trickled down to the festivities. The children old enough to go unsupervised played Black Swan just upstream of the *Kate*, while their fathers and uncles crewed boats or swam from vessel to vessel offering their services. Their female relations cheered their own men forward and heaped loud insults on their opponents.

Further along the riverbank, several dozen white families had spread their picnic blankets out beneath the hot sun, optimistic that the breeze off the water would counteract the intense summer heat. Below the Government Garden opposite, the citizens of North Brisbane and Fortitude Valley had joined ranks to do the same. Although it was not yet eleven, beer, rum and arrack were flowing freely on both banks of the river; the party promised to last long into the night.

A group of Chinese locals had set their prawning nets aside and come to observe the carryings-on. They stood in their pointed hats, discussing the merits of the different boats in their own language. Mulanyin eyed them with disquiet. Dagai were aggressive about land and could be dangerously unpredictable, but the invading British were – in some ways at least – a known quantity. With the guidance of Yerrin and Dawalbin, and daily instruction from Murree, Mulanyin was learning what he could expect from white people. He knew about those newcomers the Kurilpa considered reliable friends: the Petrie family, Mr Pugh the newspaperman, along with Mr Duncan and the Indian John Cassim. He knew too, which dagai were notorious for shooting Goorie people without a second thought. He'd been warned especially about Freddy Walker and his Native Police, a death squad of mostly southern blacks who were to be avoided at all costs. Entire clans had been lost to their murderous rampages. Yerrin had spoken of Walker in a low growl, and Dawalbin had turned away shuddering at the sound of his name.

These Chinese men on the riverbank were different again. Neither dagai nor Goorie nor Hindoo – and standing outside the class divides between free settler, croppie and diamond – they caught Mulanyin's interest. Part of him felt an instinctive hostility to those he didn't know or recognise, but he decided to disregard them. The Chinese did the same, far more interested in the boat races than in him, just one among the scores of blacks on the riverbank.

'There'll be some sorry heads tomorrow,' Murree noted, seeing the labourers of Stanley Quay already unsteady on their feet. And not just from grog, agreed Mulanyin, when a roaring Welshman wielding a broken fence paling shaped up to a Londoner twice his size. The Londoner darted back as the Welshman swung drunkenly at his head, and then used both hands to send his assailant plunging into the river. The crowd cheered uproariously and drank on.

'Yura, Mulanyin!' called the boss of the *Pirate*, a lanky Amity fellow with a sharp, penetrating gaze. 'You joining Yerrin's mob, ay? I thought you were a saltwater man. Gonna race against us, cousin?'

'I'm a saltwater through and through,' Mulanyin replied, instantly alert to accusations of treachery. 'But just watching today, cousin. This river doesn't know me.'

'Oh, you're alright.' The lanky fellow laughed. 'We're all related to Town mob anyways. But how about you come on board with us, and we show these jackaroos how to handle a kundil?'

Mulanyin shot a look at Murree, who was far from impressed at this attempt to poach his prize athlete. In the end it was decided that Mulanyin would row for Kurilpa if he rowed at all. As the *Pirate* swept away downstream, Mulanyin watched the whaleboat fade into the distance with a thrilling plan germinating in his mind. The Amity mob were his distant relations, speaking a similar language and sharing his deep affinity for the burragurra. Like his own people, the Amity mob gathered each year at the Mullet Run and loved to feast on both the whiting and the dugong. If they could own and operate a whaleboat, then why couldn't he?

Rather than slog through the clay of South Brisbane with wooden yokes biting at their shoulders, he and Murree could be real men, rocking gently past the river mouth in search of turtle and dugong and grouper. Masters of their destiny, camping at Fisherman's Island and Winnum, and no day on the bay the same as any other! Living the lives that Goorie men were born to live.

This new idea consumed Mulanyin through the entire afternoon. His own boat, yes, and work of his own choosing. When he cheered the *Pirate*'s win, really, he was cheering his own future as he watched the Amity men pull ahead of their opposition and take the two-pound prize. It was his knotted forearms and corded shoulders pulling the *Pirate* past the *Swiftsure* and in his daydream the winner's purse was stuffed not into an Amity dillybag, but into his own. With a boat, he could return to Nerang any time he liked; he wouldn't have to rely on the goodwill of a friendly captain to see his family. He would be free to travel where and when he pleased. Yes, a boat had everything to recommend it. All he needed to do was somehow gather together the price of one, and then talk Murree into a life on the bumpy surface of the ocean.

'I'll row in the blackfellow's race,' he announced suddenly.

'Now you're talking.' Murree grinned as he stood and signalled to his father that he had another set of hands to crew the boat they'd borrowed from Grandfather Andrew Petrie.

Mulanyin settled onto the seat and grasped the oaken oar of the whaleboat, so different from the light kundil paddles he was used to. He looked to Yerrin, who stood holding the rudder pole that would, hopefully, direct them over the finish line ahead of Dalapai's men. Perhaps the Ancestors would send a large wave over their opponents bow, Yerrin suggested with a cheeky grin, or better yet a whirlpool to spin their boat like a willy-willy! The Kurilpa crew laughed and when the flag on the *Kate* dropped, they put their backs into the job of beating Dalapai's crew back to the signal ship.

The splashing of the river water made the race refreshing, even under the December sun. Several sets of muscular arms rowed in unison, reaching and dipping their paddles, feeling the might of the river below their narrow craft. Droplets ran down the men's backs and arms, sweat mingling with river water, as Yerrin urged his crew on to greater efforts. Dalapai did the same, a few short feet away; at one point the competitors' oars almost clashed and a cry of outrage rose up from both boats.

'Pull harder, men,' Yerrin cried, 'this is our stretch of the Warrar, not theirs!'

Redoubling their efforts, the Kurilpa crew reached the halfway point just in front of their competition. With the wind behind them, and the crowd loud in approval, Yerrin's men pulled forward to win in the end by a short length. Mulanyin's joy amidst the backslapping and wild applause was cut abruptly short though, when he realised that they hadn't been rowing for cash. His face fell on seeing Yerrin handed a bag of flour, sugar and tobacco, which constituted the prize for the blackfellow's race.

'What's up, lad?' Yerrin asked. 'You'll get your cut, don't worry.'

'Nothing,' Mulanyin fibbed, 'just catching my breath.' To voice his disappointment would shame Yerrin and the others. It would be tantamount to saying they had deceived him, were greedy for his labour and had lied by omission to get it. But then no-one save Murree had actually come out and said that the Goories were racing each other for two-pound stakes. Murree must have assumed, like himself, that the prizes would be equal. Mulanyin told himself that other than a few blisters, he was no worse off than he had been an hour ago. And he had at least now rowed a whaleboat and knew what it took to shift one over this flat river water.

'I want you two lads to help Young Tom take the boat back to Petrie Bight,' Yerrin ordered Murree and Mulanyin, after he had distributed the foodstuffs among the crew.

The young men were halfway to Tom's home when they saw an enticing string of bubbles rise to the water's gleaming surface. Mulanyin gave a shout and plunged over the gunwale, diving down to where the turtle was grazing on algae-covered rocks. He was a strong and fast swimmer, but the turtle had been alerted by his splashing entry. After a frantic winding chase through the greenish underworld, Mulanyin ran out of breath and was forced to surface empty-handed, to the merciless teasing of his friends.

'Don't blame me,' he told them, blowing his nose and gulping air as he clung to the side of the boat. 'These Warrar bingkin are so terribly small, they slip through my fingers like grains of sand. In fact, to be honest, I had difficulty even seeing that one, it was so minuscule. I'm more used to hunting saltwater bingkin half the size of this boat,' he said, gesturing at the vessel. This brought more mocking laughter and several pointed comments about river turtles being a lot more use than no turtle at all, which was exactly what Mulanyin had managed to catch.

'There!' Young Tom shouted, spying bubbles again, this time on the far side of the rudder. 'Look!'

'Oh, go away with your Warrar bingkin,' Mulanyin sniffed in disgust, dragging himself back into the boat with the help of several strong young arms. He could fail in the hunt once and retain his dignity; to fail a second time would be a different matter, and as an eternal outsider to Kurilpa waters he had to think carefully about such things. He was welcome in Yagara country as a guest, but if he were to develop a reputation as a poor hunter that might quickly change.

'Your turn, Murree,' urged Tom. But Murree recoiled; being a man of the Turtle totem he could neither hunt nor eat the animal.

In the end it was Young Tom himself who leapt in and managed to seize the unfortunate reptile by its shell. Murree took the flailing creature from him mournfully, talking softly to it as he admired its endearing, yellow-streaked face. He had to fight the urge to release the turtle back into the river to freedom.

Seeing this idea appear very clearly on Murree's face, Mulanyin snatched the animal. 'Don't look,' Mulanyin instructed. Its legs scrabbled in the air, searching for escape but finding none. Murree covered his eyes. Then the hands holding the turtle promptly broke its neck against the side of the boat.

'I had to, brother,' Mulanyin told Murree, who sighed heavily. Mulanyin grew impatient. 'Did I complain when you had roast waterbird three nights ago?' he demanded. 'No. Because I have balls the size of this bingkin, not the pathetic little ugaris you have hanging off your cock!' The unhappy vision of the gutted bird suspended on a framework of green sticks above a coal fire and being turned by its spoon-shaped beak still haunted him. Yet he had said nothing about the bird, a close cousin of his totem, being food for others. That was simply the way of the world.

'How do you come to still be in South Brisbane, when the other kippas have left?' Young Tom intervened, questioning Mulanyin in the Yagara that was becoming more familiar with each passing day. Mulanyin relaxed. Yagara freed him from the prison of English which stifled his tongue and bogged his mind as surely as the drays stuck in the clay of Grey Street.

'Halfway through the ceremony Father got word through the Pretty Face Wallaby clan that my Waijung was sick,' Mulanyin answered. 'He left me in Yerrin's care while he went home to see to her. He reckoned it'd do me good to learn my neighbour's languages, and the ways of the Kurilpa and the Amity people too, before I marry.' He paused. His father had also told him to learn English from the dagai and to watch them carefully until he understood the depth of their rapaciousness and criminality. But Mulanyin hesitated to say that to the son of one of North Brisbane's leading settler families, no matter how many Kurilpa assured him that Young Tom was different.

'Did you get news of your Waijung?' Young Tom asked, retrieving the dead turtle from the bottom of the boat and tucking it by the neck into the waistband of his trousers. It hung there, dripping river water onto Tom's bare feet. Mulanyin gazed ruefully at the animal. Part of him hoped that it would find a home in his own grumbling stomach.

'One of Pettigrew's men saw my cousin at Pumpkin Point recently,' Mulanyin replied. 'I'm told I have a new sister, and that my Waijung has returned to good health.' His mother had been gravely ill while pregnant, however, and second-hand news from a drunken cedar-cutter offered very limited solace. 'I want to go and find out for myself, of course. The *Otter* sails soon, and I intend to be on her.'

'Better not go home till you can speak fluent Yagara,' teased Murree, who didn't want to lose his new brother. 'And good English, too. Or your fathers will properly growl you.'

'If I wait that long I'll be going in my own boat,' Mulanyin told him ruefully. Languages were not his forte; fishing was, and anything to do with the ocean. After three moons he understood Yagara well enough to get by and he had picked up some basic English along with a smattering of Gaelic. But Mulanyin still thought, and planned, in Yugambeh alone.

Young Tom's ears pricked up. 'Your own boat?'

'He wants to put Captain Winshipp out of business!' Murree elbowed his mate's ribs. 'And corner the dugong trade while he's at it!'

Mulanyin didn't deny it. He saw no reason why his head and

his hand shouldn't seek the bounty of the ocean. He had been born to do just that.

Young Tom gave Mulanyin a measured look. The kippa standing in front of him on the pier was several years his junior, but his superior in strength and stamina, if today's regatta was anything to go by. At more than six feet the lad, like most Goorie men, towered over him. He was bold, too, and ambitious with it. A man to watch.

'I intend on riding out to North Pine soon,' Young Tom said thoughtfully, 'to select a station. You might come along if you want paid work. I'll need good men to help build my house and yards and help with the stock, too, once that's done.'

'Stockwork beats loading damn heavy wool bales!' Murree exclaimed. 'And slopping water for waymerigan ...'

Mulanyin hesitated. The North Pine was even further away from his family than South Brisbane. And the Pine was Kabi Kabi land. He had no rights there whatsoever.

'I promised Father to stop in Yerrin's village,' Mulanyin told Young Tom, as a tumult of emotions took hold of him. Paid work on a station would lead him to the boat that would take him home and set him free. Station work would mean no more water-joeying for dagai housewives. No packs of bleating town goats or yapping dogs roaming the streets all night, leaving him lying awake in this foreign Country, worried for his Waijung and sisters. Station work would remove him from the confusion of South Brisbane, with its ever-swelling population of dagai, more arriving on every tide with their sunburnt faces and odd voices and their bizarre British ways.

Yes. He could escape all that. There was a lot to be said for Young Tom's offer.

But he'd promised his father he'd stay put. Had promised to remain where he was, under the care and protection of the Yagara Law. And then there was the problem of the word 'select' too, ringing harsh and worrisome in his ears. North Pine lay far to the north of the Warrar. It wasn't Country for dagai to be picking and choosing over. It already had owners, with Dalapai a leading one. Get tricked into trespassing out there and he'd be likely to end up with a Kabi Kabi spear through him. Mulanyin shot a look at Murree. Tom Petrie had grown up with Kurilpa people. He had been to the Bora ceremonies and knew the Goorie Law. Was he intent on breaking it now and looking for gullible young kippas to assist him in his wrongdoing?

'Just come along for the ride,' Young Tom pressed. 'Dalgnai will take us.'

'Dalgnai!' exclaimed Mulanyin. Dalapai's son was the perfect ambassador. Murree grinned, seeing Mulanyin's expression change.

'I have Dalapai's permission, of course,' Young Tom added, very matter-of-fact. 'I'm not just going to squat anywhere the fancy takes me.' *Like every other white man*, was the unspoken ending of this sentence.

'Come on, brother, say you'll come along,' Murree urged, 'We can get emu near the German Station and plenty of echidna, too. Dalgnai will know the best places.'

Mulanyin found himself growing more curious about Young Tom, this dagai who spoke Yagara like a Goorie. He was intensely interested to find out more about the magic that had allowed Young Tom to catch the turtle that had eluded him. It was remotely possible that this dagai urging him to join his quest for land was even some kind of wiyan, with much important knowledge to teach. The light in Young Tom's eyes promised a grand life waiting in the north for any who followed him, if they were game for the adventure. Brisbane's taverns were full of white men blathering about the fortunes to be made in what they for some reason called the 'new country'. Everywhere dagai gathered he heard them dream aloud of runs and cattle, of gold and sheep.

A land of plenty, they boasted to each other, hoiking their britches up and laughing too loud to show that no spears or waddies would stop them growing rich. Just like every other dagai, Young Tom had land, cattle and wealth in his sights; and was dizzy with the idea of the power which came from all three. But unlike the others, Young Tom's ambitions would be underpinned by the authority of Dalapai and the strength of the Bora Law. His interest aroused, Mulanyin finally agreed that he would ride out with them to Whiteside Station at the Pine – just for a look.

'Good man!' Young Tom clapped him on the back before leaping up onto the stone pier. 'Nita will be pleased with our haul, anyway,' he said, lifting the turtle in one hand as the others secured the boat. 'She told me last week she was sick of Mayne's salt beef.'

An easy life this Nita must have, Mulanyin reflected, to tire of eating beef. Game in Brisbane was nowhere near as plentiful as it was back home, where the dagai had scarcely yet made a difference to the Yugambeh estate. Occasional hunger was a new experience for him in Brisbane, and not one he intended to tolerate. His growling guts were just another in a lengthy list of good reasons to get his hands on a whaleboat and head downriver to the ocean and freedom. On the burragurra he could run his life the way a saltwater man was entitled to, on the glory of the waves. White men with rifles could steal Goorie land and employ shepherds to guard their flocks. They could even stop him harvesting kangaroo and emu off his own land. But with his own boat and a clear sky, no dagai would ever stop him from enjoying the bounty of the ocean.

8. Rough Justice

1854

Nita scraped the final shreds of meat from the bingkin shell and put her spoon down on the kitchen table. She smacked her lips, trying to convince herself that she was supremely happy. The coal-roasted turtle had been succulent, a far cry from salt beef. Yet like so much else in Brisbane, the meal seemed more like a memory of life rather than life itself.

Nita traced the bony plates of the carcass with her forefinger. She had no business complaining, even silently. Her belly was full and complaint was disrespectful to the animal, which had died to fill it. Plenty of Brisbane Goories were going about their business with next to nothing in their guts. Poor whites starved, too, for all they tried to hide the fact. But the taste of Warrar bingkin was so very different from those of her home, it was hard to feel truly grateful. And to eat alone, minus her brothers and sisters and parents, minus the sounds of the ocean wrapping around the family: minus the crying gulls, the splash of each wave onto the sand ... there was no end to the missing if she allowed herself to recall her losses. Which was why she very rarely did. She stood up, determined to clear the table and her head.

'Tasty?' asked Young Tom, suddenly appearing in the doorway, flanked by that rascal Murree. 'You're licking your lips – it must have been.'

'Tasty enough,' Nita told him, pausing as she collected the table settings. 'But next time I'll make soup. The bones are wasted, otherwise.'

'Oh, puss will enjoy those. And if not puss, then Rex. Sorry, Murree.' Murree was blanching at the idea.

'I reckon the hog might enjoy a chew on what's left,' Nita answered with a large dollop of malice. She hadn't forgotten Murree's performance at the Inn the week before. 'Those strong jaws of his'n will crack the marrow right out.'

Young Tom raised his eyebrows. 'She's chucking you to the swine, Murree, what've you done to deserve that?'

Murree scowled as the others burst into pitiless laughter.

'Who's that hiding in back of yer?' Nita asked, curious about the stranger lingering in the hall.

Tom stepped aside. 'This is Mulanyin, a saltwater Yugambeh to watch, and didn't he show it at the regatta! He'll be a ship's captain one day, you mark my words.'

'Is that right?' Nita answered drily, taking in the arresting youth who stood there, black as coal and a head taller than the other men. He was naked but for Tom Petrie's kerchief tucked into his string belt like an afterthought. The stranger met her gaze with benign ease, as though he was some kind of visiting dignitary. He was a fine example of manhood, lean and muscular from daily work with his net and spears. For some reason, Mulanyin bore the ritual marks of the Kurilpa on his chest, she observed; not those of his own clan. Seeing this, Nita grew curious. Like him, she was a Goorie living far from her birthplace and making a life among people other than her own. Perhaps she and he might understand each other?

The stranger was strikingly handsome; his presence in the kitchen was already making her heart pound in a way that other men had not. Nita found this unsettling; she was used to being chased by a horde of suitors and showing her heels to the lot of them. Why should this saltwater fellow be any different? The realisation that she was staring at him – not to mention the imperious look he gave her in response – prompted Nita to take Mulanyin down a peg or two. When she spoke, it was Tom she addressed.

'A pirate ship I take it you mean? Or has he perhaps struck gold, to be talking of buying a ship when there's plenty of souls begging in the street for a dry crust?'

Mulanyin snorted, matching her sauce with his own. 'Do you think I'd be standing here if I'd struck gold?' he asked. 'I'd be at sea, my keel crammed full of youngen and bingkin as big as this table.' He knocked the wooden table with his knuckles. 'And this saltwater will be setting sail in his own whaleboat soon enough – with or without a gold mine.'

Nita's mouth watered at the mention of fresh sea turtle and dugong. 'Well, Mulanyin of the Yugambeh,' she told him breezily, 'you can bring me the very first youngen you catch, when you get your wonderful whaleboat. I'll be waiting here with great interest. But you'll forgive me if I don't hold my breath meantime.'

'There's a challenge for yer,' laughed Young Tom.

'No challenge at all.' Mulanyin grinned. 'Provided she's still here when the feast begins.' He was supremely confident that he would earn the purchase price, buy his boat and resume a saltwater life, if not by the next Oyster Season then certainly by the following one. The boat was already rocking beneath him and the waves were glistening blue in all directions as far as the eye could see. Mulanyin fixed the pleasant image hard in his mind so as to make it more certain; yet in his guts he knew that the picture was already real. No matter how long it took, he would be leaving Murree and the Warrar in a wooden boat and returning to his beloved burragurra. He could feel the Nerang River coiled in his guts, the drag of it forever upon his spirit, pulling him homeward with every rising tide.

'Oh, Nita isn't going anywhere,' Tom interjected. 'She's part of the family.'

Mulanyin glanced at the servant girl. He found himself enchanted by her, despite her mockery.

'Then the Petrie family table will receive my first haul, Tom. And your Nita will have to eat her words that day, as well as my catch.'

'Out of the kitchen, you men!' Mary Petrie bustled in with an armful of purple and white orchids she had just purchased from Catchpenny. 'Go get me six ripe pineapples from Mr Skyring, Murree, if you want to be useful for once! Nita, can you arrange these in the sitting room?' she asked, handing the girl the flowers. 'And mop the guest quarters. We'll need three dozen oysters too. Tom, can you go and let your sister know Reverend Lang will dine with us tonight? Pineapples, Murree, I said!'

The young men fled up Queen Street past a scattering of wooden shopfronts and tents, heading for the Skyrings' pineapple plot. Before they had gone halfway, though, they discovered a raucous crowd gathered around the courthouse stairs. There were furious men yelling and various cries of alarm from onlookers. Abandoning the idea of pineapples, the kippas stopped to investigate.

Mulanyin glimpsed a stout bearded dagai at the centre of the hubbub. The man, a uniformed officer, was drunk. Flanking him were eight, no, nine black troopers in uniform, all looking as grim as death. The officer staggered about the centre of the crowd howling curses at another white man. Some of the many Goorie onlookers jeered at the drunk. Others stayed silent, seeming to Mulanyin as though they were oddly unwilling to even utter a word. Perhaps, he thought uneasily, this rum-soaked diamond has an evil magic that not everybody knows to fear? In contrast, the white half of the crowd threw out commentary without pause, their barracking evenly divided between the combatants. The effect from where the kippas stood was one of overwhelming noise and confusion, tinged with an edge of Goorie hysteria.

'What the hell?' Mulanyin asked, turning to Murree, 'Who's this cranky fellow?'

'That's him, now. Freddy Walker,' muttered Murree, staring at the enraged officer. Beads of fresh sweat burst on his brow. 'The other's Duncan, the newspaper man. And them troopers is Native Police, murderers the lot of em. Let's leave them to it, brother.'

Just then Duncan accused Freddy Walker of being a drunken disgrace to his uniform, and told him he'd see him stripped of it, if it was the last thing he did in the colony. The argument was growing shriller by the minute, for neither Duncan nor Walker seemed interested in taking a backward step. It was all very peculiar. Mulanyin shook off Murree's arm and pushed deeper into the crowd, fascinated. Despite the fully public setting there appeared to be nobody in authority overseeing this pullen pullen at all. And with ten armed warriors against a lone individual, the duel was a complete mismatch. This fellow Duncan was an angry man, or a reckless one, to fight them all on his own. Mulanyin looked around in vain for the Elders managing the duel.

'Brother! Come away! Them mob evil, they murderers!' Murree's bare chest was heaving with emotion.

Mulanyin suddenly realised that his Kurilpa brother was deathly afraid. Even at a public tournament with a hundred onlookers, he was afraid. But of what?

'We right, brother,' Mulanyin reassured him. 'What they gonna do to us here? In Queen Street, in front of all this mob?' Mulanyin turned back to the hubbub, as the 'throwing insults' phase of the pullen pullen grew louder.

Murree's face contorted with terror and grief. Mulanyin was as unknowing as an infant when it came to the Native Police. Before he could speak, though, a great roar erupted from the crowd. Women screamed as Walker drew his sword from its scabbard and flourished it wildly at Duncan, who fell backwards in shock, tripping on the wooden gutter and almost falling to the dirt. Walker's troopers instantly surged forward, forming a tight semicircle behind their leader, though whether they did so to protect him or to prevent his assault on Duncan, Mulanyin couldn't quite fathom. His outrage, which had begun to simmer when he first laid eyes on the two men, now began to jump and boil. He felt like he had swallowed a live possum. Two white men facing each other: one a defenceless civilian and the other an officer with a drawn sword, with nine black troopers to back him up. If these dagai had any Law at all, it must be a very particular one, to allow such a contest.

In the moments that followed, Mulanyin somehow found himself in the very first row of onlookers, close enough to smell the grog on Walker's breath. He could see soup smeared down the front of the lieutenant's blue jacket and grass stains on the knees of his breeches. Then to his shock, the man Duncan was standing right beside him; the crowd scattering in panic from Walker's wildly swinging blade. Without any conscious thought at all, Mulanyin stepped out, putting himself between the armed officer and the helpless Duncan. He spoke in his own tongue, his right arm raised as though to ward off the madman's blade by sheer force of will.

'Coward!' Mulanyin accused Walker fiercely. 'For shame! What sort of a warrior are you, to attack an unarmed man with no brothers stood beside him? Have you no honour at all?'

Murree's mouth fell open. He made a choking sound, but no good words emerged. Horror glued him to the spot.

Startled and confused, Walker paused his attack. Duncan, though gasping in fear, drew enough courage to resume his tirade. 'Yer not on the MacIntyre now, boyo,' he taunted Walker. 'There'll be no cover-ups in North Brisbane!'

'The black reckons you're a coward, Walker,' shouted Tom

Petrie, who was shoving his way forward through the gaping crowd. 'He's asking what sort of man attacks an unarmed opponent? Which is a fair question, I might add, as a fellow son of the thistle. Put the sword down, man.'

Walker let out an ugly guttural growl. He snarled at Mulanyin as though about to run him through on the spot.

Mulanyin didn't flinch. His contempt for Walker overrode the fear that was gradually dawning on him.

Murree crouched down and picked up a broken half-brick from the dust of the street, wedging it hard into his palm as he stepped forward. If Walker flashed his sword, Murree would swing, too, and smash his skull to smithereens.

'I'm right here, brother,' he told Mulanyin in his own tongue.

Walker took a wobbling step towards Mulanyin, his weapon high. The crowd shrieked.

'Och, come along man,' Young Tom repeated, shoving his way past Murree to stand beside Mulanyin. 'Put that thing back in the scabbard where it belongs and come and have a dram.'

The mood of the whites in the crowd hovered for a second. Then, almost palpably, it swung away from Walker and towards Tom. Cries of 'shame' and 'yellow cur', and 'pack him off to sober up' began. The Native Police, already mortified, encircled their master and began to shepherd him uphill to the barracks. As they passed by, one brushed hard against Mulanyin, meeting his eye with a cold, blank hatred he had never known before.

'Cover your arse with trousers next time,' the black trooper sneered, 'You damn ugly savage.'

Had they been five miles away, in Nundah or at Cowper's Plains, this stranger might have blown Mulanyin's head off and called it a good day's work. Here in town, with scores of British citizens as witnesses, the Native Police were forced to endure the humiliation of their boss, and thus themselves. While the troopers marched past with Walker, memorising Mulanyin's face for another encounter on another day, the kippa controlled his expression and deliberately slowed his breathing.

Show them no fear. Don't blink. Give them nothing.

Oblivious to the earlier altercation, a sulky pulled by two sweating bays trotted past. For a moment the choking dust cloud in its wake made everything invisible. Duncan took his felt hat off and used it to beat the dirt away. When the dust subsided, Walker and his murderous phalanx had disappeared in the distance.

'Walker's finished,' Tom told Duncan. 'There's no coming back from that display.'

'I might have to stand you a drink,' Duncan told Young Tom, wiping his face with a forearm as he sank onto a tree stump in front of Warry's apothecary. He looked pale and spent; as though he was dredging grateful words up out of the last of his courage.

'I think you might stand this fellow one, along with some thanks for saving your life.' Tom gestured towards Mulanyin. A dozen local Goories had clustered around Mulanyin, celebrating his courage, while at the same time Murree berated him for his utter stupidity.

'Mulanyin, this is Mr Duncan,' Tom said by way of introduction. 'Mulanyin's going to come and work on the Pine with me,' Tom added.

Mulanyin was dumbstruck when he heard this claim. He had said nothing at all about working for Tom at the Pine, yet for some reason now found himself unwilling to contradict Petrie publicly. Afterwards, Mulanyin reflected that his silence at that singular moment had somehow drawn him further than he intended into Tom Petrie's plans. The white man's claim and his own silence had melded, becoming an almost solid thing that fell over them both like a possum skin cloak. The words became a promise; and the promise bound their fates together like an incantation.

~

69

Standing in front of the Oyster Saloon, Nita was deaf to Mr Hart asking a third time for her mistress's order. Her head was full of the extraordinary scene she'd just witnessed on the far side of the street, and with the idea of Moreton Bay youngen, the wedding food of saltwater people. She smiled to herself, wondering exactly how long it would take Mulanyin to arrive on her doorstep proffering the first he caught. For there was no doubt in her mind, anymore, that he would get his boat and his dugong, too. A saltwater man to watch, Master Tom had said in the kitchen, and he was right.

She would watch Mulanyin, watch him carefully. He would work for Tom Petrie at North Pine, and with the wages he earned there he would buy himself a whaleboat. And then she would marry him, and then he would take her home.

9. All One Mob My Arse

2024

Joy fought with astonishment on Johnny's face. His crush had just appeared in front of him, a vision of loveliness in faded blue jeans and a Black Flag t-shirt. Giant Haus of Dizzy earrings dangled beneath Winona's cornrows; a canvas satchel lay flat against her very desirable left hip. She was, Johnny swooned, the very picture of a hot Murri girl enjoying her Sunday at the West End Markets. She had to be roughly the same vintage as him. More important than her age was the question of whether she was single, and straight. He'd done a quick social media stalk of her the day they first met and found exactly zero useful information. Worried that Winona would leave without even spotting him, Johnny leapt out from the back of the stall he volunteered at.

'Hey, I hope you like samosas?'

'Doctor Johnny!' Winona startled, not expecting him outside the hospital and minus his stethoscope.

'The very same. Want one? We're fundraising for Clean Creeks.'

'Since when do you work at the markets?' she asked, ignoring the tray of food in his soapy hands. She seemed far more interested in the posters of Creek Carers planting native grass on riverbanks and paddling kayaks in lurid orange lifejackets.

'Once a month since I was at State High. I guess you're not from around here – I'm on a first-name basis with half of West

End.' As if to prove his point, a passing punter called hello Doctor Jay, promising to return and buy a dozen samosas later. Johnny waved back at them without taking his eyes off Winona. Her dark eyes. Her slanting cheekbones, her gleaming bronze forearms. He could have stood and gazed at her forever.

'What?' Winona wrinkled her nose.

Johnny suddenly realised in horror what had come out of his mouth.

'I don't, I mean, I didn't mean you're not *from here*, I meant you probably aren't living around this area, in West End, I mean, like, *obviously* you're local cos, umm ...' Johnny stumbled over his words as it dawned on him that he now sounded like he was fishing for her address, which was, if anything, possibly even worse than telling an Indigenous girl she wasn't 'from here'. Christ Almighty. Just shut up, ya fool.

Winona laughed. 'Yeah, I'm from Logan, ay. But I'm staying at Nan's place while she's in hospital. Saves heaps on train fare.'

Johnny exhaled in relief. Winona was chill. He turned to his fellow Creek Carers.

'Well, this is my mate, Avelina. And that sad excuse for a human being over there's Happy. Guys, this is Winona. She's .... well, she's Winona. From Logan ...' Johnny trailed off. Calling her a friend would be pushing it, and it was against hospital protocol to identify her as a rello of a patient.

Winona smiled at Johnny's mates as she picked up a samosa. She sniffed it doubtfully, then took a bite. Her eyes widened. 'Not too bad.'

Johnny glowed. His mind was racing with possibilities. Should he ask her to come to the Dreamtime footy with him next weekend? If Winona had a partner, then surely they would have been at the markets, too? It boded well that she appeared to be here alone – *very* well, *very* promising. But then how could he ask her out when he was still looking after Granny Eddie; what was the go there? Cracking onto patients was an absolute no-no, but extremely attractive twenty-something rellos encountered outside the hospital was a grey area. What if it didn't sound like a date though? What if it was something that started out platonic – *feel like going to the Dreamtime match?* – and then turned into a date later on? Or was that horribly dodgy? Johnny felt sick, knowing that Winona would very likely take off any moment now, dateless and un-wooed, and completely oblivious to his burning desire to make googly eyes at her all night long for the rest of his life.

'I made them. Not the dhal though. Avelina's the dhal Queen.'

'You said, it, darl,' Avelina joked.

'Looks like ya found your calling, Doctor Johnny. If ya kill too many patients you can always open a restaurant, ay?' Winona grinned, but Johnny knew he'd lost her. Her attention had been caught by a didge starting to drone on the other side of the park. She flashed him a final smile and began to wander off, looking for all the world like her mild approval was payment enough for the half-eaten samosa in her hand.

'They're ten bucks for three, hey?' Johnny called, desperate to prolong the encounter.

Winona turned around. 'What?'

'The samosa ...'

'You offered it to me!' She gasped in mock outrage. At least he hoped it was mock.

'Yeah, to buy! Ten bucks for three. Or four bucks each. For the fundraiser?'

'Do I,' Winona asked through another mouthful of spiced potato, 'look like I've got ten bucks on me?'

Was this flirtation? Winona was clearly playing some kind of game but Johnny didn't know the rules. He ploughed on, trying to save face.

'You look like you've got four bucks less than you did a minute ago.'

'Bzzzzzt! Wrong!' She was laughing openly now. At him? With him? If he smiled and let it go, he'd look weak. If he didn't let it go, he instantly became a tightarse and a killjoy. All over one vegan samosa. Johnny began to sweat under his Creek Care hat.

'We're raising money to buy a thousand lomandra tubes,' he said, retreating to the safety of facts. 'To keep Oxley Creek clean, or make it clean, I should say, cos—'

'Good onya,' Winona interrupted again, nodding. She seemed to enjoy interrupting him. 'Every river in Australia's been royally rooted in the arse by capitalism. The Murray–Darling's on its last legs cos the cotton dams are full – but let's fix the climate one market stall at a time. Awesome!'

Her irony left Johnny confused. How could anyone under fifty possibly be against Creek Care? And wasn't addressing climate change a fundamental part of Land Rights?

'You got a better plan?' he shot back. 'I'm all ears.'

'Yeah, Doctor Johnny, I've got a better plan,' Winona said, coming back to stand where Avelina, a harried oncology student, was dishing out dhal and eavesdropping like her life depended on it. Winona hitched her canvas satchel up and focused her full attention on Johnny. 'Some of youse must have real boats, right? With outboards?'

'The club's got a tinny.' Johnny couldn't stop staring at her lips. The shape of them, their utter kissability.

'Okay. So, here's how to fix ya creek. Ya cook up a nice big feed of these beauties' – here Winona helped herself to a second samosa, lifting it in demonstration – 'and you grab a couple of six packs, and ya park your tinny under the Story Bridge, or moor it, whatever it's called, one fine night, yeah? And you and ya mates eat ya samosas and have a beer and look at the stars, and enjoy yerselves, okay. Don't forget the Aerogard. And when you've had ya deadly feed and checked out the night sky for a few hours, and told each other a lotta lies, and had a few hours' shuteye, then ya take ya tinny up to the Botanic Gardens past where all them other boats are. And ya chuck on hi-vis vests and some steelcap boots and hardhats, right? It's getting close to daylight now. Ya take ya fuel can, two full jerrycans if you can carry em and a lighter – make sure it's a good one, not an old gammon one that's just about fucked out – and then you head through the park to George Street and ya go and ya burn Parliament House to the fucken ground. And when ya get outta gaol in about twenty odd years, ya have yaselves another cook-up and feed, and another good look at the night sky, and then ya do the same thing all over again. And ya keep burning the cunt down till the dumb fucks inside start listening to the science.' Winona looked at Johnny with a smile. 'That's what it's gonna take, brah. Not lomandra tubes. Not samosas. Direct fucking action.'

'What could go wrong?' Johnny joked uneasily.

'What could go right?'

'Arson, criminal damage and attempted murder …'

Winona's smile vanished. 'Yeah, yeah – they real good words them words. What's climate change if it ain't arson and murder? You seen that footage of the 2019 bushfires? And the floods in Lismore – pensioners drowning in their ceilings while politicians talk about *clean coal*? Don't talk to me about attempted murder, mate.'

'I'm not gonna burn down Parliament House, Winona.'

'Guess ya creek's fucked then, Doctor Johnny.'

'Am I gonna get my four bucks or what?' Eight bucks now, really.

'Take it off the ree—ee—ent!' floated the reply over Winona's shoulder as she disappeared towards the enticing drone of the didge.

'Ouch, fuck! What's the deal with her?' asked Avelina, who had just burnt herself on the dhal pot for the second time in an hour.

Johnny untied his apron and hung it up. 'Entitlement on

steroids,' he said, leaving to continue negotiating payment for the samosas. 'Or maybe a real live revolutionary. Possibly both. I'll let you know when I've got her figured out.'

'I think she likes you,' Avelina added, turning to the first aid kit, but Johnny was out of earshot and her teasing went unanswered.

Winona weaved a path through the many bodies at the market. The young and the elderly; the able-bodied and the infirm; the slender hipsters; the defiantly fat, the tattooed, the pierced, the dull suburban middle-class and the fabulously wealthy. All these met in the mecca of the inner south, held there in the tight Kurilpa loop of the river which, having embraced you, was mighty slow to let you go. Winona wasn't much interested in the crowd; she'd been caught instead by a steady pulse, thrumming from afar. She followed the sound of the didgeridoo dragging her to the far edge of the park, eager to see if she knew the fella playing, and discover what other Blak mob were around. Hopefully, Winona thought, she'd find a little oasis of Goories there to replenish her spirit, weakened from the hours she'd spent lately in the soul-sucking hospital.

The hippy she discovered sitting on a blue plastic milk crate, his cheeks pumping, his pale dreads swaying, was not anyone she knew. A handwritten cardboard sign in front of him read:

Dreamtime Didge Experience. Taught by Master Yidaki players from Yolngu tribe, Arnhem Land. Available for Baby Blessings and Sonic Healing.

Winona folded her arms. Most of the marketgoers gave the man a small smile as they walked past uttering the mantra, 'Sorry, no cash.' About one in ten found a bit of bungoo to throw his way. While Winona stood ignoring the man's attempts to catch her eye, a scattering of gold coins and a five dollar note made their way into his upside-down Akubra.

'Who's ya mob, brother?' she eventually asked, picking up a CD: *Dreamtime Drones*. Dreamtime Drongo, more like.

The man didn't answer. He grinned and lifted his right hand in greeting as he continued to play.

Winona's nostrils flared. 'Are you a Blakfella? Cos you'd wanna be, playing that thing for money.'

The man nodded and pointed to his sign. Then gave her a thumbs up.

'Yeah. I can fucken read. Who's ya mob??'

The droning continued. A small child, encouraged by its parents, threw a coin into the Akubra.

'Are you a Blakfella or not? Answer the fucking question!' Startled, the parents snatched their child up and hurried away.

The man finally took the didge from his mouth. 'Yeah, I'm Indigenous, sis,' he told her.

'Where from?'

'Indigenous to Australia, I mean.'

'So, who's ya mob?'

'I was born on Larrakia Country. My teachers are Elders from Arnhem land and I've got their permission to play yidaki. They want me to share the culture.'

'A whitefella, in other words. Did these "Elders" tell ya they want ya busking on other people's land? And calling yaself "Indigenous" while ya taking bungoo off of actual broke-arse Blakfellas?'

'The market's open to anyone – black, white or brindle,' the man insisted, before foolishly adding, 'anyway, I don't see how it's your problem. Yidaki is men's business!'

'Men's business,' Winona repeated softly. She bared her teeth in what the man tragically mistook for a smile.

'Yep. So, if my Elders tell me I can busk and make some coin while I educate people about the culture, I will.' He put the instrument to his mouth and began to play, cheeks bulging with his circular breathing. The instrument was no longer a soothing song calling Winona to the comfort of an urban Blak community. It was the buzzing of a million mosquitoes, swarming around her head and attempting to drain her of her life-blood.

'Right,' she said, removing first one Haus of Dizzy earring, and then the other. She stowed them in her rear pocket. '*Men's business*; if that don't take the fucking cake. Dagais laying down the law to me about my own fucken culture. Now I've heard everyfuckingthing!'

She picked up the Akubra and dumped its contents into her satchel. 'What *I've* been taught by my Elders is, when ya get invaded—'

'Hey! Whaddya think ya fucking doing?!' The busker goggled as the yidaki fell away from his open mouth.

'—by thieving whitefellas—'

'Give me that back, you crazy fucking bitch!'

Winona spun the empty Akubra, frisbee-style, straight in the man's face. He recoiled in shock, crashing off his milk crate onto a pile of CDs, where his blond dreads splayed out on the ground like the head of a mop.

'—thieving, lying, *gammon* whitefellas—'

Winona seized the didge by the flared end that was closest to her and expertly flipped it. She was still enumerating the man's sins as she lifted it above her head to smite the coloniser. Seeing her murderous expression, the hippy forgot about his hat and found a brand-new set of priorities.

'You can't touch that!' he screeched.

Winona brought the didge down savagely, aiming for his grubby, trespassing feet. The hippy rolled sideways in the nick of time, yelping in shock when she raised the instrument high for a second go.

'Only men can touch the yidaki!' he screamed, stumbling into the milk crate in an effort to get far, far away from this crazy black chick. The didge cracked hard against his cheesecloth-covered arse.

'—colonising dagais, who wanna thieve ya land—'

The man made it to his feet and tried to grab his yidaki. But Winona swung it like Babe Ruth on meth. He ducked, and heard the instrument whoosh overhead with a terrifying wind of vengeance.

'—AND ya kids—'

She swung it again, this time in the reverse direction. Whoosh! The man staggered backwards, slipping and sliding on his cardboard sign.

'—AND ya culture—'

She lifted the instrument and stepped forward for another go, but the man was now out of cracking range, fleeing through the crowd in terror. He didn't look back until he was far away from the cyclone that had descended on him from a clear blue sky.

'Ey, good onya sis,' chuckled a Maori lady, nodding at her wide-eyed grannies. 'See that you kids? That's the way to do it.'

Winona shouldered the didge, breathing heavily but satisfied with her outcome. She was ready to bin the fraudulent CDs when she realised that Doctor Johnny Newman was standing behind her, gaping in the centre of an astonished crowd.

~

Some days Granny Eddie spun yarns for the sheer pleasure of seeing Dartmouth swallow any lie she told him. His fistula was repaired, and he was now an outpatient, but their regular interviews had become a habit. One she hid from Winona. The allure of company, and of being listened to about the old days – listened to by someone who made a living from listening – had proven too much to resist. Darto was an idiot, yes, but an amiable one; and he had a mysterious supply of mint leaves lollies, to boot. It wasn't like she was giving him any *important* stories. She could tell him whatever she wanted and he'd nod happily and put it all in that little notebook of his. A person could make up any old rubbish.

Today she sat in her wheelchair on the hospital balcony overlooking South Bank, which she had recently christened South Blur.

'I read that the Aboriginals would be run out of town at dusk in the early days,' Dartmouth proposed. 'By men cracking stockwhips.'

Granny sighed. Always with the violence.

'*Some* people,' she informed him with a haughty look – implying that she could name many such individuals, white historians and university lecturers and suchlike, but that, overflowing with moral rigour and cultural discretion, she chose not to – '*some* people talk a lot of rubbish about the early days, when they wasn't even around. I've heard my history straight from the Old People, see. I know the truth of what was done and not done.'

Dartmouth sagged a little in his plastic chair. 'So that didn't happen?'

'I'm not saying it *never* happened,' Granny conceded with a dismissive flick of her right hand. 'But not for very long. And there was always blackfellas camped near the Valley, right up till the war, they was never shifted off. A lot of that crowd ended up in Spring Hill and Paddington later on, stone's throw from the city. The Beehives, the Johnsons and the Wallabys. You ask Aunty Deb Beehive, her old father and uncles used to all corroboree at Spring Hill in the seventies. We'd hear em often when we was over that side of the river, clapsticks and all. And card games at Victoria Park, oh my! Biggest card games all us Murries had. No, we was a part of Brisbane alright, we was always in the thick of things.'

'And this, ah, crowd – the fringe dwellers at Spring Hill. Where were they from?' Dartmouth asked, circling back in search of stockwhips.

Granny Eddie peered at him. Not just an idiot, but blurry too. 'From?'

'Yes, originally. Before they were in the Valley.'

'They weren't *from* anywhere. They was always there.'

Dartmouth adjusted his glasses, flushing. 'Ah, yes. Of course. Of course, they were.'

'They call us mob fringe dwellers,' Eddie added, 'but Goories ain't no fringe, you whitefellas is the fringe! We always lived on our own Countries and then the dagai come and plonked themselves down next to us. Or on top of us, if they felt like it! Beehive and Wallaby mob always been in the Valley, long before John Oxley came up the damn river! Fringe dwellers my dot! That word makes me proper wild!'

Dartmouth changed tack.

'Okay, roger that, no *fringe dwellers*. Do you know much about the convict era, Eddie? Or the Petrie family?' he probed delicately. 'They say Tom Petrie grew up with the local tribe?'

'Oh, he did, he did!' Eddie sat up, enthused. 'Well, he had to. He was the first white child born in Brisbane, the only white jarjum here for years and years. He learnt the lingo from a baby, a few different lingos in fact. And he was the only one to ask. Ever.' Granny's forefinger was raised in admonition of all other colonists.

'Ask?' Dartmouth kept the facts of Tom's Edinburgh birth and his several older brothers clamped firmly inside his gob, lest he interrupt Eddie's flow.

'Yep. He was raised with the Yagara mob, so when he grew up and got married, he knew to ask where to select his land, he got permission off of Old Man Dalapai, see. Tom was a man of culture. They say he went through the Bora ceremonies and all ... my grandad knew him. And Tom's father, old Grandfather Andrew Petrie, he saved the Bunya Pines from the logging, Grandad Charlie reckoned. Cos he knew how much them trees mean to the blackfellas.'

'So, it's true the Petries were friendly with the Brisbane tribe?' Dartmouth prompted, mentally deleting his stockwhips in favour of Granny's narrative. 'And Tom was actually initiated?'

'Oh, yes,' answered Granny. 'Initiation means ya part of the tribe, well and truly,' she said, answering the second part of Dartmouth's question. Suddenly growing tired, she felt the nagging ache in her neck starting up again. 'The Petries were decent people, educated people. If everyone had been like them things could have been different alright. If the whitefellas had just *asked*.'

Dartmouth wheeled Granny Eddie back inside the ward. His mouth was agreeing with hers, but his mind was somewhere else, whirring with a new plan in which Granny literally played a starring role.

10. Riding the Marshes

1854

'It reminds me of the brolga dance,' Murree grinned as he released a stream of dark tobacco juice onto the grass. He squatted against the base of a gum tree not far from the Government Gardens. A short distance away, Mulanyin was enduring his third riding lesson.

'Oh, the lad's proper elegant,' Nita agreed, her mouth twitching.

'Like an eel,' Murree went on, loosening his torso and making his right arm into a sinuous creature. 'Curving its way through the reeds.'

Young Tom sputtered with laughter.

'Hands down brother!' he called out. 'Hands and heels down!'

Mulanyin's bare feet were pointed at the dry grass of the paddock. His splayed elbows rose almost level with his ears as the horse gathered pace beneath him. In a panic, feeling himself about to fall, he flung his hands around its neck and closed his eyes. With each pace, his upper half thumped against the saddle pommel, threatening to break a rib or damage a more delicate part of his anatomy. Stubborn, he clung on, clamping the horse's flanks with his heels in a desperate effort to stay aboard.

When the long-suffering chestnut finally lost patience, it folded its ears against its skull and put its head between its forelegs. Mulanyin very briefly did resemble a brolga then, leaving the saddle and becoming airborne, long arms flung wide, before crashing to the ground with a curse for all yarraman ever foaled and for the brainless dagai that had brought them here from England to torment him. A cluster of onlookers at the edge of Frog Hollow had gathered for the entertainment and were roaring with laughter. Several men threw Ah Yow's betting tokens on the ground as they disparaged the tall darkie for falling off yet again.

Murree ran to seize the reins before the gelding could make good its escape. The animal stood, blowing hard through reddened nostrils as it watched the workmen at the bottom of Alice Street constructing a low stone wall. Then it lowered its head and began to crop the dusty grass.

'You're improving,' Young Tom tried to soothe Mulanyin as he helped him to his feet. 'Nearly made it round that time.'

Mulanyin grunted irritably. He had Yerrin's permission for the trip north to the Pine River and now had to quickly learn to ride. It was that, or the humiliation of steering Captain Wickham's pet donkey all the way, his toes dragging in the dirt on either side of the small grey beast while Young Tom, Murree and Dalgnai galloped over the horizon to claim Tom's station. Leaving him and his donkey to be speared by landowners. That, or shot by the dagai still blazing away at anything north of Newstead that looked even vaguely like a black.

'You've hurt yourself,' Nita pointed to a bloodied wound on Mulanyin's ankle where the stirrup iron had whipped out as he fell. He poked at it doubtfully and the raw flesh dripped a little more red.

'It's nothing.' His tone was gruff but secretly his heart lifted like a bird. Nita was watching him with tenderness. She cared that he was hurt!

'It wants binding with cunjevoi,' she corrected him. 'Or at least with oodgeroo.'

Nita went over to the scrubby edge of Frog Hollow and began

stripping a paperbark branch. Mulanyin's heart flapped in his chest like a just-landed fish. The idea of Nita's hands upon him stole his breath away entirely. Or did she mean for Missus Petrie to do the doctoring? A question tantalising in its possibilities but completely unaskable. He stood in an agony of wondering and said nothing at all lest he destroy his chances.

'Ready?' asked Young Tom, bringing the chestnut over. Mulanyin put a toe in the stirrup and vaulted aloft, bravely gathering the reins in. The gelding chucked its head up in irritation, but this time the rider kept his heels and hands down and turned the horse in a circle until it submitted. Mulanyin rode around the paddock, then halted and grinned. The horse briefly pricked its ears at the arrival of some men who started kicking around a football, then lowered its head and began to graze again on the withered brown grass.

'No more bet!' cried Ah Yow, waving away the punters surrounding him. 'No more! Mulanyin proper budgery rider now!'

'Best jump off before those great Sassanach lumps send their football into us,' advised Young Tom. 'We best get your leg dressed, too.'

Mulanyin slid to the ground. Raised to disregard all physical pain as mere inconvenience, he was barely aware of the deep cut on his ankle. He did, however, affect a limp the whole quarter mile back to the Petrie house in the feverish hope that Nita would be the one to attend him. Her slender fingers, running a warm cloth along his bloodied shin, her white bodice, leaning over him as she poulticed the cut with oodgeroo bark ... he had never wanted anything as badly in his life as he wanted this. His chest hurt to even imagine it.

When they reached Tom's house, they discovered Mrs Mary Petrie standing on the veranda talking with the pastoralist Mr Leslie, come in from the country. Behind them, a starved-looking emancipist gobbled skillagee, fanning his mouth after each spoonful before hurriedly ladling down the next. The croppie grimaced when he saw the Goories and shifted his cane chair sideways a little, as if hiding behind the other visitors.

Mulanyin was ecstatic to see Tom's mother busy with company, as she so often was. The Petrie house was a magnet for visitors of all persuasions, from farming folk in town for a few nights, to the down and outs of Brisbane needing a feed and a helping hand. He shot a hopeful look at Tom, who gave him a hand signal invisible to the Europeans.

'Mammie,' Tom called, 'are there bandages? I want to doctor Mulanyin's leg for him, he's managed to cut it all to bits ...'

'Get Nellie to bind it,' replied Mrs Petrie, 'Or Nita. Mr Leslie has big news for us, Tom – Dundalli's been sentenced. They say he'll hang in the new year!'

Young Tom halted, gazing up at his mother. It was a considerable moment before he spoke. 'So Dundalli's race is run,' he muttered, barely audible to those on the veranda.

'And may all his murdering kind receive such justice!' Leslie cried in triumph. 'That savage will slaughter no more brave pioneers.'

'Dundalli may well prefer death to rotting in a stone cell,' Tom answered, in a clearer voice this time. 'And as for murder, there are those who say he fights a war. I sometimes fancy him a sable Robert the Bruce, not a criminal.'

Mr Leslie laughed in disbelief. He slapped Tim Shea on the shoulder, recruiting him. 'Did you ever hear such rot, Shea? Was he Robert the Bruce when the poor Pegg boys were murdered, or when poor Mrs Frazer was so brutally ... well,' Here Mr Leslie glanced at Mary Petrie and cleared his throat. 'We all know you are lost to the Brisbane tribe, Tom, but Dundalli's a different kettle of fish, a true vicious beast. Little wonder the tame natives fear him like the devil.'

'And how many blacks had we killed first, Mr Leslie?' Tom replied heatedly. 'Do we account for those deaths, too, or draw a convenient veil of silence? Twenty myalls, I'd reckon, for every white man lost – and those who believe the myalls don't count past five are plain fools. Let Dundalli hang if the court decrees it. But let's don't call a black man a murderer for doing what you or I would in his position. It is his people's country he's defending – Country they've called their own for hundreds of years.'

Hidden behind Mr Leslie, Tim Shea shifted again in his chair. He squinted hard at both kippas standing on the lawn below. By force of habit, he looked around for his wooden rifle, but it was leaning at the other end of the long veranda. Although he was sat in the centre of Brisbane town rather than herding ewes at Red Bank, a tremble nevertheless set itself up in his right arm.

'*Was* defending, Tom,' Mr Leslie said in a sharp tone, no longer laughing. 'Dundalli'll swing in the new year and Moreton Bay will be the safer for it. Aye, Murree? The murderer's no friend to your father's people, now is he? You'll be keen to see him dance, I warrant!'

Murree shook his head and looked away. Leslie, a leading squatter, was an enemy and an idiot. Kurilpa opinion was divided about Dundalli, with some believing that there was time, that the dagai could still be driven out by a combined show of force, and others resigned now, to sharing their land with the invader. It was a numbers game. Just as Dalapai had warned long ago, the dagai had never gone back to their own Country. Free settlers arrived at Stanley Quay in their hundreds each week, as they had since '42. The faces of Goories were evenly matched now, by the number of hard-eyed whites in North and South Brisbane. His young brothers were in grave danger of growing up a minority in their own land. They might never know what it was to hold their own estates sovereign. Was it really too late to drive the invaders away? Yerrin said yes, and he had good reason to say it, too. Other men of the Federation thought differently, and some Kurilpa would sooner shed copious blood than surrender. It was only two Mullet Runs since the Butchulla very nearly defeated the dagai in the north, after all.

Murree lifted his face to the grinning Leslie and barked with laughter, as though he agreed.

'Yoway! Let all thieves and murderers hang, by Jiminy!' the Kurilpa man cried.

'You see, Tom,' crowed Leslie. Tom and Murree exchanged a glance – not of amusement, the matter was too serious for that – but of recognition.

'Hanging's barbarism, plain and simple,' interjected Mary Petrie, 'and those who like it for their sport are no better than the worst myall who ever lived. Now, Tom, take Mulanyin out back to be doctored, and get that poor manky horse strapped and fed while you're at it.'

'Is John home?' Tom asked after his brother, leading the gelding around the corner of the house.

'He's off exploring the ridge opposite Breakfast Point. The white stone there can be quarried, he says, and good use made of it,' Mary said. Catching her first clear look at Mulanyin's bloodied ankle, she blanched. 'Good Lord, I hope that's not bone I can see. Nita – get some carbolic onto this boy's ankle before it festers, quick now, lass!'

Mulanyin followed the chestnut rump of the horse around to the backyard. The awful news of Dundalli's death sentence soon left his head, for Nita was there, waiting for him. She stood outside the kitchen door with fresh oodgeroo branches, a basin of hot water and a smile that made him unsteady on his feet.

~

From that day onwards, Mulanyin was in everything Nita saw and did. The Petries' back veranda had become a hallowed place to her. They'd spent breathtaking minutes there undisturbed, hands and arms brushing as she washed and dressed his bloodied ankle. She'd leant in close to his beautiful face to hear him whisper his secret love. Several times a day now, Nita stood and gazed at the garden arch, remembering him smiling beneath it and how close his mop of black curls had come to brushing its crossbar.

When the gardener, named Old Tom to distinguish him from Tom Petrie, dug a ditch around the orange trees in the orchard, it was Mulanyin who Nita imagined wielding the spade; and when John Petrie chased Cocky angrily out of the dining room with a folded *Courier*, it was her calm-tempered love she compared him to. The world burst with wonder, but how much more wonderful it was on those days Mulanyin came loping around the corner of the stable on an errand.

Mary Petrie roused on her for daydreaming. Nita was remorseful about the forgotten floor polish, and the burnt pork, but there was so much to consider besides her work. Did Mulanyin prefer corned beef over boiled bacon? Damper over Johnnycakes? What was he doing, and who was he doing it with? How long until she saw his smile again? Would he wear Grandfather Petrie's discarded work shirt, or should she attempt to sew him one from the coarse Irish twill off the last Sydney steamer? How did her sweetheart feel about temperance; and would he contemplate baptism for her? Had he ever gambled or drank? Had he fallen prey to the loose women of Frog Hollow, or was he unsullied by sin? Would he stay in Magandjin until next Christmas or return to his family in the south, or even run off seeking his fortune on the goldfields like Young Tom threatened to do? Could he kill a sheep, or plough a field, or drive a sulky? Had he ever touched a china plate? Seen a bible? Had he heard a piano or been inside a church? Did he know how to stand with a girl, take long strands of her hair and wind those strands around his finger to draw her close, and then nuzzle his nose to hers before his amazing lips softly met her own, gathering her close until their whole bodies met, kissing her in the darkness as though nobody else existed in the entirety of God's good earth?

If he didn't, Nita would teach him.

~

The four comrades packed their saddlebags so early that the Cry for the Dead still rang from Wilwinpa Hill as they left town. An hour later they swam their snorting horses across Breakfast Creek, then turned north along the Sandgate Track towards the old German Station. After riding half the morning, they arrived at the rain-scoured banks of the Serpentine River, and plunged in. Clumps of white foam washed from the horse's chests as they swam, then the mounts hauled themselves with great muscular thrusts of their rumps up through the grey mangrove mud on the northern shore. Back on level ground, the sodden horses stopped to shiver off the dirty water, flinging it in all directions. Dalapai's Country lay all around them now, and Dalgnai called greetings as they travelled, reassuring the spirits that his companions intended no harm.

'It almost looks like you might, for once, go a day without tumbling into the dirt,' Murree observed to Mulanyin. 'But I won't bet my wages on it.'

'That's because you haven't *got* any wages,' Mulanyin shot back, his lean body swaying loose in the saddle now that he had mastered the knack of riding.

'I have wages coming,' said Murree indignantly. 'Once the work is done. Which is much the same thing.'

'Ha! Can a man eat a fish he hasn't caught?' Mulanyin scoffed. 'He can *talk* about eating the uncaught fish, talk about it at great length, in fact. He can describe its huge size and marvel about his tremendous skill in landing it with the tow row. He can admire it, and he can promise it to his wife for dinner, and he can sing songs about how wonderful the uncaught fish tastes, all night long. The one simple thing he can't do, though, my brother, is eat it. You sound like a man with an empty net to me.'

'Your problem is you lack imagination, saltwater, even though you never lack words. See, the trouble with your short-sighted approach ...' Murree continued, as the men cheerfully argued their way north.

In the end it was not Mulanyin who tumbled out of the saddle that day, but Tom. His thoroughbred took fright at two large snakes, shining kubbil that were twisted together in battle on the road, forming first a plaited rope and then a tangled knot, and quite oblivious to the expeditioners riding past. Tom had stood rubbing his hip while his horse was recaptured, expecting one of his companions to seize the snakes for dinner.

'Leave them be,' cautioned Dalgnai. 'They are spirit snakes, not to be meddled with.'

They rode on.

The four men stuck to the track, making their way through forest alive with birdsong. Numerous fires smoked from the ridges to the north and west: Dalgnai's relatives were sending word ahead of them that the young ambassador was coming.

The riders spoke little, alert for signs of trouble. The Ancestors would be hard-pressed to provide them with warnings if they were consumed by idle chatter. After a time, they heard loud thumping ahead and soon arrived at the rough oompie of a Mr Bridges, busy fencing with his young sons. Sunburnt and scrawny, the jarjums looked to Mulanyin as though they ought to be playing with birds' nests, not a log-splitter.

'Hot work you have there, friend!' called Young Tom, for the sun had now climbed high.

'Aye, but the place won't improve itself,' Mr Bridges answered, wiping sweat. 'And I plan an inn, hereabouts.'

The adventurers looked around. Smoke rose from chaotic piles of felled timber and cows grazed among the butchered stumps. Beyond the clearing the forest remained. Enormous tallowwoods soared skyward alongside figs with upper boughs the thickness of Mulanyin's chest. Orchids and climbing vines fell from the canopies of both, joining with staghorn ferns to make a thick green curtain. An orchestra of catbirds, robins and parrots were all having their say about Bridges' plans for expansion. His oompie, plonked on the margin of the Sandgate Track, was the only evidence save for hoofprints and wheel ruts that dagai knew of this valley. It seemed a remote spot for a hotel unless the quolls and bandicoots had lately developed a taste for beer. Or unless Bridges proposed selling grog to the Goories alone.

'Strength to your arm, man!' replied Young Tom. 'We're taking mail to German Station, and then riding on to the Pine. I'm looking for a selection, myself.'

'Blacks on the Pine are pretty nasty,' warned Bridges, leaning on his sledgehammer, as though the three Goorie men in front of him had been rendered invisible by Tom's presence. 'I hear Whiteside Station's losing stock hand over foot. The savage buggers spear his cattle as they please, then run to the swamps where they can't be found.'

'Oh, Dalgnai here will be my ambassador,' Tom said cheerfully. 'I look forward to a cordial at your inn, when it's built. You'll call it Bridges Hotel, I suppose?'

Mr Bridges looked sceptically at Dalgnai, a slim serious man of twenty-five. He shook his head. 'Nay. The Kedron Inn. And I'll be pleased to sell you all the drink you want, Petrie, cordial or hard liquor as you please. You'll want the company of John Barleycorn if'n you survive the Pine with one musket. I wouldn't be caught dead in them parts without a few good Englishmen beside me, and pistols too – it's pistols you want, to take the curl out of the myall's tail. The treachery of the black buggers is beyond reckoning.'

Tom gave a small smile. 'This is for duck,' he said, patting his musket. 'Nothing more.'

'He complains about the landowners,' Mulanyin marvelled in Yagara. 'Does the fool not understand the simple concepts of trespass and theft?'

Hearing Mulanyin's scornful tone, Bridges shot a glance at his rifle, propped against the closest tree stump.

'I speak their language, Bridges, and Dalapai is a friend to my father and myself,' Tom told the man, with a warning look at Mulanyin. 'We'll press on, in any case. You have a job of work ahead of you, it seems, and so do we.' Tom heeled his horse forward and his three companions followed.

Looking back, Mulanyin saw Bridges step over to the stump of the tree he had just cut into fence posts and take his rifle up. The man cradled it against his chest, staring. Bridges continued staring until they had disappeared over the crest of the hill which the white man believed he owned.

'I'm sick of hearing English,' Mulanyin declared. For the remainder of the afternoon he refused to answer any questions put to him in the dagai tongue, even when he was teased by Murree about Nita, and heavy hints were dropped of Tom's insider knowledge of her true feelings.

'Explain to me,' Mulanyin demanded of Tom as their horses drank from a rivulet, 'what goes on in the brain of an Englishman? When he arrives in another man's country to steal his land, and water, and game, and then with a straight face, calls those he steals from *thieves*? Is this how it is in Scotland? Is this why your people have fled that terrible place?'

'It's hard to explain,' Tom prevaricated.

'It is harder to see and to live with,' commented Dalgnai, who until then had been rather quiet.

'The English have left their country behind,' Tom answered,

struggling for the right response. 'And in their ignorance, they don't understand that the land here has its own Law. They think that only their British law exists. Or is the only one that matters in the eyes of God.'

The kippas laughed in astonishment. Dalgnai uttered a curse against the English and their Law, even though he was forbidden, as an adult man, to swear.

Tom smiled a rueful smile. 'You saw the marked tree yesterday, near where the two kubbil were joined together? Well, the men and women of my father's village in Scotland once made a pilgrimage – a journey I mean – around every boundary marker of their parish, every Rogantide.'

'What is *paridj*?' interrupted Mulanyin. 'And *Rogantide*?'

'Parish means where the Church boundaries are – how far their Bora stretches, if you like. And Rogantide is a time of ceremony. Anyway, my point is that they do the walk, or they once did. "Riding the marshes," my father calls it. The English do the same journey and call it "beating the bounds". Prayers are read and girls carry flowers to remember the dead of the village. They used to do it yearly, so that each English kippa and maibin knew the boundary of their Country, and to never forget where they belonged.'

'Something like how we learn our Country!' Mulanyin answered, more confused than ever.

'Yes. Though the thick heads of English boys are knocked pretty hard against the boundary stones, I believe, to make their pilgrimage more memorable. And to get it through to their rather dim English brains.'

'Are you saying dagai people kept to their own boundaries, once?' puzzled Murree, gazing at Dalgnai who looked as sceptical as he felt.

Young Tom nodded. 'They respect some boundaries still,' he answered. 'Those that are well defended.'

What did 'well defended' look like, Mulanyin wondered, if not like a thousand Goories assembled at the Woolloongabba pullen pullen? If not like Dundalli, leading the warriors who had willingly assembled under him, from the Dugulumba to K'Gari?

'But, cousin, if a clan must constantly defend their land,' mused Dalgnai, halting his horse and frowning at the horizon, 'then they are effectively always at war.' He swung in the saddle to face Tom square on. 'Is war *normal* for the clans of England?'

'In a way, I suppose,' Tom said slowly. 'It's different, their Country holds no Dreamings to keep them at home.'

Aghast, the kippas exchanged horrified looks. They had assumed the vast majority of white men ravaging their lands were some kind of convict class – criminals, expelled by English Elders for their atrocious behaviour. But if Tom was right, and the British recognised no Dreamings at all, then England was pure savagery. Life there would be an endless nightmarish struggle for dominance over other men.

But how can men live without Dreamings, they marvelled.

'It is hard to explain,' Tom repeated, a little shamefaced.

'I'll stop here,' Mulanyin nodded at the front paddock of the German Station as he dismounted.

Tom sighed. He was impatient to deliver the latest news to the Moravians in exchange for a hot meal and a bed for the night. 'Don't be a blooming myall,' Tom retorted. 'Murree, tell him to come up on the veranda with us, at least.'

'He's too stubborn,' Murree said, knowing that once Mulanyin's mind was made up there was never any hope of changing it. 'Leave off wasting your breath.'

'It might rain,' Tom warned.

'It won't rain,' Mulanyin scoffed, not caring if it did. Something unnameable in him became uneasy when he got very near a newcomer's house. An oompie of waterproof oodgeroo and sturdy wattle boughs, with a wide opening facing his own Country, that was one thing; but the smooth bland walls of a white oompie troubled him deeply. The horror of being inside a place made by strange hands out of anonymous materials; to be in one was to be caught inside something unnatural, even sinister. The dagai oompies were cavernous and dim inside, far too much like a cave where a person could be trapped by enemies or stumble across a collection of sacred bones on a shelf and mistakenly wake the dead. And who knew what evil spells the dagai had sung into their brick and mortar? He occasionally carried timber as a favour for Grandfather Petrie, but going into one of his oompies once it was complete? Mulanyin shivered at the thought.

'I'll stop outside with you,' Dalgnai offered, with a meaningful glance at Tom. 'The Lord can do without my prayers today.'

'Come on then, Murree,' Tom gave up on Mulanyin, 'Let them enjoy their tree stumps and leeches. You and I will have to eat all the good German bread on offer.'

'Don't forget to pray for it, Murree,' mocked Dalgnai, dismounting. 'Nothing comes free at the House of Hunger. These jackaroos want us with a hoe in our hands all day and then on our knees half the night, praying to Jeejuj!' He sank to his knees, put his palms together, and piously closed his eyes.

'Vater unser im himmel
Geheiligt weirde dein Name
Dein Reich komme
Dein wille geschehe
We im Himmel so auf Erden.'

Dalgnai grinned as he crossed himself, and then together with Murree and Mulanyin burst into extravagant laughter. Three decades after Oxley, the rivers of Yagara Country still teemed with fish and prawns. His father's territory north of the Warrar was rich, still, with possum, wallaby and emu. The game animals had declined since the dagai came blundering in, interrupting the eternal cycles of burning and ceremony and harvest, but there still remained enough to live well from a few hours' harvesting each day. The newcomers disapproved. But there was no logic to the crazy white idea of endless *work*. The dagai had brought *work* with them from their own unfortunate starving Countries, and that was where it belonged, along with other odd ideas like Fences, Debt and Jesus.

'My father art at Nerang Creek,' grinned Mulanyin, 'which you may well call Heaven, if you saw the duck and gumbo we harvest at our leisure – as numerous as the leaves on the trees – and the size of the jalum that hurl themselves into our canoes each day.'

'My father is at home in our village too,' agreed Dalgnai. 'Not avoiding his responsibilities to family by living far away in the sky, after torturing his only son to death on a dead tree, mind you.'

'I give up,' Tom said as he walked with Murree towards the eleven German oompies that made up the German Station, 'but if you think I'm bringing you cheeky buggers any tucker out here you can think again.'

'We'll eat better than you tonight, cousin,' Dalgnai smiled.

Late that afternoon he and Mulanyin sat at a small fire, waiting for their eel and crays to cook. Dalgnai smoked a pipe and the sight and smell of the dense, dark tobacco reminded Mulanyin of home. Small Father would store a twisted wad above his ear, a habit he developed when the first timber cutters came to Kombumerri. Mulanyin's thoughts remained in the south. His Waijung had been large with child when he and Big Father left on their long walk to Woolloongabba. If the sawyer at Grenier's Hotel was reliable, he had a new sister. The realisation made him both happy and sad – happy that another human soul had come to his Country and family, and sad that he had not been there for the baby's welcome ceremony or simply to gaze upon the tiny face and waving fingers. He wondered if the infant cried at night and what name was being considered for her, whether

her hair was wavy like Big Father's or curly like his own. All questions that would be answered at the upcoming Mullet Run. There he'd tell his family about his adventures. He'd describe the pullen pullen to his siblings and teach them some Yagara words. Most important of all, he would seek permission to marry Nita, beautiful Nita with the eyes that promised so much, beautiful Nita with the shapely lips and delicate ears, and the unimaginable breasts that he …

Dalgnai blew out a cloud of smoke, then turned his pipe around, offering the stem to his companion. 'Smoke?'

'I don't really like the taste.' In fact, he had never tried smoking. Think hard before you pick up the things of the dagai, Big Father had warned, especially those that seem entirely pleasurable. The rum, the baccy, the woollen blankets that require no effort of hunting or skinning or tanning in exchange for their warmth. These things are like the fresh grass shoots that we grow to attract the kangaroo – sweet to taste but with savage consequences. And above all – here he took Mulanyin by both shoulders – you must *never* take flour, whether in payment for work or as a gift, from the hands of a stranger. Flour looks identical whether it is safe, or whether it contains the muckenzie that will kill you.

Mulanyin had promised.

'You really are a proper myall,' Dalgnai observed mildly, taking another draw, making his pipe's ember glow crimson. 'Except for them trousers, of course, and the fact you can muster up some English when you're forced to.'

'Oh, I tried riding bare-arsed,' Mulanyin answered, grabbing his balls in demonstration. 'But I intend to have many children, cousin, and so I accepted Tom's old trousers to save my wife's tears.'

'Good,' cried Dalgnai, suddenly passionate. 'Every man in the Federation must make many jarjums, to replace those taken by the Death Spirit. Some Goories hold to the old standard, but if we each have four we are doomed. I'm going to have at least eight, to make up for those my sister would have borne. If I don't avenge her death, my sons can.'

'May your spears fly true,' Mulanyin replied, growing sober. All of Brisbane, North and South, knew about the murder of Dalgnai's pregnant sister. Settlers had killed her and destroyed many oompies a few short Mullet Runs ago. It had been one of the many dagai attempts to force the landowners off their Country. But Dalapai persisted. His village remained at Hamilton Reach.

'I heard the new Native Police boss has gone north to Butchulla lands. But let Marshall and his curs find me here,' Dalgnai proclaimed. 'Their lives will be worth as much as that.' He pointed to the eel sizzling on the coals.

'Perhaps the Butchulla will do you a favour.'

'Perhaps,' Dalgnai agreed, 'although with Dundalli behind bars, it's hard to predict what will happen next.'

'I think what will happen next is a good feed. That eel's ready by the look of it,' Mulanyin observed, very hungry from the day's long ride. 'And the crays too, ay?'

'Oh, you can't eat my crayfish!' Dalgnai rebuked him.

Mulanyin's face dropped. On another man's estate he could eat only what was freely offered. His comment had been rude, and presumptuous. Dalgnai eyed his friend sternly while curls of fragrant steam rose from the cooked crays, perfuming the night air. Mulanyin's stomach rumbled so loud that both men heard it.

'You haff not hoed ze pumpkins,' Dalgnai went on, wagging a Lutheran forefinger high in the air. 'You haff not hoed ze pumpkins or ploughed ze potato field or built ze church or said your prayers. No crayfish for you, blackie!'

'I'm sorry, Fada,' Mulanyin grinned in relief. 'I am just an ignorant heathen. Please forgive me.'

Both men broke into helpless laughter. Wiping tears from his eyes, Dalgnai lifted the roasted crays onto a bark platter for them to share.

Though he was too far from Nita, Mulanyin slept well beneath the Milky Way that night. The fire burnt down to coals which glowed, then flickered, and finally faded to dark. The Southern Cross wheeled slowly across the sky.

~

One hundred and ten miles to the south, Mulanyin's mother woke from an unsettling dream to discover her infant daughter whimpering for milk. She put the baby to her breast, then sat gazing out at the waxing moonlight upon the burragurra. As the waves crashed onto the beach, the woman felt certain: something was awry. She sang a low lullaby and scanned the Sky Country for intimations of the future. Fearful, she sent heartfelt prayers out to the Star Camps above Burleigh Headland, asking the Ancestors to look over the journeys of her oldest son, whom she missed every waking moment. Keep my boy safe, she prayed to the Old People. Watch over him in the foreign territory of the Yagara; keep him safe from the strange Goorie nations of the north, and all enemies who would harm him. And most of all – stroking the cheek of her infant daughter while she kept an eye peeled for shooting stars – bring my Mulanyin home soon to meet his new sister.

11. LOVE OR MONEY

1854

'If that isn't a canny sight to see,' Young Tom exclaimed as he crested a small hill. The riders had travelled a winding route after leaving the German Station, fording the South Pine River and exploring the Glasshouse Mountains, eventually returning to the coast at Pumice Stone Passage. They had then circled west once more and stayed overnight at Caboolture.

Now a broad valley stretched before him, gorgeous country undulating as far as he could see in all directions. In the west lay the Bunya Country, high mountains cloaked in the sacred forests his father had long ago asked Governor Gipps to preserve. In the middle distance, a herd of kangaroo grazed beside a wetland being fished by Kabi Kabi men in canoes. Several smoking fires were visible three or four miles away where others were going about their business. The scene Tom gazed on was touched by the gold of the afternoon sun, burnishing the valley with softness and promise.

'Anywhere here, Young Tom,' said Dalgnai, with a magnanimous sweep of his arm. 'This is a good place, Murrumba. Father said to tell you that you can have your pick of the country from this ridge all the way over to Freshwater Creek.'

Tom sat stunned. He turned away for sudden tears had sprung into his eyes and he was eager to hide the fact. When he had composed himself, he thanked Dalgnai formally, vowing to take care of the Country as Goories always did; to never cut down a bunya tree or pollute the sacred waters, nor waste the life of any living thing on Dalapai's estate.

'Father would expect nothing less.' Dalgnai nodded. 'That's why you have his blessing.'

From his vantage point on the hill, Tom fenced great swathes of the country lying before him in his mind, populating it with thousands of sheep and cattle. He felled ironbarks and cypress and yellowbox, and with them he built cabins, stockyards and a spacious homestead. When the house was complete, its wide verandas wrapping around a cluster of high-ceilinged rooms, an assortment of small huts would be put up for the workmen. He installed his future wife and children in the grand house. He saw his herds multiply, saw the cattle slowly trailing across the foothills in the yellow afternoon light, with Murree and Mulanyin and a host of other capable Goorie men riding behind them. He stood on his unbuilt veranda and everywhere he looked was lush and prosperous and just. This was Murrumba; his fortune and his destiny. There was only one problem with Tom's tremendous vision. The valley in front of him already had an English name – Whiteside Station – and it was owned by the widow Jane Griffin.

'Will we light a waiburra?' Tom asked. Fire and smoke were essential diplomatic courtesies, to alert others to their lawful presence. Seeing smoke on their boundary, landowners would normally come by; then message sticks could be displayed, enabling safe passage.

'Let's cross,' Dalgnai answered, 'before my Uncle's river gets too cold. There's no danger, these mob know me.'

Hearing this, and being a young man not yet thirty, Tom surrendered to the wild torrent of emotion rushing through him. He spurred his horse towards the Pine River, whooping with joy.

The thoroughbred caught his excitement. It galloped willingly into the shallows and shortly afterwards Tom emerged on the other bank, sodden, holding on to the horse's dripping tail and looking about him at the valley he would come to know better than any other.

The others followed, their horses a little more reluctant, and soon all four men were inspecting the river flats dotted with crow's ash and hoop pine. It seemed to Mulanyin that Tom already sat straighter in his saddle, riding through the first of the ten thousand acres Dalapai had granted him access to. Tom hadn't stopped grinning since Dalgnai's arm had waved him on, and why would he? This glorious Country was as green and lush as his own. Dalapai's Country was part of the great Goorie Federation and Mulanyin considered Tom a lucky man indeed to be allowed to call it home.

Tom's exuberant yells had evaporated into the atmosphere unheard, but when the men lit a waiburra to boil the camp kettle and signal their presence, the thin column of smoke quickly attracted attention. A dozen of Dalgnai's relatives arrived, the women hanging back, the warriors on high alert, their spears aloft. Two of the old women were marked by pox, Mulanyin saw. Their severe disfiguration was visible at a distance.

An odd element of suspicion lingered among these landowners, even after Dalgnai was recognised by the warriors and had explained that the party was there with Dalapai's blessing. The Pine River People spoke the normal words of welcome and of peace, but then refused supper. Dalgnai was taken aside by a senior man and spoken to privately. When Dalgnai returned to the fire, his expression was grave. Something has happened here, Mulanyin thought uneasily, something we haven't yet been told. These people are injured in their souls.

Tom was brought into the conference then. Dalgnai introduced him as a son of the white man who had first transgressed against, and then ultimately helped protect, the sacred Bunya Forest. Dalgnai gave his word that Tom had come only with the full permission of Dalapai and that his good behaviour was guaranteed by the Yagara Bora. The local men quizzed Tom at length, and then conferred with each other a long while before they came to a decision. This son of Andrew Petrie would, they finally agreed, make a useful ally in their constant battles with Whiteside Station. With luck he might help drive the Griffins out and restore order to their lives. At the very least, any station he established in the valley would provide a safe haven from the terror that surrounded them. The atmosphere changed – smiles broke out. Tom formally thanked the landowners, promising to behave well and honour their dignity as well as the Bora Law.

Later that afternoon, as the travellers continued on to the Whiteside Homestead, two dagai horsemen appeared, bringing along a cloud of tiny black flies. The men flapped and swatted at the air continually as though at war with the atmosphere itself. The older of the two sported a magnificent brown beard and a brace of pistols, as well as a repeater rifle stowed against his saddle flap, available in an instant. Spying these weapons, Mulanyin knew at once that they had been used, and used recently, on men who looked like him.

'Griffin?' Tom extended his hand to this man. 'Tom Petrie. You know my father, of course. We planned on reaching your place by dark.'

'You'd best be with us by dark,' grimaced Griffin, shaking Tom's hand and looking hard at the thick scrub bordering the river. 'The niggers hereabouts are bloodthirsty buggers. They want dispersing, but a man can't get the Native Police out for love nor money. We've done what we can ourselves, mind.'

Sat upon his gelding, Dalgnai's face underwent a sudden transformation. Watching his companion withdraw his spirit to become an utter blank in Griffin's presence, Mulanyin knew instantly why the Kabi Kabi they had met were so wary. He felt a sensation he'd only ever experienced once before, during his initiation. It was terror mixed with sheer helplessness, of needing to endure the unendurable. He cursed the fact of not carrying a weapon. Young Tom was the only one of their party who was armed. Mulanyin ached to fling himself at the murderer John Griffin, his hands strangling the man's pale throat until the awful danger he posed lay inert on the ground. But instead, Mulanyin froze, hoping not to be noticed by the two white men whose casually brandished weapons may as well have been Goorie skulls dangling from their belts.

'I heard,' Tom replied.

'They spear what they please and then run east to the rotten ground that would bog a duck, let alone a horse,' Griffin erupted. 'Between their raids on the stock and their damn hideous yowling at night, my mother's a nervous wreck. You see,' and here Griffin motioned to his armoury, 'how we must travel about on our own land.'

'Indeed. Well, I am looking around for a selection, myself,' Tom proposed. 'And since I speak their language, I can talk to the blacks in a way they understand and get along with them alright. Perhaps you and I might come to some agreement.'

Griffin's interest sharpened. 'My mother will want to meet with you,' he replied. 'I've got business with a neighbour and will be away overnight. But go and talk to her, man. She'll sell you these lower sections and throw the niggers in for free, I'm pretty sure.' He snorted. 'It'll save us the trouble of getting rid of them.'

Hearing this, Mulanyin coughed a nervous cough, gulping for air; the sound drew Griffin's attention. Seeing the pistols poised in the murderer's belt, Mulanyin's pulse hurled itself against his throat. He quickly turned his face away, lest catching Griffin's eye be seen as some kind of provocation.

Griffin grunted in contempt, then continued issuing directions to Tom. When the two strangers had cantered away, Griffin smiling broadly at the idea of selling his problems to Tom, Dalgnai returned to life. He gave a large, involuntary shiver. Then he spat, gazing at the disappearing Griffin with a bitter expression. He and Tom had had several complicated debates in the past few days about who owned Dalapai's estate. Tom had struggled to make Dalgnai understand that the valley they rode through now belonged to the English Queen.

'Should we warn your family?' Mulanyin asked, following Dalgnai's look.

'Of what?' answered Dalgnai. 'It's no secret he wants to roll all our corpses into the river.'

As the four companions rode towards the Whiteside homestead, Dalgnai let his horse drop to the rear. He would not meet anyone's eye nor speak for some time; he was deep in thought and looked entirely disconsolate.

~

Two days later, Tom's negotiations with Mrs Griffin were complete. His party rode back to town, with Dalgnai impatient to see his home at Breakfast Creek again, and Mulanyin lovesick for a glimpse of Nita. The Yagara families they had ridden past the previous week fished and mended nets and went about their business in Dalapai's village, just as before. The same water joeys were filling buckets; the same women fished from the rocky headland opposite Tugulawa. The same labourers nailed timber on the same building sites and dug holes for the foundations of the same buildings. The weary riders entered the stream at the same muddy point they had used heading out of town.

Mulanyin spotted familiar birds in the mangroves. There were black and white darters, and the depressive outline of a sole nankeen heron staring into the shallows beneath its branch, along with a host of seagulls and oyster catchers, squawking and gossiping on a narrow crescent of sand. Some clods of black mangrove mud flung up a week ago by their horses' hooves remained on the tree trunks, as well as on certain boulders above the high-tide mark. Very likely the exact same fish were darting about in the very same shoals as they had a handful of days earlier.

But though all this was unchanged – would probably remain unchanged for months and years to come – and though the formal deeds of sale for Murrumba Downs were yet to be drawn up, signed and lodged with the Governor in Sydney, the young white man who had ridden north with Mulanyin no longer existed. The Goories returned to Edenglassie travelling not alongside Young Tom, their lifelong friend and brother, but beside Mister Tom Petrie, pastoralist, who was the putative owner – and would indisputably become the master – of Murrumba Downs Station.

Dalgnai rode home weighted down by the painful knowledge of what his people faced in the north, but thankful a safe haven would now be carved out from the dangerous wild territory of the Griffins. The moderating influence of Tom Petrie would change the landscape of the Pine forever. Dalapai's son had done his work well; the Old Man's vision was about to be realised.

The North Pine would receive no more secret corpses from Whiteside Station.

12. THE NAMES OF THINGS

1854

'Cocky's up to his old tricks,' Murree chuckled. The kippas were relaxing in the sun at Petrie Bight after their morning bogey. Mulanyin lay back on the riverbank and laced his fingers behind his head.

Cocky, an infamous nuisance, was perched in a nearby eucalyptus. Poised on a limb branching over the Warrar, the bird bobbed with excitement. Then it raised its yellow crest and screeched a command to a farmer on the opposite bank. 'Pumpkin Ho-oo!' the bird called from the tree, sounding for all the world like any other customer. 'Pumpkin Ho-oo!'

Murree chortled with glee. 'Here he goes, my brother!'

The emancipist Bribie, busy fishing the creek near the kippas, paused at Cocky's cry. He shook his head when he saw the farmer dutifully carry a dozen large pumpkins to his small wooden craft and begin pulling it across the river.

'Somebody should tell im,' Bribie muttered under his breath, as he tied two large woven fish traps beneath his bridge. On the bank below the disapproving Bribie, Murree was enthralled by the sight of the farmer labouring to town engulfed by his pumpkins. He nudged Mulanyin in the ribs.

'Check this cheeky bugger out!'

'Who?'

'Cocky – ordering pumpkins again!'

'Cocky?' Mulanyin had been daydreaming. 'Cocky's at Petries'.'

'Ah, yer head's at Petries'!' Murree observed in disgust. 'At Petries' with Nita, where it always is, along with Nita's susu, and Nita's arms to wrap around your neck, and Nita's smooth hips to run your hands down.'

Lost in memories of that glorious day when Nita had knelt and doctored his now-healed ankle, actually running her hands along his bare calves, Mulanyin didn't answer. He pulled several grass stalks from the riverbank and chewed on the ends.

'Brother!' Murree protested, shoving Mulanyin's shoulder and laughing at the hold Nita had over him. 'You are deaf to anything except gossip about that girl!'

Murree understood Mulanyin's romantic daydreams only too well. Like most of the young Goorie men in Edenglassie, he too had been infatuated with the beautiful Nita. But she had tossed her head at his sweet-talk, just as she had at the propositions of Lumpy Billy and Joe Sunshine. Well into her prime childbearing years, some of the Kurilpa Elders speculated that Nita might be one of those rare women who shunned men and marriage. But the arrival of Mulanyin had put paid to the idea of a childless Nita. Since the afternoon she first saw him in the Petries' kitchen, it had been clear that Nita was as fascinated by the southerner as he was by her.

'I'm not deaf,' Mulanyin replied. 'I'm just deep in thought.'

'Yes, thoughts of how delighted your jun will be if you can ever get her alone,' Murree teased.

At that moment the pumpkin seller arrived, pulling up to the riverbank below where Bribie stood, grinning now despite himself. As the farmer shot his oars and climbed out of the boat, Bribie gestured up at Cocky, bobbing and screeching triumphantly in the eucalyptus.

'Yer outta luck, cobber.'

'Ah fer the buggering love of Jesus! Not again!' The pumpkin seller hurled his hat on the ground and began ranting around the base of the tree. He cursed the bird to high heaven, shaking both fists. His face grew redder and redder as he raved.

'Poor Cocky!' the bird commented as the man stormed and swore. 'Poor, poor Cocky!'

Murree and Mulanyin collapsed into fits of laughter. The pumpkin seller turned and berated them, then cast about in even greater fury for sticks to hurl at the bird. But Cocky's previous victims had already cleared the ground for a long way in both directions.

'Pumpkin ho-oo!' offered Cocky helpfully. 'Pumpkin ho-oo!'

Roaring, the farmer bent to rip clods of grass from under his feet, hurling them skyward along with a great many choice adjectives for both bird and blacks. The clods fell just short of the branch where the cockatoo was pacing.

'You should be ashamed of yourself!' Cocky lectured. 'Call yourself a Christian!'

Mulanyin rolled on the grass, gasping for air.

'I'll be praying for you,' Cocky added primly in the voice of Mrs Mary Petrie.

At this, Murree nearly tumbled into the river. Cursing and raging, the pumpkin seller climbed back in his boat and began the journey back to Kangaroo Point.

Mulanyin wiped tears from his eyes and got to his feet, wheezing. 'I'm going to ask her to be my bride,' he confessed, turning to find Murree flat on his back, exhausted from laughter. 'If your Elders let me. Will they say yes, do you think?' Water droplets, still caught in Mulanyin's curls from the Bogey Hole, shone brilliant as diamonds in the morning sunlight.

Murree sat up, feeling a stab of anger in his chest. So, Mulanyin would claim Nita; a kippa who had not even set foot on Kurilpa land two seasons ago was going to claim the prize of her love and devotion. Murree recognised his anger as jealousy, and brought it under firm control. He was no small boy to be tossed around by his feelings, but a man with the instruction of the Bora to fulfil. Nita was not his promised wife; she was free to marry his friend if the Elders agreed. He had no right to be jealous.

'Brother,' he answered glumly, 'I had hoped you might wait, and marry that daughter of Darramlee.' He referred to a girl of the Black Soil People, who was still two years off womanhood.

'Darramlee would do me great honour if that happened,' Mulanyin hesitated, 'but brother, I want sons now, not in three or four Mullet Runs. Dalgnai said something at Noondah that made me think. He told me he wanted at least eight jarjums, to replace those his sister will never have. With Nita I can have many children – and perhaps if all my clan do the same, we can grow strong enough to avoid your people's tragedy.'

The kippas sat shoulder to shoulder, facing the rising current of the river as it made its way past the Bogey Hole. The Warrar churned with activity. Chinese men throwing their prawn nets, while their wives dried last night's catch on straw mats in front of their huts. A host of steamers, ketches and punts went about their business, heading up to the docks with salt from the Islands, carrying German labour to Eagle Farm or headed downstream to Cleveland Point or Dunwich with wool bound for Sydney. There were Kurilpa crew on nearly all these boats, and scores of Goorie faces on both shores, but the dark faces of Murree's people were matched in Brisbane, now, by those of the dagai. The tendrils of the white man's web stretched further beyond North Brisbane with every passing moon. Murree's people might soon become a minority – a strange and disturbing new reality to think upon.

'Tragedy,' repeated Murree, disliking the word.

'Think, brother!' Mulanyin said, his eyes alight. 'What if you came south to my Country and married a Yugambeh girl? We can grow our people; we can stand side by side and defend our lands and families – and keep our majority. There's no law saying we must simply succumb. We have every right to defend ourselves – and a duty, too.'

'I have a promised wife in the Upriver clan, as you know. And besides, it's not so simple to leave your own Country,' Murree said. 'I think I'm too attached to my own people, and to the Warrar.'

Mulanyin nodded, disappointed but unsurprised. It was highly unusual to spend as long away from home as he had. His compulsory kippa exile had ended long ago and it was the lure of Nita, now, which kept him so far from his family. A new husband, after spending several Mullet Runs in his bride's Country, inevitably returned to his own people and lived there with his wife, contributing to order and prosperity in his own land. It was women who left their homes. Adopted by Yerrin and Dawalbin, Mulanyin was welcome on Yagara land and could stay indefinitely. But Mulanyin knew he was exceptional; he was like his yuri, the blue heron, normally seen fishing alone, and prone to take flight whenever it felt the urge. Murree, by contrast, needed his mob close by. He would leave his Country only briefly, or under duress.

'I do miss my home terribly, you know,' Mulanyin said. 'Sometimes when I wake at night I feel as empty as Bribie's basket over there. Hear how soft the Warrar laps against these mangrove trunks? Like a wallaby lapping at a puddle. But in my Country the burragurra crashes onto the sand one hundred times louder; the waves are this high,' he demonstrated with a hand at his neck, 'before they curl over and kiss the beach with passion, as though they really mean it. The pounding of the surf is the sound of my heart; that and the kurrumburum singing up the dawn. Here the dagai talk fills my ears day and night, and I'm tormented by the sound of cows' mourning their calves that have been taken away. I hear stockwhips and ships' bells, and the poor chained dogs barking with hunger and misery. There are nights I wake to the clamour and would give anything to hear the waves lapping the shore at Jebbribillum.'

'Yugambeh Country sounds very different,' Murree said, struggling to remain composed in the face of this blunt critique.

'This Warrar is beautiful, brother, but my Nerang balun is beyond all compare, and my Waijung and Fathers too far away. There's a brand new jarjum waiting to meet me and except for when I'm around Nita, my time here drags. I want to hold that little baby sister against my heart and fish the waters I grew up with.'

'And yet here you are.'

'Till I get my whaleboat,' Mulanyin replied. 'And my wife. You know, my family will be at the Mullet Run. You should come, I'll introduce you and you might change your mind.'

'I'll be there, brother. But you know you'll have to fight Missus Petrie for Nita,' Murree warned. 'She's lived with Tom's people since she was small; they won't let her go easy.'

'I'll take us down to Cleveland Point,' Mulanyin dreamed. 'By the time Missus Petrie has time to get wild, I'll have Nita safely at Nerang. Will your Elders agree to our marriage, do you think?' he repeated.

Murree got to his feet. He stood alongside his brother and gazed at the disgusted pumpkin seller on the far bank, his effort wasted, his pumpkins unsold.

'You must present yourself at the waiburra and ask them yourself, brother,' Murree said as he watched. 'Only they know the answer to your question.'

~

'These need darning, Nita,' Mary Petrie said, laying a dozen socks down. 'And Grandfather's jacket is torn, again.'

Nita's needle flashed silver, repairing the damage that came with every washday. 'My husband *will* insist on feeling every new

113

wall and inspecting every new window in Moreton Bay. That man'll be the death of me yet.'

Nita murmured agreement. Andrew and Mary Petrie loved each other but you wouldn't always know it by the way the Missus talked, full of complaint about the risks her husband took.

'Mister Petrie wouldn't know what to do with himself if he kept away from his work,' Nita answered, 'and I'm sure the men would be lost without him and all.'

'I won't rest easy till John takes over,' Mary said, settling down on the veranda, lace petticoat in one hand and a needle in the other. 'Climbing ladders, if you please, at nearly sixty and blind. The man's a lunatic!' Her attention suddenly shifted to the gardener, Old Tom.

'Tom! Tom! I need those banana trees put beside the shed, out of the wind. Can you please find it in yourself to plant them today before they wither anymore.' Mary Petrie's voice descended from the veranda, more an entreaty than an order.

Old Tom grunted and kept hacking away at the lemon tree he was intent on reducing to a stump. Mary sighed. Like the rest of the household, she was mildly terrified of Old Tom. Transported for bodysnatching, he was now a free man, and a reliable if stubborn worker. But nobody was ever quite sure to what depths Tom might stoop if he took a set against you.

'Missus?' ventured Nita, balling one pair of socks and picking up the next. She poked an index finger through the hole in the toe and waved it at herself. 'Can I ask you something? Something about America?'

'America! Well of course you can,' Mrs Petrie said, peering over her glasses.

Nita drew breath and bravely went on, hardly believing what she was about to utter. 'I heard Dalapai say that the dark people in America are going to war against the white people who own slaves. And he said that the Africans will have a lot of guns to fight with … is that true?' Nita's eyes were wide. The idea of an entire army of black people fighting for their freedom was as thrilling as it was dangerous. What might Dundalli have done with equal weapons?

'Oh!' cried Mrs Petrie. 'Well, I don't know that it will come to war, Nita. President Pierce has damaged the prospects for emancipation, it's true. But there's many good Christians opposing him. And the slave states will see the wrongness of their ways in time – they must. It's against all of Christ's teachings. No, I don't think it will come to war. And Dalapai shouldn't put the idea in your head in any case, worrying you about such things on the far side of the world.'

Nita was quiet, choosing not to reveal that it was eavesdropping on Grandfather Petrie and Dalapai that had led to her curiosity.

'Yes, missus. It's just … if the slavers don't see the wrong of it now,' she eventually went on, 'what's to make them see it, other than war?'

Mrs Petrie became aware that Old Tom, standing beneath the house with his back to the veranda post, had paused in his work and was listening to them. The old shirt he wore was stuck fast to the middle of his back, his malodorous sweat plastering it to him like a shroud. Morbid, she told herself crossly. Stop seeing corpses every time Old Tom is near.

'Well, think of the convicts, Nita. Moreton Bay has been stained by our dark history, but even so we are a free colony now, and soon to be a state. No man in Brisbane wears the broad arrow today. It didn't need a war to stop that evil. We must pray a war won't be needed to stop slavery in America. It would tear that great Godly nation apart and cost thousands of innocent men's lives.'

'I hope so, Missus,' Nita replied, sceptical of prayer alone as a recipe for justice. *Liberty, equality, fraternity – or mort*, she had heard Dalapai insist to Grandfather Petrie behind a closed door; and it turned out that *mort* meant a fight to the death. She indisputably owed her own freedom to Grandfather Petrie, yes, but what of those miserable Goories still bought and sold in secret by the pastoralists of Moreton Bay? Why, just last month Missus Petrie's washerwoman – a white person – had been sold by her Irish husband for the price of a carriage! What hope did her own people have, or the American slaves for that matter?

Nita was distracted, just then, by the sight of Mulanyin appearing out of the undergrowth, his legs and chest streaked with thick splashes of mangrove mud that had dried to grey on his skin. Her beloved's spear was threaded with five fish, each as long as his forearm. In his other hand a fat green mudcrab cast about in vain for liberty.

'Mulanyin, my goodness!' exclaimed Mrs Petrie, 'You're certainly a provider. Take those around the back to Nellie, there's a good boy. Or no, wait, I'll get Old Tom to gut the fish in the shed. Tom, are you still there Tom?'

Old Tom loped around the front of the house, shovel in hand, reaching his mistress at the same time Young Tom emerged from the hallway.

'It's Old Tom I meant,' Mrs Petrie explained. 'Tom, can you clean these fish that Mulanyin caught, the clever boy.'

Old Tom stared at the longhaired kippa, muddy and naked but for his cast-off trousers, which revealed almost as much as they hid.

'Mullar … wot?' he grumbled, taking the fish. 'Rotten heathen lingo.'

'Mulanyin,' Mrs Petrie repeated firmly. 'He has a name, as we all do.'

'Melon'll do me.'

Mulanyin gazed down at Old Tom with mild contempt. The gardener could have been a stray mutt dragging its wormy arse down the middle of Queen Street.

'Don't be ridiculous!' Mrs Petrie was affronted. 'Melon. What sort of a name's that for a fine young darkie?'

Old Tom spat aside a stream of tobacco juice. 'Toby, then,' he suggested gruffly, wiping his mouth. 'I'se a long streak of a cousin back home, name of Toby.'

'He does have the look of Toby Brinkworth,' offered John Petrie, emerging from the house with Young Tom and jamming on his boots. 'Remember, in Sydney. He looked like he could run all day and not break a sweat.'

'Oh, yes!' Mary Petrie agreed, suddenly enthused by the memory of their old neighbour. Her voice rose in excitement. 'He *does* look like Toby, John, you're right. I think that's a grand English name for you to use in town, Mulanyin.'

'What's a *Doby*?' Mulanyin looked at Nita, alarmed, since Mrs Petrie had assumed the authority that Old Tom clearly lacked in this department. The giving of any name was not something to treat lightly. Those assembled on the lawn laughed and Mulanyin shot a look at Young Tom, fearful that he'd said something ridiculous. A familiar feeling rose in him of being surrounded by friendly aliens, yapping at him in their alien tongue and presenting him at every turn with their bizarre ideas, which they considered absolutely ordinary.

'A Toby isn't anything really,' Mrs Petrie explained gently. 'It's just a name, a man's name.'

Mulanyin frowned. It was ridiculous to take the name of *nothing*. There was no power in that. Or was that the point? Was this the waymerigan's secret plan, trying to diminish him and strip him of his selfhood in front of Nita so that he couldn't steal her favourite servant away to be his wife?

'Hold on, yes it is,' Young Tom contradicted his mother. 'Come inside, brother and I'll show you.'

'Do you mind?' cried Mrs Petrie, rounding on Young Tom in the doorway. 'Will you look at the state of him – mud from head to heel and stinking like the inside of a fish house!'

'Oh, surely Nita can mop up a bit of mud,' said Tom, poo-pooing her objections. 'Anyway, he's no dirtier than Father was yesterday evening,' he said, beckoning the barefoot kippa inside.

Hesitant, Mulanyin lay his fish and spears on the lawn and walked up onto the Petrie veranda where he had never stood before. There he met Nita's eye, drinking in her beauty and wishing he could stay beside her rather than follow Tom inside. Her twinkling expression warmed his whole body. With difficulty, Mulanyin managed to tear his gaze away and wipe his feet on the doormat, copying Tom. He padded behind him until they reached the drawing room; a dagai cave made from ochred wood. All Mulanyin's senses were on high alert as he stood waiting to see what Tom would reveal.

'Here,' Tom opened a cedar cabinet and took out an odd kind of container. 'That's called a Toby jug.'

When Mulanyin saw the distorted ceramic face which formed the body of the jug a spasm of horror shot through him. He stepped back, shaking his head in refusal, all his fears confirmed.

'What's up?'

'That's a debil head!' Mulanyin blurted. 'Your Waijung wants to name me after a debil?'

He fled the room, leaving behind the ugly laughing ceramic face and all Tom's feeble rejoinders.

'Mulanyin,' he announced as he strode off the veranda and snatched his spears from the lawn. Mulanyin drew himself up to his full height and looked directly to Nita. 'My name is Mulanyin of the Yugambeh, son of Yagoi! I am a man of the Nerang boollun and the great burragurra which it flows into.'

Nita gave him a nod which went unnoticed by her mistress.

'How about we call you Saltwater Toby, in that case,' Mrs Petrie proposed. 'Or Yugambeh Toby, just for a town name.'

'Your *Dob-ey* has nothing to do with me,' Mulanyin flashed a look at Old Tom that made Mrs Petrie realise he was mortally offended. And with that he was gone.

For days afterward, whenever Mulanyin remembered the Toby jug, a tremendous shudder would pass through him. He had a sense, a dimly understood premonition, that in receiving the name Toby, even briefly, he had also received some kind of clumsy curse from the bowed croppie who slaved in the Petries' garden.

~

Three figures climbed out of a rowboat at Newstead. The sun making them into silhouettes sat low and orange over the western hills; night was one short hour away. On the bank opposite, Dalapai's clan were stoking fires, cooking damper, or retrieving fish they had caught that morning and stored in the shallows with a vine through their gills. A girl used a coolamon of creekwater to rinse her infant sister's dirty backside, well downstream of the oompies. Four men were at work repairing a singed home with large rectangles of bark; the two neighbouring oompies had recently been burnt to the ground, and theirs was lucky to survive the attack. They worked stolidly, as they did every other time the dagai came across Breakfast Creek to persecute them with fire.

One of the figures from the rowboat walked towards the house overlooking the river. The other two watched him go.

'Quick,' Mulanyin urged as Tom ascended Captain Wickham's stairs. 'He'll be out soon as he delivers the mail and has a drink.'

His unchaperoned minutes with Nita were precious. This was only the third time they'd ever been alone together, and Mulanyin was determined to make it count. The young couple rushed into the shadows of Captain Wickham's garden. Mulanyin grasped his girl's narrow hand. As she willingly folded her fingers into his he felt as though his skin would burst from the pounding of his blood.

'I'll show you what I promised, and then you will owe me an apology *and* a kiss.'

Nita was entirely unconvinced of Mulanyin's claim, but excited to be alone with him, whatever his excuse. When they reached the far side of the garden, the kippa halted at a wooden enclosure.

Inside squatted a curved animal, the size of a dugong, but rounder and far more solid. Its comically flat face rested on the ground, eyes closed.

'There!' Mulanyin turned in triumph. 'The biggest bingkin you have ever seen, by far! It'd feed a family for half a moon – now tell me I'm wrong?' He drew Nita close to claim the kiss he was owed, but she put a palm on his chest to stay him.

'Yugam bingkin!' she retorted. 'You're full of humbug. Look at those feet – no bingkin ever had jinung that shape!' Her tone was one of teasing mockery. Mulanyin would work for his kiss tonight.

'Of course, it's a bingkin!' whispered Mulanyin, equally passionate. 'Nothing else has a big round shell over its body like that! What else could it be?'

'It doesn't matter what it is,' Nita countered, still smiling. 'Only what it's not – and it's not a bingkin. That's called a *tortuj*. Captain Wickham's pet *tortuj*. From a different Island Country far, far beyond our saltwater.'

Mulanyin felt his kiss ebbing away into a desert of semantics. He had expected Nita to be astonished by the huge beast.

'A snail has a shell like that, too,' Nita added for good measure. 'Maybe this is a gigantic kind of snail brought here from Muttakundrei.' Her hand still rested on Mulanyin's bare chest. His heart thumped beneath her palm.

'Is this creature soft-skinned like a snail?' he retorted. 'No. It has leathery feet – four of them! And just because dagai give something a different name, doesn't make it a different animal. They call Kurilpa "South Brisbane", but it's Kurilpa! They call me Saltwater Toby, but I'm really Mulanyin. This is a bingkin, a different shape of bingkin and certainly a different *size* of bingkin – a giant in fact – but that's still what it is. I didn't expect you to play childish games with me. Maybe you've been living with dagais too long and have forgotten how to keep a promise?'

he accused her.

'I've forgotten more than you ever knew about how names change things,' Nita told him, growing haughty. 'You seem to think you know more about Brisbane than I do. But I lived here when the Sufferers still worked the mill in chains. You arrived with the last lot of fluffy magpie chicks and haven't stopped warbling your nonsense since.'

As though produced by her words, Tom's whistle summoned them back to the boat. Mulanyin's heart sank, but he made one last stab at wooing this beautiful, impossible girl.

'I am new here,' he conceded, 'true enough. But it's a strange world everywhere these days. Yerrin says we must be strong and adjust to a life with the dagai wandering about our lands. Where kundil can carry a hundred men. Where bingkin can have stubby feet instead of flippers,' he added, taking Nita's hands and gazing at her, 'and grow to the size of an old man kangaroo.'

She met his eyes, a lump in her throat.

'Don't be afraid of change. Be brave and marry me,' said Mulanyin. 'And have my jarjums. I love you, Nita. I can take you to the burragurra again. We can watch the gowanda leaping in the foam and hear the cry of the gulls. We can fill our nostrils with salt air and hear the waves breaking all day and all night – forever.'

Nita was unable to speak for a moment.

'I've seen more change than you've dreamed of,' she whispered. 'More than even I can believe, sometimes.'

'Marry me, Nita. Come away from this place and we'll make our own changes in a world of our *own* choosing, on my Country where the dagai are few. Leave the Petries and make a new family with me.'

Mulanyin leaned down and Nita raised her face, allowing her lips to find his. They kissed for a long minute. When they broke apart, shivering with passion, she had made up her mind.

'I will marry you on one condition.'

'Anything,' Mulanyin blurted, his heart tumbling over itself in sudden joy. Hearing the words he had been dreaming of for five moons made him feel oddly unbalanced. He might be whisked into the air like a feather, should the wind blow his way. 'I'll give anything, my darling! But I know what you'll ask. You want me to be baptised.'

Nita put a finger to his lips.

'I'll be your wife, and yes – I do want you to be baptised. But Mulanyin, my only condition is this. You must never question me ...' She was looking directly at him now and could see his love for her shining on his face, transparent and real '... about my life before the Petries.'

'Of course, sweetheart,' Mulanyin said, folding her into his embrace. He would have promised anything, would have stood there all night, all *week*, pressed against her glorious warm body, nuzzling her hair, but Nita stepped away.

The fingers of her right hand were still threaded through his own as she tugged him towards the rowboat.

'Come, Tom is waiting.'

13. Fools, Rushing

2024

Doctor Johnny picked up the didge and turned it in his hands. When he put it to his mouth, the rich scent of beeswax filled his nostrils. To Winona's surprise, Johnny began to play, and play pretty well.

'Nice,' he said, resting the instrument against his shoulder. 'I might just keep it, hey.'

Winona's eyes widened. 'Don't *you* go getting any ideas about busking,' she said, grabbing it back without ceremony. 'I've just about had it up to here with white didge players.'

Johnny laughed. 'Yeah, I bet. But, um, I'm not white, hey? I'm a Murri.'

'Yawhatnow?'

'I'm Murri.'

'The fuck ya are! How come you never said? Who's ya mob?'

'Goomeroi. From Kickalong Station.'

'Huh.' Winona peered at Johnny. Brown hair, hazel-green eyes and a skin that could pass for any breed in Europe. If he was a fairskin blackfella he should have said so.

'I thought you might be Jewish, name like Newman.'

'Yeah, the surname is. My grandad was stolen and he ended up adopted by a Jewish couple in Sydney. They raised him in the faith. But after he died, we found out about his real mum, she was a Collins, so … "yaama".'

Winona sighed. Another of the thousands of claimers washing up on the shores of the Aboriginal Nations, looking for refuge and belonging. And bringing all their existential woes along with em, for real blackfellas to fix. Cos we don't have any problems of our own, nah. We live to help suffering white people with their identity crises. We fucken adore it.

'Hey, hold up! Ya don't get to be a blackfella just cos your ancestor was,' she replied firmly. 'If ya got no lived experience or living mob, then ya just another bloody white Aussie holding a vanilla milkshake, mate.'

Johnny's smile vanished. 'That's not what I've been told,' he protested. 'We've identified as Goomeroi for years!'

Winona felt the nightmare of the didge player returning to haunt her.

'Finding an ancestor does not fucking mean you're Aboriginal,' she repeated. 'You're a white man with a Black ancestor.'

'So, what – the assimilation policy was right?' Johnny argued, 'You can wipe the people and culture out and call it a job well done? I think you'll find that's called genocide, hey?'

Winona groaned. This clown was gonna be in Granny Eddie's life a while yet. She had to sort his delusions out, onetime.

'Don't talk to me about assimilation, mate. Half my fucking family are still hiding our kids from DOCS now, in 2024. And if your ancestors way back assimilated, then they fucking assimilated, ay? That means ya white. Acknowledge it. And for the love of sweet suffering Jesus on the cross, don't assume actual blackfellas don't know our own fucking history. Have some humility! If you want to be a blackfella, it takes years of work. Lotsa years. Learning shit, meeting Elders, and discovering how to even shuttup and *listen*.'

Johnny gave an ironic laugh. That was pretty rich, coming from a chick who had done nothing but lecture him since the day they met.

'Okay, understood. But let's just say I *have* been listening. What if I *have* been learning? When do you start listening to me?' he countered, trying not to sound as pissed off as he felt. 'You don't actually *know* me, or my story, or—'

'I listen to your story every week, pal,' Winona shot back. 'Lemme guess. You've always felt a bit of an outsider, right? A bit *different*? And as a kid you had this really magical connection to the bush – more so than other whitefellas, yeah? Over the years you felt drawn to dark people, to us mob, and maybe to Islanders or Maoris or whoever, and some of them told ya that you weren't like the other whites, that you really belonged with Blak people, and then someone said that maybe you were even Blak yourself. You started to feel that you had an Aboriginal heart, or an Aboriginal soul, and there was a rumour going around in the family that someone's mum or dad was a bit tanned, that maybe an ancestor might have been Aboriginal and like, you never really knew for sure, but you *felt* it was true. And then some bloody dickhead told you, "Yes, go ahead, identify as Aboriginal," cos if you feel like you're Blak you probably are, there's that many missing and murdered ancestors never accounted for. And now six months or a year later, here ya are, identifying as Blak without any lived experience, or any fucking connections – other than the existential angst of every human that ever fucking lived – and some offhand words from a kind-hearted Goorie who wanted you to feel like you belonged somewhere for once in ya fucked up colonising life.'

'Um,' said Dr Johnny Newman, gobsmacked at Winona's accuracy.

'I suppose you've done a DNA test and everything, have ya?' she went on mercilessly.

Johnny wasn't about to fess up that he had recently done just that and was awaiting the result. 'What's wrong with DNA tests?'

'Are you deaf?' Winona yelped. 'Being a blackfella *isn't about having an ancestor*. It's about who ya are, ere, now. In the twenty-first century. Plus who claims ya, and who you are in the world. It's about who you're connected to and how you understand land, and your language, and ya mob, and maybe ya Dreaming – it's a collective thing, not an individual thing. You don't get to just fucking wake up one day and decide that you're a Blakfella!'

'But that's not what happened. Ya not listening. I got claimed by a Goomeroi man first, and we went on from there.'

'Well, ya shoulda just fucken stayed white, ya ask me. As if us mob don't have enough problems.'

Johnny grimaced. He felt as though Winona's horrified rejection was slowly tearing his skin off in long, deliberate strips. Her family was properly Blak – *always was, always will be* – and so she had the power to do that, to flay him to the bone if she chose to, and apparently, she did. It was hideous, and it was fucking unfair. As though the Stolen Generations never happened, or never mattered if they did. As though genocide could be wished away. But something about her expression told Johnny that arguing at the West End market was not going to change Winona's mind anytime soon.

The two stared at each other in profound dissatisfaction.

'How long since ya grandad died?' Winona asked, breaking the awkward silence.

'Five years ago. We found out at the wake. And about that time one of my Indigenous Health lecturers picked me for Murri. He's from down that way and he knew the Collins name from Kickalong Station and we put two and two together. He told me I'd walked into his lecture that day a white man and walked out a brother.' It had been one of the outstanding moments of Johnny's life.

'Oh, that'd be right,' muttered Winona, taking a last draw before stubbing her durrie out on the grass. She looked at Johnny glumly, knowing full well he was cut. Pity, cos she actually liked him, liked how smart he was and how he genuinely cared about Gran. But facts were facts. She wasn't about to start handing out Aboriginality like a popularity prize.

'I gotta hook it in case security's on the way. Seeya when I'm looking at ya.' She pocketed her cigarette stub, shouldered the didge and jogged off into the thinning crowd.

Johnny watched her go. When she'd disappeared from sight, he stood alone, feeling that his centre had been gouged out with her every word, leaving him a hollow cicada husk, the exact dimensions of the original creature but with no substance at all. And ya wonder, he thought bitterly, why I never mentioned I'm Aboriginal before.

Winona's scorn echoed in his head: *That means ya white. Acknowledge it.*

So much for wanting to date her.

'Ah fuck it,' Johnny said in disgust, and returned to Creek Care.

~

'What's this fucking dribble?' Winona threw a newspaper lift-out on Eddie's bed, where it lay, glossy and deceitful, between Granny and Dartmouth. Her eyes flashed at the journalist in contempt. 'Who told you all this white boong bullshit, and said it was okay to write it down like you're The Venerable Fucking Bede?'

Dartmouth reared back, trying to process *white boong* and *Venerable Fucking Bede* in the same sentence.

'Settle yaself down, Missy,' Granny Eddie snapped. 'And knock orf swearing while ya at it, you swear too blooming much. I told him what to write.'

'Oh, really Nan?' replied Winona, knowing full well that Eddie's eyesight was shot. 'You've okayed all this then?'

She picked up the insert and began to read aloud. 'Many politically correct myths have grown up about conflict between black and white in colonial Moreton Bay, says Queensland's oldest Aboriginal. The pioneering Petrie family were in fact deeply loved and adopted by the Brisbane tribe. Their son, Tom, a well-known pastoralist north of Brisbane, was an initiated man and led many British settlers on their explorations into unknown virgin land with the blessing of the Indigenous population. The Petries were "really good people" says Aunty Eddie Blanket, who at one hundred and three is in a unique position of authority to speak about early Brisbane. "People talk a lot of rubbish about the old days when they weren't even there."'

'Well,' muttered Granny Eddie, her gaze not quite meeting Winona's. 'They do talk rubbish, bub. You know how people go on. Bignotin.'

'Nan,' Winona pleaded, 'my phone's lit up like a Xmas tree. Ya can't go saying stuff like that!' Her phone buzzed even as she spoke.

'Lettem come ere then!' snorted Eddie, with a flash of the spirit that had kept her Blanket family intact throughout a century of ethnocide. 'Lettem tell me to me face I'm wrong! I'm a one-hundred-year-old black woman and I know what's what!'

'Aunty Karen Beehive wants me to call her asap,' Winona read the messages in growing horror. 'And Uncle Henry Wallaby too. They not happy, Nan. Not happy at all.'

And who can blame them, added someone in the rear of the room. Eddie snapped her head around then and cried out, pain rocketing up her neck. There was a blurred figure beside the wash basin.

'Who's that there? State yer damned business!'

'What?' said Winona, looking up from yet another angry text. 'Who ya talking to?'

'Who's that where?' asked Dartmouth, coming alive in relief at no longer being the centre of attention.

'There, next to the basin. I heard someone cheeking me,' Eddie grumbled. 'These damn doctors, why can't they fix my eyes? They want to buggerise around with blood pressure and insulin, but nothing about getting me eyesight back, oh no. That's not a priority at all, is it?'

'It's just us here, Nan,' Winona reassured her. 'Who'd it sound like?'

'Dunno.'

Nan gazed about in dissatisfaction. Winona was blurred but definitely present. Same with Dartmouth. And the far corner of the room – turning her head more delicately this time – now appeared vacant. Was she hearing things? Going womba? Or was her room haunted by the unquiet ghosts of innumerable former patients?

'Seeing mooki,' she muttered, putting a hand flat on the bed to steady herself. 'Is that my Endone there, bub ... give me one will ya.'

'Want another cup of tea, Aunty Eddie?' Dartmouth stood up.

Winona shot him a look that would have killed a lesser man. 'How about you piss orf with ya *Aunty* and ya *cuppa teas*,' she snapped. 'I can make any cuppas that need making around here! Go peddle ya whitewash somewhere else!'

Dartmouth stepped back, palms up to indicate his innocence. 'I'll pop in again this afternoon, Aunty Eddie,' he said with a stab at dignity. 'When it's just the two of us.'

'What?' said Eddie, closing her eyes. 'Oh, yes, just us two. Gorn, then.'

Ngali yabra-bulla whispered the figure in the shadows.

Just us three.

14. 5 January

1855

The big man lay unmoving on a straw pallet, exhausted. Outside his window, magpies fluffed their feathers and stretched their necks to announce the sunrise, sending great loops and curlicues of sound echoing through the dusty streets. A young goat had escaped its pen overnight and wandered down to the Bogey Hole. Now, confused and alone, it bleated a rat-a-tat call for its mother as snarling mutts gathered around. In the dense scrub below The Windmill, two hundred Goorie voices chanted, as they had chanted all through the night, the knocking of clapsticks and burrang sharp now in the dawn air. The big man clung to this chant and sang with those outside. The song helped him to remember that Goorie voices would be heard here forever beside the Warrar. The ground his filthy pallet rested on would absorb today's music and hold it, and release its power when it was needed, over and over and over again, until such time as the earth itself was no more. He, like all men, was insignificant. His life was fleeting. Only the power of the song mattered, and the earth which contained it.

Outside in Queen Street, servants scurried to serve their masters and mistresses. A few workmen made their way to building sites at the Queen's Wharf and William Street, where a brand-new version of North Brisbane was being constructed on the ruins of the colony. They were building a Brisbane determined to look forward, averting their eyes from the shame of its convict past. The workmen – many wincing from injuries that would never see a doctor – glanced up at Windmill Hill as they went, clutching their trowels and hammers in case of attack. A Tanna woman emptied a shit-bucket into the gutter of Albert Street, then hurried indoors, away from the malodorous goonah of her mistress and the trouble the day promised. Brisbane's atmosphere was thick with summer humidity, but today a different kind of pall hung over the town. Mounted police patrolled the streets, their faces taut with fear.

As the sun rose higher, more and more black bodies flowed into town from the outer districts, joining the vigil on Windmill Hill. The song grew stronger with every new arrival. Smoke rose from campfires in the scrub, its tendrils curling through the streets of the town and filling every gap and crevice as though it was the song made visible. White folk smelt it and were afraid.

The magpies would sing the same chorus tomorrow morning, the big man knew, but he would not hear them. The goats would still bleat as they roamed; the labourers would hawk and spit and curse about the work to come. He would not hear them. The rays of the sun, life's great overseer, would reach into this very room and light the pockmarked stones which imprisoned him. He would not see that golden glow, nor the room either. He would never again see the ocean, nor hold his children, nor lie with his wife. He would never hear another corroboree on Windmill Hill.

He was Dundalli, and today he would hang as an example to all free Blacks.

Mulanyin puzzled over Tom's decision to avoid the hanging. Nita had been ordered by Missus Petrie to stay home, but Tom had refused outright to accompany him up the street to see the awful event.

'I've seen three men hanged,' Tom had said, screwing his face up. 'And I've no wish to see another.'

'It's our duty,' Mulanyin replied, knowing that Tom was well aware of his responsibilities to the Bora. Mulanyin was in any case eager to see the great man for himself. Everyone had heard the stories of the fearsome Dalla warrior: taking entire flocks of sheep here, scattering herds of cattle there, leading organised attacks to burn white houses, destroy white barns and fences, and killing, when killing became necessary, the Chinese shepherds and other dagai trespassing into his homelands. Dundalli was doing a General's work for the Bonyi Bora; he was their Napoleon and their Mulrobin, their leader in the field of war, and so his name was hated and feared by whites for hundreds of miles around. Many had believed him immortal. In Mulanyin's eyes, Dundalli was equal parts war hero and wizard.

Magic or not, their warrior stood condemned under British law. The dagai would destroy him to signal their triumph. Dundalli's war was over, they boasted on every street corner, and his black resistance would surely die with him. New South Wales belonged to England's God, and England's Queen. Any remaining myalls in Moreton Bay would be dead of pox or the bullet soon enough; British pluck and progress would see to that.

Mulanyin had few ties to the Bonyi Bora which had endorsed Dundalli's leadership in an era when he himself was barely off the tit. But Mulanyin was made a man at the Yagara Bora, and so any Bora business involved him. He would join Yerrin and Dawalbin and Murree and the other Brisbane mob on Windmill Hill, all those from the Yagara and Yagarabul; the Coastal and Upriver clans, the Black Soil People and the northerners. They would all join together to help sing the correct songs for Dundalli's death, and then hear what the Elders had to say about prosecuting the Law of Payback.

Mulanyin was no soldier, but he was full of love for a man so bold. If anyone tried to steal his land, he would fight to keep it. He too, would kill if instructed. Only a low cowardly dog would give in to invaders without a fight – and he was no coward. If the

Goories assembled below the Windmill decided on battle today, he would gladly play his part. The thought made his breath catch, and his heart pound. Nevertheless, he pushed up Queen Street into the crowd of townsfolk, determined to join the clans massing on the hill beyond.

The crowd roared as Dundalli was brought through the arched prison doorway in chains. White men shouted approval; their women screamed along.

His shackles clinking, the warrior brushed roughly past his gaolers on the way to the gallows, toppling one to the ground. Then Dundalli climbed onto the wooden platform, head high, as if it was his own people's Law demanding his death today. He was no snivelling coward who needed dragging to the noose. He was a man, and a leader of men.

'The great brute,' shuddered the chemist Warry in the front row. 'Savage to the end.' His wife and sister-in-law agreed, their eyes glued to the prisoner. They were anxious not to miss a moment of the spectacle.

Nearly seven feet tall, heavily muscled and scarred, Dundalli stood in the centre of the gallows and began declaiming to Windmill Hill in his own language. He ignored the white bodies below him as if they were so many termites. His chains might not have existed, he wore them so lightly.

'What's he saying, man?' Captain Wickham demanded of Jem Davis. 'And where is Dalapai?'

The flat-faced blacksmith by his side concentrated on Dundalli's oratory. 'He speaks to his wife and his family, telling them to avenge his death,' Davis interpreted. 'They must find the turncoats among the town blacks and hunt them down and execute them as payback. He says ...' here the freed convict hesitated a moment, listening hard '... he says that the British are low characters, who must use deviants to enforce their law. He refers to Green,' he added for Wickham's benefit.

The Government Resident pursed his lips. The colony's hangman was a convicted rapist; there was no getting around that unpleasant fact. How the savage came to know it was a mystery.

Davis went on: 'Brothers, crush the filth – those black foreigners who help the mothar to steal from our people. I've done nothing but protect us and defend our lands. For this they call me a criminal. For this they will take my life. Take good note, my brothers. See how there is one law for the British, and another law for us, whose lands are invaded and whose food animals are driven off. We starve while their cattle grow fat on stolen grass. Our children sicken and die while the mothar laughs, his fat, round belly full of meat. The white man prays to his alien God but knows no morality – he is without shame. There's no justice in these lands but the justice we make ourselves. Let the rivers run red with traitors' blood. Avenge me!'

A furious roar rose from the hill, drowning out the chanting of the old men. The cacophony startled the police horses, which reared and whinnied in fear, almost unseating their cursing riders. Stray dogs howled. White children clutched at their mother's skirts and wailed. Scrub turkeys fled into the gullies, heads held low. The tumult built upon itself, sounding to the townsfolk as though the bush itself was in torment. As though the hills and trees, the birds and animals, were already keening for Dundalli and what he stood for.

The hair on the back of Captain Wickham's neck stood up. 'Will they attack?' he asked Davis. Rivulets of sweat trickled beneath his thick serge uniform. His regiment had orders to fire if necessary, but a dispersal in Queen Street would be disastrous, especially with so many journalists watching, ready to tattle tales of unrest to Sydney and London. Not every white person in Brisbane agreed with this execution, and some were openly hostile to it.

The mounted troops drew their pistols, willing to fire over the heads of the crowd on the flat, into the Goories on the hill.

'Hold fire!' called an officer, looking towards Wickham for orders.

'What are the headmen saying – are they going to attack or not, man? And where's Dalapai? Don't tell me he's ranting on the hill with those cannibals?'

'I think … not,' judged Davis, scanning Windmill Hill and searching out the profiles of the clan leaders he knew. 'Very few of them are painted for war. They're cranky, but they know the taste of lead well enough by now. And it's those who grabbed him will pay the price. If the bucks don't make a move when the noose goes round his neck, I'll wager they won't take on yer diamonds. Not today.'

'Let's hope to the Good Lord you're right,' Wickham wiped at his face and neck with a handkerchief, then spoke to his lieutenant. 'Tell Green to get on with it, damn him, before the treacherous brutes get any more stirred up than they already are.'

Green lurched forward and looped the noose snug around Dundalli's neck. For the very first time, the warrior gave some recognition that this killer existed.

'You might snap my neck, you dog,' the condemned man told him in English. 'But, tonight my brothers will rub your kidney fat on their spears.'

Green stepped back, his face ashen. The chanting and yelling from the scrub rose up again; it became a deafening crescendo, obliterating all other sound.

It was at that instant of tumult and chaos that it finally dawned on Mulanyin that Dundalli was actually about to die, right before his eyes. The revelation struck him as though he had been dreaming all morning and was now suddenly awake.

'No, no, no!' he cried in horror, arms raised, as if he could reverse gravity and lift Dundalli out of danger by sheer willpower. But his words were lost in the clamour of hundreds of other voices: those who chanted the Death Song, those screaming in protest, and those cheering the death of their hated enemy. Even as Mulanyin uttered them the trapdoor fell away from beneath Dundalli's feet.

What happened next would become the awful topic of conversation in Moreton Bay for many years. The trap opened and the noose was strong, but for all that, Dundalli did not die. As though the spirit of the chanting and the clapsticks had flown, arrowlike, to the execution spot, Dundalli clung to life. His enormous body was suspended, yes – but Green had misjudged the length of the rope needed, and the warrior's toes brushed the ground. The big man hung, caught between the life behind him and the death which surely awaited, slowly strangling before the horrified crowd.

'Oh, he's gone and buggered this up alright, the cackheaded thing that he is,' Jem Davis muttered to himself.

Dundalli's eyes bulged as he flailed at the end of Green's rope. The jeering and cheering from the Queen Street crowd faltered and then stopped. A revolted silence slowly fell around the scaffold. The witnesses on Windmill Hill wailed in helpless torment.

Another terrible minute passed. Dundalli's tongue protruded, yet still he lived. A low moan escaped his lips.

'For the love of God, you useless bugger, fix it!' Wickham raged.

Not knowing what else to do, the desperate Green seized hold of Dundalli's legs. He wrapped himself around them, dragging the prisoner earthward with his own body weight. The hangman clung to the black man's shuddering body for several agonising minutes until the jerking and moaning had ceased at last.

When Dundalli was finally still, and Green understood that his job was done, he released his grip and stepped back from the horror. He stood trembling, his back turned to the sullen white crowd for fear they might punish him for showing them exactly who they were.

Grim-faced soldiers pushed past him then. They cut Dundalli down and took his corpse to a waiting dray. Miserable, Green pulled his hat low over his eyes and fled inside the gaol to await the wrath of the Government Resident.

Mulanyin, who had failed to find Murree or Yerrin in the vast crowd, stood stunned and alone. He understood now why Tom had stayed at home. Women and men wailed behind him on the hill, the Cry for the Dead echoing off every tree trunk and boulder. His lips moved mechanically, but he didn't join in the sorrow; he barely even heard the others. Blood roared in his ears. All he could think to do was flee, to run from this scene of foulness and torture, run far and fast to the burragurra. Only saltwater made any sense to him in a world that could treat a black man thus.

Wickham strode about, ordering his regiment to patrol the streets till dark. The civil police needed military backup. He'd take no chance that the savages might riot. Davis trotted along behind him, wishing he was anywhere else in Moreton Bay.

'Might I be going to my shop now, sir,' Davis ventured when there was a brief pause in the strategising. Wickham turned to see the blacksmith waiting for dismissal.

'Oh, yes, yes,' he nodded peremptorily. A moment later he called Davis back. 'One thing, man – what was that Dalla word our sable friend used? Calling us ghosts, ay? But I think he's the ghost now, somehow.'

Wickham gave a grim chuckle. A more politic man would have chuckled along in agreement. But Jem Davis had spent sixteen years in the scrub and had worn the broad arrow long before that.

'Nay, sir,' he answered, turning his hat in his hands. He squinted at the toff who ran Brisbane. 'Nay, not ghost, that term is *mogwai*. The headmen now begin to use another word.'

'Oh?' Wickham was not well pleased at this correction.

'It, ah, the new term refers to one who sets a trap and who lies in wait,' Davis struggled to express the complexity of the metaphor. 'One whose sphere of influence, or danger really, spreads far from the centre and—'

Wickham sighed heavily. 'Am I to be allowed to know this wonderful new word?' he interrupted.

The blacksmith's eyes became cold granite. 'Aye. The new word, sir, is mothar. The literal meaning is *spider.*'

15. Queen of the Warrar

2024

If ya got time to clean, Winona told herself, then ya got time to lean.

She was propped against the wall, arms folded, as the ABC technician prepped Eddie for her allotted fifteen seconds of fame. Gran's 'Big Moment', and what a moment it was. Eddie Blanket had already been lifted out of obscurity by the magic prose of Dartmouth Rice. Today, she would go proper viral: Queensland's Oldest Aboriginal right there on the idiot box for everyone to see.

The ABC tech and their colleague with the make-up bag were fussing around Eddie like she was some kind of centenarian Oprah. Revelling in the attention, Gran glanced at Winona with a look that reinforced her earlier orders: *I don't want none of your lip, now, missy. This TV show is my parade and I don't want you or your smart mouth raining on it, right? Bout time us Elders got a look-in steada you young crowd always bignotin yaselves!*

Winona winked at Gran, and grinned. As if she wanted to be on TV celebrating John Oxley's two centuries of criminal trespass. Nah. Hard pass there. The bicentenary celebrations were bread and circuses for the white working-class, and a few beads and mirrors chucked at mob. Today's spot on the news – Granny Eddie, hyped as the Queen of the fucking Warrar, if ya please – was merely the cherry on top of the whole steaming crock. Winona wanted no part of the gammon thing – she wanted her land back.

But hey, she mused, props to Gran for the hustle; it cracked her up. Butter wouldn't melt in the old girl's mouth. She had graciously allowed the bureaucrats and pollies to fete her, and then permitted the innocents in the media to crown her, and now the whole damn lot of em were pretending to hang off her every word about the Good Old Days. I just hope they don't bust ya bubble before the big day, Winona smirked. At least not until ya sail upriver at the head of their flotilla and cut their fancy fucking red ribbon for em.

Earlier that afternoon, Winona had stood on the hospital veranda with a coffee and a donut, worming her way into Granny Eddie's binung. 'Ya might wanna fess up Gran. Now, before it's too late,' Winona had advised, blowing a stream of smoke into the clear winter air.

Granny Eddie snorted. 'Elders be dropping like flies, I did that! Nah, leave sleeping dogs lay, bub, that's my motto. Least said, soonest mended.'

Winona changed tack. Gran was enjoying her stardom far too much to reveal that Dartmouth had taken firm hold of the wrong end of the stick.

'Fair enough. Stuff em, anyways, how come we gotta reconcile anything? Them's the ones what come and declared war on us. Yes, war I said. There was more dead on the Queensland frontier than Aussies killed in World War One.'

Granny Eddie's gentle smile was buoyed by fifty milligrams of Pethidine. 'Bub, even if there was a war – and I dunno where ya getting them numbers from, that don't sound right to me – it was a war us mob fought and lost. Dagai not going away! We gotta get on with them. Look down there, lah, wall to wall whitefellas.'

Winona gazed down at Vulture Street, before exclaiming. 'Hey, look! Gaja Iris just drove past – she must be back from that funeral at Cherbourg already,' she told Eddie. Psychologist Iris Brown was a local legend among the woeful and the womba.

Eddie sniffed. She pushed biscuit crumbs about on her plastic tray with a manicured fingernail, making a small beige cairn.

'And look there, at the zebra crossing – Aunty Debbie and Uncle Marcus's mob! Must be taking the grannies to South Bank,' Winona crowed in triumph. 'See? It's not all whitefellas, Nan.'

Marcus waved up at the veranda but Gran ignored him, stubbornly blind to the existence of his whole blurry family.

Marcus shrugged. 'Nanna Blanket's eyes must still be crook,' he told his wife.

'Love you Nanna,' Debbie yelled up, before grabbing her foster grannies and hurtling across the road with them while the light was green.

'It's *mostly* whitefellas. And we gotta live with em. So knock off about ya wars and ya genocide, please.' Eddie was not gonna be denied her moment of fame or the narrative underpinning it.

'That's white historians wrote that number down, Nan, not me. Professors. A hundred thousand people killed on the Queensland frontier, nearly all of em blackfellas, and I can show ya the textbooks if ya don't believe me. But if ya gonna play the bicentennial game, then at least get something to show for it. First rule of negotiation: Tell em we want our land back, or a house. A decent house, too – four-bedroom job, not like that shitty little flat they expect ya to lick their arses for.'

'Mmmm ...' Granny Eddie fiddled with the *New Idea* on her lap as she chewed on this suggestion. A *house*. A house where the family could stay any time she wanted, and where Winona could be her carer instead of the delightful but unreliable Samantha from six suburbs away. A house near a bit of bush, maybe. Or a park. Her flat looked out onto the railway line and resonated to trains roaring past twenty times an hour. She was deaf, yeah, but not that blooming deaf.

'Mmm, a house'd be good I suppose. But oh, I dunno, bub. It's a terrible lot of mucking around to get a house.'

Winona kept right on pushing goonah uphill. The old girl didn't want to make waves, didn't think she deserved a decent home after growing up with a dirt floor and an empty belly. 'Gran, we gotta bite em hard onetime, while we got the chance. Christ, why should us mob always live like stray dogs?'

'We can't be sunk in bitterness,' Granny reiterated. 'Or stuck in the past. We need to focus on the good dagais, like Cathy and Zainab and them Petries, and—'

Winona made a derisive sound. 'Hear about that little disabled Murri boy they kept naked in the watchhouse for *three days* before anyone stopped it? How's that in the past?! Fuck all's changed since Dundalli.'

'Oh, please. Dundalli was a freedom fighter. Half the mob inside are there for stealing phones for crack price!'

Winona was about to point out that there'd be no need for pinching phones or using crack if the land hadn't been ripped off in the first place. *Join the bloody dots, Gran.* She'd been interrupted though, by the arrival of the shiny-arse TV mob wielding their clip-on mics and their power packs. Eddie had barely enough time to warn Winona off her parade before she was being foundationed and rouged and blow-dried within an inch of her life.

'Fancy that,' she'd squinted, touching the dark circle of powder, 'brown pancake. I never seen brown pancake in my life. Amazing!'

'I think we're right,' the sound tech told their boss. The make-up kit was packed away. Winona stepped back out of shot, and with a majestic smile Granny Eddie was live to air.

'That sovereignty crowd can believe me or not, I don't bloomin care. The way I heard it from Grandad was, Aboriginals back then accepted that white people weren't going away. And they sure as hell knew the poor convicts were no better off than us mob. Look at Logan getting killed – they couldn't work out whether it was blackfellas or the convicts who killed him, cos they were coming from the same place, both on the bottom rung of the ladder, see?'

'That makes a lot of sense,' the journalist nodded.

'A ladder sitting on our stolen land,' muttered Winona on the sidelines.

'Grandad never served, but he lived to see his cousins enlist. Proud? He was proud as punch. No, no, he never went to the war. He had a job driving Mr Bolitho around, so he was classed as primary production. Got paid a white man's wage and everything. I think he's here today, you know,' Granny added.

The journalist's brow puckered. 'I don't quite follow.'

Granny explained live to air that her hospital room contained a mooki, a ghost that seemed friendly enough, but steadfastly refused to show itself. It spoke to her; it knocked on windows and doors, and it had turned the damn bathroom light on in the middle of the night more than once.

The journalist's eyebrows lifted half an inch. 'How *interesting*. Well, so long as it isn't, ah, bothering you too much, Granny Eddie,' she said smoothly, wondering if her Uber had been ordered.

'It is bothering me!' Eddie contradicted. 'I'm an old woman! I don't want to be bothered with mooki all hours of the day and night! Can't ya leave off,' – here she addressed the empty room, 'leave off tormentin me, Grandad. I'll be with ya soon enough, Lord knows.' Eddie harumphed, only subsiding when a fresh cup of tea was produced by an enterprising intern.

'And that's a wrap,' said the cameraman. 'Thank you so much, Aunty Eddie, you were amazing!'

'Uber's three minutes away,' the tech said, as they removed Eddie's microphone and power pack.

'I hope our paths cross again soon, Mrs Blanket,' said the journalist, closing her notebook and checking if she had time to run to the loo.

~

'The Minister is *very* excited.' Dartmouth plonked himself down beside Granny Eddie's bed and slurped his cappuccino. 'The committee too. See here, they want you sat up at the head of the flotilla, sitting right alongside the governor and the T.O.s! Uncle Henry's agreed, they reckon. How's that for stylin up?'

Dartmouth had taken to using a bit of Goorie English when Winona wasn't around.

'So Henry should agree,' scoffed Granny Eddie, remembering the night in 1946 when she had kissed Henry Wallaby outside the Annerley dance hall. She'd often pondered what might have been, if a smooth-talking fella from Grafton hadn't whisked her away the next weekend and gotten her pregnant within the month. Her children would have been traditional owners of Brisbane, rather than a hodgepodge of Bundjalung, Irish and mission breed.

'Now, about the bicentenary – they can't decide between a decked-out CityCat or a replica of the *Mermaid*, to lead the flotilla,' added Dartmouth. 'I think the replica'd be better, what do you reckon? If it's a CityCat the minister wants it painted in Kurilpa totems. Imagine that coming around Gardens Point, flanked by traditional canoes. Here, let me show you the video, Eddie.'

Dartmouth's laptop came to life and Eddie heard classical music blaring out, heavy on the trumpets. On the promo video a computer-generated John Oxley gazed imperiously from a boat in midstream. Sailors on either side of him hauled on ropes and the sails of the *Mermaid* swelled to full glorious stretch as the cutter swept under the Story Bridge and into Petrie Bight. Large digital crowds lined the riverbanks and cheered onscreen.

'Oh, hold on, that's the *Mermaid* version,' Dartmouth said. 'Wait up.' As he spoke, the screen froze and the soundtrack suddenly cut to silence. The crowds on the computerised shoreline froze along with Oxley, their mouths open and their arms raised. Without the soundtrack it was impossible to tell if the watchers were celebrating Oxley's arrival or terrified by it.

Dartmouth fiddled with the settings, to no avail. 'This bloody thing's on the blink again. The hospital electronics must bugger it up.'

Eddie lay back and closed her eyes, tired from a disturbing nightmare. It was the second time in a week she'd dreamt about Dundalli, and she really wished she hadn't. His poor tongue sticking out, the hangman dragging his legs down, horrible, horrible. It was that blooming Winona to blame, talking about the hanging, no damn wonder a person had nightmares. If only she could see her TV properly. Then she'd be dreaming about *The Bold and the Beautiful*, same as usual. Fed up to the back teeth with everything, Granny gave a tiny whimper. It was no fun being old and in hospital, no fun at all. When were they going to fix her head and eyes up and send her home? Why did everything have to take so long, and be so damn hard, at her age?

'Are you okay?' Dartmouth finally noticed Granny looking unwell.

'I'm tired today. And my neck, it bothers me too,' Granny rubbed ineffectively at the place her neck met her bony shoulder.

Dartmouth clucked in sympathy and reached for the Endone and a glass of water. 'I'll go, shall I?' he offered, closing the useless computer.

'I'm sorry,' she apologised, already growing drowsy.

'No, no apology necessary. You rest up, love.'

Dartmouth stopped on his way out to tell the staff about the extra Endone.

'Aunty is not sleeping well,' Nurse Xi nodded. 'The medication, it can interrupt her sleep pattern, and she's also having some nightmares. Probably being away from home. She's very stable though, actually. I think in two to three days she will be feeling much better.'

Dartmouth thanked Nurse Xi. Then he dialled the minister's office to let them know Granny Eddie had accepted their offer to sit at the head of the regatta, whichever vessel it ended up being. Catching the lift down to the carpark, Dartmouth frowned at his reflection in the mirrored wall. *Aunty?*

~

'I'm only acting devil's advocate,' Johnny teased. He'd forged an alliance with Eddie over the NRL tipping, and had taken to playing with fire.

'Well, here's a handy hint – how about ya *don't?*' Winona proposed, hands on hips. 'I dunno who had the bloody bright idea that the devil needs any more advocates. I reckon the devil's doing okay, meself, when I look at the state of the world.'

'But—'

'But *what?*'

'But you're gorgeous when you're angry,' Johnny added, taking a large step away from Winona's slapping hand.

'You'll keep. Cheeky white dawg!'

'Whatcha growling that lad for now?' asked Granny Eddie mildly, flicking through TV channels for something that didn't look like a Rorschach Test. While her Pethidine lasted, she was the sweetest centenarian on the east coast.

'He's getting cheeky. About culture!' Winona scoffed. 'Bloody claimer. Keeps making out he's Murri!!'

'Could well be,' said Granny Eddie, winking at Johnny. 'Look at them green eyes. His mummy's cartridge probly just run outta ink.'

'Could well be?' Winona's mouth fell open. 'Is that all you got Gran? And I'm not talking about his *colour*.'

Granny Eddie muted the TV. She patted the bed and Winona sat.

'Listen ere. Ya thinking like a whitefella again, my girl,' said Granny Eddie. 'Ya gotta remember, once upon a Dreamtime, everybody all over Australia was blackfella. *Everybody*. Being Blak wasn't a big deal back then, and being a Murri or a Goorie shouldn't be a great big, huge deal now either, bub. The only question ya ever need to ask is what sorta person they are. Black fella, white fella, yella fella, any fella ... so long as you are true fella!'

'White fella, bogus fella, gammon fella, claimin fella ...'

'Oh, see now, that's exactly what I mean. Let's say Johnny's a Goomeroi and he claims it – who's he hurting?'

'I *am* standing right here, you know,' Johnny interrupted.

Eddie ignored him; Winona flapped a hand indicating he should siddown and ning, onetime.

'Right,' he snapped back, 'Well, I've got a ward to see to.'

'On ya bike, sunshine,' Winona said and turned back to Granny Eddie. 'It's about being honest – and knowing ya place.'

'But, see, I *believe* him, bub. I like him. And I reckon he *is* honest. And he might not know his place, but ain't that exactly what they wanted when they took the kids away?'

Winona paused. Yes. Yes, it was. Of course. She knew all that. But something was missing in the equation.

'I like Johnny, too. But it don't make him a blackfella. If he's a descendant and still learning then he should fucken well shut up until he *does* know his place, steada taking up airtime and jobs that belong to blackfellas!'

Granny Eddie sighed. These young generations had such freedom. Running around all hours of the day or night, no exemptions or permits or crawling to mission managers. All sorta jobs, and finishing high school in droves, mostly with full bellies and often with clothes bought new in shops, just like white people. But oh! So much angrier than her generation had ever been. You wouldn't read about it.

'I thought I told ya to knock orf swearing, my girl! Johnny's a *doctor*. He don't *need* a blackfella job and he's not *taking* a blackfella's job. We need educated ones like him, same as he needs us to teach him his culture.'

'We got Blak doctors of our own now, Gran, and nurses. Even specialists – Gaja Iris's a psychologist, and that kid of Zamira's studying cardiology.'

'Well, we can always use more, can't we?'

Winona wrestled with this idea, turning it left and right under a spotlight as her soul screamed *no, no, no!* There was something terribly wrong at the heart of what Johnny was doing. An invasion of *her* space, *her* community, almost of her own self. And Granny Eddie giving it the nod. What. The. Actual. Fuck.

'I can't come at it, Gran,' she finally muttered. 'It just feels all wrong. Invasive.'

'Yeah, I know it does,' Granny nodded. 'But believe me, girl. You're thinking like a whitefella when ya close him out. That's not our way. We bring people in, we bring our mob Home, and we care about em. We *teach* em how to behave proper way. So, you just knock orf and be nice to him!'

But what if they're the same mob that stole our Home in the first place, Winona burned to retort. *What if they're white, Nan.*

But instead, she sat down and shut her gob and stayed ning, just like a real Goorie must do when growled by her Elder.

16. Mrs Walsh's Laundry

1855

Tim Shea was delivering ewes to the Logan, footsore and hungry, when he heard an unexpected commotion. The racket came from Joe Walsh's, a dire place consisting of a timber hut and some outbuildings on ten scruffy acres. Inside Joe's stockyard, Shea could see a roan bullock – the owner of a massive set of curved horns which almost met above its forehead – that had managed by some freak accident to encircle the neck of a second steer. Torn hide flapped on the neck of the trapped bullock where it had struggled against its imprisonment. This animal moaned, stomping its feet as it pulled in vain against the encircling horns. The roan bullock likewise bellowed in fear, backing up and swivelling its hindquarters to the limited extent that the trap, entirely of its own making, allowed.

Joe's exhausted wife stood watching the bizarre scene. Dust and desperation filled the air.

'There's a rum un,' Shea exclaimed, drawing near. 'How'd ya manage that sort of a mangling?'

The woman shrank from him. The Logan was home to a population of roaming men: lags, myalls, bushrangers. Only yesterday two emancipists had lingered at the gate till a neighbour had happened past. A woman on a farm needed eyes in the back of her head.

'Ye needn't fear me, Missus,' Shea reassured her. 'I wouldn't harm a single hair on ye head. Just tell me what's happened here, and we'll sort it.'

'Never mind the beginning of the thing,' Mrs Walsh blurted, deciding to trust Shea. She was frantic to separate the bullocks before her husband returned from town to beat her for the debacle. 'Take that halter rope, will yer – the fool of an animal won't stand and be helped.'

Tim Shea ducked under the stringybark railing and did as she asked, pinioning the nose of the offending bullock where it stood. First Mrs Walsh and then Shea attempted to drag neck from horns, but the bullocks were massive, and frightened, and cantankerous; the horns weren't for moving, no matter how they struggled. Eventually, Shea and the woman stood panting at each other from opposite sides of the conjoined beasts. Then Mrs Walsh noticed Shea's wrists for the first time. She stared in dismay before catching herself and averting her eyes, saying nothing that would shame the man or provoke him.

The hot flame of convict grievance flared briefly in Shea's chest, then dimmed as she pretended not to have noticed. 'Haven't ye a hired man about the place, nor any black boys?' he asked, irritated. The Logan was an awful lonely spot for a woman on her own. And besides, it was really none of his business how other people managed their stock. He had two hundred munkies to be moving on to Bromelton, with myall spears to be wary of, and the snakes and dingoes to consider, too.

Mrs Walsh explained that her husband was away till supper and the hired man with him. They had left her the shotgun to reinforce the pot of boiling water she kept ready on the stove as a matter of course. She didn't much mind being left for the afternoon, but then normally, she added, the stock could be relied on not to get themselves into such ridiculous conundrums. No such thing would have happened at home in Rathmore, her da wouldn't have dreamed of allowing such a situation.

'Ye'd not read about it!' she cried in sudden anger. 'I'll be having to saw the blasted pair of them apart!'

'Fer a mess of dinner I'll do it,' Shea offered, softening at the mention of Home. 'D'ye have a saw?'

'Aw, would ye? That'd be grand.' Mrs Walsh's relief was palpable as she went to her toddler, now bawling inside the bark-roofed shack.

'I'm from Cork meself,' Shea answered, ducking beneath the clothesline and following the woman as far as a crude wash bench tacked to the outside of the hut. He made his way past a pile of clothes that she'd abandoned in her hurry to separate the bullocks and kept up his end of the conversation from the foot of the stairs, trying not to stare at her soiled underclothes lying in full view on the grass. It'd been so long since he'd clapped eyes on a woman's chemise that he hardly recognised the object. Eight years – eight! – wasted on the low muddy island off Dunwich, thinking himself still a prisoner of the Crown. He'd soaked his irons in the ocean morning, noon and night till they rusted off, never realising a pardon had been issued him all the while. Driven during those eight godforsaken years to the brink of madness by mosquitoes and sandflies and mud and loneliness, and the only hint of a woman's existence the slim black girls he glimpsed in their distant canoes. Why, he'd forgotten there was any such thing as a chemise! Shea was enthralled by the sight, even one as threadbare and filthy as this one.

Mrs Walsh reappeared with the toddler on her hip and bearing a small blunt saw. She promised him mutton and damper when the uncoupling of the bullocks was complete.

'T'will do the job,' he reassured her, running a forefinger along the saw's edge, 'and if ye've any beef dripping to go with that damper, Missus, I'd be obliged for a taste. I won't stow any mutton, though.'

'We've plenty,' Mrs Walsh protested, although her supplies were in fact meagre.

The shepherd shook his head. 'I'm not fond of munkie, missus. Call me cracked, most do, but it fair turns me innards to think what we do to the poor creatures. I haven't partaken of sheep flesh for many a long year.'

'And you a shepherd!' Mrs Walsh cried, incredulous.

Tim Shea turned away, not wanting to see the familiar amusement building on her face. It seemed his lot in life to attract contempt. Chained or unchained, the mockery of ordinary folk followed him like the stench of the broad arrow. He grumbled under his breath about this as he went to release the bullocks from their strange predicament.

~

Three dozen Kurilpa had gathered on the crest of Highgate Hill. As the youngest men present, Mulanyin and Murree sat silent, their heads low. The oldest was Narbalang, a stocky fellow with white eyebrows and many battle scars who had seen over seventy Mullet Runs. Narbalang was already a grandfather when the dagai first blundered into Magandjin, but it was Yerrin who had called today's meeting.

The mood of the men was upbeat. Mulanyin was generally liked by Yerrin's clan. For six moons now, the young southerner had been energetic and helpful, quick to share his surplus catch and never shirking his duty to the village. He was fast becoming a valuable man. It helped, too, that he and Murree had forged a very strong bond. As Yerrin's eldest son, Murree had a particular status at the Bora, with clear potential to be a leader of men. Murree was a beacon of hope to the greybeards on the hill, looking down on their beloved river flats; the place where they had raised their own children entirely free of British interference. One day, the old men told each other, one day Murree and Mulanyin, along with their brothers and cousins, would reclaim their river flat and boot the British out.

Alas, the South Brisbane wharf now dominated the stretch of ground where their village had flourished. The river which since the first sunrise had known only their kundil now bustled with dagai boats; a forest of masts sprouted from these vessels like shoots reaching sunward from a pile of neglected yams. A hundred white households drew from the Kingfisher Creek that had once only watered Kurilpa mouths. Bitterest of all, goats and horses grazed and shat now on the ancient riverside cemetery of Yerrin's people. But these insults weren't inevitable, the old men agreed. The dagai could up sticks and shift! They could get themselves and their stock further back from the river, or – and this was preferable by far – bugger off entirely to their own damn Countries. How to make them do it was the question. The diamonds had many guns, and along with the other dagai, they had the clear willingness to use them. The Native Police were another type of savage entirely. Still, the old men hoped to see the river flats returned in their lifetimes. Simple justice demanded it.

Yerrin called the meeting to order. 'I stand here before you, my brothers, born of our Country and her Old People,' Yerrin began. 'Born like each of us, through the blessing of our Big Waijung who gives us All Life. And it's new life we are concerned with, today.

'Mulanyin, my adopted son, who has passed his kippa test with honour, and who lives here with my kin, wants to marry the Ngugi girl, Nita. Are they well suited? Do we consent to it? Is anyone wronged by it? By custom he should be matched with a girl from the Upriver People, just as his Law Brothers are. And he will need to be put quickly through his Third Ceremony, if they are to marry.'

The meeting considered the issue. Mulanyin's value as a fisherman, a dancer, a singer and a community member was scrutinised. They circled the touchy topic of how to break the news to the Upriver People that one of their promised husbands was unwilling. After an hour, when the grey-haired men had all had their say, Yerrin turned to the others. Tandur, a broad-faced man of twenty-five, pointed out that neither Mulanyin nor Nita were originally from Magandjin and so neither had absolutely unbreakable bonds to the Kurilpa. Where would their children truly belong? Somewhere on the Bay Islands or far to the south? It might be better if they both married Yagara-born citizens, so their children could never become alien. Another man countered that Mulanyin was an initiated Kurilpa, while Nita was more-or-less adopted by Andrew and Mary Petrie, dagai people of good standing in Magandjin. They both had strong links to the Warrar. And, of course, both had numerous relatives among the Yagara through kinship and marriage.

'In any case,' offered Yerrin, 'should the pair of them end up living among the Yugambeh or on the Islands, we can always call them back. It never hurts to have our people among friendly neighbours. The dagai are strongest in three places: here in Magandjin, at Goompie, and among the Upriver People at Limestone. So, whether Mulanyin remains with us or returns to the saltwater, or marries Upriver, the result is not so very different.'

The men nodded, seeing the sense in Yerrin's argument. Belonging to any clan of the Federation was a giant cat's cradle of family obligations and connections, stretching from the Bonyi Mountains down to the southernmost people of the Bundjalung and beyond. No one area had an exclusive claim on any Goorie person.

'Anything to add?' Yerrin asked, turning to Tom Petrie, sitting cross-legged beside Murree.

'My parents love Nita, of course,' Tom told the meeting. 'And feel responsible for her. But Mulanyin will treat her well. I support the engagement and so do my parents.'

'Good,' answered Yerrin, pleased. 'Mulanyin, come forward.'

When the kippa stood in front of him, Yerrin examined him.

Mulanyin resembled few of the others present. Most Kurilpa were heavily muscled warriors of average height. Lanky Mulanyin, standing well over six feet tall, resembled his namesake the white-faced heron, long of leg and beak with a keen fishing eye.

'Do you know the name Mulrobin?'

'A fighting man,' came the answer straight back. 'Son of T'luwubluwagopilly and a hero of this Country.'

'Yoway. And more than that, he was a man something like Dundalli, whom the dagai were afraid to meet in fair battle,' Yerrin said, nodding towards the old cemetery ground. 'He lived and died here. That's his grave tree, that tall eucalypt next to the wharf. Here's something you should know, Mulanyin, a story from twenty Mullet Runs ago, when the dagai were still quite strange to us. Back then, when we didn't yet understand who or what they were, nor why they had come with their mysterious loud weapons and their bands of Sufferers, some small children were taken from us. They were stolen without our knowledge or consent.'

He paused, allowing the awfulness of this to sink in. The mood of the meeting turned grim, remembering. There had been so many jarjums lost. Dozens dead of the pox. Some snatched up as servants and curiosities. Others stirrup-ironed by Native Police, and several who had simply vanished, never to be seen again.

'Two jarjums they snatched back then belonged to George over there. One belonged to Mulrobin. One came from a family who are now all in the Star Camps. Mulrobin found out who among the dagai had been evil enough to kidnap our children from their Waijungs. He went straight to that house along with three other warriors, swimming over to Toowong with an axe bound to his back. Our countrymen attacked that house, cutting the front door to shreds with their axes, and when they returned home they brought our jarjums with them. Tandur, stand up.'

The broad-faced man stood, proud and angry all at once.

'Tandur is one of those children.'

Yerrin peered at Mulanyin. The circle of men waited expectantly. 'Do you understand this story?'

'Yoway.'

'Nothing is more precious than our children,' Yerrin walked around Mulanyin slowly, examining him from every angle, inspecting him for hidden weakness or deceit. 'Nothing. Mulanyin, if they come to take our sons, will you fight?'

'Yoway!'

'When they come to take our girl-children, will you fight for them?'

'Yoway! To the death!'

'When they come for Nita—'

'I would kill for her!' Mulanyin erupted. 'I would spear their stomachs and rip out their kidney fat!'

Yerrin broke off as the meeting cried their assent for the marriage. There was no doubt that the young man in front of him was ready to defend his people, his future jarjums and his wife to be. That was correct. No Goorie child could be born without Guardians. Mulanyin was clever, strong and willing to fight for his family. He would pass his Third Ceremony test.

'Then we agree,' Yerrin checked with the circle of nodding men. 'I'll send word to the woman's Bora that we approve. If they agree, you will marry Nita after your final Ceremony. We will corroboree for you to ensure strong and happy children, and a loving union – I hope with no need to go spearing any dagai stomachs.' Yerrin paused, then clapped Mulanyin on the shoulder as he added, 'You are brave, son, but we must pick our battles carefully.'

Mulanyin heard nothing after 'you will marry Nita'. He grinned for days.

~

'What about these ones?' Dawalbin suggested to Nita, dabbing warm beeswax on a lock of the girl's hair.

Nita selected two green and yellow feathers from the pile on the veranda and held them up, twirling them to catch the light.

'These are nice, not too big or too small. Now, tell me again,' Dawalbin prompted as Nita rolled her eyes. 'Come on, show me you remember.'

Nita pursed her lips then recited the phrase that was so important to Dawalbin. 'Yugam ngaya wulala wahlu wogai.' *I did not give you permission to touch me.*

'Almost right. Don't mutter though, say it strong. The men will moan and wail to see such a beauty taken,' Dawalbin instructed, as she worked the feathers into her young protégé's hair. 'But you mustn't allow them to sweet-talk you. And if they try …'

Only half-listening, Nita smiled at her own reflection in the Petries' sitting-room window. Soon her whole head would shimmer with the brilliance of the parrots and the fairy-wrens, and all of Brisbane would know at a glance that she was betrothed.

'And if they try?' Dawalbin repeated, poking the girl hard in the ribs.

'Ouch! *I did not give you permission to touch me.*' This time Nita sounded like she meant it.

Dawalbin grinned. 'Make sure you remember it. And sit still while I fix your hair. How can I do it right if you keep wriggling around like an eel.'

'I'm excited, that's all.' Nita flashed a smile at her hairdresser, glowing with the attention she was getting since her engagement. Adored by Mulanyin and instructed by Dawalbin, Mary Petrie and other Goorie women in the ways of married life, she felt she was being taken seriously at long last.

'Look at you,' Dawalbin caught hold of Nita's slender hand. 'Fingers like a waymerigan who need never fish for herself.' Her own smallest finger had been ceremonially bound with sinew as a very young child. With the top two joints gone, the remaining stub was half the size of her other digits.

Nita waved ten slim fingers in the air. 'Never mind! My love catches all the tasty jalum we need,' she boasted. 'And he'll bring plenty extra for you this moon, Waijung. Flathead full of roe, and bream too.'

'The fish in the Warrar grow scarce, child.' Dawalbin shook her head. 'And smaller. You mustn't tempt fate. Did you hear the Bribie oyster banks are ravaged? The dagai took far too much, took the oysters by the barge load and burnt the lot alive, over and over again, season after season, simply to use the shell for lime. Such incredible waste, and now the banks are ruined.' She stopped decorating Nita's hair, trying to swallow the bitter lump that had risen in her throat. Bountiful oyster banks that had stretched for miles along the seacoast, carefully tended sea-fields which had fed Goories since the beginning of time. In a few short years they had been plundered to the point of no return. The greed was beyond comprehension. If a dog behaved this way, Dalapai had accused, greedily ripping into and destroying stock at random, it would be shot on the spot. But this was civilisation and progress, he had been told. It was something to be celebrated.

'Grandfather Petrie is going to talk to Captain Wickham about that,' Nita answered, handing blue-green parrot feathers to Dawalbin. 'These are my favourite colours, use these!'

'Talk, yes,' Dawalbin growled. 'Talk and talk, and more talk while our creeks are fouled with the shit of the town, and our bungwall gardens overrun by cattle!'

Nita decided to steer the conversation onto a happier topic, lest Dawalbin abandon her hair half-finished.

'There is a magical new object in the drawing room,' she announced, her eyes wide, 'just arrived from Sydney. It's called a *telescope.*'

'I've seen spyglasses before,' Dawalbin replied loftily. 'Dr Ballow showed me one long ago. You put it to your eye and it makes small things large, but not really.'

'This is different from those of the ship's captains, Aunt. It's longer and has three stout wooden legs, and it lives inside a house not on a boat. It has a magical eye which brings the heavens close to the man using it. Grandfather Petrie says that when I am married, I may even be allowed to look through it.'

'This magic eye – can it show our people's Star Camps?'

Nita paused. Last night's explanation of the telescope's powers from the Petrie men had been less than transparent. And they had been downright shifty on the topic of whether or not it could be used to see the Ancestors.

'I'm not sure. Mulanyin says it's all dagai business, built for dagai to look into, so our Ancestors will not show themselves through it.'

The two women agreed that this was very likely the case.

'But probably it will show me Jesus on his golden throne,' Nita proclaimed happily, while Dawalbin added the last of the parrot feathers to her fringe.

'A toast!' Andrew Petrie raised his tumbler of ginger beer a few evenings later. 'To the happy couple!'

'The happy couple!' chorused the household.

'Hooray! Hooray!' added Cocky, swinging from the window sash. Everyone laughed.

'You will both live here with us, Mulanyin,' beamed Mary Petrie. 'John can build you a room onto the stable. That way I won't lose my dear Nita.'

Mulanyin and Nita exchanged a glance. They had yet to tell the Petries that they planned to make their lives on the coast. Tom noticed this look.

'Nita will always belong with us,' he interrupted his mother, 'but soon she'll be raising a family of her own, Marmie. I'm sure John Lang can find you another good strong lass for the kitchen.'

'Oh, aye, the bonnie little ones!' Mary Petrie beamed again. 'It'll be lovely to have bairns under our roof again.' This was a subtle reproach to Tom for selecting land so far away. She would be lucky to see her grandchildren twice a year, she'd grumbled when he told her about his plans for Murrumba.

'You may marry here, in the garden,' Andrew Petrie announced. 'I will speak to Lang about the date.'

Nita looked out the window, irritated. She'd arrived at the Petries' door no more than a child, but she was a grown woman now and could surely decide the place and timing of her own marriage. An ancient memory came to her of the dolphins at Mulgumpin, bursting out of the waves with nothing but pure joy in their saltwater lives. Was there anything so free in all the world as a leaping dolphin?

'We'll be going to the coast in time, Mister Petrie,' Mulanyin said, 'for our marriage at the Mullet Run.'

'A heathen marriage?' Andrew Petrie frowned. 'But Nita is baptised.'

Silence fell.

'The Mullet Run will mean a week away, Nita,' Mrs Petrie sighed. 'Perhaps more. And what if you decide to stay on the coast. Whatever would I do without you?'

'A week is not very long,' objected Nita.

'Those details can be sorted out later,' Tom broke in, seeing Nita's growing anger. 'Let's just be happy for the engagement, now. We're celebrating, aren't we?'

'You're right, Tom,' Mrs Petrie recovered her composure. 'This should be a joyous day. Nita, come here to me.' She embraced the girl, kissing her on both cheeks.

'Let's pray for a happy future,' Andrew Petrie intoned from his padded armchair beneath a portrait of the Queen. He clasped his hands and bowed his head. Everyone obediently followed suit. Everyone except Mulanyin, who stared about the room in bewilderment. The Kurilpa Boras, male and female both, had endorsed his marriage. Tom had said the Petries supported it as well. It seemed, though, that the Petries and the Kurilpa had agreed to quite different things.

'Lord, we ask that you cast your blessings down upon this family. Bless especially your servants Nita and Mulanyin, and their marriage according to the rites of the Church. Guide them to the divine light of your son Jesus Christ, Lord, and away from the evil of ignorance and sin. Bless any children of their union, Lord, and bestow upon them your magnificent love and salvation. In your son Jesus' name, amen.'

'Amen,' repeated the room.

'Amen!' added Cocky.

Mulanyin stared at the floor. He wondered at what point he had stopped being a kippa jalum-bira born of Yugambeh jagun and become the property of a foreign God.

17. The Sports Day

1855

Easter sports day began as a great success. The weather was sunny, and as though in celebration of the happy event, great clouds of orange butterflies floated over Kangaroo Point, alighting on hats and shoulders and the hoods of parked buggies. John Petrie was victorious in the woodchop. Tinker Campbell beat all-comers at running with a full wheat sack on his back. A notorious loudmouth named Harrington won the half-mile footrace down Main Street, stealing the crown of the aging Duramboi who had long been known as the fastest man in Brisbane.

Just before lunch a Londoner, Mrs Thorpe, fell over a stray dog during the competition to walk precisely one hundred yards. Her skirts flew up, revealing an illicit measuring string tied between her knees, and the woman was banished; she left the field to the ribald laughter of the onlookers. When a piebald horse managed to kick itself free from its sulky and bolt the length of the peninsula, reins and broken harness flying behind it in a cloud of dust, butterflies and stray curs, it merely added to the day's excitement without causing any real harm.

The trouble began halfway through the afternoon's cricket game: Irish versus Scots. John Petrie hit a magnificent six off a ball bowled by the lumbering Patrick Mayne. There was a loud crack as Hibernian ball met Caledonian willow, and then the ball

162

soared over the open paddock, cheered on its way by the entire Scots contingent. Higher and higher it flew towards the boundary scrub. Dismayed fielders scowled as they watched the ball sail overhead; only James Murphy made any show at chasing after it in hopes of a catch. Two hundred watching Goories yelled in loud approval. Any feat of athleticism was cause for celebration, and doubly so when it was the bully Mayne being bested by a Petrie.

The cheers soon faded, however, when the ball came to rest in a giant eucalypt. Perplexed, the cricketers gathered on the edge of the paddock, craning their necks. Galahs flustered in the highest branches, disturbed first by the ball and then by the commotion below.

'Get a black up there after it!' suggested players, and someone was dispatched to find a native tree-climber. Yerrin approached, along with Murree and Mulanyin and a dozen other men.

Yerrin gazed up. The canopy of the eucalypt was at least a hundred feet from the ground. 'Hmmm, pretty big tree,' he observed for the benefit of the hapless cricket teams. 'Baal easy for climb, that one ...'

'I've seen plenty of blacks climb bigger,' argued the chemist, Mister Warry, impatient to resume the innings. 'Now how about yer get one of yer boys up there, and no more humbug?'

Yerrin grimaced and stroked his beard while he conferred with his men. They assured him they could climb the tree. What's more, they had seen exactly where the ball landed, in one of the hollow limbs used by the parrots as a home. They might even get birds for their trouble, along with cash. Yerrin turned back to the cricketers with a mournful expression.

'Mmmm. Proper hard one, this fella tree. What if blackfella bin fall out? Might be him bugger up properly, then what?' He took hold of Murree's arm in demonstration of his huge economic value to the clan. 'Goorie get all busted up, no good fishing, no good catch possum, no good carry timber, no good work longa town ...'

'Where's Duramboi?' the Irish captain retorted. 'He'll show you how to get up a gum tree.' But Duramboi had left in disgust after losing the pedestrian contest. More beard-stroking and headshaking ensued, until the cricketers finally relented, offering ten shillings for the return of the ball.

'One pound more better,' Yerrin told John Petrie, with a twinkle in his eye.

'Daylight robbery,' said John, handing over the pound. Yerrin carefully stowed the note under his hat, then nodded at his son to proceed.

Murree looped a long piece of stout lawyer cane around the base of the tree and stood holding one end in each hand. He flipped the loop several feet up the trunk and sprang lightly onto it. He leant back, still holding the cane; with a tilt forward he quickly flipped the loop upwards again, repeating the process over and over, until he was high enough to swing onto the lowest branch of the canopy. When he had retrieved the ball from the hollow he sat astride the terrifyingly high branch and held it up, grinning. The crowd broke into spontaneous applause, calling for him to toss it down.

The ball was tossed, but it was Mulanyin who caught it, not the cricketers. He cradled the prize to his chest.

'Hey!' demanded Patrick Mayne, 'give that thing here, boy. We've paid for it, fair and square.'

Mulanyin gazed at the burly Irishman and tossed the ball high in the air, before snatching it to his chest again. A dark rumble of discontent came from Mayne. He was used to deference from all-comers, black and white. Few men dared cross him.

'You don't know me, ay?'

'I know what'll happen to ye, ye don't hand it over. A pound's a pound.'

'Too right,' broke in Warry, 'the insolent bugger wants thrashing!'

'Mister John bin pay Yerrin,' Mulanyin taunted Mayne. 'You didn't pay me anything.'

'Come on, Mulanyin,' John Petrie interrupted, 'don't play the fool.'

Mulanyin glanced at Yerrin, who was observing his shenanigans beneath a furrowed brow. Before the old man could order otherwise, Mulanyin answered John Petrie.

'Lemme bowl. One bowl.' He held up a skinny finger in front of his face to underline his point. 'Then you'll get your ball back.'

'What?' John Petrie was nonplussed. Invisible to him, a butterfly landed on the brim of his cabbage tree hat, opening and closing its orange wings as though gently applauding Mulanyin's suggestion.

'I wanna bowl. At him.' Mulanyin pointed at Mayne. The butcher had no memory of flourishing his stockwhip at the skinny black boy in Queen Street six months earlier, but Mulanyin remembered it only too well. He'd been startled by Mayne that day, and worse, shamed by the laughter of the York's Hollow men who had seen him jump in fright from the curling, stinging lash. It was one of his earliest memories of Magandjin.

John Petrie shrugged. 'One ball won't make a difference.'

He proffered his cricket bat to Mayne, who hesitated before taking it with a dry laugh.

Warry shook his head in disbelief as he turned back to the field.

'You Petries are too damn soft on niggers,' Mayne grumbled, pointing the bat at Mulanyin. 'But let him bowl it. I'll send it back in the black bugger's face. See if he wants to grin at me then.'

Barefoot and shirtless, Mulanyin floated to the section of the paddock marked out as a pitch. As he went, he interrogated the contours of the cricket ball, learning its nature the same way he understood the qualities of saltwater each time he put a fishing line in, through delicate, exploratory touch. Here, on dry land, he weighed the foreign British object between his fingertips and thumb; he paid close attention to the way the tendons and muscles of his forearm responded to the missile in his hand. He raised it to his nose and sniffed.

Minyagu wahlu?

Cow.

Cotton tree.

Oak.

Underneath the visible, a hidden centre. Bark from a foreign tree grown in foreign soil in another man's Country, very far away. Mulanyin curled his long fingers around the stitched seams; he spoke without words to the woggai of that faraway tree and asked its help. If the ball did his bidding today in front of the scoffing York's Hollow mob, he would recover his honour, publicly stripped from him all those moons ago.

When he turned and faced Patrick Mayne, the kippa's eyesight, honed from years of gazing on saltwater and a lifetime of spotting wallaby and possum in thick scrub, detected something faintly askew in front of him. A tiny patch of native weed grew on the grassy pitch, five feet from Mayne's left boot. Mulanyin knew this kind of weed well; he knew it would be solidly matted at its base. He released the image that he had created in his mind. In response the ball told him what he needed to do: hit that matted base at speed, and the ball would react as though it had struck solid rock. If he hit its left-hand edge, he immediately understood, the ball would likely spin up into Mayne's face like a savage willy-willy. If he hit the right-hand edge of the matted weed, the ball might twist instead like an attacking eagle's claw, smashing its way past Mayne's bat and into the wickets behind.

Yoway. Ngaya gungalehla.

Mulanyin sucked a deep breath into his lungs. Seeing Mayne ready, he began to run at him. He flowed like a dark inexorable tide towards the batsman. When he reached the chalk mark the ball flew from his hand and rocketed straight at its intended target. Mayne swung the bat in vain as two of the three stumps behind him exploded with the force of Mulanyin's delivery. A great roar lifted from the crowd as the wickets flew in all directions. Mayne stood over the wooden shards which remained, wildly askew, his mouth agape.

In a heartbeat, brawls erupted between the spectators. Maddened Dubliners swung at cheering Kurilpa; Glaswegians roared in triumph, shoving Limerick chests and ducking retaliatory Limerick fists. Cockneys and Bavarians fell back, trying to avoid injury while retaining a good view of the entertainment. Ah Yow's contingent looked on, hoping not to become targets of the mayhem. Then Yerrin's voice boomed out across the paddock, telling his men in no uncertain terms to behave themselves, to fall back and regroup on the southern end of the peninsula. Because he'd had the foresight to ban all spears and boomerangs from the sportsground, the flurries between black and white fast petered out into Gaelic swearing and Yagara mockery. Save for a few blackened eyes and a Welshman with a torn ear, not much harm was done to anything apart from Mayne's sporting reputation.

The Scots surged around Mulanyin, cheering. Several thumped his back in joy, and one raised a smashed stump high in the air, declaring its destroyer a true son of the thistle.

'Tom'll kick himself for missing that caper,' called John Petrie. 'Ye'll be the talk of Brisbane for a month, man. North *and* south!'

Mulanyin nodded across the heads of the players. They both knew he had done something extraordinary, and that all Magandjin had been there to see him do it. The kippa headed off to rejoin Yerrin and the other Kurilpa; then he paused, and turned back to face Tom's brother. Mulanyin allowed himself the barest hint of a smile.

'I think mebbe Mister Mayne will remember me now.'

~

'Children are a blessing of course,' Mary Petrie agreed, poking at the cake Nita had just taken from the oven, 'but have you thought about when the babies come?' The Petrie matriarch crinkled her eyes at the girl. Nita's flat stomach under her apron showed no sign of being pregnant, at least, an embarrassment with which the young Mary Petrie had once been very familiar. 'Even the best bairn needs attending to, and it will interfere with your work, interfere considerably. You know that marriage inevitably means children, don't you, Nita? And that children must be supervised?'

'Yes, Missus.'

Facing the oven, Nita's mirth was invisible to the Missus. As she straightened up, she poked her tongue out at her reflection in the glass window Mrs Petrie was so proud of. Pooh! Dawalbin was right! Dagai *were* too ignorant to know how to keep a hold of the spirit babies that were wanted and how to send the others back to the woggai world before they started kicking for their freedom. As she expected her own baby would, before long.

'Well, then, how are we going to manage? Mulanyin's people are far away, and there's nobody under this roof with the milk and the youth to nurse your bairn.'

'Nobody cept me, Missus,' Nita said pointedly, beginning to fear where the conversation was headed. She fixed her employer with a stare and a determined tilt to her chin. 'While Mulanyin and I live here, Missus, our jarjums will have to stay right here with us, you see. And if that's not possible, then we'll just have to find other work.'

Mary Petrie's eyes crinkled with concern. When a woman has lost three children the dread worm of worry never entirely leaves her.

'Goodness, Nita, what are you saying? You're part of our family! I suppose we can try to muddle through with the babies somehow. Perhaps Dawalbin will come and help, or one of her sisters. And if necessary, Reverend Lang can probably find a suitable woman to mind the bairns while—'

'My babies blong with me and my husband!' Nita yelped. 'And we keep them no matter what.'

Mary Petrie was a good employer, and generous in her own fashion. But everywhere dagai went, generous or not, they were horribly prone to seizing black babies to make them into pets, or slaves, or a warped combination of both. And God help those poor black girls violated by white men on a gin spree. The sons and daughters who resulted, their lovely dark colour spoilt, were easy pickings. Dagai stole these yellow jarjums openly, reefing them away without even a pretence at consent. *Saving them*, they called it. Nita's gut churned. Frog Hollow housed a dozen such souls who had run from their saviours, preferring the opium pipe and a life of sin. Girls, yes, and the others too, for the appetites of Frog Hollow were vast. Rum and gold dust bought more there than girls if Catchpenny was to be believed.

Nita was seized by a blazing fury. She would kill Mrs Petrie before she let any child of hers be taken. Nita was astounded at how clearly she knew this to be true. 'My babies gotta stay with me,' she repeated, feeling sick in the stomach and not just from her condition. 'Only me. Wherever I am and whatever I do. We will never let our jarjums go to strangers. *Never.*'

Buying time, and more than a little startled at Nita's outburst, Mary Petrie arranged six loaves of bread on the new cooling racks which had arrived with the last Sydney steamer. She gazed at their browned tops. Perfect. After a decade of careful training, Nita had become an excellent servant; she'd be very difficult to replace if she took off for Southport or Dunwich. Housemaids were harder to come by even than washerwomen; those imported from Edinburgh and Liverpool were gangly useless items to a girl. Mulanyin and Nita's children would be useful workers in their turn, of course, but that was years away.

'Oh Nita, you misunderstand!' Mary placated her. 'I wasn't suggesting that the children be sent away, only that a nursemaid could be found, somehow, while they are tiny. And, as I said, if you want them here with you, we'll just have to muddle along.' She squinted again at Nita's stomach, hoping the marriage could be delayed, and the whole dilemma of skilled labour pushed aside for another year.

'You simply don't want to live in town,' Nita pouted from the stone wall at the bottom of the Government Garden.

Mulanyin was at work on the grassy slope below her, shaping fresh spear shafts over a small fire. He'd just revealed his plan to remain living at Yerrin's village after they married. What's more, he seemed surprised at Nita's reluctance to join him there.

'You are properly hard-headed and no mistake! Why sleep on possum skins when I have a bed at Petrie Bight with a flannel sheet and a wool blanket?'

Mulanyin sighed as he scraped bark from his spear shafts. He saw no advantage in flannel sheets. 'I'd sleep in a tar-barrel to lie beside you, sweetheart,' he soothed, flashing her his best smile. He came to the wall and took Nita by the hand. The girl was utterly confounded, but her lover wasn't about to reveal his real reason for staying south of the Warrar. Brave as he was in a fight or on rough water, the lad remained terrified of the Toby cup in the Petries' china cabinet. He intended to keep a good distance from that cursed object. If not for Nita, he wouldn't set foot in Tom's yard let alone contemplate sleeping under the same roof as the thing.

Nita snatched her hand away and inched her arse along the wall to put clear air between them. She glanced at Catchpenny, roped into acting as chaperone while Tom was out of town chasing dreams and gold dust. Catchpenny narrowed her eyes at the lovers. But because Nita had retrieved her hand and put a yard of porphyry block between her and her betrothed, Catchpenny let the indiscretion go.

Mulanyin ignored both women, gazing intently at the river. A shoal of jalum was approaching the strip of beach below. The Warrar fairly sang with their flickering presence.

'Then why not sleep beside me!' Nita cried in exasperation. 'Plenty tucker at Tom's, plenty bed, plenty work, plenty everything.' She smoothed her apron against her lap as she said *everything*.

Distracted by what the river was promising, Mulanyin seized a spear from the bundle he carried everywhere and hurled it at the current with a smooth, practised motion. The ten-foot lance pierced the surface, then quivered. When he waded in and retrieved it, a large flathead was bucking on the wire prongs.

'It takes many pounds to buy a whaleboat,' he told Nita, returning to shore and shaking the fish off onto the grassy bank where it joined a dozen others. 'When I have the price, *then* we can go to the coast and live together free of bosses. We need never worry about dagai again, Nita, except for selling them our catch. Imagine it.'

'So how long must we live apart?' Nita probed. She had no idea how much one of the long timber kundil cost to build, but they certainly didn't look cheap, even if Old Man Petrie had promised Mulanyin the wood at a discount. And why couldn't he just continue to fish and do other work while living at the Petries'? Was he planning to cheat on her?

'I've got a third of the cost already, my love. Grandfather Petrie is holding the scripts.'

'Aunty, look!' Nita said, with a burst of enthusiasm. 'Is that your cousin Nanang up the road there? With Dalapai and Captain Winshipp?'

'Yoway, but that's not Captain Winshipp,' answered Catchpenny, getting to her feet to socialise, 'he's at Norman Creek, starting Mister O'Connell's bridge.'

With her chaperone successfully distracted, Nita drew Mulanyin close, pulling him down behind the stone wall. Hidden there, they kissed, fast and urgent, breaking apart only at the very last second before Catchpenny returned. Mulanyin let out a moan of frustration.

'You won't get kisses like that in Yerrin's camp,' Nita commented, observing Mulanyin's trousers. 'At least, you better not, or you'll be in proper big trouble!'

Mulanyin faced the river and sorted his fish into a dilly until his jun went back to sleep.

'Listen up! You'll never guess what the Old Man told me,' Catchpenny announced. Normally she would have saved her gossip for the older folk, but this important news had to be shared at once. 'An Irish woman has gone and got herself raped on the Logan. And they reckon it was Goories done it.'

Nita and Mulanyin drew sharp breaths. This would stir the dagais up something fierce. 'Which Goorie men? What clan?' Nita slid off the wall. 'Have they caught them?'

'No, and nobody knows who they were. Maybe Dick Ben and Jacky are still roaming around up to no good ...' Catchpenny pursed her lips. 'They wanna be well up in the mountains by now. All the Logan mob wanna be. The dagai'll be after payback, nothing surer.'

'Native Police were called to Bromelton this moon,' Nita said, both hands on her stomach. 'They'll find them in the scrub, if anyone can.'

'Yoway,' Catchpenny agreed grimly, 'or they'll grab whoever's handy. You be off home – there's talk of lynchings in Logan Town already. Mulanyin, go with Nita, and the pair of you lie low. Hurry now!'

'But what about you, Aunty?' Nita asked, picking up Mulanyin's dillybag. She reached in and handed over the largest mullet it contained. The older woman nodded her thanks.

'I'll come down shortly with Dalapai.'

Catchpenny waited while Mulanyin got his spears in order,

before ushering Nita to the far end of Queen Street. The young lovers waved goodbye from the Petries' gate.

Catchpenny frowned, gesturing with her pipe that they should get inside without delay. Two Chinese shepherds had been speared west of Limestone since Christmas. A homestead had burnt to the ground at Cash's Crossing last November. McGrath's man speared at The Gap a month ago, and now this. A white woman outraged one day's ride south of Magandjin. The Yagara would pay dearly if the British took it into their heads to punish random blacks. Their fighting men were demoralised, with Dundalli killed and Mulrobin gone as well.

Catchpenny cast her eyes skyward in trepidation. Trouble was coming.

~

Mulanyin tossed in bed, half asleep. Through fragments of a dream he could hear the older women begin chanting the Cry for the Dead. His head was thick with slumber, but even so the mourning cry was somehow wrong. Dogs barked, or perhaps it was dingoes he could hear, howling beyond Darragh's Paddock. The noise persisted, growing louder. After another minute, Mulanyin sat up, irritated, and pushed aside the kangaroo skin door flap. It was still dark outside, even with a near full moon turning the trees to silver and the Warrar to a shining ribbon of light at the bottom of Highgate Hill. The Southern Cross sat high in the heavens; dawn was hours away. The women weren't wailing then, but should be asleep. Mulanyin rubbed his tired eyes as the dogs began to bay in earnest down at the riverbend. Human voices rose in anger. Something was definitely amiss. He snatched up his spears and went to investigate.

'Where's yer gins!' roared Tim Shea, stumbling through camp and reeking of rum. He was one of four white drunks who had made their way to Yerrin's village uninvited.

'We want gins and we'se got grog aplenty!' announced Old Tom to the world. He was several steps ahead of Tim Shea.

Two other drinkers from Grenier's Hotel yelled along in rowdy agreement. The four shared more than the madness of rum in their veins. They had known each other for years before freedom arrived in '41. Rooster Smith, a scrawny Yorkshireman with a blunt nose, aimed a kick at some growling camp dogs. He missed and tumbled to the ground with a cry. His three companions had to pull him to his feet before the curs attacked. This delay was long enough for the intruders to find themselves surrounded by a dozen Kurilpa men brandishing spears and killing boomerangs.

Confusion reigned. Four male intruders constituted a serious threat. As they had arrived unannounced and at night, they could legitimately be speared on the spot in the Goorie Law. On the other hand, these dagai were not only unarmed but almost too drunk to stand. As the Kurilpa men debated what to do with them, Murree's older sister, Ada, dashed through their ranks and picked up a smouldering branch from the nearest fire. She swung it in front of her, threatening to blind any white man who came near her daughters or herself. After putting their eyes out she would roast their balls for them, she promised, and then burn their feet to charcoal, so they could stay at home where they belonged, mourning their manhood along with their sight.

'Ah, quit ya jabber!' snapped the fourth drinker, Murphy, proffering a bottle. 'Wantem grog? Wantem baccy?'

'Course she does,' slobbered Old Tom, stumbling past Tim Shea and digging in his pocket for the twist of cheap tobacco he'd bought for this very purpose. All natives were addicted to the stuff, and any white man with a supply could easily get what he wanted in exchange.

'Ere,' Old Tom broke off a segment and held it out, grinning. 'Chomp on that!'

Far from accepting his trade, Ada spat at him. Old Tom

laughed. Then he tossed the baccy to one of the watching men, who hesitated before dividing it with his brother.

Taking this as consent, Old Tom approached Ada again. He was about to relieve her of her weapon when he felt himself jerked violently backward through the air. In an instant he was sprawled on his stomach in the dirt, with his shirt torn from his body. Tom blinked in confusion at a pair of bare black feet not six inches from his nose.

The owner of the feet was none other than Murree. He held Old Tom's decaying shirt collar in his right hand and a nail-head jabree in his left. The kippa flung the collar down at the old lag along with a number of threats of fatal violence if he dared move a finger. Tim Shea, Smith and Murphy prudently stayed where they were. It was gradually dawning on the drunks that they were massively outnumbered, and that the Kurilpa were universally unhappy to discover them in their midst.

'I said we shoulda gorn ta Frog Holler,' whined Murphy in Tim Shea's ear, swigging another mouthful of rum. This action caught the eye of a Kurilpa woman; she promptly relieved Murphy of his bottle.

'Get rid of this stinking scum,' Ada advised Murree. 'Or more trouble will surely follow them here.'

Surrounded by furious warriors, Old Tom heaved himself up to a sitting position, gasping to regain the wind that Murree had knocked out of him. He pawed at the ground for his shirt. In his inebriation he succeeded, after several attempts, in pulling the torn collar over his head, so that the ragged cotton circle ended up a ridiculous ornament sitting above his bare collarbones. Some of the young men snickered.

Yerrin and Dawalbin arrived at that instant to find Old Tom sitting in the middle of the circle of warriors. Drunken, dirty and half naked, he was a pathetic sight. Ada lifted her burning branch to illuminate the intruders for the benefit of her parents. Justice required that the culprits be correctly identified. And in the light from her flickering torch Murree saw for the first time that Old Tom carried a grim legacy.

From armpit to armpit, and from his neck down to his waist, the Englishman's back was a raised ropey mass, the thickness of Murree's palm. Murree thought instantly of the bleached coral branches that washed ashore near Fisherman's Island. Yet this was no lone branch Old Tom bore on his body. It was a messy thicket, grown dense over many seasons of floggings. It dawned on Murree, seeing this, that it might well have been Old Tom he'd heard as a child, his screams piercing the distance between Queen Street and his home, so that Dawalbin held him close and covered his ears, singing the horror away.

This drunk is a little like us, the other warriors observed, looking at each other and touching their neatly incised chests. They were remembering receiving their own marks: trophies of achievement, hard-earned in manhood ceremonies but given ultimately by the Elders in the spirit of respect and love. Tom's back was evidence only of pain, yet in the men's minds a doubt began to grow: *perhaps he is a man after all.*

Only one of the crowd was entirely unmoved by the evidence of Old Tom's terrible suffering. Ada addressed the gathering in a furious voice. 'Look at this worthless drunk! Mouth open there, heaving for air like a big old catfish dragged onto the riverbank!' she roared. 'You useless maggot! Pity the flogger didn't cut you clean in half! If my husband was here, he'd rip your kidney fat out then chuck you in the Warrar for the sharks!'

The woman's acid commentary broke the brief spell that had fallen. The tobacco-chewing brothers shuffled back, avoiding her eye.

'You know me, Yerrin,' Old Tom wheedled from the dirt. 'Us coves was just after a bit of fun. But we'll go quiet, like. Just let us up and yer won't see us fer dust.'

Yerrin turned away from Old Tom to face Tim Shea. His killing boomerang was slung loosely over his right shoulder.

'So, the Logan mob haven't skinned yer yet, Shea?'

'Many's wanted to,' Shea answered, with a choking laugh. 'But me innards is still on the right side of me hide. As ye can see for yerself.'

Shea's voice had a hysterical edge. Like all shepherds, he lived in mortal fear of being roasted and eaten in some godforsaken gully. He hadn't expected to face the same terror in South Brisbane, and he silently cursed Old Tom for leading him into peril.

'More's the pity,' answered Yerrin with a withering stare.

'We don't want trouble,' blurted Rooster Smith. 'We just fancied a couple of gins.'

'I ought to put your eyes out, you maggoty specimen,' snarled Ada.

From nowhere, the image of his Waijung's cousin shot dead at Coombabah flashed into Mulanyin's mind. He stepped forward, his spear raised. A red mist was fast falling over him when Yerrin spoke.

'Mulanyin, pull up! I've told you before, control yourself!'

Mulanyin blinked and came back to his senses. He returned to the circle of watching men – but his eyes were fixed on Smith.

'Take these croppies and piss off,' Yerrin told Tim Shea in cold fury. 'Does this village look like Frog Hollow to you? If I see you here again, I'll open your neck and let the dogs do the rest.'

Nearly weeping with gratitude, Shea hauled Old Tom up out of the dirt and dragged him away to the safety of Vulture Street. Rooster Smith and Murphy disappeared along with them.

'This type of thing gets worse,' Yerrin announced to his village, 'whenever waymerigan are attacked, anywhere, by anyone. The dagai quickly make it an excuse for their crimes. Keep your heads, you men. The next evildoers to arrive might not be as few, or as drunk.'

'And could well be armed,' added Dawalbin, holding Ada close to her. 'The Native Police are returning from Bromelton about now.' The Kurilpa women stared hard into the night, as though the next evildoers were already closing in.

Half a dozen extra sentries were posted for the rest of the night; it was close to dawn before the village settled. Wide awake, angry at the invasion, yet chastened by Yerrin's words, Mulanyin decided he may as well start the day's fishing. With the morning star bright on the horizon, he took his spears and tow row and headed for the Bogga track.

'Where are you going alone?' Yerrin asked, as Mulanyin passed his fire. With nobody yet arrested for the attack on Mrs Walsh, dagai feelings were running high. An impetuous young Goorie could easily bring down more trouble on everyone's head.

'The Yeronga Cod Hole, Father.'

'Why so far?'

'The big fish are becoming scarce here. I thought to preserve them.'

'Hmm. Well, remember – not every fight belongs to you. Keep your spears for jalum and not for croppies – understand?'

'Yoway. Ngaya gungalehla.'

18. Black Don't Crack, Baby

2024

'I've had just about enough of you,' grumbled Granny Eddie from her bed. With difficulty, she hauled herself upright and peered into the corner of the room. 'Wotcha bothering me for, Grandad? Ain't like I won't be with ya soon enough ...'

The apparition in the corner didn't speak – it never spoke, exactly – but its reply came through loud and clear regardless. Eddie understood its meaning with her entire body.

I'll leave when I get what's mine. And when you tell the truth.

'The truth? Tell who the truth? You calling me a liar?'

Uneasy lies the head that wears the crown.

'Oh, go way, ya silly old bugger! I'll get Uncle Henry Wallaby onto ya!'

They must return to me what's mine.

'Wotcha blooming mean, what's yours? Stop talking in riddles, can't ya?'

There was a long pause.

Granny Eddie harrumphed. Typical. Ask a bloke a simple question and do ya get a simple answer? No. No ya don't. A person may's well talk to the blooming wall as try and—

It is too awful to tell.

'What? What is?'

The ghost was silent.

'Oh, blow this! I'm not listening no more! Go way, Grandad!'

Granny Eddie lay back down and stared at the ceiling in exasperation. Since when did Grandad Charlie give a single rat's arse about the truth? He'd made a life out of spinning tall yarns, the bigger the better. And what did that mean anyway – give him back what was his? She was too old for all this bloomin rubbish. Far too old.

~

'How'm I doing?' asked Winona, aiming Johnny's borrowed sailboat directly at the Kangaroo Point cliffs. 'I reckon I'm getting the hang of this, ay.'

'If ya want to smash us into a million tiny pieces, maybe,' groaned Johnny in mock despair. He leant over her to adjust the rudder. 'We want to be lined up with that pylon.' He pointed at the marker a hundred metres away beneath the freeway overpass. With his hand on the rudder, the boat swung a smooth quarter-circle to face the correct spot. Winona shrugged carelessly.

'Meh. Don't be pedantic.'

'Keep going that way and we'll be beached as, bro.'

'Smartarse.'

Winona pulled her BLM cap down tight and concentrated on the view. The thick brown river, dotted with stray branches, mangrove flowers and the odd piece of plastic rubbish, swirled and eddied past the foot of the cliffs. On land, groups of sinewy climbers stood in their harnesses, pointing up at footholds and crevices that would let them ascend. Joggers and dog walkers filled the rest of the narrow parkland that ran along the edge of the peninsula. A Murri woman had been found murdered at the top of that very cliff a couple of years ago, but Winona doubted that many of the people using the park remembered her name. She spoke a few quiet words, telling the sister she hadn't been forgotten.

'Where do ya get off calling me a smartarse, love? Talk about the pot calling the kettle black,' Johnny commented.

'Ya might have a Goomeroi Ancestor, but it'll be a long fucking time before I call you Blak, Dr Johnny.'

'It'll be a long fucking while before I care,' he lied.

'Typical pop-up blakfella,' Winona crowed in triumph. 'No accountability.'

'Oh, get fucked!' Johnny was laughing, sort of. So was Winona. Sort of.

'I'm accountable to my own mob, anyways, not you,' he added.

'What fucking mob?'

'Uncle Robbie Smith recognises my family line.'

'One blackfella doesn't make a mob, Captain Oxley. Sailin in uninvited like all the other wannabes and colonisers.'

'Fuck off, we're full, ay? You sound exactly like Pauline Hanson.' Johnny rolled his eyes at Winona's ever-shifting goalposts. Folded in his shorts pocket was a DNA profile that she had sniffed at, even though it showed his Aboriginal descent right there in black and white, coming down through his grandfather's line. It was gradually dawning on Johnny that he might never be Aboriginal enough for Winona.

'How bout we leave my identity out of it and just concentrate on sailing, ay? Before I have to explain to Joe Kwong that a radical activist sent his Seaway 25 to the bottom of the river?'

Winona laughed merrily. 'Tell him anyway. Then I can slap a coat of paint on it and park under a tree somewhere upriver. Home away from home – and away from fucken Mad Max too, bonus. Old mate can whack in an insurance claim, and everybody's happy.'

'Why do I get the idea you're not even joking?'

'I'm all about the win-win, me.'

Johnny was loving himself sick being on the river. They had put in at West End two hours ago and Winona showed no signs of being either seasick or bored. Offering to teach her to sail, thought Johnny, had been a stroke of sheer genius.

'Yer Gran's not too happy at the minute. And she won't be till we get her meds sorted,' Johnny mused. 'She still thinks her room's haunted by Grandad Charlie.'

'Well, can't you shift her to another floor or something?'

Johnny looked at Winona, nonplussed. 'Why?'

'To get her away from him. Although I suppose he ain't gonna worry about lifts or locked doors, is he … nah, scratch that idea.'

'For real?'

'What?'

'Are you seriously telling me you believe she's having hallucinations and phantom pain cos of a *haunted hospital room*?'

Winona glanced at Johnny, equally nonplussed. 'Duh.'

Johnny found a seagull to contemplate while he processed this.

'You said yourself it's called phantom pain!' Winona pointed out.

'We just haven't got her meds right yet.'

'If ya wanna have any hope of *eeeeeever* being proper blackfella, Dr Johnny,' Winona chided, 'ya gonna have to let go of these dagai ideas.'

'Hey, hey, pull up right there!' Johnny interrupted. 'I don't need *fixing*, and I don't need your little stamp of approval. Eddie's hallucinating, same as other dementia patients hallucinate when their meds aren't right. We adjust the meds and the hallucinations stop. Now whaddya say we tack over to South Bank and have a coffee, instead of an argument. Or a beer – I could murder a beer.'

'Aye aye!' Winona gave an ironic salute, before slyly adding, 'Captain.'

'Fuck you!'

'You wish.'

Winona was smiling as she said this, fully smiling, with her eyes sparkly and her entire face lit up with mischief. Johnny felt a great burst of fresh hope blossoming inside him. He'd take this girl on a date one day and kiss her, if it killed him.

'What this joint needs is a lot more public art,' Johnny announced, pretending a cool he didn't feel as he moored the boat to a pylon. Tourists wandered along the riverwalk, enjoying the breeze off the water. An R'n'B concert in the amphitheatre bled through to where the donut stall was doing a roaring trade near the pool. Cyclists braked as they reached the crowd spilling out onto the boardwalk; E-scooter riders found the narrowest of gaps between local families to zip through. Tied off now, the Seaway was rocking gently against the outgoing tide. 'And a riverside basketball court.'

'Yeah, right. How many balls would end up in the river brah?'

Johnny screwed his mouth sideways, imagining a huge orange raft of lost basketballs rounding Gardens Point and headed for the bay.

'Maybe not riverside, then. But a court, somewhere.'

He leapt up onto the metal pontoon and held his hand out for Winona. She took it and stepped across onto solid land.

'Coffee or beer?'

'Charge, if ya shoutin.'

'What this place needs is a shitload more public art, a basketball court and a pub with free beer.'

'What this place needs is a revolution, beginning with Treaty, reparations and a fuck-ton of social housing.'

'Why not do both?' Johnny mimicked the kid in the taco ad.

'Some decent public art would be a revolution round here, actually,' Winona conceded.

'They've done a few murals around the place.'

'Yeah, I'm talking stuff that transforms the entire fucking joint, not five hundred bucks' worth of paint thrown at mob to keep us happy.'

On the edge of the riverwalk in front of them, a group of suited forty-somethings were being photographed in front of a plaque on a long wooden retaining wall, tiny Australian flags in their hands. They looked like bureaucrats.

'Look at these sinister cunts. Up to no good, I betcha.'

'Wanna know what that plaque says?' Johnny had been coming to South Bank his whole life and knew its fifty acres intimately.

Winona raised her perfect eyebrows.

'I very much doubt it. But do go on.'

'Where Mulrobin walked so others followed … And where once stood one hut the world would meet,' he recited, pleased to have a chance to show off his photographic memory. 'It's about the first bridge whitefellas built back in the day, and how South Brisbane grew.'

'One hut?'

'Yep.'

'One?'

'Yep.'

'Oh, fuck me roan.'

'Uh-huh. Terra nullius in bronze. Paid for by our tax dollars.'

Winona swivelled on her heel and stomped to the toilets. Johnny went and queued for the drinks and five minutes later slid a schooner of dark ale across the table to her.

He raised his beer in salute, ready to toast a successful day on the water, but was instead flummoxed to see Winona's eyes brimming with unshed tears. He took a large gulp of beer, and then another. *Fuck.* That's where gammon amateur art criticism got a bloke. He'd been trying to demonstrate he was onside, not make her cry. 'You alright?'

'Yeah.' Winona blew her nose.

'You don't look alright. Come on, let's have it.'

Johnny wasn't afraid of tears. All the years he'd worked on wards, nobody had ever *not* stopped crying, eventually. You mostly just had to shut-up and listen.

Winona made a hopeless gesture in the direction of the plaque and the bureaucrats. 'It never ends, ay. My uncle, my gran, and Aunty Elise. All the Wallaby crowd we grew up with. They've all fought so fucking hard all their lives, and for what? So whitefellas can come along and put their white supremacist shit up anyway. It's like, haven't they heard of Mabo, or sovereignty, or *anything*? Do we hafta start blowing shit up for real?'

'Sorry.'

'It's *exhausting*.'

'Yeah. Fuckers.'

They drank in silence.

'There's Uncle Neville Bonner's bridge up now, at least,' Johnny suggested gently.

'Yeah. That's what governments do, see. Give with one hand and take with the other, that's their main game.'

'What about if ...' Johnny hesitated to argue. He didn't want his head bitten off. He liked his head how it was.

'What?'

'What if Queensland's Oldest Aboriginal wanted that plaque fixed? Or better still, replaced with some kick-arse radical art?'

Winona's head lifted and her reddened eyes met his. Johnny could see the cogs spinning in her brain, the pros and cons of the idea, the likely payoff, the extraordinary difficulty of getting Granny Eddie to do something she termed *political*. The effort it'd take to convince her, as well as the traditional owners – the Wallabies, the Beehives and others – who'd need to be onside.

'I already yarned her bout hitting the minister up for a house,' Winona said slowly.

'A *house*?'

'Why not? She's been paying rent to the Housing Commission since my mum was born. She's paid for a house five times over. And still they got the nerve to plonk her beside a crackhead like Mad Max, at her age.'

'I reckon they're more likely to fork out for a statue than a house.'

It was Winona's turn to become a six-year-old Hispanic. 'Why not do both? The minister's creaming his daks about having her on his boat, ay?'

'Her face *is* all over his webpage,' Johnny mused. 'And *The Courier-Mail* ads.'

'Billboards, too.'

'They can't backtrack now, she's too famous!'

'Them mob are fucked!' Winona laughed.

They spent the next hour dreaming about art that served to remind the government just whose land they were on.

'Big-arse statue of Dundalli! Ten foot high, holding a number seven boomerang!'

'With his shield up stopping the *Mermaid*, saying that's far enough there, pal!'

'Plus, sculptures of Goories all over South Bank. Like them bronze roos in George Street. Just mob enjoying themselves everywhere ya look ... kids up in the pandanus trees ... men diving off the riverwalk ...'

'Yeah, ay ... and bronze women fishing off the pontoons. How cool would that be?'

'Cooking flathead up, with mudcrabs on the coals, and mussels.'

'Bending over the fire, mooning the Executive Building ...'

'Bahahahhahaha, fuck yeah!'

Johnny drained his second beer. 'Refill?'

'Aww ... nah, I gotta cut. Meg Pegga got out Tuesday and there's a party for her at the Boundary. Imma get her shitfaced and then some.'

'Where's that pub with free beer when ya want it?'

Johnny's joke told Winona he didn't expect an invite to kick on with her crew, and just as well because no invite was issued. But one day soon she'd want him there with her and the cuzzies, he told himself as he skippered the Seaway back to Joe Kwong's. He ran his hands through his hair and grinned into the breeze. One day.

Winona woke in the night and realised she wasn't alone in Granny Eddie's flat. Oh, fuck, no. Christ Almighty.

Ya dumb ugly dog-faced bitch of a thing, look atcha. No man, no house, no job, no bungoo, nobody even likes ya. Should hear em run ya down at the pub. They was rubbishing ya after ya left …

Fuck orf ya big hairy hole, I'm not listening to ya shit tonight.

Loser, looooseeeeerrrrrr. Nobody'd give a rats if ya chucked yaself off a bridge. Do em a favour, ay.

Shuttup, ya liar. Fucking liar!

Story Bridge not too far from ere. Gorn. Do it. Jump, boom, end it all. Not like ya got anything to live for is it?

Yeah, I do. I DO. Fuck you, I'm not listening to ya shit no more!

Maybe not today. But ya will, one day soon ya will. Cos ya useless. Fat, dumb, USELESS mothafucker.

Nah, I'm not useless, ay, ya wrong. Ya wrong, wrong, wrong, WRONG!

Winona leapt to her feet and attacked the bed with Granny Eddie's pillow, belting into the mattress and sheets and screaming dissent, as though the Voice could be destroyed that way. If the neighbours called the cops, then they called the fucken cops. She didn't give a shit. At the rate she was going, she was nearly as dangerous to herself as the blue gang was. Winona flogged the mattress with pillows till her arms ached. Then collapsed onto the lounge in front of the TV, sobbing, the enemy in her head subdued for another hour.

~

'Ay! Old Man! Ya member back before the war?' Eddie chirped as she began hoeing into her green hospital jelly.

Dartmouth frowned, peering out into the hall to see who was eavesdropping. Granny dismissed his concerns. She didn't give a rats what the nurses thought about Grandad Charlie; them young mob didn't even know they was born. No! She needed a proper chinwag with someone who knew a few things, someone *old*. And Dartmouth needed to hear it from the horse's mouth, too.

Everything was so different then.

Up for a yarn at long last. Bout blooming time. The ghost remained a muddy smear in the back corner of the room, but thankfully today there were no strident demands for truth-telling or non-specific restitution from the authorities. Ghosts were like anyone else, Eddie supposed, with good days and bad days. She had to strike a good one eventually.

'Member how Albert Street used to run straight past City Hall, fore they built the Square? Spose you woulda seen em building City Hall, come to think. When was that, Darto?'

'Depression project, it opened in the late 1920s, if I recall correctly. It must have provided a lot of labouring jobs.'

Albert Street was boggy in the early days, the ghost reflected. *There was a marsh there, once. Crab, eels, yabbies … we fished the lot …*

'Eels in Albert Street! Ya writin this down, Darto? People gotta hear this!'

Sceptical, Dartmouth rubbed his nose with the back of his hand. City Hall had indeed been built on a swamp, on the old North Brisbane watering hole in fact, but the marsh where English colonists had once shot duck was completely paved over by 1885. Grandad Charlie was either mixing his yarns up, or – and this seemed far more likely – spinning his tall tales through the vessel of Granny Eddie. Either way, an invisible informant, audible only to a one-hundred-and-three-year-old woman nursing a head injury, wasn't what he called a verifiable source.

'I *could* write it down,' he said delicately, 'but, um, who's going to believe me when I tell them my informant died in 1939?'

Granny Eddie snorted. 'That's yer trouble right there, see,' she commented. 'Lazy. Ya write it down and then ya go find out who believes ya, not the other way round, mate. You wouldn't know hard work if it bit ya on the bum!'

'You could be right,' Dartmouth agreed. Eddie had gone out as a domestic at twelve, and not for good people either.

'Course I'm bloomin right,' said Eddie, smacking her lips on another spoon of jelly.

~

Winona ran her fingers through her hair as Nan's shower rained down on her head. Bliss, with her cornrows removed and her locks all loosey-goosey for the first time in months. She rested her head on the tiles and shut her eyes, trying to think only of Nan's hot water. The Kingston rental she shared with four other shift workers was sporting a shiny new real-estate sign in its front yard. The lease had just expired and homelessness loomed in her future like a motherfucker. Probably her best option would be to camp on Nan's loungeroom floor, look after the old girl. Give up the idea of going to uni, or the traineeship Gaja Iris had told her about at the Indigenous Medical Service. The flyer for that one still sat beside the kettle: Certificate III in Health Services.

'My, ah, own mental health's not all that flash, Aunt,' she'd confessed to the older woman. 'I kinda … hear weird stuff. Sometimes. Not all the time. But, enough. It's not too good …'

'Yeah, I thought that might be the case, bub,' Iris had replied. 'A lotta people do, it doesn't mean you're womba. You know we can help you with that?' She slid a piece of paper over to her: www.hearingvoices.com.au.

Mortified, Winona stuck the paper in her bra and picked up the flyer about the Cert III. She'd spent the rest of the appointment talking about tweaking her meds and career options, avoiding the hard stuff.

'You come back and see me tomorrow, bub,' Iris had ordered her gently. 'I'm not done yarning with you, ay? We got plenty of time to talk things through. And please keep on with the meds – they work, but ya gotta take em.'

Something in Winona had felt suddenly safe. She nodded that yes, she would come back.

~

Dartmouth put an illicit loaf of banana bread on the table and Eddie's eyes lit up.

'Oooh, quick Darto, cut me a bit before anyone sees!'

'I got you this, too,' he told her, dumping his laptop and papers, and dragging out a stick of forbidden gold-wrapped butter from his Woolies bag.

'Not as good as my brother's fruitcake. But pretty good,' Granny nodded with childish glee after her first bite. 'Oh, I miss his fruitcake. Sometimes I think I miss it more than I miss him.' As she oohed and aahed, Dartmouth recounted his latest finds off Trove.

'So, it turns out *Pugh's Almanac* didn't kick off until the late 1860s, but it's still got just about everything you'd want about early Queensland. And I found a really strange story from 1855, as well. Does the name Warry mean anything to you?'

'There's Warry Street in Spring Hill.'

'Warry was the first chemist in Brisbane; it'd be named for his family if it's not specifically named for him. He had a shop in Queen Street and his brother had one, too. But the brother had a grocery, I think.'

'The first *white* chemist.'

'Oh? Oh. Well, yes, I suppose ...'

'Us mob been using our own medicines for sixty thousand years.' Granny wasn't budging. And truly, Darto ought to know better after nearly six weeks of careful instruction. Slow learners, his mob.

'Absolutely, that's right. And I need to investigate that some more, actually.' Dartmouth began making a note on his iPhone to look into local bush medicine, then shook the device. 'Bloody thing. I've got the luck of the damn Irish when it comes to technology.'

'Winona says computers can sense weakness,' chuckled Eddie, dabbing cake crumbs away from her mouth with a tissue and shooting a glance at the corner of the room. 'I'm just glad I grew up before all that business came in.'

'No iPhones when you were young?' Dartmouth joked.

Eddie snorted. 'iPhones! Ya were lucky if yer had a pair of shoes! People today have no idea what it is to be poor. To live on a bit of bread and dripping twice a day. They wouldn't even know what bread and dripping is. No, it's all Uber Eats and Macca's, this young crowd!'

'When *did* you get your first pair of shoes?' Dartmouth cracked open his laptop. He sensed a yarn coming on.

'Oh, I don't know. I don't remember much ...' Granny began. This was her inevitable disclaimer which started every interview, or as Dartmouth had come to think of them, struggle session.

'All I know is, us mob all went to school barefoot, summer and winter. We was tough, see, raised tough. On really frosty mornings the boys' jinung would get so cold they'd have to – you know – so they didn't get chilblains.'

Dartmouth looked blank. 'Have to what?'

Granny made a vague gesture towards her stomach.

Dartmouth shook his head. 'I'm not with you.'

Granny rolled her eyes at his stupidity. 'They'd go jull. You know, piss.'

'On their *feet*?'

'Yeah. Warm them up. Course us girls couldn't do that. Even though the cold went right through ya bones.'

'Fascinating.' He pushed more cake towards Granny. 'And your first shoes?'

'Well, let's see. We weren't ever church people, so I think it must have been when I started my second job. Oh, that's right, I used to have these old men's shoes when I did the Bolithos' laundry! I 'member walking to see the Story Bridge the week it opened, cos they gave me terrible blisters. The laces always used to break, and I'd tie knots in them till they looked like blooming carpet snakes that had swallowed half the hens in the chook house. I wonder who Mum got them from?'

'Mr Bolitho?'

'No, no. He always passed his old boots on to Grandad Charlie – and they were both real big men, with big hoofs to match. No way they would have fit.' Granny wriggled her toes in demonstration. 'Size six, me. I'd always get nice comments on my feet and ankles when I went out dancing, later. I had women's shoes by that stage, mind.'

'A far cry from hoiking to school barefoot.'

'Oh, yes,' Granny Eddie developed a faraway smile at the memory of the Boathouse. 'I'd go dancing every night of the week if I could. Loved it. Especially when the Americans arrived. Christmas 1941. Us girls joked they were our Christmas present, with their nylons and their uniforms. Handsome!'

'You would have been, what, nineteen?'

'Best years of my life. I was a looker back then, Dartmouth.'

'You still are,' he fibbed.

'Oh, shut up, you fool of a man! I'm a dinosaur!'

'Well, you certainly don't look like you're a hundred and three,' he judiciously amended his flattery. 'What's the secret? My full- ... I mean, my *friends* in the Territory told me they use goanna fat to soften their skin, but I can't see you doing that, somehow.'

Granny laughed and pointed to a large bottle of Nivea skin cream beside her bed. 'That's my urban goanna oil. And anyway, haven't you heard? Black don't crack, baby.'

~

'We're seriously thinking,' Winona beamed at the minister's advisors, 'of setting up a GoFundMe for Granny Eddie. She's homeless, poor darlin, or as good as.'

'Come again?' The advisors shared a look.

'Mmmm, Queensland's Oldest Homeless Elder. Forced onto the street by crackheads at one hundred and three … that yarn should raise a few bucks, ay? Pull a few heartstrings. Especially with her smilin up on all them billboards near the airport. Do you think maybe the minister could chuck in towards a few nights in a motel?'

The older advisor winced.

'That might not be necessary,' sighed the dyke in the navy suit. 'Let me make a couple of phone calls and see what I can sort out with Housing.'

Winona winked at her. This one wasn't as dopey as the others.

'Good answer.'

'Mercedes has the same Latin root as mercy,' Winona grinned as she sipped sweet coffee in the nurses' lounge. 'They both come from the word for payment.'

'See, I knew you'd give me shit. This is why we can't have nice things.'

Johnny already regretted revealing his lust for the red XL convertible. He'd been humming Janis Joplin all day. 'I didn't expect ya to be chucking cartwheels.' Johnny searched in the cupboard for the Arrowroot biscuits. 'But I didn't expect Latin roots, either. Did you swallow an encyclopaedia at birth, or what?'

'I got into these online Latin lessons …' Winona slurped, accepting a biscuit '… ta … during lockdown. The best way to understand any culture is through its language. And Latin is the root of English, hence of all evil, so …'

'Know thine enemy?'

'Yep. And understand its trinkets. Exhibit A: the Mercedes sports, the ultimate neoliberal emblem of capitalist wank.'

Johnny fake-yawned. It never ceased to amaze him just how wide Winona threw her net of critique. Language. Sport. Gaming culture. Consumer goods. Gender. Film. Almost everything slotted into her vast well of political opinion. No wonder she was so *angry*. He checked his watch. Three minutes till he had to be in a consult.

'Well, okay, but what if you flip it? That'd mean anyone fluent in an Aboriginal language is Aboriginal, in some sorta way.'

Winona blew a giant raspberry.

'Naah, gammon! There's a big difference between understanding a culture and *belonging* to one. I learnt Latin but I'm not Italian, am I? I could go learn Gaelic, but it wouldn't make me a Gael.'

'Maybe, but ya gotta factor in attempted genocide. Nobody tried to wipe Italians off the face of the earth lately. Anyway, Uncle Dave told me Aboriginal culture's different to coloniser cultures. We bring outsiders in and assimilate them, always have and always will. Because everything on Country needs to have its place or everything gets right outta whack.'

'Yeah, I've heard that argument,' Winona replied, not revealing who she'd heard it from – Granny Eddie. 'But it's a philosophy from a different time, ay? A time before white supremacy arrived on boats and started stealing shit.'

Johnny desperately wanted to point out what changing a fundamental cultural tenet implied, but he had an even more desperate need to piss. It was an urge he'd been suppressing for a good twenty minutes just to sit with Winona while she cheerfully argued about nothing at all.

'I've gotta go jull,' he said, getting to his feet, 'before my bladder blows up. And then I've got consult meetings till three. But text me later about the new house.'

'Oh, it's looking good. Old Girl don't want me camping in ere any more'n I do.'

Winona pointed her lips at the vinyl daybed in the nurses' lounge, where she'd been sleeping. Mad Max made living at Fairfield Road a nightmare, and it was easier to just crash up the corridor from Eddie.

'My offer still stands, ay?' Johnny mentioned on his way out the door, trying to make it sound casual. His sofa bed at home had her name written all over it.

'Yeah, nah. I'm good.'

'Too Blak for my place, are ya?' he teased.

Winona gave a wry smile. 'Something like that, yeah.'

Five minutes later, washing her coffee cup up in the sink, Winona gave a sudden grunt of surprise. Johnny had used the word *jull* and she hadn't noticed. Hadn't even blinked.

~

The next night, Johnny cracked open a beer and flopped onto his lounge. On the screen in front of him were a multitude of open tabs, with an array of Collins family trees, GEDmatch numbers and ancestry profiles harking back to what seemed like half of Europe. Hidden deep among these profiles were his Blak ancestors – the ones who had turned the Australian continent on his ancestry map to blue – but hidden where? That was the sixty-four-million-dollar question. No way to search the giant database by ethnicity. He had to examine every bloody Collins tree he'd matched with, and there were hundreds of the bastards, most of them fifth cousins from Tipperary or Aberdeen or Chicago.

'Like looking for a needle in a haystack,' he muttered to himself. 'A haystack made of needles ...'

Scrolling idly down the long list, he was seized by a random thought. Returning to the home page Johnny entered: Gender – female; birthplace – Brisbane, Queensland. In the box below he carefully typed – Eddie Blanket.

When the results appeared – a long list of ancestral names,

dates and birthplaces – Johnny squinted. As the meaning of what he was reading slowly sank in, he began to grin, and then to really laugh, long loud bouts of hooting laughter that brought Avelina to his door with a quizzical smile.

'Oh, my frigging Gawd,' he cackled. 'I don't believe this!'

'Did you find your Aboriginal family?'

'Nah,' Johnny chortled, blowing his nose. 'But I found something else pretty good. Hey, any of those samosas left?'

19. Hunger

1855

Nita was up to her elbows in suds in the outdoor laundry; Mulanyin leant against the doorframe, entranced by this most mundane of tasks. The slosh of bubbles in the tub reminded him of the waves below Jellurgal, tumbling in frothy surges against the boulders at the foot of the mountain.

'When we marry,' he dreamed aloud, 'we'll have six jarjums at least. Three boys, maybe four, to help me work the boat, and a couple of girls too. Three girls would be alright, if you want three. Provided I get my sons for the fishing.'

Nita hauled John Petrie's sodden cricketing shirt out of the tub, examined it, then resumed scrubbing, rocking back and forth with both arms extended to reach the washboard. She hadn't yet told Mulanyin that he would become a father several moons hence. It pleased her to keep the news secret for now.

'Only two sabbaths to go,' she said, flashing him a smile. Then their lives would be transformed by Reverend Lang, who had agreed to baptise Mulanyin on the morning of the nuptials.

'I can't wait that long! Two sabbaths feels longer than two Mullet Runs,' he complained, aroused by the swaying of Nita's body as she worked. On impulse, her betrothed stepped into the dim room and put his arms around her waist from behind, stilling her. Nita turned to face him, her soapy hands held out to the side, and they kissed. She felt her breasts burn at his touch, and her breath grew ragged.

'I *really* can't wait, I mean.' Mulanyin began to unbutton his trousers.

Nita giggled in alarm. 'Someone might come looking for us!'

'Exactly. No time to waste!'

His lips were on her mouth again, then on her neck, her breasts. Desire flared between them. As Mulanyin lifted the hem of her dress, Nita, feeling mischievous, teased him for his impatience.

'But what if it's my time?'

Mulanyin shied away. He fled the laundry and only stopped when he was well across the yard.

'Are you insane?' he accused. Terror roiled in him, looking for an exit. It had never occurred to him that Nita could be dangerous.

Nita laughed. The moon was no more than a pale gum leaf floating in the sky. 'I'm only teasing.'

Mulanyin narrowed his eyes. He could have slapped her. 'Is this your idea of a joke?'

'As if I would allow you to touch me then,' she scoffed. 'Or even approach me.'

'Are you absolutely sure?'

'Of course, I'm sure! I know my own body, Mulanyin. There's no danger whatsoever.'

'Then why put such an idea in my head?'

Nita was stumped. Perhaps the tedium of washday had affected her. Perhaps she was overwhelmed by his desire for her, or her own for him. Whatever the reason, seeing Mulanyin out in the yard, diminished by fear and doubting her love, Nita was full of regret. She beckoned him. 'I don't know. It was just a silly joke. Are you coming in, or will I go back to this damn shirt?'

Still wary, Mulanyin let himself be drawn inside the laundry. In a short while the pair were entwined once more, and this time it was Nita who reached for the hem of her dress.

'You musn't ever joke that way again,' her lover reiterated as he rebuttoned his trousers a short time later. 'My life isn't a joke to be taken so lightly, my love.' He forced a smile, then picked up his fishing spears and left, still shaken.

Bemused, Nita watched him stride away to the river. Something must have been missing in what Dawalbin taught her when she first became a woman – or had she misremembered the lesson? Perhaps Mulanyin's people felt more strongly about such things than the Yagara. She turned to the washboard, casting her mind back to the older woman's instructions as she scrubbed shirt after shirt.

Dawalbin had taught her at length about how and why children came to be. The safe times, and the times it was critical to keep away from men, lest her menses prove fatal to them. How to attract a baby spirit or bring twins. The medicines needed for an easy birth, or to return pregnancy to the spirit world, if need be.

The idea of twins made her startle suddenly. For if a second child spirit chose to come to her today, helped along its path by Mulanyin, what would this dreary conception place – a cobwebbed laundry full of endless work – imply for that child's life? Would such a baby be forever doomed to servitude? To never be free?

Nita hurried outside and stood at the garden gate, braving the scrutiny of Old Tom. A saddle horse trotting to Fortitude Valley left a trail of shining green manure as it passed. The rich grassy aroma, not unpleasant, filled her nostrils even as it attracted a horde of pale tan coloured flies. At the far end of the street, Chinese workers bathed in the Bogey Hole beneath the giant fig tree. Nita barely had time to wonder where *their* spirit children would come from, when Mary Petrie called out from the sitting room. Was the laundry finished? It was well and truly time Nita went to Mayne's for boiled bacon and pigs' trotters. And could she make a start on tonight's rice pudding, too?

Nita sighed. Her body was no mystery to her, but how to live in it sometimes was.

~

Mulanyin stood at the Queen's Wharf, dismayed at what he saw. Or rather, at what he *didn't* see – the Kurilpa canoe that belonged there and was glaringly absent. He searched the nearby mangroves, hoping to be wrong. But a long narrow scar on the muddy bank, already half-hidden by the incoming tide, was the sole evidence he could find of the canoe's existence. A scattering of boot marks told him who was responsible.

'Thieves, again!'

Yerrin had gone twice with Dalapai to complain to Captain Wickham about this ongoing pilfering. An edict had been issued, yet the thefts continued; as usual, croppies had no compunction at all in taking what wasn't theirs. Kurilpa canoes had sat unmolested on the riverbank since the time of the Ancestors, allowing people to cross at will. Now the kundil were fair game.

When I have my whaleboat, Mulanyin vowed for the thousandth time, I'll take Nita and leave this cursed place for Nerang, and live a *normal* life among decent people who understand stealing is forbidden. He looked up to see the unsmiling ferryman steer his vessel in. When the man had tied up, the boat rode high against the wooden pier.

'Gimme a ride across?' Mulanyin requested.

'Whatcha offerin?'

Mulanyin held up one of three small bream he had speared since leaving Nita. Good-sized fish were growing scarce. All Brisbane was taking from the river these days, and Brisbane held a great many empty mouths.

'Right ye are,' the man grunted, taking the fish. 'Come back when I've stowed me grub.'

While he waited for the man to return from his lunch at the

Lord Raglan, Mulanyin built a small fire on the riverbank. His remaining bream had been for Dawalbin, but he gambled on being able to spear more that afternoon. Grilled fresh on the coals, the fish would make him a fine meal right here and now. His stomach rumbled at the thought.

'Any morsel spare, fer the wean, friend? A mouthful is all I ask …' A white wraith had materialised half a spear throw away.

The beggar woman stood on the track leading to the Commissariat Store. A moment after she spoke, a government clerk brushed past, berating her for an eyesore and a harlot before shouldering her off the path. She stumbled closer and Mulanyin stared. An infant's brown foot protruded from the grubby swaddling cloth tied around the woman's waist. He felt a stab of pity for this tiny child, held in the arms of a white woman who was little more than skin and bone herself. A Goorie mother would have sent her baby back to the spirit world unborn rather than bring it into a life of such unhappiness.

'Please, mistah. A skerrick fer the wean …'

It was hard for Mulanyin to make out the woman's speech, bursting at the seams with foreignness as it was. But there was no mistaking what she wanted. Her thin orange hair was plastered against her skull; her cheekbones were razors. She closed her eyes in infinite weariness.

'Where's your husband?'

'I have no husband with breath in him. And my family is very far from this … paradise.'

Mulanyin blinked. He knew what it was to be far from home, yearning for news of your people. He would embrace his mothers and fathers at next moon's Mullet Run, and yarn with them late into the night, sleep beside them at the same fire. But this waymerigan might never see her family again. Touched by her sad dignity, he lay a bream down on the ground between them.

The woman's expression grew wary.

Mulanyin gestured. *Take it.*

She darted forward and seized the jalum. To his amazement, the woman, her baby still swaddled against her, began devouring the raw fish right where she stood. She tore and gulped at it frantically, pausing only to spit out scales. Soon there was nothing left of the bream but its skeleton, and a coil of gut floating in the river, loosening as it was attacked by a cloud of translucent prawns. Mulanyin was astounded.

The woman swatted away flies and faced him with the courage of one whose belly is half-full. 'I can see what yer thinkin. But it's all I've ate since two nights past, and my wean must have milk or surely perish.'

His last remaining bream lay on the grass like an accusation.

The river suddenly puckered with movement. Fish had joined the prawns feeding on the discarded guts. Seeing them splash and lunge in front of him, Mulanyin grunted and gave the last bream over to the woman. Then he picked up his spears to begin doing what he did best – fishing. It seemed the logical thing and had the added advantage of allowing him to turn his back on her shame.

'Oh, bless yer, son, bless yer. Yer a proper Christian under that sooty skin and may the Lord bless and keep yer fer yer kindness ...'

The woman stashed the bream beneath her clothes before shuffling away. The only evidence of their encounter was a host of fish scales, gleaming on the riverbank like a scatter of diamonds.

20. The Dugong Camp

1855

Small waves lapped the beach at Teerk Roo Ra. Plop, plop, plop. The ocean had transformed recently. Normally a brilliant blue, the small crescent-shaped bay, thick with chewed dugong grass, had turned a dull khaki. Mulanyin had never imagined a place or time when saltwater would leave him unmoved, yet he was utterly miserable. He sat on Peel Island facing the distant mainland as his expulsion from Brisbane played over and over in his head.

'Aren't your hands scorched with shame?' Yerrin had thundered in front of the whole village, refusing to listen to any explanations. 'An honourable man will never take what isn't freely given, nor what isn't his to take! And as for brawling in the street, in front of white men? You behave like someone without a family!'

Mulanyin burrowed his feet into the beach sand until his legs looked like blunt black sticks. He seethed with the injustice. Exiled to hunt dugong with the coastal mob of the Bay Islands; pushed away from his life on the Warrar and the work that would buy him his boat; and worst of all – unspeakably worse – banished far from Nita's love and her warm body pressed against his in the laundry. Their marriage was postponed, Yerrin had roared, until such time as Mulanyin showed himself capable of restraint, capable of living in Kurilpa lawfully, no matter what trivial provocations might come his way from the Warries of the world.

203

'Why did you do it?' Murree had whispered after the meeting.

'I did nothing wrong!' Mulanyin snapped. 'I was simply going to visit Nita when I came across Billy on his knees outside Warry's shop. Surrounded by dagai, laughing and jeering at him.'

Murree had waited. Mulanyin kicked at a stray bit of bark. He'd been walking towards Petrie Bight quite carefree, joyful at the prospect of seeing his girl, before the encounter with Warry made his blood run hot.

'They were mocking Billy for begging. Laughing at him.'

'There's no shame in begging when a man's had his land and livelihood stolen and is hungry,' Murree objected.

'Perhaps. But Warry,' Mulanyin's jaw tightened on the hated name, 'that dog Warry had Billy on his knees in Queen Street. Reciting the Lord's Prayer for half a cup of rum.'

Murree winced. 'Won't Father believe you?'

'You heard him. Knocking the grog to the ground was wrong, he says, since it wasn't mine to spill. And pushing Warry over is nearly as bad, apparently. But Warry told the *Courier* that "blacks had been brawling over rum in Queen Street" and they printed the lie …'

Murree grimaced. Only last week, encouraged by Grandfather Petrie, Dalapai and Yerrin had begun composing a Proclamation of Demands to the Governor. The manifesto outlined the wrongs done to their nation and pointed out in forensic detail how the behaviour of the British was criminal as well as unchristian. Now Mulanyin had gone and made an awful spectacle of himself. His behaviour reflected badly on the Yagara, and negotiations with the Governor would have to be delayed.

'Did Grandfather Petrie believe you at least?' Murree asked, 'And Tom?'

'Thou shalt not take hard liquor,' Mulanyin spat. 'Tom's still on his way back from the diggings, and that's all Mister Petrie had to say.'

'Will you go to Tëerk Roo Ra?'

'What choice do I have?' Mulanyin replied. 'Father won't welcome me when Yerrin's ordered me to the Bay. I have to spend three moons with the Island mob, working at their dugong camp. For *free*.'

'Three months's not so long,' Murree fibbed. 'And the coast mobs have fine flathead and oysters, not just bingkin and dugong.'

'But I'm to marry Nita at the Mullet Run!' Mulanyin had blurted, close to tears, 'And I could see my family there, and am so close to owning my boat! Three moons is not even something I can make sense of in my mind!'

Murree grabbed Mulanyin then and hugged him, squeezing as much love as he could into his brother.

'My only chance of happiness is gone,' Mulanyin mourned against Murree's shoulder. 'I'll never really be free.'

Murree stepped back and took his brother's right hand, pressing it against his own heart. 'Rubbish. There will be another chance to marry very soon, perhaps at the Bonyi gathering. You'll get your whaleboat, and you'll live well off it. So, bring back a huge saltwater bingkin,' Murree encouraged him, 'for us to share. Concentrate on that. Three moons will pass soon enough.'

'Yes,' Mulanyin said, looking wretched. 'That's if Nita's still talking to me by then.'

During his first month at Peel Island, Mulanyin moped. His body might have been on the coast, but his mind remained at Petrie Bight. Daydreaming about Nita, he made several silly mistakes that meant torn tow rows and lost dugong. His colleagues in the fishing camp were unimpressed, mostly ignoring him except when his long arms were wanted to rob a beehive or a bird's nest. The kippa did his daily work for the Island mob, but he baulked at dancing with them, or laughing very much at their jokes, and he took little part in their evening yarns around the fire. The senior Teerk Roo Ra man nicknamed him 'oyster'.

'He's lovesick,' the dugong hunters told each other. 'Leave him be'.

In his second month on the island, Mulanyin began to open his ears, and occasionally to grin ('a miracle – the oyster smiles'.) He joined the others around the fire at night and heard stories of Goompie and Mulgumpin, of Jumpinpin and Karragarra. He learnt the history of the great tournaments and corroborees of the past. His body relaxed, becoming attuned once again to ocean breezes and the constant cry of gulls and curlews; and the softer he became, the more Mulanyin understood the ways of these Island People – his own family's neighbours and close relatives of Dawalbin. He was educated about the places which fed and mothered them. He listened to talk of the very first Sufferers arriving on their shores; of the escapee Tim Shea hiding mad and alone on his little island for years, of brutal missionaries and wretched lepers. He heard rumours of mainland children stolen, taken by boat through Goompie to live among white strangers in the north. He wondered if those stolen children were Yugambeh, and whether or not their families had avenged these dreadful kidnappings.

In the Season of the Cold Winds, Mulanyin saw the full moon rise for a third time over the shining waters of the bay. He rowed offshore with Island men who held up lanterns to attract their prey. The hunters stood alert as fish clustered towards the light: bream, mullet, curious stingrays. A sawfish with its extraordinary nose. And down very low in the water beneath all these, Mulanyin glimpsed something that made him catch his breath.

A giant shimmered there, beneath the boat. *The Matriarch*. A shout went up from the other men as they spotted her, for in the bending light of their lanterns she seemed as long as their spears.

'I know this fish,' announced Mulanyin. 'I know her very well.'

'Try and hold the boat steady, you shitty-arses,' commanded the senior Teerk Roo Ra man, leaning over the side with his weapon in his right hand.

'Uncle, no!' cried Mulanyin, surprising everyone as he clutched at the man's elbow. 'Please! Leave her be!'

'Behold! The oyster can speak after all,' someone marvelled. The others laughed.

'I know this Grandmother fish,' Mulanyin spoke fast, pushing down his fear of ridicule. 'My people don't hunt her, she's too old. I once caught her as a boy and had to return her to the ocean. Please, Uncle – I beg of you. Spare her life ...'

The Teerk Roo Ra headman swivelled to face Mulanyin. His brow developed deep furrows, hearing the kippa's plea. 'Strange words, when killing is how we live.'

'She's off!' cried another man. 'Headed south to the Dugulumba.'

'I'll replace her value in other jalum,' Mulanyin blurted, sensing an opportunity, 'Or in youngen. But please, she is ancient, and important to my clan.'

'When the oyster speaks, he asks a lot,' commented someone at the back of the boat.

The older man shifted his grip on his spear and peered into Mulanyin's face. Then he laughed hard, from his belly. 'If you want to do my fishing for me, oyster, I won't complain.'

The man gestured to the oarsmen to keep rowing. Dugong were their real goal, and the incident of the mulloway was soon forgotten. But Mulanyin was comforted by their encounter. He dreamed of the Matriarch many times that month, imagining her secret journeys from Jellurgal to Teerk Roo Ra and back again, travelling past the mouth of the Dugulumba, her Dreaming Track entirely below the waves and invisible to him except in his sleep.

~

Dawalbin rocked with laughter, slapping her leg hard as Murree mimicked the latest dagai antics.

While his clan watched on, Murree stiffened his limbs and clenched his jaw to become an enraged white man marching at speed along a bush path. He flung his head back and worked his mouth violently, chomping on the different arguments he was about to unleash. His hard eyes darted from side to side as though anticipating attack from all directions. The man came to a juddering halt in the middle of the bush track. Here he accosted a much taller opponent.

'You stand there all high n mighty, like yer better'n me!' he shouted, casting his arms about in fury, 'ya snobby bugger! Spying on a feller, day and night!' He stood heaving for breath, overcome.

'But yer won't lift a hand to help a cove do his bloomin work, will yer?' The watching Kurilpa roared approval. Camp dogs howled along. 'I've had about enough of yer insolence, damn yer,' Murree threatened his invisible enemy. 'I won't be spied on by the likes of you no more! I'll finish yer before yer finish me, by Gawd I will!'

The man turned away, starting back along the same track he'd travelled, then thought better of it. He spun on his heel, a cunning grin plastered over his face.

'Hah! Thought ye'd catch me off guard, ay? Let's have at yer then, yer blaggard!'

Murree pranced on the spot, shaping up with one fist far in front of the other. A maniacal gleam entered his eye. 'Just cos yer ten times my size,' Murree panted as he danced, 'don't think I'm afeared, cos I ain't! I'll knock yer on yer arse as soon's look at yer! Yeah – that's right! You better step back and yer best keep steppin, too, mate, if ya know what's good fer ya!'

Weak with laughter, Dawalbin pleaded with Murree to stop. Her son burst into giggles himself then and dropped his fists, turning back into a Goorie. Imitating the lunatic who argued with a eucalyptus tree ten times a day on Windmill Hill was fine entertainment, but he had something more important to do. He needed to head to town and find Tom. Rumour had it he was back from the southern diggings with a satchel full of gold dust. Nita would be able to tell him if these rumours of Tom's astounding riches were true.

~

'Oyster, come here. I want to talk to you,' the Teerk Roo Ra Headman called. Mulanyin was at the water's edge watching a sea eagle bathe in the shallows. He'd seen mirrigimpa do the same at Tallebudgera and it had always struck him as odd – a creature so purely of the air, standing up to its feathered thighs in the ocean, washing.

'Yoway, Uncle?'

'You asked last week that the mulloway be spared,' the Headman said, crossing his white-haired arms. 'A large fish worth many shillings.'

'Yoway. And I'll provide her value in other jalum, as I promised.'

The Headman harumphed, his eyes narrow. 'Do you really think my people are savages, to go plundering the ocean of her Elders?'

Mulanyin smiled, unsure of what was going on.

The man smiled, then, too. 'You've been suckered, young nephew.'

Mulanyin pursed his lips in disgust. What a fool he was, offering to catch so many extra fish for no reason at all. The Elder clapped him on the back and slung an arm around him as they walked back to the camp. He had news for Mulanyin, big news. The sea eagle paused at their departure, before it continued its preening and splashing.

'Never mind. The trade you offered will have to wait,' the Headman said, coming straight to the point. 'Yerrin's summoned you to return to Magandjin. As soon as possible.'

Mulanyin could hardly believe his luck.

'The *Otter* sails from Goompie at noon.' he blurted.

'Yes, you must be on her. There's no time to waste.'

Mulanyin's face cracked open in a giant smile. He sprinted down the hard sand, yelling and whooping, tossing himself into a string of dizzying head flips that ended with a somersault into the freezing ocean. There, oblivious to the cold, he stood spinning in circles, hurling handfuls of wet sand as hard as he could towards the mainland.

'I'm coming, Nita!' he shouted through cupped hands, 'Your maibin is coming back, my sweetheart – get ready to eat plenty of bingkin and to become my wife!'

The rest of the morning – first the whaleboat trip to Goompie carrying a fine fat turtle, then the endless hours it took for the *Otter* to arrive from Cleveland – was the longest wait Mulanyin had ever endured.

~

Nita was peeling pumpkin when the message arrived. In her condition she was especially sensitive to such things. The butcher bird hopped onto the windowsill and cocked its head at her, before carolling an exquisite song. A surge of electric energy tingled through her body and she knew beyond any doubt – Mulanyin was coming home.

That night when the baking dishes were washed and the whole house mopped, she lay in bed on the veranda looking to the heavens. The skin of her belly was stretched tight, silver streaks on it marking her transformation into a Waijung. Nita yawned as she put her palms on the small globe and felt her baby kick.

'Soon, my little one,' she promised. 'Soon your Big Father will come and you'll hear his voice again. He'll come with wedding turtle for us, little one, your very first taste of saltwater bingkin.'

She patted her stomach, then lay back and began to snore.

~

210

Mulanyin stood on board the *Otter* at Cleveland, bursting with impatience. To help the time pass, he watched workmen pole cedar logs towards the waiting vessels. Cleveland harbour was awash with felled timber; several dozen massive logs floated each side of the jetty where the *Otter* had tied up, all with their owner's brand burnt into them. Men with spikes laboured to bring the cedar and oak onshore after floods washed them down from the hinterland logging camps. Some massive logs would never make it to Cleveland, let alone Brisbane or Sydney. Some that did make it downriver were washed away and lost in the open ocean; others again would sink to the floor of the Bay or rot in the mangrove mud far from any town. The dagai somehow seemed to not care about this tremendous waste, happily toppling a hundred trees in order that forty or fifty could find their way to Pettigrew's Sawmill in town.

'Want a job, mate?' called a timber cutter from the wharf. 'They're crying out for men on Yellowwood Mountain.'

Mulanyin shook his head. He was no more inclined to harvest cedar than he was to herd Tom's stock at Murrumba. Dagai flattened the forests for their strange wooden houses that were beginning to dominate the landscape. White men's oompies were almost as common now in North Brisbane as trees. On their high stumps these houses looked like long-legged animals, desperate to run away from the noise and stench of town but compelled to remain there. Many were built of timber from the Logan and the Nerang, and Countries even further south. How must these poor trees feel, imprisoned in such foreign ground?

'I'm off to Petrie Bight to marry my promise,' he called, 'and then take her home to Nerang!'

'Plenty of work on the Perry for a man who can swing an axe.'

Mulanyin simply shook his head again and crossed to the other side of the boat to watch workers loading maize. The ripe cobs had waited a while on the wharf and had already begun to sprout.

'The sooner Separation comes the happier I'll be,' complained a timber merchant to Captain Freeman. 'It's our best hope of British labour.'

'Some hope,' Captain Freeman scoffed. 'This damn government will keep any new felons for themselves. Transportation won't benefit the likes of us.'

'You might be right,' the timber merchant agreed. 'And then what's a man to damn well do? Hire coolies or starve on principle?'

As the dagai grumbled to each other about their woes, Mulanyin became aware of a stranger staring at him from the far side of the jetty.

'Do I know you?' Mulanyin asked in the language of Teerk Roo Ra, but the answer came in his own tongue.

'No, no, we've never met,' the boy said, quickly drawing his prawn net up out of the water and walking off. Mulanyin frowned. If the lad was Yugambeh and had overheard him talking about going home to Nerang, he was quite rude not to stop and yarn.

'What's your name, cousin?' he called. 'Which of the five rivers is your home?'

'The Dugulumba,' muttered the youth, darting behind a bullock dray and disappearing. Mulanyin was exasperated. He wanted news of his family, especially of Waijung and her newborn. He noticed the workers had almost finished loading their sacks of maize. Was it worth risking his place on board ship to chase the young Logan River lad? He hesitated, torn between asking the captain to wait a moment, and simply leaping ashore. Then the young Goorie reappeared, walking with an older man. They stopped on the wharf opposite and greeted him. Relieved, Mulanyin began to recite his name and affiliations.

'We know who you are,' the older man interrupted. 'I'm Billy Monday. Your grandmother was cousin to my grandfather. In fact, she saved his life once, when he was about to drown in a riptide. My grandfather spoke very highly of her.'

'That's a relief, Uncle! I couldn't decide whether this lad here had run from my ugly face or taken off to fetch some men to fight me!' Mulanyin said, making a feeble joke of the young man's disappearance. Billy Monday didn't pretend to smile. The atmosphere grew strange and awkward. The younger man was sucking the meat from a prawn, and looking anywhere but at him. Billy Monday's eyes were deep-set liquid pools, and something desperate hid in their blackness. A chill fell over Mulanyin.

'Your young countryman ran away,' said Billy Monday very carefully, 'because of what he feared to tell.'

An onshore breeze sprang up, racing past Mulanyin, tangling his hair and blowing strands across his face. Even though the noonday sun was warm on his shoulders, he shivered where he stood, waiting for the blow to fall. He already knew, by some dread instinct, that the news concerned his Waijung. He would never see her beautiful face again, nor hear her laugh, nor see her smile with pride at his accomplishments. She would never meet and love Nita, nor cuddle the grandchildren Nita bore. At home, Big Father would be inconsolable with loss; and his young brother and sisters would need to turn to Second Waijung for their daily care.

Standing on board the *Otter*, Mulanyin was flooded with regret and shame for ever leaving Nerang, wasting his life in a foreign land so far from his family. He had to return home, immediately. He'd collect Nita and leave without waiting for a damn Christian wedding or a time convenient to the Petries. His own people needed him. That was all that mattered. The *Otter* would arrive at Queen's Wharf by dinnertime; curfew would force him to remain at the Petries' overnight. Then he and Nita could leave on the first boat south and be at Father's camp by nightfall.

'My Waijung – she has passed to the spirit world?'

The man nodded. 'Yoway. She is finished.'

'How long ago?'

Billy Monday hesitated. 'I'm terribly sorry to bear these bad tidings, cousin. My heart is like a stone in my chest to have to tell you, but last sabbath at Murry Jerry Station,' said Billy Monday in a low, grave voice. The man paused, seemingly paralysed by the weight of the news he was duty-bound to pass on. He dropped his chin and gave a choking sob.

Seeing this, Mulanyin pressed his palm heels very hard against his temples. Hard enough to hurt. It was important to focus; to contain his crumbling world until the man had finished telling what he knew.

After an eternity, Billy Monday heaved a sigh, then spoke once more. 'The head dagai at Murry Jerry Station invited your family for a feast. There had been a lot of bother about a missing bullock or two, and this was to be a feast of peace and friendship ...' The man trailed off then, lifting his face and fixing Mulanyin with a look of despair.

An odd sensation started up in Mulanyin's gut, a whirlpool of anguish and confusion spinning just below his navel. An unravelling. He didn't understand what was happening. Couldn't grasp the meaning in what Billy Monday was saying. Mulanyin struggled to recognise any connection whatever between this stranger's words and the plain fact of a Waijung dead at Nerang. A feast was a good thing. Friendship and peace – these could only be good things. There had obviously been some mistake.

'They gave lots of tucker to your family that day, plenty fresh beef and damper for everyone, but oh, cousin ... the damper ... the flour they used ... the muckenzie ...'

And so Mulanyin understood, now, why the young man had run.

'My Fathers, also?'

'Yoway.'

'My brother and sisters?' he whispered.

'All dead.'

'The baby?'

Billy Monday's mouth was a black cave of agony.

'Everybody is finished.'

21. Waste

1855

Mulanyin flew above the *Otter* as she forged her way towards the river mouth. In the west, the distinctive sharp triangle of Peak Mountain rose from the horizon. As his blue-grey wings flapped with slow, deliberate beats, he gazed down on the seamen hauling at the canvas sails that would carry the boat to Brisbane. His round yellow eye fell on the boat's captain, and on the sacks of sprouting maize, and on a few Islanders bound for Maryborough. Last of all his eye fell on the kippa standing alone at the rear of the boat, facing the roiling ocean. This youth seemed to belong to another world entirely than that of the seamen and captain, who shunned him. The youth stood by himself during the journey up to Fisherman's Island, his back to everyone else on board, keening in low desperation to the birds and the fishes. If the other men on board heard him, they gave no sign.

From certain angles, Mulanyin saw as he flew, the noonday sun turned the kippa's dark face, wet with tears, to a shining silver. Dipping and tilting in the breeze above the ketch he saw the youth's features come in and out of focus, at one moment seeming like those of any ordinary man on any ordinary day, and in the next transformed, slick with pain yet devoid of detail, becoming a blank silver plane, all reflection and refraction of the blinding light. A slippery customer, then. The kippa disappeared a thousand times during the voyage, falling with every wingbeat into the blinding anonymity of the sun and reappearing each time Mulanyin made a feathered prayer of himself against the dense blue horizon.

The kippa remained a stranger to him until the moment the *Otter* nosed the jetty at Fisherman's Island. When Captain Freeman hurled a rope to a waiting sailor, Mulanyin felt compelled, suddenly, to draw his wings in close and spiral down, folding himself elegantly into the person of the kippa who, he now saw, was abandoning ship, renouncing his prized bingkin to dive overboard and make for land. The young man was staggering out from the shallows of the river mouth and shoving through mangroves, wading through the dense dark mud that hoped to hold him fast in its embrace, frantically searching among the fishing shacks for a boat to steal or a horse to borrow, any means at all that could take him south to discover the truth about his family and the life to come.

A skinny bay nag was tied to a fencepost, asleep. He ran to it, undoing its halter rope with shaking hands, then climbing the rails to mount and head home through coastal Country he had only heard tell of. Mulanyin was astride the gelding when its owner ran out of a nearby hut, cursing and hauling him off, pulling the horse away with a swift kick at Mulanyin's face for good measure.

When he returned to consciousness, the horse-owner's curses had faded. All he could hear was the gentle slap of waves and the cries of the gulls. Mulanyin sat up and wiped blood from his mouth. The *Otter* had sailed and the inlet was empty. Realisation came flooding back – *everyone is finished* – and he was sorrier than he had ever been in his life. If only he'd stayed unconscious on the sandy hillock, innocent and unknowing. But his stupid innocence was at an end. He got shakily to his feet, knowing only that he had to find a way home, and find it fast. A boat to take him down the coast, or a passage on the next Sydney steamer or a horse that would carry him back to his river and his village and his—

His what?

Everyone is finished.

Mulanyin sank to his knees. A stone's throw from where he knelt, the river flowed past Fisherman's Island as it always had and always would. The sound of it lapping the banks was as normal to Mulanyin as his own breath, for he had never slept a night without hearing water shifting against land. Entirely familiar, and yet for the first time since leaving home Mulanyin truly understood its voice, this wide river that was not *his* river, in this Country that was not *his* Country. Some things should never be spoken of, the tide advised him, whispering with every ripple that reached the shore and hissed up the sand:

Shhhh shhhh. Don't mention the Terrible Thing.

A string of small islands dotted the ocean in front of him, islands he had grown to know well in his months in the dugong camp. On the mainland, a long line of fires stretched south into the distance, each one tinier than the last, until the furthest was a mere thread of smoke. The mark it made against the sky resembled those wisps of spider web he'd seen floating through the air as a child. Fires of his people? Or was it the smoke of his enemies he saw, the killers of his family?

Exhausted, he let his arms drop slack at his sides, suddenly wanting nothing more than to curl up on the grass like a babe inside the womb. But no. He must not think of babies, or of wombs. Best not to think of anything at all. Best to simply move his body and set something – anything – in motion, rather than allow in the thought of what had been done to his people.

Mulanyin found neither boat nor horse; instead, he ran all afternoon, stumbling upriver for brutal hours to reach Nita. Thorny bushes tore at his limbs and stones bruised his feet, but he felt none of it. Inside his agony, too deep for realisation, was a hope that Nita might be able to reach down into the abyss of his existence and change the past. He staggered into Kangaroo Point just as the stockwhips were cracking curfew in town.

Sweating and numb, Mulanyin went to the top of the rough-gouged cliffs and looked across the river at Petrie Bight. A scatter of boats were visible, returning from Eagle Farm or Limestone or the Bay. Others had already moored for the night near the Customs House. He could recognise some of the men on the far shore, going as they pleased between shops and inns and other places of business. These white men stood on street corners, ignoring the stockwhips. They laughed with their friends and strolled in pairs and threes to the various hotels. They climbed on and off boats moored at the foot of the Government Garden, heedless and unafraid. These white men lived in another universe than him, one without murder at its core. Or thought they did.

It occurred to Mulanyin that he was standing directly opposite the spot where Murree had rolled with laughter at Cocky's mischief. If he could fly like a white cockatoo he'd be across the river and holding Nita close in the time it took to spear a bream. But he was no cockatoo. The Warrar and the stockwhips stood in his way.

At the bottom of the cliff directly below him, Ah Yow's wife squatted near her oompie, smoking and scoffing at a comment from her sister. Several of their children chased each other in play on the sandy beach. A white billy-goat was attacking a stray dog which had veered too close, while Chow the opium-seller watched on unconcerned.

Upstream, a little past the Woolloongabba Swamp and the fig grove, the smokes of Kurilpa cooking fires rose in a score of white pillars against the western hills. Unlike those of the steamer chugging downstream, these smokes rose vertical in the still air. They reminded Mulanyin of the bars which had imprisoned Dundalli in Queen Street. Kurilpa women would be gathering their jarjums in close before true dark fell, cooking the day's harvest, and yarning with their husbands and sisters. Yerrin and Murree and the other men would be tarring fish nets, mending their oompies, or perhaps skinning winter possums to add to the store of bedding in the village. Older people would rest by the fire and smoke their pipes as the hum of family surrounded them like a warm and comforting blanket. Everything with the Kurilpa would be unremarkable, while here he stood a mile away in a tumult of grief. The contrast bewildered Mulanyin. How could the rest of the world possibly continue unaffected? How could things continue at all when Waijung and his Fathers and …

But no. He could not allow himself to think on it.

Yerrin had summoned him home from the dugong camp. That meant he had been forgiven his brawl with Warry. The Teerk Roo Ra men would have sent word back to South Brisbane, given a good account of his behaviour, and his reward was to be allowed back at the Kurilpa village. Yerrin would welcome him back.

Mulanyin had a sharp realisation.

If he had misbehaved on Peel Island, if he had been rude or lazy or unhelpful in any way, he'd still be in the dugong camp and blissfully unaware. His family would still be alive in his imagination and his biggest problem would be being too far away from Nita. Would that ignorance have been better than knowing the truth, though? The question was unanswerable. He *did* know what had happened. There was no going back, not even to the bright innocence of that morning when he'd rowed with the others away from Teerk Roo Ra, on fire with dreams of the family he and Nita would build. The kippa who'd woken today expecting to hunt dugong for another half-moon at least was a very different one from the man standing high on a cliff among vines and orchids, where the winter wattle was blooming. The honey scent reached him on the rapidly cooling air, reminding him of the day he'd first arrived at Woolloongabba. Could it really be only one Mullet Run since he'd come to Brisbane with his

Father and witnessed the great pullen pullen? Only one Mullet Run since he'd gone through the ceremonies which had turned an ignorant boy into a man?

The Father who had brought that ignorant boy to Brisbane was dead. The boy was gone too, replaced by a kippa with the marks of responsibility etched forever on his chest. The ash rubbed into those scars by Yerrin's hands came from Yagara trees grown in Yagara soil; this river Country he stood on could never leave him, nor he it. He carried it over his heart, and was proud to; but, oh, how his spirit yearned for the land of his own people, where his placenta was buried in Yugambeh soil.

Mulanyin stood above the Warrar and wept, a man divided.

The Petries' front door slammed. Nita startled awake and sat up, putting her hands on her belly. Something was amiss. In Nita's dream Mulanyin had come to her with his eyes wild and his feet bloody. She had to find him and help him – but where was he?

The water bags hanging from the veranda beams creaked to and fro on their straps, buffeted by the breeze that had picked up just as John and Grandfather Petrie arrived home from the School of Arts. The moon was a mere sliver. Nita drew her blanket up, shivering. The song from her dream was still trying to reach her, but the noise of the men in the kitchen wouldn't let it find its way.

'A hundred bronzewings!' John exclaimed, 'A man'd choke on pigeon pie!'

'Knowing Hanlon he'd have given half of them away,' said Grandfather Petrie, his walking stick tap tap tapping against the floorboards.

'Hanlon's a good man, I'll grant you, and keeps a good table. But what he said about Wide Bay – do we believe it?'

'We do,' said Andrew Petrie gravely, 'and we must have an inquiry, sooner rather than later. A full inquiry, mind, John. The

Burnett boys are terrible for the gins, it's hardly a secret. I'll write to Sydney tomorrow.'

When the Petrie men had retired for the night, Nita crept inside. She couldn't risk a lamp, and so felt her way in the gloom, purloining the brandy bottle from the cabinet. Needing strength to face whatever was coming, she gulped down a couple of mouthfuls of the burning liquid. Then, clasping the bottle to her chest, she tiptoed outside again. She slid silent as a cat past Old Tom's lean-to, where the empty boots of Tim Shea told her the two old lags were inside up to their usual sinning. She inched the garden gate open, holding her breath, and then headed towards the Government Garden, borne there by a fearful pull that only intensified as she approached the dark vein of the river.

The breeze rose into a gale as she walked, whipping through the trees to let her know the Ancestors were watching. Gum leaves blew in her face and long dangling vines danced from the fig boughs like restless spirits. A bandicoot scuttled in the undergrowth, then suddenly shot out beneath her feet. Nita let out a cry, afraid of both the living and the dead in the dense bushes of the riverbank. She gulped another mouthful of brandy. It was madness to be out after midnight, let alone by herself, let alone heavy with child and unable to flee. If discovered breaking curfew she risked arrest, or worse. Far worse. Still, something untellable drove her on: Mulanyin needed her. Wherever he was, and whatever had happened, she had to find him. She began to tremble, but whether from the cold or from fear she couldn't have rightly said. As she continued, Nita began to recite the first prayer she had ever learnt at Mary Petrie's knee.

Breathing *amen*, Nita arrived at the bottom of the Government Garden. She stood on quivering legs opposite the Kangaroo Point cliffs and something happened then, that she would later tell her children and their children in turn, in a new century. Gazing out on the ripples of the river tiding downstream, she begged the

Ancestors for a sign. She asked them to show her where beneath the great canopy of Star Camps she would find her love. In the deep night, the only illumination came from the mangroves fringing the river – their low rounded branches shining with hundreds of fireflies. The swamp at her back roared with life. Standing there big-bellied at the edge of the Government Garden, Nita felt as though the wide current of the river was flowing somehow not past her, but through her. She knew suddenly that she was nothing more than a vessel; completely empty and yet absolutely full in the same moment, and the thing that she was full of was the world itself. Armed with this strange understanding, her terror evaporated.

With her fear vanished, Nita could sense Mulanyin waiting somewhere on the far side of the Warrar, near the cliffs. She felt her way down the stone steps to the river and clambered into an empty dinghy she found as much by touch as by sight. Breathing heavily, she threaded the oars into the oarlocks and pushed out into the current, making for the faint lamplight of the Chinese prawning camp. Somewhere there in the blackness of night, her love was waiting. As she began rowing across, leaving the forbidden night streets of North Brisbane behind, Nita discovered an old familiar tune rising in her throat, a song of freedom that would not be denied. As she approached the middle of the channel, she began to sing.

> *Amazing Grace, how sweet the sound,*
> *that saved a wretch like me,*
> *I once was lost, but now am found,*
> *was blind, but now I see.*

To her joy, Mulanyin called out, screaming her name. She rowed towards the sound, singing her way over so her love would know she was coming, that she would never abandon him.

When we've been here, ten thousand years,
bright shining as the sun,
We've no less days to sing His praise,
than when we first begun.

When she reached the tiny beach below the cliffs, Mulanyin waded out to her. They fell shuddering into each other's arms.

They clung to each other, kissing in the dampness of the stolen boat. Then Nita rested her forehead against his, breathing in his breath as she traced Mulanyin's scalp with her fingertips. She discovered a large lump where the horse-owner's boot had struck, and she sat back.

'What's this lump? Are you hurt?'

Mulanyin put his face in his hands, mute. It was too much to ask – that he shatter her with his news. That their love be contaminated by it. Far better to hide behind his hands and pretend. He began to weep.

Confused, Nita groped in the dark for his forearms, trying to pull his palms away from his face and down onto her stomach. He resisted, but Nita finally made him lower his hands. Whatever awful thing had happened, whoever had assaulted him or hunted him still, her husband was with her now. He deserved to know the joy of new life that awaited them. Mysteriously, though, when she held his hands, spread wide across her rounded belly, rising and falling with her every breath, Mulanyin's sobbing grew more intense. He collapsed forward, resting against her, as though sitting upright was beyond him.

'What's wrong?' she asked in bewilderment, cradling his head. 'Tell me, sweetheart, are the Northern tribes chasing you? Or the Native Police? Speak to me! What's happened to your head?'

It took an age, but finally Mulanyin sat up and met her eye. What she saw there in the faint glow of starlight gave Nita pause.

She had seen such a look before, and she caught her breath. 'Oh, my love,' she whispered uselessly. 'Is it your family?'

Mulanyin turned away then, trembling on the wooden boat seat. Facing the high darkness of the cliff, he spoke the only word he could bring himself to utter. 'Muckenzie.'

Nita flinched, but she knew she had to act; had to wrap herself around him, herself and the baby too. As she pulled the man into her she breathed out a first long wail for his dead. It was a sound that contained all grief, and all love, and the unavoidable knowledge that the world was full of pain, shared and isolate. They wept together for a long while, until finally Nita asked, 'When?'

'Last sabbath. After Church.'

'How many?'

Mulanyin's eyes were wild. Tears streamed down his face, collecting at his jawline. 'None survive. I am an orphan.'

Nita thought fast. When Mulanyin stopped crying he would collect his Yagara brothers and go south. He would avenge his family's murder, or die in the attempt, and if he should die, he would burn in hell for all eternity. She had to stop him.

'You have people still, my love. It's a great tragedy, and you must mourn your family, we all must. They will have ceremony, of course. But remember – your people are here, now, too,' she insisted, pressing his hands hard to her stomach and holding them there. 'Whatever has happened, you have brothers and sisters and parents among the Kurilpa. You have a new son or daughter waiting to meet you.' She pointed at the slender crescent hanging overhead. 'Perhaps in the next moon. You have me, and Yerrin and Murree. And your life *must* be here now, Mulanyin.'

It was as though she hadn't spoken.

'I'll leave at first light. The Dugulumba clan will help me mourn them, and perhaps the Pretty Face Wallaby People. You'll come too.'

'Your Waijung and Big Father – both are perished?'

'Are you deaf, woman? I told you, already, none survive!'

'How can you be so sure?'

'The man who told me had no reason to lie. He spoke as though it cut his tongue out to tell it.'

'Oh Mulanyin, my love, my love ...' She handed him the brandy and he drained the bottle in one swallow.

With his head sunk in her lap, Mulanyin keened like the Elder women who cried each dawn for the Dead. His sobbing echoed in the night, booming off the stone face of the cliffs. The Chinese prawners downstream woke at the sound and lay in bed wondering what was amiss. His cries reached across the river to the frogs and owls in the Hollow, and the slum-dwellers asleep in their shanties. Stray goats bleated unhappily hearing his pain; the fish asleep in the river took his mourning cries into their dreams. In the scrub just south of Kangaroo Point, the dingoes heard him, and their neck hairs quivered. Knowing the sound of Death intimately, they stood, and in respect for Mulanyin's loss they pointed their noses at the moon, answering his terrible grief with their own. The howls of man and dog echoed over Darragh's Paddock, reaching the Kurilpa village in a symphony of sorrow for the slain.

While her man keened and the dingos howled, Nita used her oar blade to push the dinghy back into deeper water. She began rowing upstream to the Kurilpa village, knowing she'd need Dawalbin and Yerrin in the coming days and weeks if Mulanyin was to be kept safe from himself. If she and her unborn child were to have a future.

'It's madness to go alone!' Nita erupted early next morning, 'And look at me – I'm in no state to go to Nerang!'

She and her man stood around the fire with Dawalbin and a small cluster of others, stomping their feet against the frost. Yerrin and Murree were both away at Murrumba with Young Tom and many of the other men; they would doubtless return as soon as they could.

'I'll send for you when it's safe. Dawalbin can care for you until then.'

'They'll shoot you dead in your tracks! And you'll go to Hell, and I'll have nothing and nobody. Is that what you want?' Nita raged. Mulanyin was undeterred.

'Was Waijung's life a worthless thing? And the lives of my fathers and brothers and sisters? Think about what you're asking of me. What kind of man would I be to sit here idly in Kurilpa village and do *nothing*?'

'Wait for Yerrin, then – at least seek his advice before leaving.'

'No, I won't wait.'

Nita and Dawalbin exchanged a worried glance. Mulanyin was very far gone in grief to refuse Yerrin's counsel.

'Wait to take Murree with you, if you must go. You owe that much to your unborn child …'

Mulanyin rounded on Nita. 'Our unborn child is safe here in town, while the spirits of my family wander in torment! Where are their mogoy, Nita? Can you tell me that? Is there a goanna at Murry Jerry Station chewing on my Waijung's thigh? Or did her killers chuck her in the river like a pine log for the crabs to feast on? My blood must be put to rest – can't you understand!'

Mulanyin was dishevelled, his eyes red and sunken, with the mud of his journey to town still smeared across his chest. He had barely slept. Nita doubted he had eaten in two days. There was no strategy in the man: there was only madness and pain. All she could do was attempt a delay.

'The dagai will be on guard for retaliation,' she argued, putting a hand on his arm. 'But if you wait for your brothers, you can strike harder and with less danger. Leave it for one or two moons – the killers will begin to relax and get lazy. Our child will be born. And then, husband, with only one firestick—'

'You don't understand,' Mulanyin reeled away from her touch. 'There's no solving this. It's a catastrophe.' Nobody could reach him through the fog of his grief, nothing could undo such atrocity. Eleven people murdered – and for what? Nita was worried for their baby, of course she was; but his betrothed had no idea of the pain crushing the breath from his lungs. The brandy she fed him barely touched the sides of his agony. Every waking second he felt like knocking himself out cold against a tree; that would be bliss compared to this unending nightmare. 'Can you stop talking about what you can't understand,' he growled. 'My entire family has been slaughtered by vile criminals and all you do—

'But Mulanyin, she does understand,' Dawalbin interrupted very gently. 'She understands everything.'

Nita gave a moan and collapsed onto her haunches beside Dawalbin's fire. She covered her face with her hands and began rocking back and forth where she sat. Ada and a second young Kurilpa woman knelt and curled their arms around her shoulders, whispering in her ear and moving with her as she rocked.

Mulanyin blinked. Dawalbin met his gaze without judgement. He saw strands of her hair being tossed by a light breeze. Watching her curls lift and fall he came back to himself. 'What?'

'Nita understands.'

'How can she possibly?' Mulanyin broke off, looking at Nita, whose rocking had now intensified along with her moaning. The sound was attracting attention from others in the village. 'The baby?' he asked. 'It comes so quickly?'

'No,' said Dawalbin, still gentle. 'Not before next moon. She sits and rocks at my fire for a different reason. Your pain is immense, Mulanyin. The loss tears at your stomach like a ravenous dog that can't be sated. It overwhelms you, but know this, son – you are far from alone. Do you think you are the only one bereaved in our lands? Nita survived hidden in a creek bed, along with one other small child. The stockmen who shot her family sold her to an Irish sawyer for a tin of jam. That sawyer kept her for three years, until

Grandfather Petrie discovered it and bought her freedom for two pounds.'

Nita cried out, lamenting, 'And now you know my shame! Leave me if you must, Mulanyin, and your unborn child too. But take the advice of one who knows – there is no way to live looking back. Your life must lie in front of you, or believe me, you will lose your mind along with your family.'

Wretched, she struck her belly with both hands. 'This is the only future we have.'

22. Edenglassie

2024

'… and forty-nine hundred, and that's your five grand,' Johnny finished counting out hundred-dollar notes into the old bloke's hand.

'You know what yer buying, mate?' The man's rheumy eyes crinkled with concern. 'She looks sound in the shed, but you hit rough weather, I dunno she'll stand up to much. Needs recaulking, I'd say, at a minimum.'

'Oh, I've been restoring old boats since I was a kid,' Johnny reassured the old man. They had just drunk litres of tea; Barney's wife, Joan, had fed him scones and jam in a kitchen smelling of Pine O'Cleen and White Ox baccy. 'She's in safe hands. I'll even take you out on the Bay when she's tidied up, if you like!'

The old man wheezed with laughter. Lungs like cellophane. 'Oh, Christ, son, I get terrible seasick! Couldn't think of a worse thing.'

Johnny smiled, feeling rather puzzled. 'You're not a sailor then?'

'No, no! It was me old Aunt what had her built. She named her too. Said *Edenglassie* was a prettier name than Brisbane by far, and a pity it hadn't stuck to the place. No, you go and have a good time sailing, young feller. Send us a photer if ya see any crocodiles!'

Johnny was behind his steering wheel ready to pull out onto the highway when Barney waved at him to stop. Johnny lowered his window and got another whiff of White Ox. Not long for this world, old mate wasn't.

'Ere. May's well take the tarp, too, I got no use for it. Been in the shed since the old Aunt went into Eventide in ninety-one.'

'I'm telling ya, bud, it's like Lehman Brothers, too big to fail. We got em over a barrel onetime!'

Winona was jubilant at the tiller of Johnny's newly restored sailboat. It wasn't the *Edenglassie* she referred to, though, but the statue they had somehow persuaded the Bicentenary Committee to install at South Bank. Their brainchild would sit proudly facing Gardens Point, reminding all white eyes that they were still on Aboriginal land, and that Cook had been nothing more than a Yorkshireman too fond of trespassing on the wrong side of the globe.

'Well, ya wanna be sure. Ya Nan's eyesight's come back like there's no tomorrow,' Johnny warned as he lay back against the rigging, slurping down Buderim ginger cordial in a gesture towards the Dry July he had failed to complete. 'Now that the old girl can clock what's what, she's reading the riot act to the whole bloody ward. Nurse, orderly or CEO – everyone's copping it.'

'Us Blankets always been a pack of standover merchants,' Winona grinned.

'Ya don't say.'

'Hard to believe, I know.'

'Speaking of ya Nan. You know all those mad yarns she's got for Grandad Charlie – how much of that do ya reckon's fair dinkum? I mean, *obviously* he never drove a Rolls-Royce around a burning farmhouse at top speed to save it, but—'

'The fuck he never! I looked it up on Trove!' Winona protested. 'He was a proper clever man. Fix anything, drive anything, ride anything, track anything. Spoke fluent lingo, too. Nearly all of them yarns is for real. Like the one about when he was working on a station out near Warwick breaking in horses, ay.'

'Did he put his undies on one leg at a time though?'

'Bushmen got no use for jocks, brah! Anyways, they was breaking in yarraman, and there's a badarse little gelding there called Nigel, with an evil look in its eye, and the cowboys all too scared to hop on him, ay. Gran reckons Grandad Charlie wanna go and bignote himself, see, impress the doobs, and so he starts doing the big hero act. He dampens down the arse of his trousers—'

'Ay?

'Geez, I thought doctors are sposed to be hejimicated? To help him grip the saddle! So, he damps his trousers down and grabs a hold of Nigel's ear ...'

This time Johnny kept his confusion to himself.

'... and swings his leg over. Five seconds in the saddle and Grandad's there all grinning up at the girls, too deadly me. Then Nigel – BOOM – fucken explodes underneath him. Grandad's got just enough reptile brain activated to kick his feet outta the stirrups; then he's soaring majestically through the air with the greatest of ease. He nearly eats shit but somehow the jammy prick manages to land at a running stumble in front of the whole damn crowd. While he's in orbit his cowboy hat's gorn sky-high of course, and so he looks up and spots it and catches it on his index finger right before it hits the ground. "And that, friends," Grandad goes to the mob, spinning the hat back onto his head, "that's how to get off before you get bucked off!" Bahahaha! Showman or what?'

'Being a standover merchant's not the only thing that runs in the family,' laughed Johnny, 'Sounds like a fair dose of bullshit does too.'

'Nah, true story, bra, I swear ta god.'

'Prefer it if ya don't go lyin and blasphemin too hard before this boat trip's over, thanks. I told the old couple I bought it off that I'd look after her, not make her a target for the wrath of Yahweh.'

'Yahweh? Sounds like yoway,' replied Winona absently, coiling a rope on the deck. '*Yahweh, yoway,* spose there's only so many sounds a human mouth can make. The wrath of yoway, the curse of saying yes too often …'

'I'm more worried about the wrath of Granny Eddie. She's gonna twig real fast when she sees that statue, and I reckon she'll be gunning for ya.'

'So long as she don't clock it before Sat'dy week. Be a done deal then. And whaddya mean, gunning for *me* – your arse is on the line too!'

'We'll both be dodging her!' Johnny grinned a broad, mischievous grin. Winona had suckered him into her sneaky campaign to get the sculpture erected just in time for Bicentenary Day. The enormous artwork – informed by an artefact Johnny had spied years before in a drawer at a Sydney university – now lay prone under plastic sheeting near the Goodwill Bridge. Three metres long and made of polished stainless steel, the gigantic Dundalli, complete with shield and raised spear, was almost ready to be hoisted onto a high pedestal facing North Brisbane. The warrior would stand as a potent symbol of a culture fully alive in the twenty-first century. Fuck the Expo needle, they had told the bureaucrats, this is a deadly blackfella with his spear up ready to defend his mob, and it's what's happening. *Granny Eddie said so.* The fact that Dundalli's spear exactly resembled a sharpened kangaroo bone was left unsaid. No whitefella would recognise it as such, nor realise what it meant for the riverside expressway named after the first dagai pirate to arrive on Yagara land.

Winona had lain awake many a night, willing her daring plan to come to fruition.

The *Edenglassie* had almost reached the river estuary now. Thick mangroves clustered against both shores. In a carpark on the southern bank, two fisherwomen worked to free a pelican from tangled line someone had been too ignorant or lazy to take home. In front of Johnny's sailboat stretched the river bar, and then Moreton Bay and its many islands; a saltwater highway that the Goories from hundreds of kilometres around had been criss-crossing for millennia. Johnny took a deep breath, sucking the sea air into his lungs. It smelt of seaweed and sun and freedom. Good medicine.

'I love this view of the river. The way it opens out and you've got the whole world waiting for you,' Johnny said.

'If Gran beats me to death with that old stick of hers, at least I lived long enough to sail this far,' Winona agreed.

'Maybe we should just hook it right past Fisherman's Island and head to Aotearoa?' Johnny joked.

'Ya know yer a blackfella when yer shit scared of a hundred-year-old blind woman in a wheelchair, ay?' Winona agreed.

'She might be frail and old, but she got her jabree and she proppa ready to use it!'

Both of them cracked up, knowing the ferocious force of nature that was Eddie wielding her fighting stick. Winona tilted her head at her companion. This fulla was deadly smart and funny – and sounding real Blak lately too. 'What's with all the code-switching bra? You sound more Goorie than I do.'

'Aw, hanging around with Uncle Robbie's mob'll do that.'

'So long's yer not bunging it on.'

'Didn't realise I needed yer permission to talk Blak, jij.'

'I told ya before – biggest standover cunts, my mob.'

'True fucken story, ay.'

Winona laughed. She flipped her BLM cap around, facing into the breeze with her eyes closed, relishing the briny scent of the ocean and the warmth of the sun on her face. 'You get anywhere with that DNA stuff?'

'Yes and no. Spent five hundred bucks, and all I've found out is that every bloody convict in Australia's related, if ya look long enough.'

'Sounds like us mob.'

'Mmmm, well I'm still waiting to meet my magic seven per cent of Goomeroi. Found plenty of Irish. And French and Lithuanians, too. Even a bit of Indian. Did I tell ya the latest ancestry update made me one per cent Punjabi?' Johnny rolled his eyes.

'I think Punjabis are from Pakistan.'

'All I know,' Johnny said, ducking under the boom as the wind shifted, 'is this lady I matched with had a Punjabi ancestor in Ipswich in 1860. Only we can't find how we're connected.'

Winona grunted. 'Must have been a heap of Indians around back in the day. Gran's family line's got some, remember?'

Johnny stared. 'I thought you meant like Pocahontas Indian. Native American.'

'Nuh, the other sort. What's the surname you matched?'

'Oh, lemme think. Not Brown, all my Browns are Irish. These Indian mob are, oh, I can't remember. Soda, Sohdee, something like that? But it's not even definite. There was a lot of Hindus come here and finding the right one's like winning lotto.'

'The perfect pyramid scheme,' Winona reflected. 'Kiss ya bungoo goodbye.'

'Yeah, ay. More bungoo than fucken sense, me.'

They both laughed again. Winona pointed her lips at Johnny's cordial. He passed it over silently and sat watching the movement of her glorious throat as she tipped the bottle and swallowed. One day he'd kiss that throat, he promised himself. Then opened the tackle box and began baiting squid onto hooks.

An hour later, an Emirates jet roared above the side channel where they had anchored to fish. For a full minute as the jet went over Winona was mouthing at Johnny silently and in vain. He shook his head and shrugged, pointing up.

'I said that's a special place,' she repeated when the noise stopped, gesturing towards the mouth where the waves of the bay met the ripples of the outgoing river. 'Not as special as it used to be, of course. The airport mob seen to that, had to fuck up the island to build their bloody stupid runways, and the Law Story with it.' She bit into her sandwich, and chewed enthusiastically, leaving a constellation of white crumbs on her singlet and a dab of Vegemite on her cheek. Her honey skin was pale against the jet-black paste. This doob really is only one shade darker than me, Johnny mused, taking his hat off and feeling the sun bite his face. Could he *tan* his way into being more of a Blakfella? Nah, gammon, he'd just get skin cancer. Wake up to yerself Johnny. 'Ya cheek,' he brushed at his face in demonstration.

'Ay?'

'Vegemite. Ya look like Darto, with his drowning mark.'

'His what?'

'That mole. On his face.'

'What's moles got to do with drowning?'

'It's from *The Tempest*. We did it at school. "He hath no drowning mark upon him, his complexion is perfect gallows." The Poms called a facial mole a drowning mark, back in the day. They believed if you had one, you could never drown.'

'Well, well, ain't you the deadly culture vulture, spouting Shakespeare?'

'Pretty much. You gonna let that Vegemite just sit there, are ya?' Johnny wet his thumb with spit and moved closer. To his delight, Winona allowed him to carefully wipe the smear away. Thrilled by this intimacy, Johnny went on, 'I dunno what it has to do with drowning, I mean obviously moles can't stop you drowning. Some sorta old wives' tale, I guess.'

'Old wives got a lot to teach us, bunji. Them old girls is the crones, the dirrigans.'

'Ooh, scary! Better chuck this on then,' Johnny threw her the lifejacket she'd refused when they set sail that morning. Outfoxed, Winona shrugged the lifejacket on and even let Johnny do the clips up.

'What do you reckon it means?' he asked, but she had now become fixated on the dense vegetation of the inlet where *Edenglassie* was anchored. They were tucked away from the main channel, with no jetskis or commercial shipping nearby to bother the wildlife. Herons and egrets poked under the mangroves. Every few minutes a big fish jumped to remind them that their empty lines were their own fault, not that of the river.

'So beautiful, ay. Woulda been absolute magic before Oxley rocked up with that dickhead Parsons. Look how clear the water is. Anything could happen at a place like this.'

'Anything? Like you agreeing to a date Saturday night?' Johnny posed the question for the second time that month.

'Hah!' Winona brushed herself clean of crumbs, toppling them into the river. 'Palo solidarity gig Saturday night. And I already told ya, anyway, I don't date whitefellas.'

'Oh, right,' Johnny was momentarily paralysed. Then Uncle Robbie's voice kicked in: *Never listen to identity shit, son.* 'I forgot I'll never be Blak enough for you, cos ya keep shifting the goalposts on me.'

'If ya worried about anyone else's goalposts ya playing the wrong game, sunshine.'

Winona suddenly flapped both hands at the Amity water taxi motoring past the inlet on its way to the Bay; the Straddie jarjums on board all excited to see their Aboriginal flag flying from Johnny's mast. One day, she reflected, this Goomeroi fulla might stop worrying about her definition of his identity, because he would have grown strong enough into his own. But that day had not yet arrived, and she couldn't waste time waiting for him to blacken up. She had an ailing grandmother to spring out of Ward B, a Community Health Worker course to complete, and a long white coloniser's expressway to curse with a stainless-steel kangaroo bone.

'Bout time we was heading back, bunji. Help me get this bloody anchor up, will ya?' she asked. 'There's sharks from arsehole to breakfast time round ere and I don't wanna fall in and feed em.'

23. A Fork in the Road

1855

On the next full moon, the Kurilpa gathered to celebrate the new child of Mulanyin and Nita. They spoke about the future awaiting this infant girl, Annie, and her place in their clan. Even though this baby's blood originated from east and south of here, they proclaimed, this jarjum belongs to us by Law, and so she belongs to our Country also. Despite this generosity, Mulanyin struggled to find any joy in fatherhood. Grief still bowed the corners of his mouth towards the earth. Even when Yerrin offered Annie the gift of a significant Yagara name, Mulanyin had to fake his appreciation. His mind was always in Nerang, now. If he had just stayed home then maybe the disputed bullock would never have been speared, and the poisonous feast might never have happened. If he hadn't stayed in Kurilpa so long, captivated by Nita, if he'd gone back to his own clan, then perhaps they might all still be alive.

If! If! If!

His daughter – a tiny scrap peeking from her possum-fur blanket, with Nita's huge eyes and his own shapely lips, was adored by everyone. Mulanyin allowed Annie's tiny fingers to grasp his own. He even laughed when occasionally he held her in his arms and her tiny mouth sought his flat nipple. But the moment his jarjum was back with Nita or Dawalbin or another of her Waijungs, he remembered. And whenever Yerrin was nearby, the insult flung at him months ago by the Elder crashed around Mulanyin's brain like a wounded wallaby in the scrub. He roamed the river, the swamp and the town, spending long days alone.

'Why are you avoiding Father?' Murree finally asked one morning at Kingfisher Creek. 'Is it because he forbade you to go to Nerang?'

Mulanyin trod water in the deepest part of the creek. He had an outraged turtle clamped in each armpit, as well as one clawing for freedom in each hand. The distress of the turtles perturbed Murree enough to pose the question that had been bothering him for the better part of a moon. Mulanyin turned on his back and kicked over to the creek bank, where he handed the animals up to another man, Tandur.

'Well?' Murree insisted.

'I'm not avoiding him. He's busy helping Tom at Murrumba most of the time. I'm busy here. It's just how it is,' Mulanyin fibbed.

In reply, Murree hurled a large handful of mud at Mulanyin's head. His brother ducked under the surface and came up spluttering, rubbing his eyes.

'Don't bullshit me,' Murree went on. 'Every time Father appears in the village you take off with some weak excuse – what is it? Is it because he sent you away to the dugong camp, are you still angry about that? Or is there something else you haven't told me?'

'It's certainly hard to forget his criticism,' Mulanyin muttered. His pride had been mortally wounded that day, when, for the first time ever, Yerrin had made him question whether he really belonged in the Kurilpa camp.

Murree nodded. The public roasting had been lacerating, no question. But, he explained, it was only because Yerrin had such hopes for Mulanyin and such a high opinion of him before the stupid fight with Warry. And his father's reputation was on the line too. Having taken Mulanyin in, put him through the Bora

Law and then adopted him and promised him his third ceremony, Yerrin was not about to be shamed by stupid brawling. He had been forced to tell Dalapai that his Proclamation of Demands needed to be delayed, Murree pointed out, a situation just as embarrassing as Mulanyin's humiliation at the meeting, if not more so. In any case, he'd done his penance on Teerk Roo Ra. The matter was finished now, forgotten by everyone except him. Sulking did not become an adult man, Murree added.

The kippas fished until dusk, and when they returned home their dillybags were full of bream and eel, and half a dozen duck eggs to boot.

'It may not be the dugong you grew fat on in the bay,' Nita teased, arranging several of the eggs on the coals, 'but I suppose these'll do for dinner.' Her eyes were tired from night feeds, yet her spirits were high. Between them, she and Murree had persuaded Mulanyin to delay his revenge expedition. Almost two moons had passed since she rowed to meet him at the foot of the cliff. With every sunset, Nita's hopes grew that Mulanyin would remain safely in town where he belonged. Going south would help no-one, she told herself, and would endanger everybody.

'I asked him why he avoids Father,' Murree told his Waijung that evening, 'But he just makes excuses.'

Dawalbin smiled at her oldest son and took his hand in her own. 'Murree, you love your brother, but you can't live his life for him, nor see through his eyes. Remember what he's lost. He's in great pain.'

'I just don't understand him anymore,' Murree complained. 'He's finding fault all the time, and he's been no fun since—'

'Yes. *Since*,' Dawalbin nodded. '*Since*. He's suffered a tragedy, one I pray you'll never know. As for avoiding Yerrin – who was it that sent Mulanyin away to the place where he first heard his family were murdered? In his mind, being exiled and finding out about the murders will be all mixed together in one big, tangled story. It's less than two moons since he found out, which is nothing at all. Give him time, and kindness and patience, the way you've been taught, son. The old Mulanyin will return, though it may take several Mullet Runs to meet him again.'

Dawalbin spoke these words louder than usual, and she was careful to face the oompie of Nita and Mulanyin as she did so. At rest in bed with his wife and daughter, Mulanyin heard her clearly. As the mullet jumped and splashed in the river below the village, he lay on his back, listening to them. If he concentrated hard enough on that sound, he thought, and on the night cries of the plovers, he might be able to blot out the awful sentence Yerrin had roared on the day of his exile.

You behave like someone without a family.

~

'Hoy there! Mulanyin!'

Mulanyin stepped inside Chow's establishment, ignoring the familiar voice behind him. The opium hut next to the Kangaroo Point abattoir held a dozen stoned bodies of various races, asleep on blankets or resting on low daybeds. All their problems were obliterated, briefly, by the clouds of sweet smoke which hung beneath the ceiling of the grimy store.

'Ah, Mulla-yin, good to see you,' Chow smiled. 'You want to bite the cloud again?'

'Mulanyin, don't you ignore me, you rude southern bastard!' Tom Petrie stuck his head inside the hut. 'What are you doing here with these bloody degenerates? Come and have a noggin with me,' he insisted, hauling Mulanyin away under protest to the Logan Inn.

The inn was considerably more lively than Chow's. Mulanyin peered in from the street and saw a crowd of drinkers gathered around a man reading from the *Courier*.

'The accused claimed to have released the sheep from the yards on philosophical grounds, believing, he told the Court, that the eating of their flesh was an abomination. Shea was sentenced to thirty lashes and two weeks in gaol, in lieu of restitution which straitened circumstances prevented him from supplying to the owner of the flock ...'

The crowd roared with laughter and urged their literate friend to keep the entertainment coming.

'Not the first time Tim Shea's been scratched by a cat,' Tom remarked drily as he and Mulanyin made their way to the yard outside, bottles in hand. 'And likely not the last if he wants to go around freeing Mayne's wethers.'

The previous year Tom would have roared with laughter along with the rest, reflected Mulanyin. Now he spoke like a pastoralist, as though sheep and cattle were sacred objects, not to be interfered with on pain of a flogging.

'I didn't know you'd taken to visiting Chow's,' Tom accused, once they found a couple of stumps to perch on. Mulanyin brushed his question away like a mosquito.

'Ah, it's nothing. I've only gone there once or twice, no different from this,' he said, raising his bottle.

'A man can drink beer and still work his twelve hours next day,' Tom argued. 'But those living skeletons at Chow's'll be lucky to ever work again. You're walking a dangerous path, brother.'

'*Work*,' spat Mulanyin. 'Is that all you care about these days? Chasing damn cows around in circles?'

'Yerrin asked me to come and fetch you.' Tom sidestepped the question of what he cared about. 'He wants you to come to Murrumba for a while. I need all the men I can get, brother. The lambing's about done, and when it's over we'll muster Griffin's cleanskins. You'd be doing me a favour.' Tom eyed Mulanyin over the brim of his beer bottle. Yerrin's wishes had been very clear: don't return to Murrumba without that kippa. Left to his own devices, he will kill himself with opium and despair. He needs work, and to be among friends, far away from Chow's hut and the sleazy taverns of South Brisbane.

'My Waijung lies unburied in the south,' Mulanyin said bitterly. 'Why on earth would I ride north when her ceremonies need to be completed, and her death avenged?'

Tom sighed, and Mulanyin bristled. Tom had a wife of his own now, along with a living mother and father and a houseful of siblings. His brother John was about to become Mayor of North Brisbane. With his family intact and his ten thousand acres secure, Tom had not the slightest inkling what it meant to be orphaned far from home, the solitary victim of an unrecognised atrocity.

'There will be an Inquiry, brother. There has to be. And Father is still holding the scripts for half your whaleboat,' Tom encouraged. 'What if,' he went on, 'you come and work at Murrumba for a moon – perhaps two, if it works out that way. When the mustering is done and the cattle sold, I'll loan you the remainder. Then you can build your boat or buy one ready-made, and sail home with Nita, the way you've always talked about.'

Mulanyin grunted non-committedly. Hearing Tom speak, the fisherman in him realised that deep down he still craved a life at sea. But the idea of heading north to get it, travelling away from his responsibilities to his murdered family, was impossible. His people needed ceremony. Each step towards Murrumba would feel like betrayal.

'Home? I don't know where home even is anymore, brother,' he muttered. 'Dawalbin buried Annie's placenta beside the Warrar. My family line at Nerang is broken ... and really, so am I. What good am I to anyone?'

'Brother,' Tom responded, choosing his words with great care, 'I have something serious to tell you. Listen to me. Dalapai heard something two nights ago from his nephew, just back from

Goompie. Now, mind what I say – I have no idea if his information is true or not.'

Mulanyin stared at his feet. What new horrors might Tom be about to reveal?

'Dalapai's nephew heard some talk that two Goorie girls were kidnapped recently by a Hindoo named Brown,' Tom went on. 'He was told they were taken to the Wide Bay as servants. Well, *servants* – we may as well say slaves. My point is, they are said to be Nerang Creek girls of perhaps eight and eleven.'

'My sisters?' Mulanyin blurted, leaping up and spilling his beer. For a moment, he remembered what it was to have hope. Then suspicion took hold of him, and he scowled. 'Is this true? Or just a tricky means of sending me away to Murrumba? If you lie to me about these Nerang girls, I swear I'll—'

'We have no way of knowing if the rumour is true,' Tom interrupted. 'But all I've said to you now is exactly what's been passed on to me. Do you really believe I'd lie, brother, just to get your labour? About your only remaining *blood?*'

Mulanyin gulped the dregs of his grog, then tossed the bottle aside. It rolled downhill to the end of the yard, clinking against the mound of others at rest in the long grass. He squinted at his companion. Tom might not deceive him to get his labour, no, but he might lie in Yerrin's service. He especially might lie to lure him away from the meagre comfort of Chow's pipe. Mulanyin was desperate to believe that his sisters might be alive in Maryborough. But the price of false hope would be horrendous. 'You want me to abandon my duties on a rumour,' he muttered. 'And leave my parents unburied to chase a fantasy.'

'You don't know for certain your people are unburied. Other Kombumerri may have performed their rites, or the Minyangbal, or the Pretty Face Wallaby People … and think hard on this, too, brother: you took the word of a stranger that all at Nerang are finished. This new rumour is much the same – the word of a stranger, passed on by Dalapai's nephew, who we both know is a man of the Bora, and cannot lie to me on pain of death.'

Mulanyin folded his arms, shaken by the possibilities Tom presented. It was something to hope for – his sisters, alive in the north.

The Native Police were often in the Wide Bay now, hunting landowners across great swathes of Country. Goories had been dispersed from K'gari to Cabulture, a trail of butchered bodies in Marshall's wake, the new Commandant carrying on Freddy Walker's legacy with terrible zeal. And the Maryborough township was very far from Brisbane – a day by steamer; four days ride, at least. While not one hundred steps from where Mulanyin stood was Chow's hut.

'True enough. But you might think on this, *Mister Petrie*,' Mulanyin replied, stepping around Tom and heading back to the lane. 'Who would you believe? If it was all your family slaughtered and you stood in my place, an orphan, with only your tears and a pipe for comfort? Tell me Tom – whose yarn would you believe?'

~

Several days later, Mulanyin arrived home at dusk holding a wood duck by the neck. It was not a fat wood duck, nor was it a large one. He found himself glad that the twilight was dim.

'Hmmm,' Nita pursed her lips from where she sat beside the fire. 'Give it here, then. I'll stuff it with lemon myrtle leaves, if you got any.'

Mulanyin lay the bird on the sand, then silently flicked his palms downward to show that no lemon myrtle seasoning was on offer. Nita rolled her eyes as she began to encase the bird in clay.

'Is there a problem?' Mulanyin snapped.

Nita didn't reply immediately. 'Tom sent word,' she said a minute later, attempting to lift his spirits with her own cheerfulness. 'He leaves for Murrumba in two days. Asks you to go with him and meet his new bride. He reckons you'd better meet her in case you ever inherit her. Apparently, he's shaved off that long beard and he looks like a different man!'

Mulanyin twisted his mouth sourly. As if any waymerigan would understand the Law of the Federation or keep to it if she did. Anyway, dagai women of the Petries' class had their own families to support them in widowhood. Be damned if he'd take on another mouth to feed should Tom somehow be killed. It was hard enough providing for the family he already had.

'He can send for me all he wants,' Mulanyin responded. 'I'm not planning on becoming his damn servant.'

Nita sighed. Mulanyin had stayed away from Chow's for three days and had been sleeping at the village where he belonged. On the other hand, he was now avoiding the river, for reasons she couldn't fathom. Her husband's run got smaller day by day, and his catch with it. She wondered if it was farfetched to put this behaviour down to the river being the avenue to the Bay; and the Bay being the place where the Murry Jerry murders had been revealed to him. Whatever the reason, Mulanyin was now struggling to bring home the food his family needed. The Woolloongabba Swamp was raided day and night by all manner of men, and even that rich landscape failed when the old rules were ignored. Only this morning, she'd seen a man openly eating kuril and then laughing when an Elder woman chastised him.

'Don't bloody sigh at me!' Mulanyin erupted. 'I'm no white man's fucking slave! And I'm not yours, either!' He lunged forward, grabbing at Nita's wrist and attempting to pull her to her feet. Nita pulled back, resisting strongly, and without thinking Mulanyin raised his free hand high as though to strike her.

Rather than flinch, Nita looked down at his fingers encircling her forearm. 'Yugam ngaya wulala wahlu wogai,' she pronounced icily. *I did not give you permission to touch me.*

246

Mulanyin stared at her for a long moment, unblinking. Then he dropped her wrist.

Nita got to her feet and went over to the stone slab where women still occasionally processed bungwall. She picked up the wooden basher and began thumping a few tubers into pulp. How dare any man seize her in anger! How dare he! She breathed heavily as she worked, trying to make sense of what had just happened.

Hearing his woman pound the tubers, Mulanyin recalled the very same sound echoing up and down Nerang Creek while his Waijungs laughed and yarned over their work. He clutched at his temples, knowing he would never hear his mother make bungwall damper again.

'I won't be sent for by any dagai,' he repeated fiercely. 'For any reason. Even Tom.'

Nita did not forgive his transgression. 'You can go now.'

Mulanyin stood helpless.

'Don't stand there staring at me like an owl that's seen a kuril. I have work to do. Someone has to feed this family.'

Mulanyin's nostrils flared. 'I'm so pleased,' he began sarcastically, 'that you can provide for us. Thank goodness. When all I can bring to our fire is crab and duck and mutton flaps, how wonderful it is to know we won't starve for want of bungwall.'

'I haven't eaten crab for days,' Nita countered. 'As for mutton flaps, I wouldn't even remember what they look like if not for Missus Petrie. You are deep in grief, I know. But husband, we have a growing daughter to feed. Please, tell me you're going to fish the Warrar again, instead of the damn swamp! Every other man goes to the Warrar, so why can't you?'

'Because I saw ... something.'

'Saw *what?*'

It was Mulanyin's turn to heave a loud sigh. The gleaming dark muscle of his chest rose and fell. He pressed his palm heels into his eyes and grimaced. 'It is too awful to speak of.'

'I don't understand you anymore, husband. You snap and growl and sulk like an old dingo with rheumatism, but you won't tell me anything I don't already know.' Nita hadn't slept. The night feeds and walking long hours to soothe Annie left her with nothing in reserve. Her patience with Mulanyin finally expired. 'Perhaps I should take Annie and just go back to work at Petrie Bight?' she threatened. 'Where I'm wanted, and sorely missed, and the food is always heaped on—'

'I saw a dead infant,' Mulanyin interrupted, his eyes welling. 'Last moon. It was bobbing on the high tide at Stanley Quay, his little white body … oh, such cruelty! The tides which used to bring our people bounty now bring only horror and death.'

Nita's mouth fell open.

'What has this life become?' Mulanyin cried, his face contorting with misery. 'What sort of world is it, Nita, where tiny infants can be discarded to rot, and a People be slaughtered for the loss of a single bullock?'

Nita had no answer. She put down her bungwall pounder and spent a moment collecting the fern-root dough in her hands. She stood, patting it into a sphere while she thought.

'Where will the spirit of that poor dead child rest?' Mulanyin cried.

'Its spirit will rest where the tides take it. Perhaps back to its Muttakundrei,' Nita replied, trying to comfort him. 'And besides, husband, who knows who that baby could have grown to be, anyway? Another good man like Tom Petrie? Or would it have grown to do evil? It might have been another Freddy Walker, or a Warry. And if not an evildoer, then one like most dagai, those who see evil done and say nothing, and look in the other direction at what's easy to see. Don't stand there and ask me to mourn an infant that could grow up to laugh at our people's fate.'

'I didn't think of it that way exactly,' Mulanyin said slowly. 'But you're right.'

'We'll have so many children, man, six or eight or ten! And our sons and daughters will each have many descendants. And that's how we'll replace every Goorie shot, or poisoned, or starved to death for want of a Country. We'll win this war and the dagai will have to go home if we can just stay strong. Then there will be no dead babies in the Warrar and no murders of landowners either. The Law will be honoured. And maybe, Mulanyin, just maybe, your sisters *are* alive, still, and waiting for you to find them …'

She went to him then and led him into their oompie where they lay together. 'Find me another child spirit,' Nita whispered in Mulanyin's ear, 'give me a son this time, as brave as you are, and with my strong heart.' When their lovemaking was over, they rested in each other's embrace and cried, tears of pain and joy and hope mingling on their faces. Annie stirred and gave a little cry, then settled back into slumber on her possum-skin rug.

'She's such a good baby,' Mulanyin glowed. 'I can go on, for her,' he said, getting up on his elbow to watch the child, 'and for you, my love. I'll find strength enough to go to Murrumba and work a moon. Then buy my boat and sail to the Wide Bay and find my sisters.'

'Good. I'll wait for your sisters to come and meet their new daughter,' Nita answered, her heart lifting. As she spoke, Mulanyin used his forefinger to lightly trace the tear tracks on her face, wiping them into invisible patterns that only she would ever feel or know about. She closed her eyes at the pleasure of his touch.

'Be safe while I'm away,' he blurted. 'Make sure Dawalbin or Yerrin know where you are at all times, and don't leave the village. Or maybe you *should* go back to the Petries until I come home,' he fretted. 'You'll be safe and well fed under their roof.'

Nita laughed. 'Haven't I done ten years' hard labour for Missus Petrie already?' she teased. 'I think I know how to manage without mopping floors and peeling vegetables. Besides, it's relaxing here. I don't have to speak English, and everyone dotes on Annie.'

'South Brisbane's changing,' Mulanyin cautioned, 'with more strangers coming in on every tide …'

Nita promised her husband she'd stay well clear of the immigrants at the dock, and the myriad drunks surrounding the inns. In her heart, though, she felt his worry was ridiculous; it was Mulanyin going up to the dangerous territory of the Wide Bay, not her.

24. An Intelligent Wife

1855

'Nita's certainly a canny lass,' Tom offered, as his horse snorted and propped at one of Dalapai's dogs that had followed them up Queen Street. 'You've done well to catch hold of her.' He shouted at the mutt to go home, then spurred his mare forward.

Mulanyin shook his head. Had Tom forgotten his manners completely while away on the goldfields? Any Goorie man talking that way would be asking for a spear.

'And your wife is no doubt considered attractive by many also – for a waymerigan.'

Tom stuck his tongue hard into his cheek before deciding to laugh this comment off. 'Fair call,' he grunted.

The two men were headed to Murrumba, despite heavy overnight rain turning the river brown and transforming the roads into muddy streams. Tom had decided that morning not to wait any longer for John Logan's band of Yugambeh workmen to arrive. He didn't entirely blame the Logan crowd for failing to turn up. Pastor Haussman at Waterford had first claim on their labour. And although the Logan and Kurilpa were allies, quite willing to work alongside each other, Murrumba was a long way to travel for an unfamiliar boss, as Dalapai had pointed out over breakfast. He'd advised Tom to cut his losses and leave without them.

Now, trailed rather comically by a string of stray goats, mongrel dogs and even, for a short distance, the Petries' elder cat Gilbert, the two riders headed off for the Sandgate Road. Tom's mood was sombre. His initial euphoria about owning Murrumba had lately come hard up against legal complications to do with land title, and the harsh reality of building an entire working station from scratch. His slab house was complete now, and his new bride installed, but there were dozens of workmen's huts still to put up, several cattle yards and a shearing shed to finish, not to mention the constant rounds of mustering, branding and fencing essential to keep his stock his own. Tom had a dozen workmen at Murrumba, but the ongoing labour shortages in Moreton Bay kept him awake at night.

He changed the subject away from wives, extolling the virtues of the champion collie he was about to import from Melbourne. The five-year-old dog would form the foundation of a line of working sheepdogs that would outrun and outwork any in New South Wales, he claimed. A well-bred collie was easily worth three shepherds. The dog would earn him a pretty penny at stud, to boot. Tom was confident the investment would pay off.

'Not that we'll be living in New South Wales for long,' he went on, 'our children will grow up in their own State, brother! We'll be independent of Sydney and chart our own course.'

Mulanyin's brow crinkled at this. Dagai names for Country mattered very little to him, and he was distracted in any case by the sight of Commandant Marshall and six of his troopers washing muddy packhorses over in Wheat Creek. A spring-cart full of trunks and wooden casks rattled past the black troops on its way to Fortitude Valley; two hungover men on riding hacks were returning to town in the opposite direction, both riders tipping their hats to Tom.

'What's them ugly foreign bastards up to now?' Mulanyin pondered, speaking Yugambeh as he often did now with Tom. His companion shielded his eyes from the glare off the creek.

The Native Police had stopped washing their horses and stood alert, watching them go by. Radiating arrogance and hostility, they clearly recognised Mulanyin from their encounter in Queen Street all those months ago, before Freddy Walker was sacked in disgrace. Tom nodded curtly at the new Commandant, Marshall, who nodded back from the far side of the stream. Mulanyin felt the stares of the black troops land on his skin and bristled. He was relieved to be by Tom's side as they headed out of town. The Petrie name held weight everywhere in Moreton Bay, and with Tom next to him the Native Police were near powerless to do him harm.

As they left the tents and huts of Spring Hill behind, Mulanyin began musing about the Chinese prisoners they'd heard when passing the gaol.

'What a strange situation the Celestials find themselves in,' Mulanyin began, 'far from their own Country, trying to organise themselves into unions, and hated by so many. Why come here, for so little reward?'

'The same reason any men leave home, I suppose. Looking for a better life.'

China must be unbearable, Mulanyin decided, if slaving on dirty building sites for dagai who loathed them was preferable to staying home. Shepherding stupid sheep in the scrub would be even worse, given the spears and waddies of angry landowners, which had ended so many Celestial lives.

'There are thousands of Chinese down south,' Tom went on, 'creating all sorts of jealousy and havoc. The British send them packing when they can, but they multiply anyway – the roads to the Victorian diggings are a river of Celestials, along with the Americans of course. Even though the government has slapped a surcharge on them, they keep coming and taking gold out of the hands of white men. It'll end in more bloodshed, no doubt about it. The red ribbon brigade won't be pushed about.'

'The Americans in the south, are they white or black men?'

Tom laughed. 'White, of course. The black Americans are not free to travel. But the dagai Americans come in droves. I shared a tent with one who had lived for a time with the natives of his homeland.'

'Which place?' Mulanyin was interested in the Goories of all Countries, but he had never heard that there were any in America.

'In his part of America, called Kansas, there are great flat plains full of game, antelope and buffalo. The native people there live in strange, pointed tents and worship horses, he said. And they believe that the thunder is a god speaking to them, and that if a man kills a spider, he will make the rains come. The government there is trying to drive them further west, and they are fighting to stay on their Countries.'

Mulanyin was fascinated by these ideas. Resolving to explore them at length that night, he switched to another topic.

'What do the southern landowners do about these Americans and Chinese, all coming to dig the gold from beneath their land?'

'They aren't happy,' Tom said. 'But what can they do in the face of European civilisation? First, they were settled by the likes of McMillan. And now invaded by Chinese, who transform their land with such industry they hardly recognise it. But they're an interesting lot, the Koories. A Christian mission has been set up for them, where many have converted and found safe haven. There is even a native man down there who has invented a remarkable system for communicating by radio waves – using a kind of electric box. A Koorie man, I mean.'

'They should all stay home on the far side of their rivers,' sniffed Mulanyin, thinking again of the staring black troopers they had seen earlier. 'Nobody asked them to come up here and murder us.'

'Most *have* stayed at home, brother. Though their numbers grow fewer, and the half-castes are on the increase. I met one senior Elder in Melbourne, a keen strategist,' reflected Tom, 'and a student of the human spirit. He put me in mind of Dalapai, or my father. One of those old grey men, the thinkers who have truly seen into the heart of things.'

This was highfalutin talk from Tom, whose conversation since his return centred on cattle, labour and the prospect of Separation. It gave Mulanyin hope that his erstwhile companion might not have become a complete philistine after all.

'A pity they didn't send their great Elder up here, then, instead of the murdering scum we passed before. But when you say the Goorie man has invented a way of communicating with an electric box, do you mean ...' Mulanyin paused then, hearing horses cantering up behind.

He and Tom both turned to see Commandant Marshall drawing near, with two troopers in his wake.

'Mornin, Petrie.'

Marshall was a man of average height with no fat on him, Mulanyin observed. He knew Native Police detachments spent long weeks and months travelling the bush, living on dry rations and kangaroo, and whatever foodstuffs the local squatters were prepared to sell them at the low government rates they paid. A hard and hungry life, reflected Mulanyin, for a band of miserable assassins, who deserved much worse for their sins.

Marshall and Tom exchanged some banalities about the weather and Mulanyin grew distracted. Just above the line of the Commandant's beard, he noticed, the man's left cheek bore an inflammation. Probably a bush tick had burrowed into the flesh there and a hard permanent lump had formed around the bite. The angry inflammation drew the eye; looking at it made Mulanyin's own face begin to itch. How, he wondered, did the detachment get on in the scrub anyway, their thick uniforms horribly hot and scratchy, a veritable cage for all sorts of burrowing and biting insects. He knew that when the troopers were hunting Goories they shed their uniforms, going naked through the scrub except for the peaked caps they wore to avoid shooting each other in the chaos.

Both the black troopers lounging here on their horses, almost close enough for him to touch, had surely murdered innocent people. He shivered. What must it feel like to kill somebody from far away with a rifle, he wondered, instead of at close range with a spear or waddie? Although rifle butts and stirrup irons were said to be used very often, to save wasting bullets out in the scrub where—

'I'm arresting your black, Petrie,' said Marshall. 'In the Queen's name.'

'What? On what charge?' Tom laughed.

'Rape.'

'You're joking?!'

'Rape of a white woman – I don't call that a joke.' The Commandant began to unhook the handcuffs from his saddle.

Tom shot a look at Mulanyin, who was poised to flee into the scrub of Green Hills and take his chances. 'Best not run,' he said quickly in Yagara, 'or he will surely shoot you. Let me handle this.'

Mulanyin paused a second too long, the troopers drew closer, and his chance to flee had passed.

'Rape of a Mrs Walsh, at Logan,' Marshall went on. 'He was seen in the area with an accomplice.'

'Don't be ridiculous,' Tom fired back. 'I know this fellow very well and he's of upstanding character. Seen by who?'

'The woman's husband, returning from Canoe Creek. Your boy and another nigger were seen leaving together along Slacks Track. When Walsh got home, the woman was distressed, having been violated by both blacks. He matches her description perfectly.'

Marshall made a curt gesture and the two troopers grabbed Mulanyin, forcing him down from his horse and handcuffing him to their bosses' stirrup with an air of righteous satisfaction. In a daze, Mulanyin saw one of the troopers lift the reins over the head of his gelding and hand them to Tom.

'What's happening?' Mulanyin cried to Tom. 'Stop them, brother, quick! I'm a dead man if they take me in!'

'You won't die over this rubbish,' Tom frowned. 'Commandant, you're making a serious mistake. This man is my worker and I'd trust him with my life. The Walsh woman is either mistaken or a liar.'

'Ballow signed the warrant,' replied Marshall, waving a warrant at Petrie. 'And the Court will decide if she's lying, not you or I.'

'Help me, brothers!' Mulanyin screamed into the scrub of Windmill Hill. 'I'm being murdered! Brothers! Help me!'

The troopers glanced into the bush either side of the road, unconcerned. Dalapai's people were two miles away at Breakfast Creek and any Goories working in town were well out of earshot in the other direction.

'Callem bit louder,' sneered one trooper. 'Mebbe Yerrin bin hear you longa Kurilpa.'

Mulanyin stared at this bald-headed southerner, committing every detail of his appearance to memory. 'I will execute you,' he swore in Yugambeh. 'I'll kill you the very first chance I get, you lying criminal piece of shit, and your accomplices too. And I'll stomp your kidneys to pulp and toss your beating hearts to the dogs.'

The troopers laughed open-mouthed, showing him their contempt with their teeth and tongues. They didn't need to speak Yugambeh to recognise Mulanyin's threats – they had heard many such speeches in their bloody careers. They knew, too, that angry words are the tool of the weaponless and the weak.

'Harm him and you'll have me to deal with,' Tom told the black men curtly. He went on to inform Marshall that he was going to be in a mess of trouble before the day was out. Not only was Mulanyin an honest kippa and a close friend to the Petries, he was sorely needed for the upcoming muster at Murrumba, as was Tom himself. Being delayed was a huge impost.

'Be that as it may,' the officer answered, tucking the warrant inside his breast pocket, 'my orders are clear. He's wanted for rape and he'll go to trial. I don't doubt he'll hang.' With that, the Commandant turned and trotted towards town, dragging his manacled prisoner along beside his polished boot.

'Don't panic, brother,' Tom told Mulanyin as he cantered past, also heading in the direction of town. 'My father'll straighten this out, and we'll both be at Murrumba by Friday.'

~

Five Chinese prisoners sat and talked in the open yard of the gaol, their clipped tongue sounding to Mulanyin like Ah Yow's abacus, or the clatter of ceremonial burrang. Sounds with plenty of meaning to them, but little music. In the neighbouring cell, Tim Shea raved about sacrificial sheep and myalls, and of needing to be washed in the blood of the lamb. Mulanyin paid little heed to either conversation. He stood on the stone floor of his cell, trembling with fury. His options were to escape, or else submit to the white man's court in the hope he'd be found innocent and his life spared. A choice that was no choice at all. Luckily for him, Warder Armstrong was an infamously bad shot.

The aged brick gaol was a low building with wide arches at its front to admit men and horses from Queen Street. It faced the Wilwinpa scrub and the Windmill. If Mulanyin hauled himself up by the bars to look out, he had a clear view of the spot where Dundalli had been put to death. It was not a comforting sight. He preferred to sit and gaze instead at the pockmarked stone of his cell which other convicts had dug from the Kangaroo Point cliffs years ago.

Mulanyin could see where desperate inmates had picked at the mortar binding the stone blocks together, using sticks or tools, perhaps even their fingernails. Everywhere the white men go, Mulanyin thought, they mark their passage in stone and iron, for there is no softness in them. All they understand is guns and whips, shackles and steel. All their world is built on cruelty. He closed his eyes, shutting out the noise of Tim Shea and the Chinese, concentrating instead on what he could hear outside.

He longed to hear his own people's voices, or birdsong, or at least the wind in the trees. Petrie Bight was two minutes away – he dreamed he might hear Nita, or indeed any of the Petries, if they called out to someone in the garden or the street. But he only heard the conversation of strangers and a dog barking at a builder's dray lumbering past. The banana grove on the street corner opposite the gaol rustled in the breeze. Workers pushed wheelbarrows between shops and houses, one whistling 'Loch Lomond'. The regiment were drilling up at the barracks, and in the distance a child laughed. Birds called: crows, wrens, a pair of king parrots. He imagined he heard Nita calling his name.

He opened his eyes to find Nita, not imaginary but real, and standing in the street below his barred window.

'Nita!' he cried. 'Where's Tom? What's happening? Is he getting Grandfather Petrie to free me? Where's Yerrin? And Dalapai?'

'Tom's gone to fetch John from Albion,' she told him. 'And Grandfather Petrie has already left for Newstead to see Captain Wickham about freeing you. Tom and John will meet him there. Yerrin's at Canoe Creek, not back till tomorrow. Are you hurt? Did they bash you?'

'Not much,' Mulanyin lied. The native troopers had delivered a score of stunning blows to his skull and body, with threats of far worse to come. He had a splitting headache and his ribs were on fire. 'I'm alright. Nita, my love, go to Petrie Bight and stay inside. Don't go out. The dagai will make a victim of you too. Hide there till I come for you – one way or another.'

'What are you talking about?' Nita was perturbed by this hint of escape. 'What if the warder understands?' She came around the corner of the gaol and glanced in at Armstrong from the front of the gaol.

'What's your name?' she asked in Yagara.

'Wot?'

'Where are your people from?'

'Quit jabbering, yer savage. Speak English!' He stared as though Nita was a talking dog. Relieved, she went back to the side street.

'The mortar's weak in places,' Mulanyin continued. 'All I need you to bring me is a nail or a piece of strong wire. I think I can loosen a window bar.'

'But Grandfather Petrie will insist you are freed!' Nita was deeply agitated now and working her apron in her hands. 'Husband, listen to me – even if you did get away alive, you'd need to stay hidden. We'd be driven apart – and what if they take Annie?' Nita's throat constricted. The young couple had never made their Christian vows. Mired in grief, Mulanyin had refused point blank to convert, and so their beloved daughter was a bastard in British eyes. Annie could be taken by any white family in need of a black doll to decorate their home. If her father was an escaped convict, the danger would never end. Nita felt faint. A few hours earlier she'd waved Mulanyin off to Murrumba, concerned only that he might be gored by a bullock or drown in a flooded creek. Now *this*!

'Grandfather Petrie's probably talking to Wickham right now!' she pleaded.

'And if they kill me tonight?'

'They know the Petries are our friends,' Nita begged. 'They wouldn't dare murder you, husband. Don't be rash, *please*. I'll be back in town as soon as I collect Annie from Dawalbin.'

She gave the bread and meat she had brought to the warder, and ran; she couldn't free Mulanyin, but she could take her daughter into her arms and never let her go.

~

260

Nita was right, Mulanyin told himself. Infuriating though it was to be caged like a pig or a goat, and however much he wanted to choke the life out of Warder Armstrong, he needed to exercise patience. Better to sit still for a day than risk death escaping. He would listen to the dogs bark and the carts wheeling past. The flies buzzing. Smell the familiar stench of tar drums burning outside the shanties in the side streets. Hear children screaming at Frog Hollow and smell the tobacco smoke drifting in from a gentleman's pipe as he passed by. He could picture the scene outside: could hear the cries of the gulls in Petrie Bight and the thump of carpenters nailing a roof near the Bogey Hole. Tom would surely come soon, and Grandfather Petrie, and Yerrin. The cell door would swing open and this insult to his character would be wiped away, no more than a bad memory.

He waited for tedious hours as the sun climbed high, his thoughts whirling and zigzagging around the accusation of rape. Who had really violated the waymerigan at Logan? And how could he prove it wasn't him, but some other long-limbed Goorie breaking the sacred Law forbidding rape, and managing to land him in this mess of confusion and peril? Had a genuine mistake been made by some careless dagai who'd mistaken his identity – or was an enemy intent on engineering his death at white hands? Maybe he'd brought this fate on himself? Perhaps this was punishment from the Ancestors for failing to avenge the murder of his family. Mulanyin clenched his fists then, at the thought of his parents dead at Murry Jerry Station; he began hammering at the rough-hewn walls as he cried out in useless rage.

Eventually he slumped to the floor, head in his hands, imprisoned by his guilt and terror as well as by massive blocks of stone. But he had powerful friends, he told himself, and must above all be strong. His life had made him strong, and the Bora. He was not a town dandy nor a criminal, but a man of the Law. Tom would arrive soon, and Yerrin, and Grandfather Petrie, and all of them would help him. The door would swing open. He would be free.

~

On the third day of his imprisonment, Warder Armstrong shoved a plate through the bars of Mulanyin's cell. 'Ere, monkey.'

A mess of cold skillagee, along with some bungwall tubers. Nita had failed to clean them properly and a few tiny clods of dirt still hung off the narrow fern roots. Mulanyin looked at the meal with an unimpressed grunt.

The Warder chuckled. 'Oh, yer gin brung some mutton flaps, too, but I saved yer the trouble of eatin em. Very tasty, they was.'

Mulanyin scowled. He would rather die than rise to the taunts of a man like Armstrong, an incompetent as well as a bully; too old to run far, and notoriously unable to hit the side of a barn at twenty paces. Dimly aware of his inferiority, Armstrong had developed the compensatory habit of standing at Mulanyin's cell door, asking him every hour whether he was a monkey or an ape. At first Mulanyin responded at length, outlining in Yugambeh the ways he planned to avenge himself on Armstrong and any family he might happen to have, but yesterday evening an emaciated Upriver man named Billy and his coughing sister, Poll, were brought in on charges of fowl-stealing. Now Mulanyin spent his time conversing with them. All three Goories made a point of completely ignoring Armstrong.

How long would it take to run the twenty paces to the wall of the prison yard? Mulanyin gazed down at his long legs. Could they carry him fast enough to save his life? And would it be best to swerve and duck in the open yard as he ran, or to simply sprint in a straight line for the wall and hope Armstrong's pistol missed as he climbed to freedom? These questions went round in his mind endlessly, as they'd done the entire time he'd waited for Tom to secure his freedom. Wasted time, as it turned out. Mulanyin was beginning to suspect that of the Petries, only Tom truly believed in his innocence.

'Father's written to the Governor,' Tom had said the previous afternoon. 'If you're sent to trial in Sydney over this, my word and that of Father and John will stand you in very good stead. And there *must* be an Official Inquiry into the Native Police as well. Everyone in Moreton Bay knows what they do in the regions and the mood is fast growing for reform, and for justice.'

Mulanyin's heart had skipped a beat, hearing this fatuous speech. Did Tom actually believe that any Bora composed of dagai would want the truth, or care one jot if he was hanged for another man's crime?

'Words are just that,' he had muttered. 'No piece of paper will save me.'

'We'll prove your innocence, brother. Believe me, we will! The woman claims she was attacked not long after Easter, when I was still away. Do you know where you were, then?'

Mulanyin shrugged hopelessly. Nita had taught him what Christmas meant for the baptised. And of course, he knew Sunday, the day when blacks must stay out of town, and the dagai wore clean clothes if they had them, and the church bells rang thrice: first with the magpies and then when the sun was high, and lastly with the call of the kookaburras at dusk. But his life was measured not by church bells but by the blossom of wattle and oodgeroo, by the cycles of the planets and the stars. Summer and Winter Solstices, the Mullet Run, the emergence of the goannas from their burrows when the cold earth grew warm: these were the markers of Goorie life, not the white man's paper nonsense brought from a far distant land.

'I wasn't at the damn Logan,' Mulanyin told him, losing patience. 'Father told me to stick by Yerrin and that's what I've done.'

'Listen,' Tom cocked his head towards the barred window, 'Dalapai's people are back. They sing on Wilwinpa Hill.'

'I heard them corroboree last night.' Mulanyin paused. Dalapai's people would always circle back to the hill above North Brisbane. 'Tom, listen to me – I've made a decision: I'll not die as the Dalla warrior died. I dream of him, night after night – his face as he stood on the gallows, that terrible noise he made at the end. I wake up screaming in the very cell that held him. Do you understand?'

Tom was afraid to respond.

'I refuse to finish that way.'

'But we'll prove you innocent, man!' Tom cried. 'Don't talk about dying! I'm long overdue at the muster and can't stay, but John and Father are both agreed: we'll leave no stone unturned to free you. I beg you my brother – be patient just a few more days.'

Tom stood up to leave, hat in hand, his face downcast.

'Don't trouble yourself about me, Tom,' Mulanyin made a contemptuous gesture at the stone walls. 'My life won't end in this cursed box. I'm going to go and find my sisters and bring them home.'

'And then? Where will you live, if you do manage to escape?'

'Where does the wind live, Tom? Where does the tide live? I am a free man, and I'll live like one.'

Tom had clamped his hat on then and put both his forearms through the bars, taking hold of Mulanyin's. They stood that way a minute. Then Tom turned and left for Murrumba.

Putting these bittersweet memories aside now, Mulanyin gave a wry smile and picked up the bungwall that Armstrong had flung at him. He rubbed the dirt away from the tubers, giving thanks for such an intelligent wife. He nibbled at the roots, taking great care not to damage his teeth.

When he was done, a square-head horseshoe nail lay secreted in his palm. The handmade nail, blackened and a little bent, would be his salvation. It might be his life. And if it wasn't, he thought grimly, then let all Brisbane fall. He lifted the nail, pointing it in the direction of the Barracks, the Windmill; at Mayne's butcher shop and Warry's chemist, condemning the entire town as he pointed. Let fire and flood and pestilence follow my murder, he muttered. *They can all burn.*

On the sixth day of Mulanyin's imprisonment, soldiers came and dragged Chow's friend, Zhang, from his cell. The yellow man fought hard, biting and kicking, protesting the entire length of the stone walkway leading to the main gate. 'I won't die,' he screamed. 'I won't die.'

They hanged him anyway.

Words are one thing, Mulanyin reflected as he witnessed this, and deeds are another thing entirely. A great calm fell upon him. The Ancestors had sent him the sign he had needed.

When dark arrived that evening, he cast off his ragged trousers and smeared his entire body with the mutton fat Nita had bribed Armstrong to allow him to keep. He stowed his horseshoe nail deep in his hair and prayed to the Ancestors for their help and guidance in whatever followed. Then Mulanyin reached up to yank out the loosened window bar, and slithered out into the prison yard.

He ran for the high stone wall as Armstrong fired.

At the sound of the first pistol shot, Nita woke on the veranda at Petrie Bight. At the second, she leapt to her feet. When the crack of the third shot came, she collapsed on the veranda. Her nightdress pooled around her like a shroud.

'Did you hear that?' Andrew Petrie asked as he entered the parlour. 'Three pistol shots, I think?' Mary looked up from her sewing and agreed that yes, she had. They listened intently to the yapping of the town strays. But there were no more disturbing sounds, and once the dogs had quietened, no sign that anything was amiss.

'I hope nobody's been hurt,' Mary said, examining her

embroidery for puckers. She undid her last few stitches and turned the lamp up higher.

'I've got good news about Mulanyin,' Grandfather Petrie announced cheerfully. 'Although somewhat confusing news, to be truthful. John ran into Tim Shea being released this afternoon, you know, the shepherd. Apparently, he passed by the Walsh farm on the day the woman says she was assaulted.'

'Oh?' Mary looked up.

'He stopped and helped her. An odd story – two grown bullocks had become entangled by their horns and had to be sawn apart, can you imagine it? But the point is, he says Mrs Walsh was in good spirits that noonday, and alone but for her bairns. He also said he saw her undergarments waiting to be washed, and, well – according to him it was her time of month. He put it far more crudely, of course, being the type of man he is.'

Mary gaped at her husband.

'But no native man would ever touch—'

'Exactly my point,' Andrew Petrie agreed, beaming. 'Mulanyin's innocence is proven, along with the innocence of every myall in the district.'

25. Bicentenary Week

2024

'Funny thing,' said Granny Eddie to Dartmouth, cheerfully sipping her last mouthful of tea, 'mooki. You'd think a hospital would be full of em, hundreds. Thousands. But there's only Grandad ere that I can make out.'

'Is he back again?' Dartmouth asked, taking Granny's food tray and putting it in the corridor. A pragmatist, he had entered a neutral zone of neither belief nor disbelief in Granny's invisible companion. It saved argument.

'Yeah, but he's gone a bit quiet, cept about what's owed to him,' Granny said, rolling her eyes. 'Be different if he'd *tell* a person what he wants. I mean he was always full of stories. Jokes, yarns. You'd never shut him up. He's like a bloomin oyster now, compared to back then.'

My life's not a joke! retorted the ghost, still indistinct in the rear corner. Granny swivelled in bed where she sat and immediately began to topple sideways. Dartmouth grabbed her just in time to stop her sliding onto the hard floor.

'Yer putting words in my mouth now,' she accused when she was upright again. 'I said nothing of the sort! You *really* can't see him, Darto? Well, but how? His legs are sticking right out from behind that blue curtain, right there?'

Dartmouth peered into the back of the room, his mouth

watering at the mention of oysters. He'd love a dozen fresh Sydney rock oysters with a slice of lemon squeezed over the top. There was nothing to see in the rear corner, he told Eddie, but an ugly vinyl chair, a blue privacy sheet hanging off a metal frame and the concertina room divider that had been tied back against the wall for the entire nine weeks of Eddie's stay.

'Nothing I can see, sorry.' Then Dartmouth decided to try something rather radical. He addressed the vacant room himself. 'What is it you want, Grandad Oyster? Grandad *Charlie*, I mean?'

I'm no damn oyster! The ghost erupted in sudden rage. *Nor a tree! I have a name given to me by my Grandfather.*

'Jesus Christ,' stammered Dartmouth. 'It's, it's real – I can hear him! Fucking hell, Eddie!'

'Of course, he's damn well real, I told—' Granny Eddie pursed her lips, realising that Darto had been humouring her for weeks. Bloody whitefellas! Never listen. Winona was right, she should have gotten rid of Darto at the start, before he wormed his way in and somehow turned into a friend.

'But what does he mean, not an oyster or a *tree*?' Dartmouth interrupted. Granny could see the pulse in his neck going nineteen to the dozen. Darto wanted to get on some blood pressure meds onetime, or he'd be pushing up daisies before she was.

'Whatcha on about, Grandad?' she posed the question. 'Talking bout trees? Can't ya take a joke no more?'

You insist on calling me jali, but my yuri is no tree. It is the blue heron.

Eddie's teacup fell from her hand and promptly broke in half on the polished linoleum. The china pieces rolled out of sight beneath her bed. As Dartmouth automatically bent to retrieve them, Eddie clutched at his arm. Sweat had broken out on her top lip, and her hand trembled as she stared at the figure obscured by the curtain.

'Grandad's totem wasn't the blue heron! Are you Grandad Charlie or what? Who the hell are you?'

I am Mulanyin of the Yugambeh, Old Woman, adopted son of Yerrin and Dawalbin, and I will not leave this place till I get what's mine.

~

Johnny groaned. 'How can you be in such a good mood at this hour?'

'Oh, I bin laughing meself silly since we ripped them suits,' Winona handed Johnny an extra strong espresso and plonked herself down on the end of his bed. She crossed her legs and stuffed half a croissant in her mouth. 'Them mob didn't know if they was Arthur or Martha by the time we was done. They even had the fucken caucasity to try and school Nan about massacres.'

'Oh, no!'

'Oh, yes. But don't worry, we set em straight, real fucken quick.'

Despite his hangover, Johnny managed a laugh. That would have been something to see.

'The big boss tried to get a bit mouthy about the massacre plaques. I told him straight up, well let's have one at Bulimba, for starters. And South Brisbane. And Nudgee waterhole. And the Ekka Grounds. Cribb Island, out where they put the airport. Cleveland. Beenleigh. Murrarie, K'gari, South Maclean. Oh, and Pine River, don't forget that big one. Maidenwell, Caboolture, Moreton Island. Beaudesert, not three kays from town, Witheren, Waterford. And Mudgeeraba, course. Stradbroke Big Hill. Kilcoy. Maryborough. A field of skeletons at Ipswich. Google it, I told him – a fucking *field*. Dreamtime Beach at Kingscliff. Outside Boonah, some mob reckon maybe two hundred killed. How many *snipe shoots*? How many *fox hunts* after Sunday church? I said, I'll tell you how many, mate – there was six thousand of us Goories when Oxley dropped anchor. And thirty years later less than a thousand blacks collected blankets on the Queen's Birthday. Say there was three times that number still alive, from Maryborough to the Tweed. Half our fucking population wiped out. And the other half being told ever since that we're criminals for living on our own land. For walking around, for having the temerity to *breathe*. I told him straight – if you whitefellas could parcel up the air itself ya would. Ya should have seen his face, the little gammon prick. Didn't know whether to shit or go blind.'

'What'd Nan do?'

'She proper backed me up, I couldn't believe it. And so, in the end, it was all "Yes, Nan, no Nan, three bags full, Nan." She even conned em into giving her a chopper ride over to Queen's Wharf instead of the fucken boat ride up the river they been planning for months!'

Johnny grinned and gulped at his coffee, then let out an anguished cry. He fled into the ensuite where Winona could hear him spitting the coffee out and rinsing his mouth with cold water.

'Oh, yeah, sorry, it's pretty hot …'

More agonised rinsing. Johnny reappeared, wiping his mouth, mournful as a stray dog.

'It's the thought that counts, right?' Winona chirped.

Johnny grunted. He took his cup into the bathroom and replaced half the contents from the cold tap before sculling it.

'Shoulda stuck to lolly water like me and Paddy,' Winona lectured.

'Shoulda, woulda, coulda. That's fuck-all use the morning after, ay?'

'You're gonna have a ball today, brah,' Winona laughed mercilessly. 'Them Yugambeh boys go hard.'

'Last-night-Johnny shoulda given that more thought. The dumb dawg.'

'Get in the shower while I make ya some Vegemite toast.'

Ten minutes later a young person with a shaved head and a rainbow wristband banged on the screen door.

'Ya lift's ere,' Winona called.

'Hey sis. Doctor Jay ready to roll, or what?' the Goorie asked.

'Yeah, he's coming. He's grogsick, but.'

'Oh, we'll soon sweat that outta him. You're Winona, ay? I seen you and ya man getting around West End. I'm Lucas, I'm a Walker and a Gray.'

'Yeah. I'm a Blanket and a Robertson – but Johnny's not my *man*,' she replied. 'We're just mates.'

'Oh, sorry, shouldn't assume. Here he is! Let's hit the road, cuz, that mountain's waiting for us!'

Johnny brushed past smelling of mouthwash and deodorant, backpack over his shoulder and hiking boots in hand. He gave Winona a look of despair. 'I'm never drinking again. Swear ta God.'

'Have a deadly bushwalk.' She smirked as the screen door banged shut. Johnny had polished off a bottle and a half of red last night after several post-shift beers. Hiking up a steep mountain with Uncle Robbie's men's group was gonna really sort out the gammons from the maibins.

'And stay hydrated!' she yelled, 'I ain't driving to New South Wales to rescue ya!'

'Winona ya doob or what, cuz?' Lucas quizzed Johnny, who was pulling his boots on in the back seat.

'Nah, just mates. I wish she was my woman, don't get me wrong.'

'She's cute man, ya wanna ask her out before someone grabs er.'

'I asked her like four times already, ay. Anymore and it'll be harassment. But she reckons we can't date anyway cos we dunno if we're related.'

'Oh, bro, tell me about it. I bin looking for a hot single Blak man who's not a rello my whole damn life!'

'Yeah, and cos of Grandad being Stolen Gen I can't rule anyone in or out.'

Stolen himself in 1969, Uncle Robbie turned around from the front seat. 'Best way is to go over west and find a Nyoongah, son.

Or an Island girl, or a Maori one. Us stolen mob can't mix our bloodlines, too risky.'

Johnny flopped against the window and groaned. First Winona wouldn't date him because he was a whitefella. And now that Uncle Robbie had pulled her up sharp about that, and she had finally, grudgingly accepted that he was indeed some kind of a Blak man, he *still* couldn't date her. Unbelievable.

'I'm too crook ta think about it.'

'Grogsick, are ya? You wanna stick to that wotsername drink, young brother,' advised Uncle Robbie. 'Sobah. Hangover ain't gonna do ya much good up on our mountain.'

~

The minister was apoplectic. 'What do you *mean*, Granny Eddie won't be on the fucking boat? She's the centrepiece of the whole shebang! Her face is all over the fucking billboards!'

'So,' winced his senior advisor, 'it turns out – and nobody knew this, *obviously* – that she's got a phobia about boats. But the Traditional Owners Association have nominated, ah, Uncle Henry Wallaby to take her place. He turned one hundred last month.'

'Oh, that's bloody wonderful, that is. Queensland's second oldest Aboriginal. Doesn't have quite the same ring to it, does it? Why wasn't he thought of earlier?'

'Apparently he, ah, ripped up his letter of congratulation from Buckingham Palace and sent it back with a demand for eighty billion dollars in back rent.'

The minister dragged his hands over his face. 'Are you shitting me? A hundred-year-old political ratbag?'

'But listen,' the advisor went on, 'I think it'll be fine. I'm told it was a joke. Well, mostly. We can put Uncle Henry on the boat, if he agrees, leading the way as the senior traditional owner. And then Granny Eddie arrives by chopper, with the media on the rooftop, as Queensland's Oldest Aboriginal. Problem solved.'

'Fuck me, it's like herding cats. I'll be glad when I can go back to worrying about the Olympics.'

~

'You been sniffing around my ancestry page?' Johnny accused. 'That's private.'

'Well ya left it open and I wanted to look up Nan, like ya offered. It's not cheap ay, all this "find ya family history"?'

'Nah. Addictive as hell, too.'

'Like I said, the perfect pyramid scheme. Anyways,' Winona continued, 'I found this yarn in there for Nan's Nan – I dunno if it's right but. It says she lived next to Frog Hollow with her four kids, two black and two so-called half-castes. Archibald Meston himself signed their removal papers, the dog-faced genocidal prick.'

'Spose ya looked up my tree too, did ya?' Johnny braced himself. *Mister Seven Per Cent. One good nosebleed and ya outta the tribe. Claimin ya Blak now there's money in it.*

'Oh, chillax. We both know you got fuckall blackfella in ya. I thought ya got over that blood quantum bullshit.'

'It's hard when some people don't wanna let ya get over it.'

'Well, fuckem. Ya heart's one per cent of your body weight, hey, but you'd be rooted without it. Keep doing what ya doing with Uncle Robbie and you'll be right.'

'He was talking about hearts,' Johnny mused, rinsing out his folding plate and drink bottle, and resisting the temptation to correct Winona's biology. 'Bout how the colonists used to steal blackfella organs and put em in the Old Museum at Herston. His mob never ever went in there till recently. And his own parents didn't even drive past the building, he said. How fucked up is that?'

'Colonisation 101: your body is not your own.'

'Wonder where they ended up? The bodies?'

Winona made a disgusted face, looking in the cupboard for dinner ingredients. 'I reckon a lot of em ended up just over the road in the Medical School. That's what I been told. Basement's full of our Old People's skin and skeletons and shit.'

Johnny paused, struck by a sudden realisation.

'What?'

'I've got the code to the Herston research lab.'

'Oh, no! Good go, yer on yer own there, pal! I'm not going near any fucking dead people!'

'We could repatriate a lotta mob all in one hit,' Johnny suggested. He imagined himself on the TV news and in the *Koori Mail*, a hero to mob all over the country. *Dr Johnny Newman, a Goomeroi man, has taken back from the oppressor what was stolen, a century before ...*

'Oh, please!' Winona scoffed. 'Sit round ere with a house fulla dead bodies not knowing who they blong to or how to go about getting em home safe? Haunted from arsehole to breakfast time?! Yeah, nah. There's no need to go being a fucken hero just cos ya got a lab code.'

'Meston, then,' Johnny grinned. 'Take a shovel to South Brisbane Cemetery and resurrect the old Protector himself.'

'Yeah – whack his skull on a spike in the middle of Musgrave Park, see how he likes being the main attraction,' cackled Winona, '*Now* you're talking!'

'Would ya? For real, though?' Johnny was suddenly serious. 'Cos I would. Do our bit for the bicentenary.'

Winona took a slug of pepperberry Sobah, grimacing at the idea of disturbing a grave, even that of a body-snatching mongrel like Meston. She shifted a large pot of salted water onto the stove and splashed in a generous dollop of olive oil. 'Nah,' she said slowly. 'We'd never get rid of the murdering arsehole. Plus, Nan'd have a stroke.'

'Okay. But I've still got my medical skeleton,' Johnny proposed. 'With a bitta dirt rubbed on it'd look pretty realistic ...'

'As in, let's not dig Meston up but say we did?' Winona's eyes gleamed.

'Bicentennial basketball in the Mall, Goories versus Murries. Guess whose skull we're using for the ball?' Johnny agreed, turning into Patty Mills and sinking a three-pointer with his right hand.

'You're going straight to hell, you are!'

'I've seen too many cadavers to believe in hell. When I drop dead, or fall out the boat and drown, that's it baby. I'll be shark shit, nothing more.'

Winona gave a wry smile. Johnny still had a long way to go. He would have to learn for himself about the spirit world. She measured out three cups of wholemeal pasta and began bruising cloves of garlic with the side of her knife.

'Hey,' she replied, 'speaking of drowning, I asked Nan about that drowning mark thing.'

'Oh?'

'Yeah. She'd never heard of it.'

'Oh.' Johnny was crestfallen.

'Hold up, dickhead. She'd never heard of it and neither had Darto, but Nan reckons it's obvious.'

Johnny waited. Winona kept chopping garlic and dicing tomatoes.

'So are ya gonna tell me?'

'Nope. I had to do the work to figure it out. Why should you get a free ride?'

'Fuck sake.'

'You got a brain,' Winona waved her knife in the air. 'Get outta my way and go use the damn thing.'

'But it makes no sense.'

'Not if ya think like a white man, no.'

'Shakespeare was white.'

'Was he? How white was anyone in the sixteenth-century Stratford?'

Johnny's brow furrowed as he left the kitchen, wanting to begin an argument about Othello but refraining. Ten minutes later he reappeared, triumphant. 'Sailors back then couldn't swim. Not English ones.'

'Keep going.'

'If they fell overboard, that was it. So, they needed their superstitions to protect them, stories about no women aboard, and all that. Plus, God and Jesus and hell were completely real, in their eyes.'

'Yeah. And?' Winona wiped the kitchen benchtop with a Chux, leaving the dark granite surface gleaming.

Johnny stopped. That was as far as he'd got – Shakespearean lives ruled by superstition.

'Taste this,' Winona tossed the Chux in the sink and presented him with a spoonful of kangaroo bolognaise. Birthday cakes were her speciality, but she could knock up a pretty good pasta when she tried.

'Yuuum. Maybe a touch more salt,' Johnny passed her the tall salt canister from the dining table. Winona held it for a moment, deep in thought. Then she very deliberately poured a handful of white grains out onto the benchtop. Johnny looked at the mound of salt, then at her, and then at the mound again.

'Why'd ya do that?'

Winona didn't answer, but instead began singing 'My Island Home' into the canister as though it was a microphone.

'You're cracked, you are.'

Winona eyeballed him. 'And your complexion is perfect hanging, mate. What's land to a sailor?'

'I dunno. A place to start from, and get to? Safety? A beginning and an end?'

'Don't be lazy. Really think about it. Think like a blackfella.'

Johnny stared hopelessly at the benchtop. He had no idea what Winona wanted from him. How did 'blackfellas think'? He cast

276

his mind over everything he'd gleaned off the mob at uni, and what Uncle Robbie had taught him in men's group. How Goories didn't egotistically name mountains and rivers after individuals like the colonists did, cos blackfellas had no need to curry favour. How all Aboriginal landscapes and peoples and sentient beings were connected across the continent, tied to each other in a thousand ways by names and totems and songs and dances and stories. How everyone somehow belonged to everyone else, before colonisation. Nothing alone, nothing ever in isolation, but always as part of a larger whole extending out to the air and the stars and the planets. How could a mole on the face of an English sailor possibly fit in?

He gazed at the tiny white island of salt. The charcoal granite benchtop became a sea streaked with paler swirls. The light parts of the granite looked a bit like cresting waves. *No man is an island.* Understanding glimmered at the edge of his consciousness but couldn't quite manage to surface.

'Nuh.' He shook his head, defeated. 'You're not gonna tell me, are ya?'

Winona closed her eyes and tasted the sauce again.

'I should cook roo more often.'

26. Resurrection Men

2024

'Oh, Iris, come in, sister!' Eddie beamed, overjoyed to have a visitor she wasn't constantly explaining things to. 'I love your headscarf!'

'Saltwater colours for my favourite saltwater patient. How's the head today?'

Improving, Eddie said, and her eyesight almost back to what it had been before her fall. The doctors were useless, but she'd managed to survive their incompetence. Next week she'd be in her new unit with Winona. About blooming time.

'God heals and the doctor sends the bill.' Iris smiled.

'Johnny's the only one I trust, but he's so young ...'

'Funny world when a thirty-year-old can be in charge of people's lives. Robbie's taken him under his wing, I hear.'

'Yeah, and Johnny listens, you know. Binungs ain't painted on like most of em. Tell me, sis, how's that poor Maori family going?'

Iris reassured Eddie that the missing placenta of a newborn Maori boy had been safely returned to his grandmother. Some fool in the birthing wing had tossed it in a rubbish receptacle and the family had gone into deep shock.

'Awful,' muttered Eddie. 'They got no clue, this lot. No culture and no clue.'

'Speaking of culture, I wanted to ask you about this statue,' said

Iris, in a tone that made Eddie's chin snap up. 'Dundalli's War. Over the road at South Bank, there.'

'Dundalli's War?' Granny looked blank. 'You better ask Aunty Deb Beehive, sis. I never heard nothing bout it.'

'Really? I was told you were the one who wanted it?' Iris frowned, her suspicions all but confirmed.

'Somebody's got their wires crossed, I dunno nothing bout it. Oh, look, here's Darto, that journalist who's writing my memoir for me. This is Gaja Iris.'

Darto thrust out a hand. Iris looked at it briefly, then picked up her handbag.

'Yeeees. Well. Look, Aunt, I'm going to go confirm your discharge for Tuesday. And I'll see what I can find out about this Dundalli's War business, too.'

'Oh, isn't it marvellous?' Dartmouth rocketed into the conversation uninvited. 'The big man himself. Right at the top of South Bank, recognition for our First Nations struggles at last!'

'*You* know about it?' Granny Eddie shot back. 'How come *you* know about it, and I don't?'

'Oh, but we talked about it, remember? With Winona and Johnny? The minister put it through Cabinet quick-sticks about three weeks ago.'

Iris and Granny Eddie looked at each other blankly.

'Aunt didn't know which end was up, three weeks ago,' replied Iris. 'No offence, Aunt, but the amount of Valium you were on. And they wanna go and talk about informed consent!'

'Tell Winona I need to see her, onetime,' snapped Granny, rapidly caught up in Iris's disquiet. 'Cheeky little sod going behind my back.'

'Texting her now,' Iris held her mobile up in demonstration as she left the room. 'I'll be back shortly.'

Pleased to be alone with Eddie, Dartmouth cracked open his laptop. 'Hopefully this damned thing decides to work. Now, where were we yesterday? Oh, I was going to fill you in about the Warry incident. Quite bizarre, it is, he must have been some sort of head case.'

Gaja Iris walked down the corridor then stood waiting for the lift to arrive. She blinked in surprise as the shadow of a bird suddenly passed over her, and just as suddenly vanished. A large type of bird, like a pelican or heron, making the overhead lights flicker with its impossible presence inside the hospital. A moment later, she was gripped by the certain knowledge that Granny Eddie was in danger.

'Warry was the chemist, remember? So according to Trove, in 1855 a young man called Saltwater Toby was arrested and taken in—'

'Zip it, mate!' Iris's index finger was in Dartmouth's astonished face. 'What the hell do you think you're doing?'

'*Excuse* me?'

'Have you heard this yarn, Aunt?' Iris turned to face Eddie. 'About Saltwater Toby?'

'No-o ... I mean, the *name* rings a bell. Maybe from Grandad Charlie, when I was a little pitcher with big ears.'

'Right. You – out.' Iris blazed at Dartmouth. 'Before ya do any more bloody damage. Git.'

Dartmouth protested in vain. Iris needed him gone, and so out he went.

'That yarn's not yours to tell, mate,' Iris said as she banged the door shut. 'To anyone, let alone *Granny Eddie* of all people. The nerve!'

'What's wrong?' Eddie had never seen Iris so angry. 'Is it men's business, this story, or what?'

Iris gave Eddie a weary look and touched her index finger to Eddie's ancient shoulder. 'No, Aunt, I'm okay to tell you about it. It's just, well, let's wait till the Dundalli stuff's sorted, hey? One thing at a time. Cuppa?'

'If you don't mind, love.'

More better if a Yagara person told it, commented Mulanyin, who had now shifted outside the sliding glass door onto the balcony. *But this healer will have to do.*

Granny Eddie squinted at him. 'The sun's right in my eyes, there, you know,' she complained. All she could see below an enormous halo of gold was the ghost's lower half sitting cross-legged on the plastic veranda table. 'Am I ever gonna find out why you keep humbugging me?' She went on, 'And what it is you think yer owed?'

There was a long pause. Eddie thought Mulanyin had decided not to answer. When she finally heard him, he sounded rather forlorn.

It is too awful to speak of – and yet it must be told.

'Sorry I took so long, Nan,' Winona panted. 'Had a job interview at Yarrabilba.'

Granny Eddie was on her high horse, and not about to dismount in a hurry. 'I've heard all about this Dundalli statue of yours, missy. Some bright idea that is! And I can tell ya one thing for free,' Eddie began as she meant to go on, 'he *definitely* ain't gonna be holding no damn *pointing bone* making out it's a spear. I mean Christ Almighty! You young people go messin about in culture, willy-nilly, when ya got no damn idea what yer playin at!'

Seeing which way the wind blew, Winona collapsed beside the abashed Johnny and offered no defence. Iris sat on his other side as Eddie read her granddaughter the Riot Act.

'I dunno where ya think yer mob's from! America, hey? Or Africa?! All them other mobs –' and here Granny Eddie flung her arm around the room, indicating a whole universe of alternative Blackness '– they got their own spiritual ways and laws, not *our* ways, not *our* culture. Is that what you been taught is it, to go round on other people's land chucking poison around willy-nilly, lettin curses loose? Who went and give you permission to be cursing anything? At your age? Are you even listening to me?'

Head down, gazing at the grey hospital lino, Winona nodded that yes, yes, she definitely was. Johnny was astonished to see his favourite terrorist so meek. But if Granny Eddie kept raging, he worried, the old girl was gonna be looking at a TIA. He could see the death certificate now – Cause of Death: *Young People Today*.

'This ain't blooming Ukraine or Afghanistan or, or ... Belfast. I mean, do you think—' and here Eddie became heavily sarcastic '—d'ya think that in ten thousand generations *maybe* us mob worked a few little things out? How to not bugger things up? Do you think, *maybe,* it might be worth asking some Old People before you go and do something so damn stupid? Jesus wept, Winona. You get on the phone right now and tell that government crowd that Dundalli's not gonna be pointing no spear, *or any blooming bone*, or I dunno what I'll do. You'll be the death of me!'

'Orright, Nan, I will. I will. But ...'

'But *what!*'

'But then how will there ever be justice? When whitefellas don't listen?' Winona argued.

'I don't care two hoots what whitefellas do,' Eddie replied. 'Anymore'n I care what the neighbour's cat does. *Protect all life.* That's our Law. Not just Aboriginal life, not *some* life, as we see fit. *All living beings.* Very simple.'

'Oh, okay, I got it now. White lives matter,' Winona retorted with a flash of anger. 'No matter what they do to us or how many of us get murdered.'

Johnny flinched, waiting for Granny Eddie to blow a gasket. To his surprise, her voice grew not louder, but quieter.

'Don't you twist my words, bub. This is Law I'm talking about, not stupid racist slogans. There's consequences to everything. Consequences that can't be avoided. And if whitefellas don't wanna listen, then that's what's coming to them. Am I right, Iris?'

'Yes, Aunt.'

Winona sighed heavily.

'What if,' Johnny bravely intervened, 'what if Dundalli still held the bone, I mean spear, but pointed downwards. Like the rifles on the white war memorials?'

Granny Eddie shot Johnny a withering glance.

'That'd be even worse. Now youse two clear out and get it fixed – onetime!'

~

That evening, the lights of the CBD shone in brilliant columns beyond the river. Those at South Bank seemed almost close enough to touch. The green helipad was lit up too, by four giant halogen towers, one on each corner. From where they had gathered in the dazzling light on top of the hospital, all anyone could see in the sky above them was the moon and the faint outline of the Southern Cross.

'H for help,' muttered Winona, cocking her head at the helipad.

'And for Home,' nodded Gaja Iris, somehow hearing her from the far side of the circle. Winona blinked. Iris Brown certainly had a knack of commanding your attention. She reminded Winona of a butcher bird. That steady gaze.

'Come in closer, everyone. Johnny, bring Aunt in a bit.' The group shuffled closer until their shoulders bumped. 'Good. Now Aunt, I wanted you to hear this yarn up here on the roof, away from any strangers, and to hear it from a blackfella, because it concerns your family.'

'Ay?' Granny Eddie was startled. 'That's news to me.'

'Yes, so I gathered. It's a sad thing, strangers sometimes know our family stories when we ourselves haven't been told them yet.'

'You ain't a stranger, though, sis,' Granny corrected Iris, who smiled.

'Of course not. I do apologise, though, for being the one to tell you this yarn about your own great-grandfather. I only wish it was a happier story.'

Winona did some rapid mental calculations.

'You're right, bub. Better to know these things.'

'Thank you, Aunt. Well, we all know how important our stories are. All us mobs: Goories, Murries, Koories. People all over the world keep their stories close. Middle Eastern people believe,' Iris continued, 'that by telling a story you can change the world, and that nothing is as powerful as the right story at the right time. The Hikaye, the Seder, terribly important.'

Johnny was nodding away sixteen to the dozen, Winona saw.

'But stories can harm, as well as heal. That's why our Law stories ain't for messing with. This story now, it's not sacred like that. But it's a yarn of what was done to one Goorie man in the early days. And because of what was done to him, his story's been put away, see. Only whispered about. And I'm guessing, Aunt, that's why you maybe haven't heard it fully in your life.'

'But how did you come by it, sis?'

'I heard it first from Uncle Dugong, Aunty Deb Beehive's cousin-uncle, at his grandmother's wake. That old fella said I was to pass it on only if there was benefit in the telling, and I never have, till now. But when I heard that journalist fella with your Ancestor's name in his mouth this morning, I had to talk up.'

Johnny wondered how long these preliminaries would take. He glanced at his watch.

'You on-call?' asked Gaja Iris.

Johnny shook his head.

'Not all stories are sacred, Johnny. Some stories are just for fun, or to teach a little lesson. But the telling itself is a sacred thing. So, when you've been invited to hear a special story, you open your binungs and ya forget about the clock. Right?'

He nodded, chastened.

'Right, then. Let's all imagine it's 1855. Whitefellas only been here about thirty years. There's no hospital here, no helipad, no high-rises. Cars haven't been invented, or bitumen. The river's still chock full of fish, swamps are still full of game. The big Kurilpa village is up on the side of Highgate Hill just there. Woolloongabba pullen pullen over to our right, and a handful of pubs and houses where South Bank is. Over in town the streets are all dirt, covered with horse and cow manure. Big fig tree where the Treasury Building is, and there ain't even many streets really — mostly it's our old Goorie tracks leading out to Breakfast Creek and Herston and the other places. Most of the buildings are wood, all bar the Commissariat Store — see it over there — and the big old Barracks and the Parliament. Maybe a few churches and flash houses might be stone. The tallest thing around's the Windmill. There's just as many Goories getting about as there is British, at least till four in the afternoon when the stockwhips come out. And sitting in the Queen Street Gaol, there's a young black lad, Saltwater Toby. He's proper scared, too, sitting in that white man's gaol.

'Young Toby's been living with the Kurilpa mob. He's been put through their ceremonies at the Woolloongabba Bora, and he's ridden north to Murrumba Downs with Tom Petrie when Petrie first selected his land there. This young Toby, he's a new father, he just married a Ngugi girl from Moreton Island, called Nita.'

Winona's head snapped up. *Ngugi!*

'Your Nan's great-grandmother,' Iris nodded.

'We never knew,' interrupted Eddie in excitement, 'where Granny Nita was born. She lived here from a kid, with the Petrie family, they adopted her. We useta think she mighta been Yugambeh or Yagara, but there was always this idea that she married a Moreton Island man who died. You say *she* was the Ngugi?'

'Yes, Aunt. Your Granny Nita has her own story, of course. About surviving the invasion as a little girl and being trafficked

285

into slavery before Grandfather Petrie rescued her off the timber gang who held her captive. Then falling in love with Saltwater Toby, and later on leaving the Petries, living at Frog Hollow with her two jarjums. Having another baby to a Hindu fella there, and later a fourth to an Irishman after the Yagara mob saved her life in the Great Fire of Brisbane. But it's her first husband I need to tell you about tonight.'

Just then a helicopter came thundering in from the east, lights directly in everybody's eyes, so that the group was made temporarily blind as well as deaf. Turning away from the blazing headlights and putting her fingers in her ears, Winona saw Gaja Iris's grey hair fly in all directions. A crinkled soft drink can made a noisy run across the concrete towards the stairwell. The chopper flew past to land on the top of the Princess Alexandra Hospital, a kilometre down Ipswich Road.

'Medivac from the M1,' murmured Johnny. 'That prang at Caboolture.'

Gaja Iris lifted an open hand to the chopper's flight path and spoke a blessing in language too softly for anyone to hear her.

Death is so close, shivered Winona. Death had been on her mind a lot, spending so much time at the hospital, and hearing Johnny's doctor stories. You leave home and you never think about it – that final touch of the doorknob, the Weet-Bix bowl you left unwashed on the sink – that could be the last one ever. She gazed out over the silver ribbon of the moonlit river winding around Gardens Point, the shaggy figs on the riverbend, the soft round outline of the mangroves hugging the shore. Even the lights of the cars on the freeway were pretty from where she stood. Touched by the compassion of Iris's blessing, or perhaps by the serene tone of her storytelling, Winona softened and let the beauty of the night soak into her. Then she tensed, knowing that it was at moments exactly like this that the Voice liked to start up.

But the Voice was silent.

'Saltwater Toby was arrested for rape,' Gaja Iris continued. As the healer spoke, it felt to Winona as if the older woman's voice, strong yet gentle, was creating a kind of invisible web around her. As though Iris's words deliberately built a cradle of meaning that she, Winona, could return to whenever she wanted – weaving her own protective layers into, over the days and weeks to come. And when the structure around her was complete – a nest made from particular language words and key memories and stories of her family, and, somehow, from the underlying *rhythm* of Iris's yarning – then the Voice would find it utterly impossible to penetrate. For the first time in years, Winona felt the unfamiliar sensation of hope welling from deep within her.

'Supposedly he'd committed this rape with an accomplice, but nothing was ever proven. The so-called accomplice was never even identified, and I'm sorry to have to tell you, Aunt, that Toby was killed escaping custody. He left behind his young wife and their two babies: an infant girl and a boy born eight months after Toby died.'

The group was silent, digesting this.

'I'd be interested to tell this story,' Iris continued, 'as just one example of why some of our mob are frightened of doctors and vaccines. Why we see them as enemies, sometimes, and stupid rumours spread so easily.'

'Doctors?' Eddie asked. 'I don't follow ya.'

'It's truly horrible, Aunt, this part. Just awful. Your great-grandfather, this young fisherman with his life in front of him, and his wife he loved and his two babies to raise, put in prison for a crime I'm pretty sure he didn't commit – well, he was mutilated. He was almost certainly beaten to death trying to scale the wall of the gaol. They say the warder was a bad shot. When they took – I'm so, so sorry to have to say this to you – but when they robbed his grave and cut Toby's head off later that same night, there was no bullet hole in his skull.'

Granny Eddie gave a short and terrible cry.

'Will I stop?' Iris asked.

Eddie shook her head. 'I need the truth.'

'Why would they cut off his—' Winona began, and then caught herself. Phrenology. Eugenics. And all the other wonderful fucking reasons Europeans ever invented to cut the heads off the natives. Yagan, Pemulwuy, and now as it turned out, her own great-great-grandfather. *Your body is not your own.*

'It's almost unspeakable, Aunt. But they used your Ancestor as a ... I can't even think of the right word. It was the town chemist, Warry. He paid workmen to dig up Toby's body from the Milton Cemetery, and then bring his head back to town as a specimen.'

'Body-snatchers.' Johnny muttered beneath his breath. 'Resurrection men, they called them.'

'Yes. Well, this Warry, I don't know what the hell was wrong with him. But he held a dinner party that night, with a big silver dish as the centrepiece. When his guests were all sat at the table, he had the dish uncovered, and there in front of them was Saltwater Toby's head on a plate. With a paper frill around his neck, they say, and two dozen red roses decorating his curly hair.'

As Iris's words sank in nobody knew what to do. A paralysis descended on the group, as if to move would risk exposing further horror.

Granny Eddie broke first. She leaned forward in her wheelchair and let out a great wail of anguish that echoed back at her from the river. Winona went to her side and held her, joining in, and the two women clasped each other, keening, while Johnny watched on. Iris sang a low tune as the women wept, tapping clapsticks which had appeared in her hands as though conjured out of the ether.

A nurse in scrubs appeared at the top of the stairwell to investigate and was quickly shooed away by Johnny. When their first round of sorrowing came to a natural end and the women had wiped their faces and blown their noses, they realised a ghostly figure had appeared on the edge of their circle.

It was the long, lean figure of a young Goorie man, a man with bands of scarring across his broad chest, another scar on his ankle and a blank patch of night air where his head should have been.

Everyone stared.

I ran for my life that night, the mooki conveyed without words. *I heard shots, then I tripped and fell. Armstrong was quickly on me, beating at my head with his rifle butt. And then I knew nothing and felt nothing, for the longest time, until the dancers came.*

'Tell me, young brother,' said Gaja Iris. 'Who were these dancers?'

They were Yagara men. They spoke Yagara, anyway, even though they reminded me of the burragurra and the whale. The pounding of their feet woke me and I stayed awake long enough to remember my name, and that I had a home and a people. But then they left and I slept once more.

The mob looked at each other, baffled.

'Suncorp Stadium!' Gaja Iris exclaimed. 'Suncorp Stadium's built over the old Milton Cemetery! He must mean the dancers at the Dreamtime footy.'

I had stirred briefly once before. I had the feeling that an island man from very far in the north had done something tremendous and I almost woke, but the dream slowly faded. Without meaning to, I returned to the silence. The second time, when the dancers came, I woke properly, long enough to gather my strength and my thoughts, and fly south across the river into the top of that old grandmother tree. I would have kept going, only I realised that I had left my poor lost head behind.

Mulanyin pointed across the road at the grove of giant figs.

When you fell over the root of that tree, Old Woman, the ground quivered. The tree herself swayed like a bullrush in a summer storm. I was knocked from my branch and I followed you inside the building here. Something told me you'd be my path home, Old Woman, but I didn't

289

realise we were kin. And now that you know my story, I still must retrieve what's mine!

Everyone shared the feeling then, that the ghost was almost happy, even smiling; though how they knew it when Mulanyin had no head was a mystery.

'Your head, you mean?' Eddie ventured.

Of course, my head. Then I can return Home.

'We could ask Uncle Henry Wallaby, I suppose,' said Granny Eddie dubiously, 'He might know where to start.'

'Actually …' said Johnny slowly, 'I've got a fair idea where it might be.'

'Nan, you don't look real flash,' Winona interrupted, with a horrified look at Johnny. 'Let's get you back to bed, ay, before ya have a stroke.'

It was agreed that Granny Eddie would go back to bed and have a good sleep. It had been a very big day and an even bigger night, and in less than forty-eight hours she was due to chopper across to Queen's Wharf and have her photo taken with the Premier.

Early the next afternoon, Winona wheeled Eddie through the hospital doors and out into the noise and traffic of Vulture Street. Eddie gave a whoop of emancipation, waving her jabree as they reached the traffic lights in front of Emergency.

'Yeeee haaaa!' Winona joined in, 'Freeeeedom! How bout that, ay, Nan? How's it feel?'

'I was starting to wonder if I'd ever leave the damn place, bub. I'd get down and kiss the ground, if I could.'

'I know ya gotta go back for that MRI,' Winona commiserated as they made their way down towards the CityCat terminal. 'But Monday I'll spring ya out for good, I promise. And we'll never go back. Hey, look, there's that Maori family, the ones with the baby boy!'

The Kiwi mob waved madly from their van, heading back home to Runcorn with their newborn son.

'You know Iris got permission for them to give him the middle name Dundalli, Nan? Too deadly, ay?'

'We're lucky to have her,' Nan nodded.

A couple of minutes later they stood facing a villa in Dock Street. 'Nah, bub,' Eddie complained mildly, looking about her at the units and the luxury cars parked outside them. 'This can't be it?'

'Wanna bet? One, twenty-three Dock Street. This is it, alright.'

'Can't be!'

Winona pushed Eddie up the short ramp from the street and then spun her wheelchair around on the front patio of the retirement unit. Granny Eddie gave a holler of joy. Before her lay a sweeping view of Petrie Bight and Gardens Point.

'That's more like it,' Winona smiled. 'Shame ya had to wait so bloody long is all.'

Granny Eddie clutched her jabree. She was still secretly convinced that they were at the wrong address but was too afraid to push it. All she'd ever wanted was for her family to be safe and to live near the river Grandad Charlie had told her stories about. The villa was the culmination of a lifetime of dreams. *If* it was real. She summoned up all her internal fortitude. 'Is this ... are you *sure* this is the right address, bub?'

Winona laughed and showed Granny the paperwork in her satchel. Granny squinted and managed to make out the number and street name. It *was* real. She was going to live in a two-bedroom villa with a lawn and geraniums, and a proper tiled patio with a view of the fig trees on the riverbend. She looked up at Winona and quietly began to weep.

Winona squatted down. 'What's wrong, Nan?'

'I'm just so happy, bub,' Eddie sobbed. 'To be near South Bank and them trees, and the riverbend right there, and the cliffs. You dunno what it means to me.'

'Aw, Nan, don't cry. You deserve it, ay? You worked ya guts out all ya life, cooking and cleaning and minding kids for bugger all pay.' Granny Eddie dabbed at her nose with a tissue.

'No, no, stop.'

Winona paused. The first sight of Nan's new home had to be joyful. A day of happy memories, not one to argue about her stolen wages.

'Okay. I'm glad you like the unit anyways, Nan. And I'll be staying on with ya for a bit to look after you like we said, yeah?' Winona stood up again, enjoying the view. It was something alright. Uncle Neville Bonner's bridge boomeranging over the river upstream; CityCats and other boats whooshing by; cyclists on the footpath beneath the freeway. And West End just a fifteen-minute stroll from it all. Sweet.

Granny Eddie thumped the ground with her stick. 'Clean ya binungs out, girl! You *really* don't know what it means to me, I mean. Push me into the shade up there,' Eddie pointed to where the footpath was shaded by the massive figs on the far side of the road.

Winona obediently rolled her wheelchair along until they were directly opposite the top of South Bank. She kicked the brake on and found the water bottle, offering it to Eddie first.

'That's where I tripped over. Right there,' Eddie said, swallowing a mouthful and pointing with the water bottle, 'that day. Just up from the museum. Near old man Dundalli waving his flag at everyone. I don't reckon it was any accident, either. It was meant to be. I coulda finished up right where I fell, but I never.' She paused. 'That spot's like a sacred site, bub.'

Granny gazed around, taking in the scene. On the far side of the road, students and other visitors wandered past the maritime museum towards the Wheel of Brisbane, its red Channel Seven sign looking for all the world like a giant killing boomerang. Some passers-by were oblivious to Dundalli and the Aboriginal flag he brandished at the river. Others, though, stopped to read the plaque about his campaign of resistance and what had been sacrificed in defence of Country.

'Lest we forget,' Granny Eddie murmured.

Winona grew concerned. Of course, the spot where her Nan fell was highly significant. She might well have died there if the Malaysian students hadn't come to her aid. Seeing it again from the front porch every day would conjure all kinds of emotion in her grandmother's ancient mind. She wondered whether death became less or more frightening the older you got. But that was a question for another time.

'You weren't meant to finish up that day,' Winona encouraged. 'The Ancestors made sure we got to keep you a while longer, ay?'

Her grandmother wasn't listening. The old woman's attention was fixed on the statue of Dundalli. Eddie pointed her lips towards him and the fig trees he stood beside. 'See them grandmother trees?'

'The figs?'

'Mmm. Goorie women been putting their jarjums' woggai there forever.'

The hair on the back of Winona's neck prickled.

'Old People put em there to bind em to Country. Them trees is holding all them jarjums there, keeping em safe.'

Winona froze.

Woggai. Line, or string. But the deeper meaning was *connection.* Winona's knuckles clenched white on the handles of Eddie's wheelchair as understanding dawned. She was a fool. A fucking infant. Nan wasn't telling her about the place she'd had an accident. About tripping on a tree root and *falling over.* Granny Eddie was talking about the dawn of civilisation itself. A million births were connected to the ground beneath the fig trees. A million placental cords had been buried in that sacred ground, over tens of thousands of years.

Eddie looked up into her granddaughter's face. 'If I'd let you put that bone thing there, in a power place like that, cursing innocent people – well, it woulda all gone to poison, bub. I woulda had to disown you, and I didn't wanna do that. Ya with me?'

Winona nodded, very slow, as it dawned on her what she and Johnny had stupidly, ignorantly, blundered into. The damage they would have done.

'Yoway. I understand.'

~

'Here comes the great white whale,' Winona announced. 'Kiss goodbye to civilisation, y'all.' Her words were swallowed by the roaring of the crowds along the riverbank as the replica *Mermaid* sailed under the Story Bridge and into Petrie Bight. With her sails billowing, the schooner led a great horde of other vessels towards Queen's Wharf, catamarans and motor launches, kayaks and CityCats. The citizenry of Brisbane cheered her on while media and police choppers buzzed overhead like giant mosquitoes in a cloudless sky.

Around the next bend in the river, a contingent of traditional owners had assembled beneath the Neville Bonner Bridge in their bark kundil. Each boat held a coolamon of smouldering gum leaves ready for the arrival of the *Mermaid*. White columns of smoke rose up from their canoes, looking, some onlookers commented, as though the Yagara had somehow conjured a grove of tree trunks in the middle of the river.

Winona, Johnny and Dartmouth stood beside the hospital helipad with an eagle's-eye view of the action below. All three had their fingers jammed in their binungs because Granny Eddie, Gaja Iris and Nurse Xi had just been packed into the chopper idling on the green H.

'My little friends still coming?' Granny quizzed Iris for the umpteenth time, and for the umpteenth time was assured that yes, the Malaysian students who had saved her were waiting over at Queen's Wharf with everybody else. Eddie gripped her jabree and peered out at the commotion. On the northern bank of the river the huge cloven foot of the Executive Building was shining in the sun. Somewhere over there the minister was waiting for her arrival, and the Premier too. Funny old life. If only Bridget from Grade One could see her now.

'No room, mate,' the pilot yelled at Darto, signalling him to step back from the chopper door as the engine clattered louder still. The machine began to tilt. Eddie gasped and took Iris's hand, as together they rose up, up, up from the good Yagara earth. The chopper threw its shadow down onto South Bank as it crossed the river, a great bird flitting high above the chaos of the crowds.

'H, for have fun!' Johnny shouted, waving goodbye.

'H, for how do I get over there in time for the welcome?' Dartmouth complained.

'H, for how the hell did she get away with it?' Winona yelled in Johnny's left ear. 'At ninety-seven years of age?'

'You wanna keep that thing well the fuck away from me,' Winona warned as the *Edenglassie* sailed downriver against the flow of Bicentenary traffic heading towards town. It was just past noon, and the old wooden box Johnny had repatriated from the Herston Medical School at one a.m. was still creeping her fully-the-fuck out. Only Mulanyin's pleading had convinced her to have anything at all to do with Johnny's wild idea.

'We need more time, time to ask all the proper Elders,' she'd argued, the knowledge of the statue disaster they had almost created fresh in her mind.

These Elders, Mulanyin had despaired, *are they one hundred and seventy Mullet Runs old? No? And have they waited almost that many Mullet Runs for what is theirs? And in any case, it's my head! Who can possibly have more say over it than me?*

'I reckon he's right,' Johnny added. 'What happened to *your body is not your own?*'

Winona had finally relented. The sinister box now sat at the rear of the deck, secured between the Aboriginal and Torres Strait Islander flags fluttering from the stern. On top of it sat Mulanyin – cross-legged, joyful and expectant. Today was going to be momentous.

'That box is as far from you as I can get it,' Johnny replied, 'without swimming behind the boat carrying it on my damn back. I love ya, but I'm not swimming out to Moreton Bay for ya. Specially with all these bicentenary pissheads around.'

Johnny's mobile gave a loud ding, allowing his 'I love ya' to slide right on by.

'Is that Nan?'

'Nah, it's ancestry updating. I've set ya Nan's texts to sound like Birdz.'

'Ya wanna check it?'

'How can I?'

Winona took over the rudder, allowing Johnny to unlock his phone. Mulanyin looked on, bemused by the way Johnny looked so openly into his hands to divine his future.

'Huh.'

'What?'

Johnny kept scrolling. A minute passed, and another.

'Huh! Bugger me.'

Winona glared at a motorboat passing too close, flying a giant blue ensign on its way to town. Fucken rednecks.

'Happy Bicentenary!' the passengers cried, stubbies and champagne bottles raised high. With one hand still on the rudder, Winona swiftly turned and pulled her daks down to her knees, mooning the partygoers. They and their colonising bullshit could kiss her caramel fucking arse. A rousing cheer from the drunks told Winona her protest had not been received the way she'd intended. She sighed heavily. Pack of deadshits.

'Well,' said Johnny, looking up, having missed the entire incident. 'There ya go, it's official. We can't be related.'

'Gammon we can't be,' answered Winona, to hide the fact that her heart had leapt. 'Who says?'

'Ancestry dot com says. That latest update just deleted all the Indian DNA from my profile. This blackfella is officially Goomeroi, Irish, Scottish, French and Lithuanian. So now ya hafta marry me.' Johnny grinned.

'Oh, fuck up, Johnny. As if I wanna marry anyone,' Winona scoffed, lowering her sunglasses against the glare.

Johnny saw himself reflected there. 'Unbelievable. Ya know how many med students wanna marry me each week? You said you want to change your name and stop appropriating Turtle Island lingo. So, change it to Newman,' Johnny upped the ante. 'We'd make beautiful babies, you know we would.'

'Yeah. Beautiful milky babies. Vanillarigines.'

'Ah, get over yaself,' he teased. 'Colour ain't no thang.'

'Or we could just stay mates. It's a lot harder to find a solid mate than a baby daddy.'

'Why not do both?'

Winona laughed, and it was then that the wash from yet another speeding motorboat reached the *Edenglassie*, rocking her roughly from side to side. The old wooden box Mulanyin sat upon lurched forward and hit the mast, bursting open to reveal its uncanny contents.

Mulanyin leapt to seize his lost skull from the deck. By the time *Edenglassie* righted herself, he was whole again.

A short time later, the *Edenglassie* reached the bar where the river transformed into Moreton Bay. Johnny peered up into the rigging, shading his eyes with his hand. From where he was perched on the top of the mast, Mulanyin called out joyfully, greeting the distant islands of the burragurra as his old familiar friends. Winona craned her neck too. When Mulanyin waved down at her, smiling, she had a sudden stab of terrible foreboding.

'He's happy now,' she whispered to Johnny. 'But what about when he gets to Nerang? When he sees what they've done to his Country?'

'I don't think he's seeing what we do,' Johnny reassured her. 'He's not reacting to the speedboats or the Gateway Bridge or the Port buildings ... not any of it. It's like the modern world's invisible to him.'

'Maybe he sees Brisbane how it used to be,' Winona pondered. 'When he was alive.'

'I think so, yeah.'

'He can see us, though.'

'Well, we're blackfellas. And you're his blood.'

'True.' Winona brightened. 'Christ, what a relief. I thought we'd really fucked up for a second.' She beamed at him.

In for a penny, in for a pound, thought Johnny.

Oh, look, look, *look*!

I can see so far from up here, and it's the strangest sensation, *seeing*. These waves, the sky, the gulls. Like being reborn, after so much endless blankness, and everything in this moment coming bright now, so perfect, so fresh and pulsing with brilliant colour, oh yes! All things intensely alive, and oh, that blue of the ocean against the hull! I never forgot you my burragurra, the pure beauty of you. And the taste of salt in the wind, the breeze from the south Countries reaching my face again, filling my lungs. Am I weeping? Yes, I am weeping. I see the Bay opening before me, as I used to so long ago.

The pale kippa steers this boat well; this *Edenglassie* – strange, an old word I've not heard since my very earliest Kurilpa days. And this boat of his so much like those at that first regatta, back when I thought Young Tom had some strange magic to him and was not just a man like all other men.

And you – you Island Countries stretching low in the east – oh my friends, I know you so well. Do you know me? Do your waters run black with the mullet, still? Does the sea eagle soar above the shoal? Do the Coastal People net dugong off your beaches? I greet you, dear friends, all showing me the path towards south, and home. I see you too, Wollumbin, perched on the western horizon. And is that – can it be? The Matriarch swimming beneath us, yes! I see you, Old One. The kippa and the girl see you now, too!

Forge the way for us, Grandmother, bless us with your knowledge of these waters.

But what's this now? The kippa giving the boat over to the girl! *She* is steering us; she seems to know how! And she's laughing with joy at her skill, to turn us here at the very spot where saltwater meets fresh, and they are both whispering together and smiling now, yes, yes! Like that, have courage and take her in your arms, pale kippa – yes, hold her and kiss her. Yoway, good, that is the beginning, yoway, yoway! And she is laughing, and you are happy, we are full and laughing glorious with life, we three, and there

– now –

do you feel it? The change of the tide, the wondrous ocean slowly turning to face the day, this burragurra longing to carry us to Nerang? I can feel it, the rush and swelling of her huge desire come to take me there at last. Do you know the ocean is our great beginning, kippa? Remember it; she is our only source and will not be denied her blood, she will never be denied her saltwater people. And here am I, whole again and my long exile almost at an end.

It is time, now, yoway. Our sails swell with wind. I have waited too long in foreign lands and my heart yearns to see my people gathered at Jellurgal. I saved your life two times, Grandmother – save mine now. Come, lead us home.

Author's Note

I am grateful to have received support at different times from the Australia Council; the Jumbunna Institute at University of Technology Sydney, and from a H.C. Coombes Fellowship at the Australian National University.

A lot of Goorie people have offered me time and encouragement in the creation of *Edenglassie*. I would particularly like to thank Yagara-Yugarabul Traditional Owner and Senior Custodian Gaja Kerry Charlton, the late Yugambeh Elder Ysola Best, Ngugi Custodian and Elder Gheebelum Robert Anderson, Mrs Patsy O'Connor, Aunty Mary Graham, Aunty Deb Bennett, Uncle Lafe Charlton, Aunty Rhoda Roberts, the late Uncle Sam Watson Snr, Aunty Delta Kay, Uncle Herb Roberts, Aunty Robyn Williams, the late Aunty Eileen Williams, Aunty Dawn Daylight, Leanne Levinge, Michael Aird, Dr Judy Watson, Uncle Des Sandy, my brother Uncle Victor Hart, Dr Maureen Newton, Aunty Duck Williams, Aunty Lilla Watson, my brother Jonathon Slottje, Zamira Tyson, Dr Jackie Huggins, Aunty Linda Biumaiwai, Fred Leone, Dr Sandra Phillips, Uncle Michael Williams, Aunty Sharon McIvor, the late (great) Auntie Maureen 'Mook' Watson, Uncle Wesley Enoch, Uncle Alec Bond, Tawny Jay, Leesa Watego and family, Uncle Les Collins, my sister Gladys Willis, Boe Spearim, Dr Odette Best, and lastly my friend Aunty Betty McGrady, who held a short stick at primary school. I hope my mistakes in these pages are few and forgivable.

Yagara language and cultural references have been used with the guidance of Custodian Gaja Kerry Charlton. Yugambeh language is used with permission of senior Custodian Mrs Patsy O'Connor and the assistance of Yugambeh linguist Shaun Davies. The Murry Jerry incident was related to me by senior Yugambeh Custodian Ysola Best in 1990, along with some detail that I have chosen not to include. I am indebted to Mananjali poet Lionel Fogarty for his pioneering work with Yugambeh language. (Elders and linguists should always be consulted about use of First Nations languages.)

I thank Boe Spearim for his groundbreaking podcast *Frontier Stories*. I also thank Professor Ray Evans for his lifetime of brave scholarship, and for the spider reference in his essay, 'The Mogwai Take Meanjin'. I acknowledge the invaluable work of Dr Robert Orsted-Jensen, whose seminal text *Frontier History Revisited* was a key resource, along with 'The Proclamation of Dalapai', republished in *Southerly* by Lionel Fogarty and Ali Cobby Eckermann (eds) along with Constance Petrie's classic biography, *Tom Petrie's Reminiscences of Early Queensland*. Ken Blanch's book, *White Lies, Black Blood: the Awful Killing of Kipper Billy* was another resource. The work of various other historians contributed significantly, including but not limited to Timothy Bottoms, Libby Connors, Ray Kerkhove, Ros Kidd, Henry Reynolds and Jonathon Richards. Thanks also to Peter Eedy.

Thanks to my editor Jacqueline Blanchard, and to Madonna Duffy for going the extra mile. Grace Lucas-Pennington gave advice on a late draft, as did Professor Julianne Schultz and Mirandi Stanton.

There are, of course, numerous birthing, burial and other sacred Indigenous sites throughout Magandjin–Brisbane. The setting of the fig trees is fictional, as is that of the burial platform at South Brisbane. (Records tell of graves desecrated at Kangaroo Point in the colonial period.)

The 'unfortunate Foreman boy' hints at an 1866 incident, transposed here to 1854. English child Edgar Foreman was riding near Griffin's Whiteside Station when his pony fell, its hooves tangled in an Aboriginal skeleton. The historian Peter Osborne in his 2003 essay 'Contested Histories: frontier conflict and reconciliation in the local museum' writes that Andrew James Gold, the son of another early North Pine colonist, said of the Whiteside property that 'Griffin claimed to have poisoned so many (Aborigines) he was sick of dragging them to the river and rolling them in.'

Again, this is a work of fiction. Certain key events occurred at times other than portrayed. John Wickham was in Sydney at the time of Dundalli's hanging. Tom Petrie was married when he selected Murrumba Downs in 1859, not 1855. Dalapai was in northern Queensland, not Brisbane, for much of late 1855, not Brisbane. Yerrin is a fictional headman. He should not be taken as representing an actual individual. In contrast, Mulrobin, Dalapai, Catchpenny (a notable Yagara identity, whose real name was Gwai-a), Dalgnai and Dundalli are actual historical personalities.

Goorie villages were repeatedly invaded during the Frontier Wars. The campaign of sustained attacks on Aboriginal civilians across the Australian continent from the late 1700s can only be viewed as constituting either war crimes, or as terrorism. The total numbers slaughtered are staggering. According to historian Professor Robert Orsted-Jensen, the death toll on the Queensland frontier alone rivals the total number of Australian soldiers killed in World War One. Massacre maps are now being compiled to tell the truth of Australia's hidden colonial history, and can be found online.

Mulanyin and Nita are fictional characters, although Mulanyin's story does draw on the life of Kipper Billy. It's not known today which clan or people the innocent Kipper Billy belonged to. The grotesque behaviour of the chemist Warry is well-documented fact. Minor aspects of Nita's story have been taken from the life of my great-grandmother, Christina Copson, whose unpaid servitude began with her removal from her Goorie family as a child of eight.

I wish to pay respect to the thousands of brave First Nations people who survived through the Frontier Wars in our various Countries, and who in various ways resisted the century of attempted ethnocide that followed.

To those who have stubbornly kept Goorie culture alive for our shared benefit today: baugull wonyi – deep thanks.

Lest We Forget.

ML
Magandjin–Brisbane, 2023